T.C. WEAVER

Whispers of Chaos

Book One of the Chaos Series

For God, family, friends, and the reader.

"Believe nothing you hear, and only one half what you see."

—Edgar Allan Poe

Contents

Whispers Of Chaos

Book one
The Chaos Series

T.C. Weaver

1

Bloody Beginnings

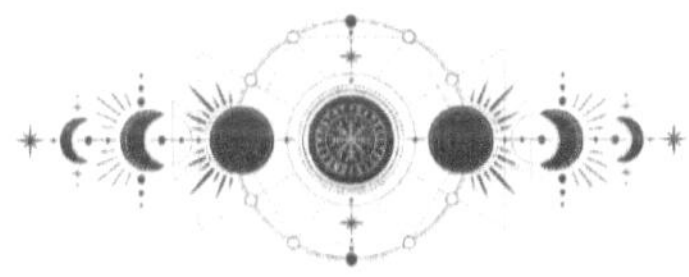

9/09
1:43 A.M.

The black Challenger roared into the gang's concrete garage, situated beneath a small two-bedroom apartment.

As the engine fell silent, the cabin doors swung open, allowing two men to exit. Both were clad in black, not even their faces visible, covered by dark ski masks.

Aside from attire, the men couldn't have been more different.

"Aw yeah, Kain." The man at the passenger side laughed. "We just scored twenty-five K!"

"Show a little couth, Saul." The driver frowned. "It wasn't free this time around. Nathan's dead."

"Kain, that kid was dumb." Saul waved his hands, dismissing the loss. "When a security guard's aiming a nine your way, you probably shouldn't stick your head up. He was a liability, and now he's not. Problem solved."

Kain shook his head, not in the mood for an argument. "You realize that now we're a man down. Whether you liked him or not, we needed the numbers."

"He won't be that hard to replace." Saul chuckled. "A good dog would do it. You know the right kinda' people, Boss. I wouldn't sweat it."

"Can't really argue with that." Kain sighed. *"Just mildly inconvenient when Nathan already knew the drill. Stupid kid. If Saul had been just a second quicker..."*

"Doesn't matter now." Kain looked to Saul. "I'm going up. Let me know when the others get here."

"Will do." Saul held a thumb up.

As he started up the stairs, Kain tugged away his mask, revealing the face of a twenty-nine-year-old man. He ran a hand over his messy black hair, brushing away the static of the mask.

"Who do I want to bring in to replace him?" Kain rubbed the back of his neck. *"Damn, this was a lot easier when I worked alone."*

He nearly smiled as he looked back on his career. Lifting liquor from gas stations when he was fourteen. Mugging the crippled guys for the thirty or forty bucks in their wallet at fifteen. Holding up the closing staff at the very same gas stations at sixteen.

*"Take a lot of cripples to match what we raked in tonight, but shit if these guys aren't a pain. Can't even get **here** on time for their money."*

* * *

2:55 A.M.

A full hour and ten minutes late, four black street bikes joined the Challenger in the garage.

As they came to a stop, Saul couldn't help but shake his shaved head, fixing the riders with the hardest eyes he could muster.

He hoped that it had the desired effect as the riders kicked down the stands on their bikes. Hope was the best he could do though, as he stared into the visors of their helmets.

"Happy the rainbow squad could make it." Saul spat as he looked over the group, each with a different colored helmet.

"Ooh. He's mad." Rick mocked as he raised his hands, snickering through his red helmet.

"Pete's sake." Saul fumed as he realized they were one rider short, and he wasn't wasting time thinking of Nathan.

"No green helmet."

"Rick, where's Dalton!"

Pulling off his helmet, Rick's sunken eyes fell onto Saul, succeeding where Saul had failed only moments before.

He put a tongue to his lower lip, visibly considering whether or not he wanted to kick the life out of Saul.

"Don't get lippy with me, Saul." Rick settled for a growl. "He was Carson's partner, maybe ask him."

Put in check, Saul collected himself before turning to Carson.

His orange helmet wasn't yet completely clear of his face when Carson answered. "Can't say for sure. A bar perhaps? It was his first big one, and I'm fairly certain he had never seen the inside of a person's head before."

"That's not good." Levi spoke through the plastic of his blue helmet. "Can't really afford to lose another one. I don't think he'd flip on us. He's pretty solid. I'll give him a call, check in on him."

"Aww, are you worried about him?" Aaron's blubbering voice carried from beneath a pink helmet.

"Oh, shut up, Pinky." Levi shook his head as Aaron flipped up the visor on his helmet.

"It is not pink, it is salmon!" Aaron fired back.

It didn't take long for the ensuing argument to rise to a raucous, trying the young Saul's patience as he put a hand to his face.

*"Maybe we could just replace them **all** with dogs."*

* * *

2:05 A.M.

A sudden racket inside the residence of 411 Pine Street had prompted a

911 call from a citizen walking their dog. Only a few minutes later, a squad car came up the street, lights flickering red, white, and blue, illuminating the dark suburbia.

The cruiser came to a stop in front of the house in question and the driver's side door swung wide open, making room for a pasty 40-year-old cop who had eaten his fair share of donuts. The buttons of his light blue shirt looked ready to pop as the lights reflected rays of color off of his badge.

It was an ordinary rental home with white exterior walls and a coat of dark forest green paint on the front door and shutters. There were no obvious signs of maltreatment on the property, and no present indication of altercations.

A single black motorcycle rested on its stand in the drive, a bright green helmet hung from the handlebars.

Next to the door a trashcan stood watch, typical seeing as the neighborhood trash pick-up was on Friday morning in the early A.M.

His radio crackled as dispatch called in to make sure everything was under control. A woman's voice, the dispatcher, screeched over the microphone next to his head. "What's your twenty, Bryan?"

Pursing his lips in frustration, Officer Bryan White sluggishly reached up to compress the button on his radio.

"I'm at 411 Pine Street," Bryan muttered. "Everything seems to be fine on the outside."

"Probably just another young couple having spats and throwing dishes at the walls." He thought to himself.

Leaning against his car, he surveyed the property for a few moments, considering whether or not it was a prank call, or perhaps a neighbor that wasn't overly fond of the potentially loud street bike.

Bryan had already decided that it was probably nothing, but to say he tried, he figured he should at least knock.

With the grace of a potbellied pig, he heaved his weight off of his vehicle and waddled up the front walk towards the door.

As he drew closer, the broken doorframe became visible, no longer disguised by distance. Bryan froze, the situation suddenly turning.

"Dispatch," Bryan slowed his voice, ensuring he was clearly heard, "Officer White, signs of forced entry at 411 Pine. Standby."

Slowly, Bryan reached down to his waist, unclipping his holster and resting his hand on the standard issue pistol, while the other pulled his flashlight from its pouch.

Clicking on the light, Bryan slowly stepped up to the door, peeking through the crack. Despite its small size, Bryan detected no movement.

"Kirkwood P.D.!" Bryan called. "Got a call for a disturbance at this address! Everyone okay?!"

No response echoed back to him and he put a cautious toe to the door, gently pushing it open. "I'm coming in!"

With the door completely open, Bryan shined his flashlight into the front room.

His jaw dropped as he found no signs of life, rather a destroyed living room, not even the walls having been spared. Deep scores had cut clean through the drywall.

His eyes locked onto the damaged walls, overlooking the mangled couch and recliner, and the coffee table that was broken in two.

The beam of his light hung on the wall, illuminating two sets of four enormous gashes.

His feet carried him towards the scars as he contemplated how they could've been made.

"What happened in here?" He looked back, taking in the bloodless carnage around him.

He looked away from the wall, his hand moving to his shoulder mic. "Dispatch, Officer White. Signs of a... struggle at 411 Pine. Haven't located any residents. I'm checking the rest of the house. Better get another unit out here."

"Copy that, Bryan."

"Keep going." He fought to muster his courage, shaking off a feeling of uneasiness.

He looked to his right, up the stairs, before turning to look towards the dining room.

"Check the main floor first." He swallowed as he talked himself through the paces.

He ever so slowly stepped into the dining room, taking quick stock of the place. It was a typical dining room, housing a small composite-board table adorned with matching salt and pepper shakers and two simple wooden chairs.

A short hall branched off of the room and looking to its end, Bryan could make out a lavatory, though nothing called attention.

Bryan turned to his right, shining his light into a perfectly clean kitchen. There was obviously no disturbance here. The counters were in order, center island still in one piece, and no gouges in the walls.

He returned to the butchered living room and advanced towards the flight of stairs, cautiously peering up them. He took his first step, shining his light across the white walls bearing silver handrails on either side.

Only one stair from the top an eerie feeling crept through the officer's bones.

The sixth sense of being watched.

Bryan slowly turned around, shining his light back down the stairs, checking his retreat. It was clear, but that feeling was still there.

Standing sideways, still looking down the stairs, he was convinced he was suffering from anxiety. He turned, pointing his light ahead of him, and took the final step.

No sooner had his foot landed than he felt his shoe sinking into wet carpet, the audible squish of liquid displaced by his boot.

The beam of his light darted to the floor, revealing that he had made a poor choice of footing.

He was standing in a crimson pool.

In blood.

In shock he stepped backwards, clear off the stairs. Slipping through the air he clawed at the walls, losing the light as he grappled for the railing. His outstretched hand slid on the rail before clamping shut like a vice as the flashlight thudded on the step behind him, shining at the wall.

Holding tight to the railing, Bryan steadied himself, fighting off tremors of queasiness as he bent down and picked up his light, squeezing the handgun ever tighter.

His body shuddered and he shook off his nerves, talking to himself.

"C'mon Bryan, it's just some blood. You've got a job to do, so do it!"

He stepped back to the top of the stairs, sticking to the right side of the hall in hopes of avoiding the blood, despite the fact that one of his boots was already leaving tracks.

The radio on Bryan's shoulder crackled. "Bryan, what's your status?"

But Bryan wasn't listening, deaf as his eyes locked onto what lay before him, a hand and the visible portion of an arm that disappeared into the darkness between a door and its frame. Both were laying in the middle of a foot-wide blood trail that led all the way to Bryan's feet and back to the pool at the top of the stairs.

Snapping to, Bryan's shaky hand flew to his shoulder. "Dispatch, I need EMS to 411 Pine, right now. I've got a lot of blood and at least one individual down."

He released his mic and drew the sidearm from his hip, no longer thinking this was an average lovers quarrel.

He took a step forward, towards the darkness behind the door, just as a low, nearly inaudible growl reached his ear. The rumble became louder, as he swore he heard, felt, footfalls behind him. The hair on his neck stood on end, goosebumps dotted his flesh. Fear began to rise within him. Not the rational fear of someone with a gun, but a fear born of gory horror films.

Choking the pistol grip to the point of numbing his hand, he spun round, a coarse grunt escaping his clenched throat.

Nothing, his light revealed nothing, only empty space.

He shuddered. *"No more scary movies."*

Turning back to the door, he advanced down the corridor.

"Body drug down the hall, nothing left but an arm of the last meal, the unlucky person who checks it out becomes the next dinner course."

Again, goosebumps plagued his skin and again he cursed himself.

The door was only a foot away now and with a gentle push, it swung open.

Following the arm, he made a horrifying discovery. The arm truly had been severed from the body, which lay three or four feet away, and he realized that the arm wasn't the only thing missing. The other arm was also gone from the elbow down, the rest of it nowhere to be seen. His right calf had been torn in two, and his stomach ripped open, revealing his organs.

Next to the body was a small pool of blood.

"Wait... no..."

The officer walked a little closer, and suddenly his blood turned frigid, a cold sweat breaking over his body.

This was no pool of blood, but a print, like that of a giant dog, that would've easily fit his hand inside of it.

"Dispatch," Bryan's voice wavered, trying to comprehend what was in front of him.

He looked up from inspecting the mark and he heard it again.

The growling.

It came from the door.

He spun on impulse, and the sight pushed the blood run from his face, leaving a pale ghost in its wake. He opened his mouth to scream, finding fear had robbed him of his voice. He tried to run, yet terror had left his feet rooted.

There, standing in the doorway, its back nearly touching the top of the doorframe, was a monstrous gray wolf. Its eyes reflected red in the light, as blood trickled on its gleaming white fangs. It took a step towards the petrified cop, and the floor groaned.

The officer brought up the pistol, steadying it.

He pulled the trigger.

Click!

The firing pin had struck an empty chamber. Bryan studied his pistol for a moment. "Huh..."

The whites of his eyes showed as they rolled into the back of his head, and he fell unconscious to the floor.

* * *

4:30 A.M.

The fifth and final motorcycle rolled into the garage where Saul and the others stood waiting.

A near furious Saul took a step towards the braking motorcycle. "Where have you been, Dalton?!"

The rider shook his head, concealed behind his helmet and reached both hands into his jacket.

The rider's hands suddenly shot out, and the four bikers collapsed to the floor, each with a small throwing knife in the center of their throats.

Saul's breath caught as he took a step back, preparing to bolt as another, larger, knife took flight.

Before Saul could move, the blade plunged into his heart, the force driving him to the wall as he yelled in pain.

Barely holding himself up, Saul looked down to the handle of the blade, finding his shirt rapidly growing wet.

"Kain..." His mind screamed. *"I've got to warn him!"*

Saul clenched his eyes as he took a deep breath, sure to be his last, in an effort to save the last remaining robber.

"K–" Saul's voice was muffled as a hand covered his mouth, and opening his eyes, he found his own scared reflection in the visor of the green helmet.

Saul's eyes widened as a second blade jerked across his throat, leaving in its wake a crimson torrent.

In Saul's last moments of life, he felt the first blade wrenched from his chest, just before crumpling to the floor, watching a murky red pool grow around him.

The garage cleared, littered with bodies, the visor of the helmet turned to face the stairs.

The knives, wiped clean on the late Saul's jeans, returned to their sheaths before a pistol was drawn.

He made no sound as he advanced up the concrete stairs, closing in on his objective, just on the other side of an already open door.

Kain, undisturbed and unaware of the happenings below, was still sleeping, tossing and turning in the visor's reflection.

"It begins." The man behind the mask thought.

Kain's eyes shot open, revealing irises of menacing yellow. No longer was he only a man, but a creature whose ferocious power knew no boundaries.

The pistol raised to Kain's head.

"And it ends."

Kain briefly returned to consciousness, staring down the barrel of a silenced pistol. With the twitch of a finger and a silver bullet, Kain and the creature within, ceased to exist.

His mission completed, Dalton's imposter finally pulled the helmet from his head, no longer needing to ensure his identity would remain hidden.

None remained alive to witness him.

He tossed the helmet onto the bed, gently coming to rest against the departed Kain's leg.

"Time to go." He nodded in thought.

As he reached the bottom of the stairs however, he encountered something he hadn't anticipated.

The man's eyes fell on the back of what appeared to be a young man, kneeling next to a fallen biker not far from the Challenger.

"Did I miss one of them?" The killer thought.

"No, not possible." He knew how many there were, and he had killed them all.

The youth hadn't yet noticed that he wasn't alone, and as the young man stood, the pistol focused on his back.

"Stop there, kid." The killer gruffly ordered. "Don't turn around."

The youth silently obeyed, giving the man time to take stock of the situation.

This kid had stumbled onto something that he never should have seen, and now he couldn't be allowed to simply leave. There wouldn't be enough time to make a clean getaway if he notified the authorities.

The executioner found himself in an uncalculated dilemma. Two options were before him.

Either kill the kid, or detain him somehow.

The first option was dead in the water. The young man before him didn't belong here, he was simply in the wrong place at the wrong time. He wasn't some murderous robber, nor was he a member of the hunted. The young man before him was innocent, at least believed to be so.

"Detain it is." The man pulled his hood up, cloaking much of his face in shadow before drawing a black bandana from his pocket and covering the lower portion of his face.

"Turn around, kid."

Again, the youth did as he was told, and the killer's eyes rested on a young face.

Green eyes stared back at him from beneath messy light brown hair. The small amount of stubble on the kid's face was another indication of his young age.

The man moved to the passenger door of the Challenger, keeping the gun trained on his hostage.

"Drive."

2

Rainer Hemming

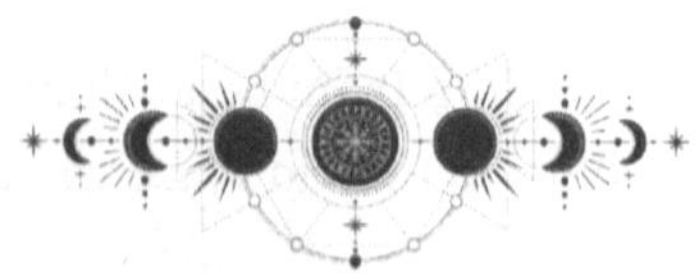

9/24
7:05 A.M.

The ever dutiful rooster crowed outside my bedroom window, a rattled cry announcing the new day.

As my eyes opened, glimpsing golden rays of sunshine, a groan of contempt escaped me, wishing nothing but ill will for the avian herald.

I reached for the ceiling as I sat up, stretching away any remaining sleep.

Another shrill call drew my eyes to the rooster, comfortably perched on my windowsill.

I offered the flimsy wire screen a gentle tap, drawing a beady little eye my way.

"Keep it up," I pointed, "and you're gonna' crow your way right into a skillet."

It seemed he knew my threat was empty though, as he was quick to let out another chorus.

"Alright, alright." I swung my feet from the bed, glancing at the old alarm clock on the nightstand.

7:10 A.M.

"Well," I turned back to the rooster, "looks like I might get the skillet before you."

Quickly as I could, I set about pulling on my clothes, already late for the morning chores.

Turning to the mirror on my dresser, I chuckled at the tan lines cut by my ball cap. From my hair line to the bridge of my nose, a pale half moon stood in contrast to the tanned skin of my cheeks and neck. Shaking my head, I vainly tried to flatten my unruly brown hair.

"Screw it." I thought. *"Gonna' wear my hat anyway."*

Finishing the lower buttons on my outer flannel, ignoring the top few, I snatched my cap and stepped for the door.

I had just put my hand to the knob when I smelled the unmistakable aroma of coffee and fresh cinnamon rolls.

I looked back to the alarm clock, suddenly doubting my eyes.

7:16.

Mom was still inside.

"Dang." I thought as I simply held the doorknob.

I knew what this meant. It meant that a "talking to" was coming my way in short order. I doubted it'd be a proper chewing, those were reserved for dad to deal out, even though he wasn't very good at them.

I took a deep breath as I pulled the door, grimacing as the top hinge, item three hundred and seventeen on the to-do list, quietly squalled out its plea for oil.

"Good morning, Rainer!" Mom called down the hall.

I couldn't help but smile. It wasn't easy to get one over on Mom, not impossible, but certainly not easy.

"Morning, Mom!" I gently called as I made my way to the kitchen, bracing for the inevitable.

"Bit of a late start this morning, love." She calmly stated as she pulled a silver sheet of steaming cinnamon rolls from the oven.

"I know." I nearly frowned, knowing that Dad and Kathryn were likely pulling up my slack on the farm.

"I'm gonna' get on out there." I thumbed at the front door leading out of the kitchen. "I'm sure Kat–"

"Ah, biscuits!" Mom pulled her hand away from the hot rolls on the counter, quickly inspecting what I could only assume to be a burned thumb.

"Are you alright?" I managed to keep my chuckle suppressed, not finding humor in the injury, rather her favorite stand in for curses.

"I'm fine, Sugar." Mom smiled as she wiped calloused hands on her white apron before she fully turned to face me. Brushing a few stray blonds from her face, she revealed concerned eyes. "And I'm sure you're sister can wait just a little longer."

"Sit." She nodded to a chair at the table, quickly joining me with two cups of coffee.

As she set the mug down I looked into the still swirling dark brew, refusing to look at her gray eyes. I had no desire, though perfectly able, to lie.

"Rainer," she gently spoke, "please look at me."

I just barely raised my eyes to hers, earning a warm smile in return.

"More nightmares?" She ducked her head, tracking my elusive eyes.

I frowned as I nodded, counting my first lie of the day. Surely not the last.

Her face saddened as she placed a hand on mine. "Rainer, it's been four months. Nearly every night you have nightmares, and some nights you wake the whole house up. I've tried not to crowd you, Rainer, but we can't keep going on like this. Everyone is worried about you."

"I know, Mom." I smiled as I looked up to her, loving her, and hating myself.

The nightmares weren't a lie, more often than not, the nights that I didn't wake the house, I'd wake with bloody recollections.

The past week however, things had changed and now the nightmares provided a convenient scapegoat.

I still hated myself for lying to them though.

"Would you please consider going to see Doctor Richards?" Mom asked. "It'd make us feel better too, Rainer, knowing you could rest, and if it's the cost… Our insurance will cover it."

"At a sixty or so dollar co-pay." I thought. *"Nearly the price of a tank of fuel."*

I couldn't ask that of them, not with things how they currently were.

"Alright, Mom," I lied once more, "I'll think on it."

"Thank you, Rainer." Mom smiled, and though the endearing gesture remained, pain hung over her eyes.

There was more she wanted to say, maybe ask, but she wasn't sure how to do so.

"Well," she suddenly stood, heading for the counter, "you'd better get out there, Rainer."

"Yup." I sighed, not exactly looking forward to running into my sister.

"Take these." She placed a pair of cinnamon rolls on the table, neatly wrapped in a paper towel. "May keep Kathryn from skinning you."

"Thanks, Mom." I smiled, turning towards the door with my peace makers.

"Make sure you get to keep yours!" Mom called through the slamming screen door.

"I will!" I called back over my shoulder as I stepped from the front porch.

"Dad's probably already bringing in the cattle." I noted the smell of rain beneath the looming thunderheads.

Weather outstanding, it was a beautiful late September morning, though that was pending Kathryn's demeanor. And with her, you never knew what you were gonna' get.

I paused at the door to our largest barn, a soft tune floating through the weathered boards.

"Well, she's singing, maybe this morning I'm dealing with 'it's alright little brother' Kathryn."

I opened the door, and the singing abruptly ended.

"Maybe not."

Quick footsteps announced her advance, fixing me with a scowl as she rounded the corner.

She was shorter than me, around five foot four while I, at nineteen, stood over her at six feet, but that didn't mean I was safe, and I knew it.

To say that she could intimidate me was an understatement, and that was when she didn't have quick access to a pitchfork.

Her curly blond hair caught a passing breeze and fluttered a bit, just before she tore into me.

"Hate to tell you this, but the beauty sleep ain't helpin' little brother." She chastised.

"It's just now after seven." I smirked.

"And you know that the horses get fed at six." She put her hands to her hips.

Looking into the stalls, I saw three of our horses, each munching grain from their troughs, and furthermore I knew each horse to be fat as a tick. They could likely roll faster than run.

"Because our horses are so famished that they couldn't make it having breakfast an hour late?"

"No, but by this time, we should be on to the birds." She noted the ducks and chickens that also needed feeding, and the eggs that were in need of gathering. "Now, we play catch up."

"I'm sorry," I shook my head as I extended the pair of cinnamon rolls, "but I did bring you a–"

Before I could finish, she had swiped both of them from my hand.

"Hey!" I chuckled as she took a hearty bite of the first. "One of those is mine!"

"Was." She shrugged as she spoke through the cinnamon roll tucked in her cheek. "One is repayment. The other is interest."

I sighed as I took the handle of a nearby shovel, pretending to be aggravated, in honesty completely fine with her eating them both. Giving her my cinnamon roll was the least I could do.

"If you're *really* sorry," She bit into the second roll as she made for the door, "you can muck the stalls, I'll get on to the birds. Maybe we'll be able to get out to dad at a reasonable time."

"Sounds like a plan." I nodded as I began down the long hall, bearing stalls to the left and a large holding pen to the right.

I turned left through a stall door, beside which sat an empty wheelbarrow, waiting for its next load of manure.

I hadn't been scooping long when I felt the presence of another.

It could only be one of two people, and I chanced a guess as I heard a heavy footstep. "Mornin' Alan."

"Morning, Rainer."

My best friend, though more of a brother, Alan, was always around on the farm, or had been in the time I was there.

Six years, though it felt longer.

Six years ago, my real mom and dad had been claimed by an automobile accident. With them being my only living relation, I wound up with an adoption agency.

Though it took a little time, given I was thirteen years old and most folks looking to adopt generally sought younger children, I finally met the family that I now knew.

They were a good family, and if I had been adopted at a younger age, I never would've questioned if I was really theirs. The people I came to know as mom and dad, since day one, had only ever treated me like an equal to their very own daughter. I was the son and brother the family had never had, but always wanted.

I met Alan within a week of moving to the farm, and we meshed together like the pieces of a puzzle.

He only lived a few miles away and, while he had never admitted to me, I was fairly certain that he was sweet on Kathryn.

His looks hadn't really changed in those six years either. Flat blond hair, bleached by the sun, laid in contrast with his sunburn, though it nearly matched the white sunglass rings around his eyes.

"Aren't we supposed to be helping your dad round up the cattle here soon?" He leaned on the stall door.

"Yeah." I scooped up a yet steaming mound of manure. "There is a distinct possibility that I may have overslept."

"Meaning Kathryn covered your hide."

"Yeah." I swatted away a fly.

"Been a bit of that here lately, Rainer." He said, not making an attack, simply an observation.

"Yes, there has." I frowned, both at the comments truth, and the horse apple I felt squish under my boot.

"Everything okay?" He raised a brow in concern. "Nightmares?"

I nodded, in this instance actually aggravated that one of my plethora of issues seemed to now be common knowledge.

"Maybe you ought to say something to your folks, Rainer. Maybe they could get you in to see a doctor, someone has to specialize in that kind of thing."

"I *have* talked to my folks, Alan." I tried to keep my tone neutral. "Mom is going to make an appointment with Doctor Richards."

"Ugh." Alan scoffed before painfully over enunciating. "Doctor Dickie."

I chuckled as I nodded. "Yeess, Doctor Dickie."

"I hear he does good work." Alan offered with a shrug.

"The guys a quack, Alan." I paused shoveling long enough to look at him. "How can someone who is a professional in quote unquote 'dreamscape' analysis ever be wrong? How do you argue with a diagnosis?"

I continued in an airy voice that left no room for doubt as to my confidence in Doctor Dickie.

"Tell me what happens in your dreams. Oh, you see a white full moon that turns red and then you're drowning in iron water, surrounded by the bodies of your friends and family. Then they all grow sharp teeth and pointy ears. You must have moonaphobia." I scoffed. "Please, Alan."

"That was," Alan paused, "*strangely* specific."

"Just a part I remember." I unloaded the shovel in the wheelbarrow, finishing the work on that particular stall.

"Besides," I carted the wheelbarrow to the next stall, "that kind of thing costs a pretty penny."

"Insurance won't cover it?"

"It will, but I'm sure there's a nice little co-pay for it."

"Money's still tight then?" Alan asked.

I sighed, suddenly regretting bringing up the family's finances.

"Nobody will admit it. Mom doesn't want to worry Kathryn and I, and Dad's too proud. Fact of it is, the price of cattle has bottomed out, and fuel is atrocious. We're getting closer and closer to not breaking even."

"I'm sorry to hear that, Rainer. I really am."

"Yeah, well, it is what it is. We'll make it, it's just gonna' be slim pickings for a while."

"Speaking of *slim*." Alan perked up. "Where's Vivian this morning?"

"Desiring some quality time are we?" I jabbed at him, though I was infinitely grateful that he used the horrible wordplay to guide the conversation elsewhere.

"We both know why she's usually the first one here. Has to get her one on one time with a certain someone here on the farm." Alan lightheartedly retorted.

"Oh, shut up." I smiled.

"You know damn good and well that she's sweet on you, Rainer. Eventually you're gonna' have to give her a chance."

"Why's that? So I can cement what I already know and give her false hope?"

"I swear Rainer… She's attractive, she's nice, and you know what, you might just make a good couple."

"She is sweet, one of the kindest people I've ever met, but that doesn't matter, Alan. I've told you, I don't see her that way."

"Not anymore you mean." Alan quietly came back. "Just a few months ago we spent the better part of a night talking about the fact that the feelings might actually be mutual. What happened, Rainer? What's holding you back?"

What was holding me back? It was more a case of what I was holding back, what constantly pounded at the doors of my mind.

He wasn't wrong. Just a few months ago, a few as in five or six, I was contemplating it, asking her out.

Not anymore.

"This chance won't last forever, Rainer." Alan said following my lack of a response.

"I know." I somberly replied. "In fact I'm counting on it."

"Counting on what?" A smooth voice asked as Vivian stepped through the door, fixing me with smiling emerald eyes.

My breath caught in my throat, certain she had overheard our conversation. We hadn't exactly been speaking quietly.

"Rainer," she smiled, "you okay?"

I nervously chuckled as I spoke through the lump in my throat. "Yeah, I'm alright."

"Correct me if I'm wrong, but aren't you normally done with this bit of chores by now?" She cocked her head just enough to send a wave through her golden hair.

"Normally." I resumed my task.

"Another late night." Alan explained, conveniently omitting my claim of nightmares.

"Oh." Vivian looked away from me, failing to conceal a frown as her slender face flushed.

"Out with someone special?" She suddenly looked back to me with a ravishing smile, mounting an instant recovery.

"Not hardly." I scoffed.

Despite the fact that her feelings weren't mutual, I still cared deeply for her, though I'd never be able to let on.

Alan had long been of the opinion that Vivian felt strongly for me. Whether or not that was so didn't matter. I knew that if I told her I cared for her, she wouldn't hear the 'as a friend' bit that followed.

I couldn't do that to her.

Something else I'd never be able to tell her, was how much I truly enjoyed her company.

Quick to laugh and possessing a contagious smile were only two of the innumerable qualities that made her a joy to be around.

"So, it was someone *not* special." Alan continued to meddle. "A late night flix and chill?"

"That's a no." I cast a mischievous eye his way. "More up your alley isn't it?"

"How would you know?" Alan countered. "I'm not one to kiss and tell."

"Can't say the same for the girls you've kissed." Vivian came to my aid. "And your reviews are a little lacking."

"Who said I'm a bad kisser?! I demand a name." Alan stomped the ground, though his beaming grin conveyed that he took the joke lightly.

Vivian was only too happy to oblige his request. "Well there's Rosa Sharon, Violet, Daisy–"

"Stop naming flowers!" Alan laughed.

"Pretty sure Rose of Sharon is a shrub, Alan." I leaned against the wall, dying for Vivian to deliver the killing blow.

She never started this witty banter unless she had a bombshell at the ready.

"But when it blooms, the shrub is flowering. Ergo, 'tis a flower." Alan replied.

"Then what about Tulip Poplars?" I retorted. "They get blooms."

"That's a *tree*, Rainer, how could it be a flower?" Alan replied as if I had spoken nonsense.

I raised my hands. "Well, it worked for the bushes."

A fiendish smile crossed Vivian's face. "Something Amy said you needed to trim, Alan."

"Hey!" That time, Alan sounded serious.

Solely at Alan's expense, Vivian and I shared a laugh.

"I have to go into Davenport for some stuff," Vivian settled down, "and I was going to ask if you wanted to go, but I guess you're going to be a while, huh?"

I nodded. "And after this, we've gotta' help dad with the cattle."

Vivian sighed with a smile. "Okay, well I gotta' go. Is it okay if I come by later?"

"You've never asked before." Alan answered for me.

Vivian cast him a glance of mild annoyance before turning her eyes to me, awaiting my answer.

I couldn't help but smile as a part of me, a very foolish part of me, thought that maybe, just maybe, I might be strong enough to hold it down.

"You're always welcome here, Viv." I smiled. "Still gonna' check fences this afternoon, and pending any nasty weather, it might be a nice evening for the horses to stretch their legs."

Vivian nearly glowed, to the point that if someone were to walk through the door at that moment, they surely would've thought I'd asked her out on a date.

"What time do I need to be here?" She asked with unmistakable excitement.

"Three or four." I nodded. "I'll make sure Skipper is saddled up and waiting on you."

Deep dimples showed at either side of Vivian's smile. "I'll be here."

As Vivian departed, I let out a breath of something akin to apprehension.

"Trying to give me whiplash, Rainer?" Alan turned to me with a raised brow.

"What?" I looked to Alan with narrowed eyes.

"You all but invited her just now. Hell, you said *you* would saddle her favorite horse and have him on standby."

"So, I've done it before. I've never been rude to her, Alan." I shook my head as thundering hoofbeats caught my ear.

"No, but you haven't catered to her in some time either. You know you'll have to catch Skipper. You've had a hard time getting near any horse here lately, except–" Alan closed the stall door as he looked over my shoulder. "Brace."

I felt myself stiffen, just before a soft thud landed on my back.

I had heard the hoofbeats, could've turned around, but I knew Jet enjoyed this game.

I turned, finding a long midnight face a few inches from my own.

"Hey youngin.'" I reached up to scratch behind the young horse's ears. "How we doin' this morning."

"Except that one." Alan chuckled as he finished up his earlier statement.

"Yeah." I nodded. "Just started maybe four months ago. Before that I could walk out to any horse in the pasture, then next thing I know Jet's the only one that'll let me near him."

"Maybe they smell something on ya' man." Alan offered, not knowing how close to the truth he was.

"Nah, the rest are just silly, ain't they, Jet." I rubbed the gelding's jaw. "If they could smell something on me, so could he."

"Maybe." Alan chuckled. "Maybe Jet just feels sorry for you."

"Pfft." I smiled as I scratched Jet's belly, causing him to straighten his neck, hitting just the right spot. "He's just a good horse, maybe one of the best, with a little time and effort of course."

"Careful, Rainer." Alan sang. "Sounds a bit like what you said about–"

"I know," I softly silenced Alan, "but *she* was the best. I think he's got the same stuff though."

"Hmm." Alan hummed. "Think you'll ever run barrel's with him?"

I shook my head. "Nah. The only reason her and I ran 'em was because she knew what she was doing. I mean I knew how, but there's a difference between knowing how and *knowing* how. And she knew."

"Oh I remember." Alan humorously raised his brows. "Nearly launched you right out of the saddle first time ya'll practiced."

"Sure did." I smiled, warmed with recollections of the old mare. "No, Jet n'me will probably just stick to cuttin' cattle and checkin' fences. He's still green, and I'm only just more than that."

"Rainer." Alan chuckled. "You do realize that you're supposed to be cleaning stalls, not playing with your horse."

"Don't listen to him, youngin'." I shook my head. "He's just in a hurry to see Kathryn."

"Hey." Alan sharply muttered. "No need to get personal about it."

I smiled, knowing both of us were right. I was supposed to be cleaning stalls, and he was definitely in a hurry to see Kat.

"Tell you what," I patted a bit of dust from Jet, leaving a beige handprint on his coal coat, "you knock out the next stall and we'll get Kathryn and go help Dad."

Alan smiled only briefly before turning to the next and last stall, belonging to a horse that more or less was his.

A handsome Paint named Lucky, though somewhat soft boweled.

"Why is it," Alan didn't turn from Lucky's stall as his hand absently searched for a shovel, "that I frequently find myself cleaning this stall?"

"Well he is more your horse than anybody's, Alan." I raked the last pile of crap from between Jet's feet.

"Right, right, I follow you on that." Alan's hand finally found the shovel. "But he lives here, so he's technically all yours."

"Consider it a… finder's fee then."

"Finder's fee?" Alan grimaced as he lifted a particularly soupy specimen in his shovel. "My Lord, how does he do this?"

"Yeah, a finder's fee." I turned my attention back to Jet, gently scratching along his mane.

"And what, pray tell, ugh," Alan sloppily emptied his shovel, "are you finding?"

"Whenever you get done whining," I smirked as I took cover on the far side of Jet, "Kathryn."

Alan turned to me with a loaded shovel, the very real consideration of catapulting it my way plastered across his face.

"Ah!" I pointed over Jet's back. "He's black, it'll stain."

"Chicken-shit." Alan insulted as he deposited the shovel load into the cart.

I smiled to Jet as I scratched his nose. "That's a good boy, keeping me covered."

"Oh, you'll be covered alright." Alan continued his work. "Especially if you keep runnin' your–"

"Morning, Alan." Kathryn rounded the corner. "Hey, nice to see you lookin' after Lucky."

"Oh," Alan quickly nodded as his rate of work increased exponentially, "well, yeah. I mean I feel like I spend the most time with him."

With a mischievous grin, I looked at Kathryn from the corner of my eye, finding her likewise looking at me.

"Almost time to go help Dad, Rainer." Kathryn said, fully aware of the effect. "I'd say we'd wait on you, Alan, but I think you've got the better part of a day's work there."

"Nah." Alan shook his head. "Just a few minutes."

"If you say so." Kathryn turned to leave, speaking as she went. "I'm gonna' saddle Sunny. Be outside in ten?!"

"Better make it five!" I called, playing along. "Dad's probably getting tired of waiting."

"Challenge accepted." Alan muttered, feverishly scooping.

I chuckled as I stepped from Jet's stall, heading to the tack room for all his gear.

As I returned I couldn't help but notice the lack of Alan's accuracy with a shovel, as well as the rapid rate of sweat dropping from his face.

"Easy, Jet." I gently lowered the saddle and blanket onto the horse's back. "Hey, Alan."

"Hmm?" I could hear the shovel furiously working.

"That's supposed to go in the wheelbarrow, you know that right?" I grinned as I softly bumped the curb bit into Jet's mouth.

"Alright." Alan heavily breathed. "Done."

I couldn't believe my ears. "There is no way–"

I turned to find Lucky's stall mostly clean, though the same couldn't be said for the bottom of Alan's jeans.

"You were saying?" Alan mocked with a smile.

"I was gonna' give you some crap." I took Jet's reins, leading him from the stall. "But I think you gave yourself enough."

3

Cattleman

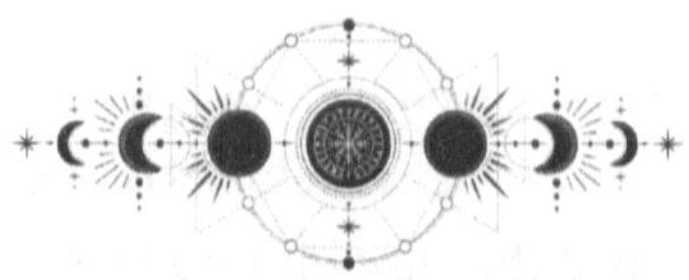

9/24

11:05 A.M.

The skies had improved some by the time we started making our way into the pastures of the farm.

I discovered that day that Alan could corral and saddle Lucky nearly as fast as he could muck a stall.

He still hadn't quite caught up though, as Kathryn and I rode side by side through the waning tall grass.

Kathryn continuously giggled to herself, periodically checking over her shoulder, watching the rapidly approaching Alan, though still a fair ways off.

"You're an ornery cuss, you know that?" I smiled as I looked back to Alan.

"I do," Kathryn giggled, "but he makes it so easy."

"Heaven forbid the poor guy think you hung the moon and stars." I couldn't help but start to feel bad for him.

26

"Oh come on, Rainer. He's sweet," she nodded as she patted Sunny's red coat, "and handsome, and I figure the next time he asks me out I'll say yes."

I smiled, happy for the pair of them because I knew that they already had a good foundation, and also because Sunny wasn't being too squirrely with me next to him.

"Good." I smiled. "Here I was worrying that you were just gonna' toy with him."

"That's rude of you to say." She scoffed. "I'm not you."

"Now *that* is rude, Kat." I swayed with Jet's gait, never turning to face her. "I don't toy with Vivian."

"Yet you knew exactly what I was referring to, didn't you?" She fixed me with an obnoxiously smug smile.

"Walked right into that." I fumed.

"Why do Vivian and I seem to be a concern as of late?" I heard Lucky's hoof beats gaining.

"I'm just saying skillet, don't call the pot black and expect not to get called on it." She said matter-of-factly. "Vivian thinks of you the same way Alan thinks of me."

"Yes," I nodded, "but the inherent difference is that you just said you'll say yes next time he asks."

"You *really* think she'd say no?" Kathryn skeptically turned to me. "Or are you saying you're not gonna' ask?"

"Haven't yet." I breathed in annoyance.

"Well maybe you should." She offered, her tone full of her typical spunk.

"Not happening." I quickly rattled as Alan caught up, for some reason breathing hard himself, as if he had run the distance.

"What's got you so gassed?" I chuckled. "Lucky did the work."

"Sympathy breathes." Alan's wide eyes set both Kathryn and I to giggling.

"What happened, Alan?" Kathryn collected herself.

"Agh, Lucky ran through a covey of quail. Took off like rockets, scared the hell out of him *and* me. Winded myself trying to hold on."

I shook my head. "Good Lord, Alan. What're we gonna' do with you."

"Give us a surprise flock of birds and I think we've got a shot at the

Kentucky Derby." Alan chuckled.

"I'm sure you'd beat 'em all." Kathryn laughed. "For the first twenty yards at least."

"So a couple flocks of birds." Alan smiled as I allowed them to pull ahead of me, their incessant banter dimming away as I thought on what Kathryn had said.

Was I leading Vivian on?

I grimaced as I realized Kathryn may've been right. I wasn't intentionally doing it though. The truth of it was that I adored her, and Alan had been very truthful when he'd said that I had considered asking her out.

It felt childish to call it a crush, but that's exactly what it was.

"That was before though. When I was just me."

I couldn't claim to be only myself anymore, and I couldn't put her in danger. I wanted nothing more than to keep her at arm's reach, but I found I was absolutely terrible at that concept.

I didn't have it in me to tell her a lie, that I had only ever seen her as a friend. She, and I, would both know that wasn't true.

"What am I supposed to do? We can't be."

It just wasn't possible. Not now. Not a chance since the changes of the last four months had occurred.

I was sure Doctor Dickie would provide some clever diagnosis, as well an equally clever named prescription, but the fact was, I didn't need him.

I knew why I dreamt of full moons, what the blood and teeth meant. I knew why most of the horses wouldn't allow me near.

They could smell it, and self preservation kept them away.

The only reason Jet allowed me near him was because he'd known me from birth.

Dad always said the complete trust of a horse was a hard thing to get, but with Jet, I had.

A ways off, past Alan and Kathryn and their growing lead, I spotted the first of the cattle trickling from the woodline.

"Well, there's one. Only seventy-nine more to go." I allowed myself the distraction.

"Come on, Jet." I gently put my heels to his sides, quickening his pace as Kathryn looked back over her shoulder.

"Alan and me will move around the left side, Rainer!" She called. "Go wide right and try to find Dad! Watch for any stragglers!"

"Don't forget the bull!" Alan quickly added.

Kathryn turned to Alan, and though they were still a ways off, I heard her quiet words.

"Believe it or not, Blackjack doesn't mess with Rainer anymore. None of the cows will. They see him coming and they all give him a pretty wide berth."

"That's weird." Alan said as they disappeared into the trees.

"Guess it would seem that way." I patted Jet's neck as we rode into the trees on the opposite side of the growing herd.

"Thanks for trusting me boy." I smiled down at the gelding, hoping he actually did trust me, and didn't just have a bad nose.

As we navigated the tree trunks, bearing wide of the cattle going the opposite direction, I let out a heavy breath.

How long could I keep this a secret? How long before it got the best of me? How long before I wasn't able to hold it back?

How long before I hurt someone?

A flash of movement caught my eye as a yearling steer darted in front of us, rejoining the herd with a cry of alarm, smelling a predator.

"Rainer, that you?!" Dad's voice rang through the trees.

"Yeah!" I spied Dad's white horse, Spooky, moving through the trees. "I see ya'!"

"Any breakaways on that side?!" He called.

"Didn't see any!" I replied as I reined Jet in Dad's direction.

"Good job." Dad nodded as we pulled up alongside him, Spooky taking a sudden step away.

"Easy now, Spook." Dad's blue eyes smiled down on the pale horse.

"Any trouble with them this morning?" I asked.

"Not a one." Dad shook his head as he smoothed his brown mustache, a couple white hairs dotted within.

"Good deal." I nodded.

"Everything taken care of up at the house?" Dad asked, his mind keeping to its normal track, farm business.

"Yup." I nodded. "Get the herd moved into the lot and check the fences and we should be done for the day."

Dad leaned back in the saddle as he looked to his right. "Kathryn on the far side?"

"And Alan." I nodded.

"Good." Dad said as he looked back to the herd. "Between the four of us we might make it back in time for dinner."

I smiled, Dad's old school terminology amusing me.

He was still of the generation that referred to lunch as dinner, whereas supper was the last meal of the day.

"Missed you this morning." Dad suddenly said. "Did you slip past me?"

"No." I shook my head. "Slept late."

He knew I had, had to have.

"Mmm." Dad softly hummed. "You talk with Momma' this morning?"

"I did." I smiled, knowing that he and Mom had talked over what to do about me. "She asked about going to see Doctor Richards again."

"I know you don't put much stock in the man, Rainer, but if he can help you–"

"I told her I'd go, Dad." I looked over to him, finding him smiling, grateful for me finally deciding to go.

"Thank you, Rainer." He looked over to me. "It's been weighing on your mom pretty hard. All of us truthfully."

"I know." I nodded. "I'm sorry I was stubborn about it."

"I know why you were, son, but no amount of money is worth you suffering." He quietly spoke. "Mom and me'd give everything we have if it meant you kids were taken care of."

"That's because you're a good mom and dad." I thought, wishing with all my might that the money they'd spend on the doctor would fix me.

For a time it was quiet, just the sound of heavy hooves and the occasional grumble out of the stock.

It wasn't an awkward silence between Dad and me, rather a peaceful lull in the typical noise of the day.

A bit of rest, just swaying on the horses and even though we were working, it was relaxing.

Dad seemed to have that effect on people, somehow able to put them at ease with only his presence.

A bit of thunder rumbled overhead and I looked up through the branches to a graying sky. I took in a deep breath, my lungs filling with the smell of rain.

"Think we'll beat it?" Dad asked, and I turned to find him smiling.

"Probably not." I chuckled as I found myself wishing I had brought my duster along.

"Here." Dad opened his saddlebag, pulling out his own.

"No. No." I shook my hand, grateful for the offer, but refusing all the same. "I knew it might rain. I just didn't think about grabbing mine."

"Alright." Dad raised his brows as he returned the duster to the bag, knowing fully well that rain was likely only a few minutes off.

I knew that Jet was the only thing that saved me from Dad throwing it over to me. Had he tossed it at me, he probably would've scared the hell out of Jet. Spooky wouldn't have minded. Of course he really didn't seem to mind anything, going so far as to tolerate even *me,* so long as Dad was close at hand.

As the first sprinkles began to fall, chilly specks that pattered around us, Dad chuckled.

"What?" I half-heartedly laughed myself.

He smiled. "Just thinking about how this is what you want, rather than go to some sort of school to make something of yourself."

"Nothing wrong with being a cattleman, Dad." I defended my position on the matter, a claim I'd made nearly a year ago.

"Didn't say there was." Dad continued smiling as he shook his head. "Just that you could go to make a lot more money than cattlemen do."

"Maybe, but I'm good at this, and honestly I enjoy it. I realize that I should probably be moving out soon, but this is still what I'd like to do.

It's an honest living."

"That it is." Dad nodded. "Lot of dirty hands."

"But clean money." I smiled over at him, finding him smiling back. That was one of the first things he'd told me when I started working cattle with him.

It wasn't a glamorous life, most days your hands were gonna' get dirty, but the money was clean.

At the time I didn't really understand the words, of course I was thirteen then. I didn't give much thought to the corruption that infested the world.

It was one of the numerous lessons that I had learned from Mom and Dad.

The thing about it was, despite being adopted at thirteen, the people I called my mom and dad were the closest things to parents I'd ever known.

My real parents both worked for the same company, and the job required them to travel quite frequently. I was more or less raised by one of their "very close" work friends. She was nice, but she wasn't a substitute for a mother or father.

Mom would make it in every other weekend or so. Dad might make it home once a month, and all holidays and birthdays.

Though it had only been six years since their passing, it pained me to realize I had largely forgotten what they looked like.

I chalked it up to God. I think maybe he realized he might've made a mistake, putting me with them, too busy to contend with raising a child.

So, then he led me here, to people who could show me what it meant for me to be part of a family.

And I was eternally grateful for that.

They were my God given family.

Maybe God hadn't made a mistake at all, maybe he just wanted me to know a good thing when I saw it.

I definitely saw the good here, and I saw the benefits to living life as clean as I could.

"Keep your heart on God," Mom occasionally said, *"And your nose on the grindstone."*

I smiled as I recalled the words.

"What's got you grinning?" Dad chuckled.

For a moment I waited for him to say something about Vivian, and I exhaled relief when he didn't, simply awaiting my response.

"Just grateful for all of this." I smiled. "Thanks for making me a cattleman."

He just smiled as he pushed ahead, leaving me alone. Alone with my intrusive thoughts.

The thoughts that told me I would never be a cattleman, nor would I be strong enough to protect them forever.

"Four months ago, maybe. Not now."

4

Riding Fences

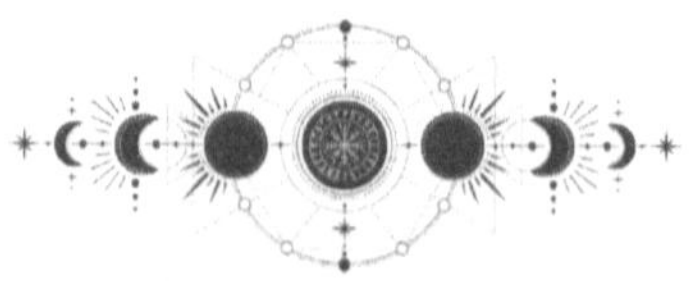

9/24
2:46 P.M.

The early afternoon found the weather only marginally improved, but the fences still needed their daily checking.

It was a relatively new daily chore, riding the fences, brought on by the suddenly dying ash trees.

Dad said it was some sort of beetle killing them off. It was only made worse by the fact that ash trees were fairly common on the farm and a fair number of them stood along our fences.

And so, most evenings found us making at least one round on the perimeter. Most of the time Kathryn and I would just take a pair of quads and each start in a different direction, meeting in the middle.

Today though, I thought the horses might enjoy it.

It took some doing, but I was finally able to coax Skipper into his stall. It cost me a full bucket of sweet feed and a half hour of sweet talking, but the handsome buckskin finally allowed me to saddle him.

"Why am I doing this?" I asked myself as I cinched the belly strap round Skipper, Kathryn's words repeating in my head. *"I'm not trying to lead her on. It just can't be. Maybe before Vivian and I could've been something, but not now."*

My brow furrowed with frustration at the number of times I said that to myself on a daily basis.

"But what the Hell can I do about it? There's no cure for this. There can't be. Hell if there is, it's sure to be a bullet. Probably why no one's ever heard of it. Am I the only one?"

I knew the answer to that. There was at least *one* other. The one who had done this, put this monster in me, leaving me to wage a never ending battle within myself.

During the day it seemed naturally suppressed, allowing me to breathe easy, but being the night creature it was, it viciously returned every evening.

"I will find you." I remembered the night, but not her face. Only her scent. *"And I will ki–"*

"Rainer?" A soft voice called me from the void of my mind, leading me to turn to Vivian, just ahead of Alan and Kathryn all chatting away.

"I was so deep in my head I didn't even hear them coming." I shook my head, grateful that I wasn't prone to speaking out loud.

"I'm here." I smiled to Vivian. "Skipper's ready for you."

"Well," Kathryn frowned as I noted the pair of lever action rifles in her hands, "you may want to take a quad instead."

"What do you mean?" I turned to my sister.

"Dad says we're one yearling short." Kathryn replied. "It must've got separated sometime before we pushed them in, first thing this morning, if not earlier. We didn't lose any on the way in."

"Mmm." I frowned. "We'd better find it quick then. Come morning–"

"Might not be much left to find." Alan nodded. "That's what your Dad said too."

I shook my head, knowing there was a fair chance the calf was already dead.

Mountain lions weren't unheard of, though it wasn't quite late enough in the year for them to be showing up. More recently, a small wolf pack had started taking calves.

A handful of local farmers had the notion to start picking them off, but as far as I knew, they hadn't taken any yet.

I looked to Jet, a stall over, fully geared and ready to go.

"It's up to you, Viv." I turned my eyes to hers. "Whatever makes you more comfortable. Horses can travel in tighter brush, quads won't get spooked."

Vivian looked to Skipper, clicking her tongue and drawing the geldings eyes.

"He seems like he's ready to go." She smiled. "Shame for him to go through the trouble of letting *you* saddle him just to get stuck at home."

I smiled. "Horses it is."

Even if we never could be anything more than friends, attempting to push her away wasn't the answer, I knew that. She didn't deserve that hurt.

I couldn't very well tell her the truth though. She didn't deserve that either.

One day, soon, I knew I'd have to find the words to let her down gently, but those words were yet to come to me.

"For this evening, can't I just pretend to be me? For just one more day?"

I was pulled from thought when Kathryn grumbled, obviously aggravated with our decision.

"Be careful will you?" She held a rifle out to me. "The killings have started again, and just a few days back the wolves were seen at the Davidson place."

I nodded as I took the rifle. The Davidson farm bordered the south side of ours. The prospect of finding a healthy calf had just grown much slimmer.

"You guys do the same, alright?" I leveled my eyes with Alan's, wordlessly saying to take care of my sister.

In understanding he nodded. "Since you guys are taking the horses we'll take both the quads, have a spare in case one breaks down."

"You doubting my maintenance work, Alan?" I smiled as I slid the rifle into the scabbard on Jet's side.

Alan shrugged. "Better safe than–"

"I was kidding, Alan." I chuckled. "Ready, Viv?"

"Ready." The leather gently chirped as she pulled herself into the saddle.

"Alright." I nodded to Kathryn. "We'll start on the east fence line. You go west. If we meet at the back pasture gate and none of us have seen the calf, we'll make a plan from there."

"Sounds good." Kathryn nodded.

I spun Jet around. "See you soon."

I joined Vivian outside the barn and took no time in starting along the five strand fence running east.

For a short distance the fence ran through fields, then dropped into the trees, where the quarters grew tight, also where a separated calf might bed down.

On the grimmer side of it, also where predators might stash a kill.

If it's dead, I should smell it well before we're in sight of it.

"Think we'll find it?" Vivian asked as she rode up next to me, surprising me with her serious demeanor.

"Dunno." I shrugged. "I'd say a fifty-fifty chance."

"Either we will or we won't?" Vivian said.

"Yup." I nodded. "You sure you wanna' go along on this? Could be a little gnarly. You remember three years ago."

"And miss the chance to take Skipper out on such a pretty day?" Vivian smiled.

I chuckled as I looked up. It was still overcast, thunderheads building, rain in the air.

"Not quite what I'd call a pretty day," I turned back to her, "and if the killings have started back up, well…"

"The day is what you make of it." She replied, maintaining her smile, her eyes saying it was more than just riding that made her day enjoyable. To her, whatever risk we were taking was worth the time together.

"Fair enough." I sighed with amusement as the tall grass brushed my boots.

As we neared the trees my eyes darted to the shadows, searching for the calf, or anything else.

"Spooked, Rainer?" Vivian almost laughed.

"Just looking," I replied, "but just for my peace of mind, stay next to me will you?"

"I think I can do that." Vivian hit me with a stunning smile, putting flight to my stomach.

Side by side, we rode the fences, talking about everything and nothing.

Not once did she ask about my nightmares, opting for sunnier topics. Colleges, the farm, the pending relationship status of Kathryn and Alan. We spent quite a while on that one.

At the end of it, we both agreed they'd be a good couple, if Kat didn't duct tape his mouth shut.

Of course that led into the conversation of whether or not he might be into that kind of thing, and according to Vivian, as his closest friend I should know.

I could happily say I didn't.

I didn't notice us round the corner of the fence, didn't notice the trees dissipate back into fields, I was too busy talking.

It was nice to talk, to ramble, to not feel like she wanted some answer I was unable to provide.

Honestly, it was nice just being there with Vivian, a bittersweet note, knowing that my feelings for her hadn't changed.

But I had.

Suddenly I found we were approaching the gate to the back pasture, and my pulse quickened, though it wasn't due to Vivian.

Kathryn and Alan both awaited us at the gate, the former bearing a scowl, the latter looking rather puzzled.

"Please, don't tell me they went into the pasture." My breath rattled as I bumped Jet with my heels.

"Took you long enough." Kathryn crossed her arms.

"Thank God." I exhaled relief.

"We were just being thorough." Vivian nodded.

Alan coyly smiled. "Bet you were."

"Ugh, *Alan*." Kathryn looked over her shoulder to find him snickering.

"Find the calf?" I smiled over Kathryn to Alan.

"Yeah." Kathryn shook her head, obviously perturbed with Alan's humor. "She was bedded down on the west fence line."

"Hmm. That's odd." I replied.

"Why's that?" Vivian asked.

"West fence line's wide open, nothing there but tall grass." Kathryn answered. "No trees or real cover. Something pushed her there."

The tone of conviction in Kathryn's voice, her certainty, left a question on my lips.

"What kind of something?" I asked.

"Something that can put three gashes on a calf's hind quarters." Alan sombered up.

"Rules out the wolves." Kathryn concluded.

"Mountain lion?" Vivian asked.

"Could be. Little earlier in the season than normal, but maybe this one's starving? But with the killings starting up again–" Kathryn shifted uneasily. "I really don't know. I'm assuming the fences are good on your side?"

I nodded.

"Good." She continued, trying to conceal the worry in her eyes. "Let's go then. Alan's been talking about Mom's chicken n' dumplings for the past forty-five minutes and now both of us are starving."

While Kathryn was quick to use Alan as an excuse, I had seen her eyes. She was on edge, and it was starting to infect even myself. The fields no longer felt as safe as they once had.

"Look," Alan raised his hands defensively, pulling me from thought, "your momma' said not to drag our feet so supper didn't get cold."

"Let's not keep her waiting then." I looked to Kathryn.

She met my eyes, and I offered a quick nod, consenting to quickly leaving the fields.

She silently mouthed her thanks.

"Wanna' take the trail?" Alan asked, referencing the cattle trail that cut through the woods. It was faster getting back to the house, but it would have us going through some pretty thick brush.

"Not today." Kathryn smiled, and I could see her trying to keep her worries to herself. "It might take a little longer, but we'll go through the fields."

As we started back to the house I smiled over to Vivian. "You're staying for supper right?"

Once more she all but glowed. "Wouldn't miss it."

"Great." I smiled. "I–"

"Rainer." Kathryn called, her quad still silent. "Need to holler at you for a minute."

I nodded to Kathryn before looking to Vivian and Alan. "You guys go ahead, we'll catch up."

As Alan put his quad in gear, leaving Vivian trailing behind, I nudged Jet up next to Kathryn.

She didn't look at me when she spoke, instead looking over the back pasture.

It was a fair sized field, a couple football fields worth of grass that would soon be baled for winter feed.

It was unused at the moment, courtesy of several trees laid over on the fences, nothing in it but a rickety old barn and its contents.

Over the field, on a gentle downward grade, the back of the Davidson farm and its fence lines were visible.

"Last kill was just on the other side of that fence, Rainer." Her tone was serious, as it should've been. "I'm sorry if I sounded mad when you guys rode up. I was just–"

"Worried." I nodded. "I understand sis, and I appreciate it."

"Been six kills the past two weeks. All the same as last time." Kathryn stood on the foot pegs of the quad, getting a better view of the field. "Stay out of the back pasture, alright?"

I nodded. "No reason to go in. Nothing in there."

"Thank you, Rainer," she nodded with a small smile, buying my lie, "and thanks for backing me about the trail."

"I saw your look, Kat." I chuckled, hiding the guilt I felt for my deception. "You might think I'm an oblivious idiot, but I do pay *some* attention."

"Well," she patted Jet's muzzle, "you do play the part."

"Now who's being rude?" I laughed.

5

The Last Supper

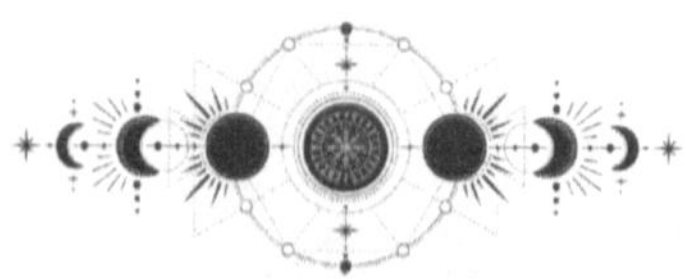

9/24
5:00 P.M.

That evening found us gathered round the kitchen table over a steaming pot of chicken and dumplings.

Alan seemed torn, per usual, his eyes darting between Kat and the food.

He was faring pretty well to be honest, able to maintain a conversation, keeping up the guise that he wasn't dying to tear into the pot.

"What do you think happened to the calf?" Vivian, sitting next to me, whispered as she tapped my foot with her own.

Before making it back into the house, the four of us had stopped by the barn, where Dad had stalled the injured heifer.

True to Alan's words, the calf bore three long narrow gashes on her left flank.

Fortunately they weren't terribly deep, doing little more than rip the hide.

When first I'd heard Kathryn's recount, I had assumed a big cat was responsible for the injury. After seeing the wounds with my own eyes though, I wasn't so certain.

Tearing through cow hide, even that of a calf, was no small feat, but the meat hooks of a mountain lion should've, would've, cut trenches into the young calf. At the very least, the calf would bear more damage, sustained as the cat was wrestling for the throat.

The rest of the calf was untouched however.

It was odd enough that I briefly considered that she may have gotten tangled up in the barbed wire fences.

That theory was quickly disproved though, the lack of bent posts and stretched wire detesting the notion.

With those ideas exhausted I was at a loss as for what could have happened, and that uncertainty left me inexplicably shaken.

Something was hunting in our fields, the fields we worked daily. While I wasn't so much worried about myself, my family was another matter.

The lack of damage on the calf would've been explainable if the animal was sick or injured, but that in itself changed everything.

It wasn't unheard of for weak or sick animals to make attempts on people.

I knew this. So did Kathryn and our dad.

It hadn't happened for a while, three years back to be approximate, but I figured any nightly activities at the farm were about to cease.

Three years ago, a string of cattle killings ran across the countryside.

It was a weird thing.

The corpses were all nearly the same. Bits and pieces of the kill had been claimed by scavengers, but what really struck the local farmers was that the kills looked as if they'd been dead for a while, dry husks.

That wouldn't have been hard to grasp if it wasn't for the fact that most of the farmers kept a close eye, and a closer count, on their livestock. When one came up missing, they'd track it down, and absences were rarely let go for more than a day, not enough time for a kill to completely dry out.

We didn't lose any cattle during the time of the killings, but Mom and Dad still thought it best to keep us indoors during the dark hours.

And now, according to Kathryn, the killings had started again.

Coupled with Dad's silence regarding the heifer, a blind man could read the writing on the wall.

"I don't know, Vivian." I replied just as quietly as she had asked, not sure what was responsible, but still aiming to keep her nerves down. "Maybe Kathryn's right and it's a sick puma. Or really young and inexperienced. I really don't know, Viv."

"A-hem." Dad quieted the table, bowing his head to say grace as we all followed suit, clasping our hands.

"Our father," Dad started, "thank you for the blessings you've given us. Thank you for the family and friends gathered here tonight. We ask that you bless this food, Lord, so that we can keep doing our honest works. We ask that you bless the farmers that grew it and fed it, and the hands that prepared it. Amen."

"Amen." The table said in unison.

"Thank you, Dad, that was nice." Mom stood as Dad sat, delivering food to plates and passing them round the table.

Once everyone had a plate, Mom included, Dad finally took his.

I had never seen anyone go hungry on the farm, and I often wondered if dad grew up with much less, and if his dad had done the same.

I never could bring myself to ask though, it just seemed too rude a question.

Whatever the reason, it just added to the things I admired about the man I called Dad, and further stoked my desire to help not only him, but my entire family.

Fortunately, that was something I was now in a position to do, though I was unsure how to go about it.

I looked to Alan across the table.

If there was someone I could count on to give me solid advice on a sketchy situation, and then not sell me out, it was Alan, and that was exactly what I needed right then.

He was pretty fox-like when it came to cleverness, the trait I was relying on here.

Unfortunately, though a very admirable trait, attached to that cleverness was the honesty of a saint.

It would take some work to convince him, but there had to be a reason this landed in my lap. The only problem was the impending setting of a curfew.

* * *

6:30 P.M.

A little later, after the evening's dishes had been cleaned and returned to their cupboards, I managed to pry Alan away for a few minutes.

With Vivian preoccupied visiting with Kathryn in the living room, I knew this was likely the best chance I'd get with him.

I knew how it was going to come off, but at best we only had an hour and half of daylight left, and I didn't really want to be out there after dark.

With myself or whatever else might be out there.

I had to hurry, for both of our sakes, even if it left him asking more questions for me to answer later.

"Alan," I spoke quietly, "you remember the money thing we were talking about earlier? Being tight and all."

"Yeah." He nodded, caught off guard as I knew he would be.

"I may be able to help, but I'm not sure how to do it."

"What?" Alan's eyes narrowed. "How? I mean just this morning–"

I nodded. "I know, just– I'll show you, but we need to hurry. I want to be back before dark."

"Or you could just tell me." Alan smiled a bit skeptically.

"No." I shook my head. The idea had become rooted in my mind, and now to wait a moment more was more than I could bear. "Just follow me."

As we stepped from the porch, headed for the barn and the quads, a voice called after us.

"Rainer?" My Dad gently shouted.

"Yeah, Dad?" I turned with a smile.

"Where you boys off to?" Dad asked as he lifted his face.

"Just gonna' go for a quick spin through the pasture." I smiled.

"Okay." Dad smiled. "Back before dark alright?"

"Will do." I gave him a thumbs up.

Alan followed me as I climbed aboard a quad, and soon we were headed towards the back pasture.

Alan was quiet for the majority of the ride, which to be honest was probably for the best. It would be much easier to answer his questions when he could see that I wasn't being hypothetical.

As I stopped to open the gate, my eyes rested on the old barn within the pasture, intended to be shelter for the stock during storms.

Now, however, the barn held no cattle, though I suspected there was now more horsepower inside than ever before.

I hurried us towards the unpainted structure, and Alan observed the state of the fences.

"I'm surprised you guys haven't gotten the fences back up yet." He said, barely audible over the engine.

"Just not enough time in the day." I replied. "Dad's hoping to get to it later in the year."

"Better hurry, not much of the year left." He added.

"Believe it or not, Alan. This pasture not getting used just might save us."

"How's that?" He asked.

I was silent as I came to a stop in front of the wide door, made to accommodate numerous cattle, though it served my purpose well.

Within, sparkling in the shafts of light that managed to break through the old tin roof, was a black Challenger.

Alan's brows rose in surprise. "Where did you get this?"

I frowned as I struggled to answer the question I knew would come, but was still unsure what to say. I had hoped that there would be a bit of time before this particular question came up.

Naturally, it would be the first Alan asked.

"I was in the wrong place at the wrong time, Alan. Somewhere I probably shouldn't have been." I managed. "*Definitely* somewhere I shouldn't have been."

"That doesn't explain the car, Rainer." Alan raised his brows, well aware that I was trying to skate around the question. "Where were you?"

"I was in Kirkwood, and I got lucky, Alan." I leaned against the fender of the Challenger. "The owners… they didn't need the car anymore, and I was pretty far from home at this point, on the other side of Kirkwood. It was made clear that I needed to leave, and the car was ultimately left to me to use as I saw fit. In all honesty, I had meant to ditch it on the way back, but then I looked in the back seat and after that I couldn't just get rid of it. Not with things the way they are here."

"You're painting a really vague portrait here, Rainer." Alan started to get aggravated.

"I feel like the less you know the better, Alan." I frowned. I wasn't trying to keep him in the dark. It was more a matter that if push ever came to shove, his lack of knowledge might protect him.

Alan sighed as he put his hands to his hips. "What the hell's in the backseat?"

"Take a look." I nodded towards the car.

Alan stepped to the door, peering through the open window to the back seat, finding five olive green duffel bags.

"Open one, Alan." I said.

He obeyed, pulling a bag to the front seat and working the zipper. As the bag opened, his eyes widened in disbelief. His jaw dropped but he said nothing, failing to produce the slightest sound.

"That was my response too." I nodded. "There's somewhere around twenty-five thousand between all the bags."

He looked up at me in wonder. "I don't understand?"

"I really don't know." I shrugged, unable to answer anymore with full certainty. "What I do know is that this would definitely help, it's just that–"

"Rainer," Alan turned to me, nothing but serious in tone, "tell me you didn't rob a bank."

"What? No!" I shook my head. "Why would you think that?"

"You remember that bank robbery two weeks back in Oakstone? This car matches that car, down to the dollar. If this car was 'left' to you, it's because they got scared and wanted to drop the evidence."

"Alan," I felt the conversation drastically veering away from where I'd intended, "the money–"

"Is dirty, Rainer, people died in the robbery." Alan paused, visibly grasping for words as he shook his head at me. "After all the talk from your dad about clean–"

"I didn't end their lives, Alan. All I know is that this will help us, all of us."

Alan Shook his head with a frown. "Yeah, I just don't know if a judge is gonna' care about that part, Rainer."

6

Break Out

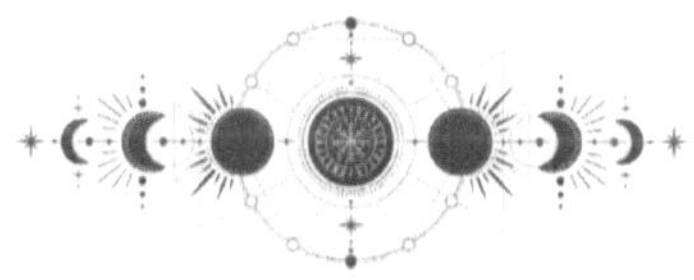

9/24

11:05 A.M.

It was the first morning back for Bryan White, just returning from a two week leave of absence following the events of 411 Pine.

His return found him driving his old patrol route with longtime friend and fellow officer Devin, a middle-aged black man of matching stature to Bryan.

Bryan's thoughts had never lingered far from that night two weeks past. This morning was no exception. The images flashed through his mind as if on film. The body mutilated, torn to pieces, and the wolf he had seen before falling unconscious.

Bryan glanced over to Devin. "Did you ever get around to going over the evidence from 411 Pine?"

Devin sighed, Bryan had been talking about this all day. "Yes, Bryan, for the fourth time."

"I just keep seeing it, over and over." Bryan said.

"I know, Bryan." Devin replied, mildly annoyed.

"What could leave a track that size?"

Devin sighed, having covered this particular item several times, still though he tried to be gentle. "Bryan, there was no track, remember? The carpet was chewed up."

"But don't you think it's odd that it was only that spot that was torn up?"

"No, Bryan, I don't." Devin shook his head as his patience left him. "It wasn't cut away like someone was trying to hide something. It was literally *chewed* away, like someone's dog had got a hold of it, and it wasn't a small spot either, it was three or four feet, Bryan, much larger than the print you reported."

Bryan grew quiet, knowing he'd worn away his friend's patience. "Sorry."

Devin sighed again, glancing down at his watch, then over to his driving companion. "Come on, let's hit the station for a bit. Supposed to be some stuff on the case coming in anyway, maybe doing something with your hands will put your mind at ease."

* * *

Thirty minutes and two coffees later, the pair were sorting through old 411 Pine evidence at the Kirkwood police station.

Sifting through papers and clear evidence bags, Devin shook his head. "Doesn't look like they've found anything new with this stuff."

"Didn't you say that new evidence was coming in today?" Bryan asked, almost frantic.

Devin nodded. "Yeah, but that may have gone straight to forensics."

"Let's call, maybe they've matched some prints or somethin'."

Picking up the desk phone, Bryan punched a few keys, impatiently waiting for an answer.

An older gentleman with glasses was furiously striking at his keyboard when the phone rang.

Without moving his head, he shifted his eyes to the phone and picked it up. "Ah, Bryan. I was hoping you'd call. I'll fax what I've found. Let me know when you get it."

There was a delay of perhaps a minute before Bryan returned to the line.

"Rainer Hemming." Bryan spoke as he looked at the picture, a driver's license, and found the face of a young man with brown messy hair and dark green eyes. A bit of stubble hugged his face accompanying an expression of enthusiasm, as is common when receiving one's first driver's license.

"This was just found at the crime scene, after some more tedious investigating." The elder stated.

"This only proves he was there, Clint, not that he committed the murder."

"True," Clint replied as he tapped more keys, "Check your email, I just sent you a video. It's certainly enough to bring him in for questioning."

It only took a few moments for Bryan to follow the commands.

Footage began to play on screen, captured by a video camera mounted on the house, overlooking the door.

"The victim, Dalton Williams, is already inside," Clint said, "that's his motorcycle in the drive."

A figure approached the door, a pack slung on his shoulder. His face was shrouded by the hood of a jacket, though his build seemed to be that of a male. The individual moved to the door and turned about, observing his surroundings. Bryan expected the man to pull a gun and was bewildered as the man stepped back from the door. He quickly reeled back a leg, firmly driving his boot into the door that was off screen. The man darted into the house, and suddenly the picture began to shudder, as if the wall was shaking.

The video fast forwarded to Bryan walking up to the house.

"When did he leave?" Bryan asked Clint.

"He hasn't yet." Clint replied.

Again, the video skipped ahead, only briefly, finding the man leaving the house, now wearing a green helmet, before stepping onto the motorcycle.

Not long after, a young man in a jacket came up the walk. Nearing the door, the young man observed, as Bryan had, the broken doorframe. The youth looked around, happening to look in the direction of the camera.

Rainer Hemming.

He was only inside for a moment, and when he left, he was in a hurry. Bryan knew what he found.

"Next activity is your precinct and an ambulance arriving." Clint said.

"Anything on the other guy?" Bryan inquired.

"Not even a hair." Clint sighed. "Guy was clean. But we have Hemming's address, thanks to the license, must've dropped it when he hightailed it out of there."

"Well," Bryan thought, *"We know he's not the murderer. And we know he isn't the–"* His mind stopped, unable to even think what followed.

The question remained however, what was Rainer Hemming doing there?

Bryan pulled out a small notebook jotting down the address as he heard it. "421 Cross Road."

He looked to Devin. "Better run this past the Chief."

* * *

Most of the remaining daylight had been spent with Alan and I debating the outcome of the money, and while he understood my logic, he held fast to his opinion that it should be turned in.

Reluctantly, I was beginning to agree with him. My folks wouldn't want this, they'd probably be abhorred that I even thought of it.

I couldn't just get rid of it though, knowing that it could help us. Weren't things like this supposed to happen? The good are rewarded? Good things come to those who wait?

In the time we spent speaking, Alan decided to further investigate the car, looking for proof, one way or the other, as to the car's origins.

I played along, even though I knew the grisly truth. I'd already picked it apart.

It didn't take long for Alan to spot the bolts and rivets inside the car, where additional metals had been integrated, creating an armored vehicle.

Not long after, Alan took note of the windows, much thicker than stock glass. No doubt bulletproof as well.

The same could be said for the tires, much heavier ply than necessary, intended to take a round and not immediately shred out.

Finally, the last nail in the coffin for my defense, Alan discovered a panel of weaponry behind the rear seat.

I cringed as he flipped the seat forward, revealing an array of firearms, ranging from handguns to several automatic rifles. Adding to the discovery, was the vast quantity of ammunition.

Alan whistled as he looked to me. "I rest my case, Rainer. Now, I'm saying you should turn it in not only because it's right, but also because if you get caught with half of this stuff, you'll be going away for a very long time."

I drew a heavy breath. He was right, of course he was right.

"Alright, Alan." I conceded.

Alan nodded, satisfied with my answer, though a new question occurred to him.

"How are you going to do it? I mean I'm happy you're going to get rid of it, but you can't get caught by your folks, or by the authorities."

I nodded towards the east side of the field, where another gate stood. On the other side was a dirt road that we used to bring trailers in for the cattle. The other end came out only a short distance from the highway.

"I'll use the dirt road to keep it out of sight from my parents, that's how it got here in the first place. As far as avoiding the police, I'll wipe everything down, and once I get far enough away from the farm, I'll ditch it."

Alan approved the ramshackle plan with a nod.

"Alright," I said defeatedly, noting the sinking sun, "let's get back to the house. We're losing the light."

"I'm sorry, Rainer." Alan managed as we climbed back onto the quad. "I know you were just trying to–"

I silenced him as I rolled the engine.

I wasn't angry, I was just disappointed, more with myself than Alan.

I should've known better.

As I closed the gate of the pasture, I found myself facing the unsettling prospect of returning in the wee hours of the morning. I wouldn't be able to ditch the car during the day, it would be too easily noticed. I'd have to do it under the cloak of darkness.

The ride back to the house was quick, and the dying light found Alan and I just barely making it into the barn on time.

As we each stepped from the quad, Alan put a hand to my shoulder.

"Are you alright, Rainer?" His quiet words hummed with apology.

It wasn't that he was sorry for telling me to do the right thing, it was an acknowledgment that he understood why I chose to do what I had.

"I'm alright." I nodded as I put my hand to the barn door. "I'm sorry for dragging you into it."

As I stepped through the doorway, I spotted a police cruiser parked in front of the house.

My stomach dropped, and my fingers dug at the wooden door.

"What are the cops doing here?" My brain fired. *"Maybe it's about the cattle killings?"*

I wanted nothing more than to dip back into the barn, but both Alan standing right behind me and the fact that the officers had already noticed me prevented it.

So had my parents, both standing on the porch.

Dad raised his face to me, gently waving his hand for me to join them.

As I got closer, one of the officers locked his eyes to mine, a portly fellow. His name plate read "WHITE".

"Evening." He smiled. "I'm Officer White. Are you Rainer Hemming?"

I nodded. "Yes sir."

"I thought so." He held his smile. "We've got some questions we'd like to ask you son. I've already explained to your folks that you're not in any trouble, and that once our questions are answered we'd be more than happy to bring you back home. Is this something you think you can help us with?"

"Questions?" My mind spun as a fist took hold of my gut. *"What's this– Is this about Kirkwood? That's been two weeks. Do they know about the car?!"*

I swallowed a nervous lump as I nodded, trying to keep myself cool. "Of course, Officer White. How long do you think we'll be?"

"Few hours." Officer Whited shrugged.

"Okay." I nodded. "Can I talk to my folks for a minute?"

"Sure, son." He smiled.

As I moved to the bottom porch step, Mom's wide eyes demanded an explanation.

"What's going on, Rainer?" Dad quietly asked, his breath short.

"I don't know," I shook my head, "they said it was just some questions."

"And you're sure you're not in trouble." Mom asked hurriedly.

I nodded, smiling in an effort to keep everyone, including myself, together. "I haven't done anything wrong, Mom. It shouldn't be too long."

"Son." Dad's eyes glistened with worry. "Pick your words wisely. I need to know now, do I need to get a lawyer down to the station?"

"No, Dad." Fear ripped at my insides as I hoped that I didn't need a lawyer. "I'm not under arrest."

Dad nodded just before Mom wrapped me in a hug.

It couldn't have been easy, seeing one of your kids tied up in something. Even if I wasn't officially in trouble, getting called in for some information must've been unsettling.

I had a feeling that the time for my late night excursions had come and gone.

As I slid into the back seat of the cruiser, I noticed Vivian spying from the kitchen window.

She looked worse than Mom.

As we pulled away, I turned in my seat, to the faces of my family. Every one of them were in shock, and who could blame them?

It had been a normal day, just going through the motions. I suspected the questioning I'd receive when I got home would be more intense than I'd undergo at the station.

I rocked my head back against the seat as the house faded into obscurity.

It was already getting the better of me, driving me out into the night trying to find the one that did this to me.

"What am I going to do when I find her? Kill her? So that I actually do

something that screws me for the rest of my life?"

He was already consuming me, devouring my ability to keep him locked away. He sowed the intrusive thoughts I struggled to keep at bay, the feelings of anger that set bloodlust in my mind.

As if on cue, the soft pitter-patter of rain danced overhead as the car sped towards the police station.

"Just keep it locked down. A few more hours." I braced myself as the sun dipped beneath the horizon. *"Don't lose tonight."*

* * *

I found myself in a mostly bare interrogation room, seated across the table from another pair of chairs, behind which was a large window. It reflected a mirror image of the room, and I knew that there were likely people behind it, peering in.

Across the room, tucked high in a corner, a single camera looked at me, a red light shining bright.

For what seemed like hours, I sat in isolation, and I suspected that this was some unspoken form of interrogation.

Finally the solitary door into the room opened, giving way to a man in a black suit with a manila folder.

He said nothing as he sat in front of me, leveling his round face with mine, and I gathered he'd been a cop for a while.

His expression was flat, no sign of any emotion, just doing his job. Above tired hazel eyes, neat hair, parted at the side, made him look as if he was about to disembark towards 1943 Europe.

"Mr. Hemming, is that correct?" He asked politely.

"It is." My stomach rolled. "You can call me, Rainer, sir."

"That's quite alright, Mr. Hemming. I am Detective Pierre." He opened the folder, keeping it tilted enough so that I couldn't see its contents. "411 Pine Street. Two weeks ago."

"I'm sorry?" I asked. I had been in Kirkwood two weeks past, but it wasn't like I'd checked the addresses of the places I went.

Detective Pierre nodded as he plucked a blown up photo from the folder, placing it before me. I saw myself, standing before the door of a house.

I knew what was in there, a wrecked house, a lot of blood, and a very unconscious officer.

Suddenly I doubted that this was just about questions. My blood ran cold as I realized I might be looking down the barrel of a murder charge.

"You have the right to an attorney son, would you like to make the call?" He asked.

"So there's–" I swallowed. "This is more than just questions then?"

"I know you were there," Detective Pierre continued, "and while I could put charges towards you, I'm more interested in anyone you may've seen in the vicinity, anything out of–"

The door suddenly burst open, and I looked to find another man standing on the threshold.

Water dripped from his black raincoat, the dark hood still raised, obscuring all but his face and a bit of his hair.

"Detective Pierre?" The man asked as he stepped inside, closing the door behind.

The sitting man nodded. "I am, and I'm a little busy if you can't tell, Mister?"

"Francis Butler, Federal Bureau." He quickly brandished an I.D. card before looking at me with hard eyes. "I am here for him."

My chilled blood suddenly turned to ice. *The F.B.I.?!*

"Pardon?" Pierre asked.

"Where are we at?" Francis asked as I noted his stony looks. He had a stern face, sporting a dark business-like beard and mustache. Black hair hung down in spider-like tendrils, ending just above dark brown eyes, a stark contrast to his fair, yet weathered skin.

"He was about to answer me as to whether or not he'd like an attorney, Agent Butler." Pierre said.

Francis smiled as he leaned against the wall, directly below the camera.

"But you wouldn't need a lawyer unless you've got something to hide? Do you, Mr. Hemming?" Francis asked.

The arrival of a federal agent sank a nail of fear into my heart, and my voice hung in my throat.

"Well," Francis said, spurred to words by my lack of, "we've already got enough to put you away for murder. You were caught on film entering the residence at 411 Pine. When you left you were in one hell of a hurry, and the man within was dead, killed in a most horrific manner. So, here's the thing, you can confess, and the judge may go a bit easier on you, or you can fight it, in which case you'll still go down and get a much harder sentence."

"Agent Butler," Pierre turned around with angry eyes, "I don't know how *you* do things, but this is not how *we* do things. You and I need to step outside for a moment."

Francis frowned, and appeared to be mustering a response when a series of loud thuds echoed on the door.

"That'll be for you, Pierre." Francis said, remaining beneath the camera.

"What the hell is going on here?" Pierre shook his head as he stood.

His hand had just landed on the doorknob when Francis lashed out, wrapping his arm around Pierre's neck.

With wide eyes, and no shortage of panic, I watched as Pierre attempted to wrench free of Francis, driving a solid elbow into Francis' side.

My panic turned to terror, matched by Pierre's, as Francis chuckled at the blow that would've found others with at least one broken rib, probably more.

Pierre began to kick wildly, his eyes slightly bulging as a pale bluish tinge took to his face.

Suddenly he went limp, and Francis gently let him down to the floor before pressing two fingers to his neck.

He nodded before looking up to me, giving only whispers. "Let's get a move on, he'll be awake soon."

Quickly reaching beneath his raincoat he drew a pistol, training the barrel on me as his arm shot straight out, almost too much.

He was overextending himself.

He smiled at me, bringing his free hand to his face and holding a finger to his pursed lips.

His eyes gestured to the camera above him and I realized this was a show.

"What the–"

"On your feet!" He barked through his smile as he slapped a set of cuffs on the table. "Put these on."

"What am I supposed to do? He's got a gun on me, he's smiling like he's nuts."

For a moment I wished for the wolf to surface, to save me from this fresh hell.

I felt it shuffle around inside my core, but nothing more.

"Shit."

Slowly I stood before ratcheting the cuffs onto my wrists, and Francis gestured to the door with the gun.

As I stepped to the doorway, Francis fell in behind me, grabbing my shoulder with his free hand and shoving the gun into my spine.

"Forward." He growled loudly before whispering. "The gun's empty, you are in no danger, Rainer. I'm here to save you, but this has to be convincing. You are not alone. I know you understand what I mean by that."

As the meaning of the words sank in I stepped from the door, being driven along by the pistol.

"Did he mean–"

"Hang a right, son." Francis calmly whispered.

As we continued into the reception area, I found the area devoid of officers, replaced by five people clad in black clothing and tactical vests. Each of them held a long gun, several with shotguns, others holding what appeared to be assault rifles.

With a nod from Francis the five gunmen lead the way to the front door.

"The officers?" I asked with concern.

"In a holding cell." Francis whispered before speaking up for the camera's. "The black car outside, get in!"

I had just shouldered the door open when the last of the gunmen climbed into the backseat of a black SUV. The door had barely shut before the vehicle sped away, splashing through still forming puddles.

"Alright, Rainer. Time for us to make tracks." Francis opened the passenger door, allowing me to slide in.

"If I wasn't in deep before," My head screamed, *"I sure am now."*

Francis quickly joined me in the vehicle, reaching down and starting the engine.

The car lurched into motion as we left the police department behind us and made towards the outskirts of Kirkwood, windshield wipers feverishly swiping away raindrops.

Francis looked over, finally pulling down his hood. "Very sorry about that Rainer, but it looks better this way. An abduction opposed to an escape."

I could provide no response, blankly staring at him, trying to sort out recent events.

"Abduction opposed to an escape? Was that an escape?"

Francis looked over to me. "I'm sorry that I couldn't clue you in more, time was short. You can snap those cuffs now."

"You're–" I started.

"A wolf, yes." Francis smiled. "Just like you, Rainer. That's why I had to get you out of there. Now, are you going to free yourself?"

With nothing but uncertainty, I pulled against the metal but found I could do little to break the cuffs.

"I can't." I grunted under the effort.

"You can't break those?" Francis questioned. "That's odd. Any wolf should be able to break free of human bonds. Just sit tight I suppose, we'll sort this out."

"What are you talking about?" I asked.

"You are a wolf, the strength you possess should easily free you of those handcuffs."

"How do you know I'm a wolf?" I whispered. I gathered he was no cop either, so how had he known I was in custody? "How did you know where I was? How do you know anything?!"

"I have my ways of knowing things, Rainer Hemming, like I know that utilizing your wolf, you can break those cuffs."

As we exited city limits, I tried again in vain to set myself free. "Well, I'm telling you I can't, Francis."

The man behind the wheel was quiet for a moment, staring through the drumming wipers. "You haven't learned to control it yet."

He seemed to be speaking more to himself than to me.

I looked out of my window knowing exactly what he was saying. That I hadn't learned to control the animal within. To control the wolf.

He made it sound like a gift, but it was far from that in my opinion, more a curse, no good capable of coming from it.

It was something that I had fought every moment since the night I'd been changed.

It was an omnipresent power, a force that shouldered for total control, to do its own will.

While I could count the instances that it had won on a single hand, of those instances, I recollected nothing. It was a blank slate to my memory, a black void that I could only speculate on with dread and anxiety.

The most solid defense I had found was that I could feel it coming on, the change. It always started the same. First there were subtle stirrings, as if it was waking from slumber. Soon after it would test the doors of my mind, like a dog gently pawing at a closed door, politely asking to be let in. When the doors remained bolted however, its demeanor turned much darker.

Claws and fury tore at my palisades, no longer requesting entry, now demanding surrender as he put pressure to my head. More than once I swore I could feel his jaws on my skull, and there was little more for me to do than wait for my head to explode.

At this point, all that I had left was to hold fast against my walls, fighting until I either failed, or was saved by the light of day.

Failure had only happened twice.

The first time was when he had made his presence known, and the second had been around two months ago.

He was particularly ferocious that night and from the onset I was worried I couldn't hold him. If I had to venture a guess, it was when I questioned in myself if I had already lost.

I didn't want to change, I didn't want to face that void. I didn't want to stumble into my home to find that my nightmares had spilt over into the real world.

I still managed to put up a fight, pushing back against the beast with all the strength I could muster, pulling from everything I knew to give me support.

My family, my friends, Vivian, the farm as a whole, things that usually bolstered my resolve.

That night, they were useless.

I called to God. I prayed for his strength, to push back this demon in my body, this creature I fought with every thought and breath. I begged for him to kill it if he could, to kill me if he couldn't.

God was silent that night.

The pressure in my skull drove me to my bedroom floor just before my world faded to black.

The next day I came to in my bed, stark naked, with a bit of blood around my mouth.

As quickly as I could I pulled on my clothes and tore through the house. Everyone was alive.

Later that day, Kathryn and I were checking fences, and we found what was left of a whitetail. The leaf litter was cleared in a wide swath, leaving Kathryn to believe a pack of coyotes or wolves had taken the deer in the night.

My early morning vomit featuring strands of brown hair and raw flesh made it very clear that it wasn't coyotes, and it wasn't the wolves that Kathryn believed.

That was two months ago, and though the wolf had growled at the door since then, never again had it been so aggressive.

I wondered what had pissed it off that night. Had it just been too long? Like a caged dog that needed to run?

The answer still eluded me, as I figured it always would, much to my aggravation.

"No, Francis." I returned to the present. "I haven't learned to control it yet. Best I can do is keep it down."

"Well," he replied, "that can be easily changed. And enough of this Francis stuff, that is not my name."

"What is your name then?" I asked.

"That does not matter at the moment." He cranked the wheel, turning onto a desolate country road lined with trees.

The car came to a stop, the engine and lights all shutting down as my rescuer stepped into the dwindling rain.

Wasting no time, he moved to my door and yanked it open.

"Out." He demanded.

I stepped out into the night; the moon concealed behind a sheath of thick clouds. As the door of the car slammed shut, I found myself in total darkness.

"Follow me." My companion ordered gruffly.

In the pitch, it was impossible for me to see him, and for a moment I hoped I'd be able to follow his footsteps. This wasn't to be however, as only the opening chorus of chirping crickets offered sound.

"I can't see you." I whispered.

"Yes, you can… You just won't allow it."

"How can I see you?!" I nearly hissed, this game wearing on me. "I don't have night vision."

"Oh, but on the contrary, you do, the wolf does. You simply haven't learned to control it. You only see the night when you allow the animal to take hold, but you haven't learned to keep it from overwhelming you. Fortunately, I can show you, as I am right now."

"How?" I questioned the voice that called from the night.

"Do you trust me?" The voice answered my question with another.

"Well, I don't really have another option, do I?" I whispered into the darkness.

"Allow the wolf to take hold. Maintain your absolute control, but let it come in and possess a small part of you, let it help you in your time of need."

"You're sure about this? If I fail, there's no telling what will happen."

"Don't make me regret saving your life, Rainer Hemming." The voice harshly replied.

I closed my eyes and steadied my breathing, feeling a darkness begin to creep into my soul. A warmth wrapped itself around me. It felt as if I were in the embrace of another. A low flame overtook my body, letting me feel the curse as it covered me, and I felt it grow from a spark to a scorching inferno that threatened to consume my whole being.

The stranger's voice reached me. "Fight it back."

The warmth willed me to give in, the heat that blanketed me beckoning me to surrender. The rage of the beast began to fuel the flames and I could feel myself begin to change, to turn.

Bones crunched as they expanded and grew in length. Muscles changed positions under my skin, forming a muscular frame far more powerful than that of any man. I was becoming the animal.

"Are you this weak?!"

From the back of my mind an image appeared. It was Mom. Straight blonde hair descended to kind eyes. Despite my shortcomings I knew that she and Dad loved me, and that they always would. What would they think of me now, in this state? I knew what they'd think, it couldn't be anything else, because it was true.

They would think me a monster.

Slowly, she faded from my mind, and I felt myself burning away as her departure angered the wolf within.

I felt myself wavering, I felt the turn completing, fur tore through my skin, my skull broke down, my teeth grew long and sharp.

A heavy blow landed on the crown of my head and I felt no more.

7

Finding An Ally

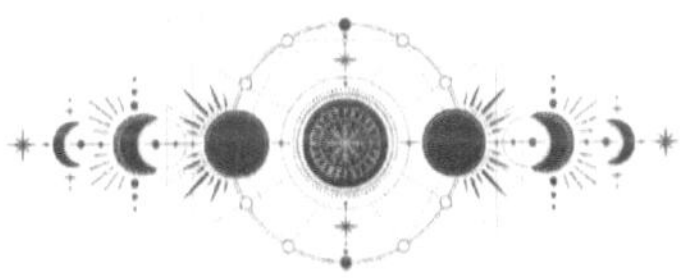

I came to with a pounding headache, laying on the floor in a fair-sized bare room. Nothing but four concrete walls and a gray ceiling. I looked up and could see the man who I knew only as Francis sitting in a chair before me, though he'd told me Francis wasn't his name.

"How long have you been a wolf?" He asked, blankly staring at me.

"Nearly four months." I replied as I pushed myself up into a sitting position. "Guess I didn't beat it."

"No, you did not, Mr. Hemming, but rest assured, you hurt no one. I saw to that."

"That explains the headache I suppose."

"I did what I had to." Not Francis paused. "While you haven't learned to control the wolf, I will commend you on the fact that you haven't eaten your entire family. Four months is a long time in regards to holding in a werewolf."

"I wouldn't say I held him in the entire time." I clenched my eyes, moving to lay on my back, deciding that until the headache retreated, I was stationary. "He's made it out twice."

"Still. That's only twice in four months." Not Francis' words stalled, as if he was expecting me to regain my feet, seemingly puzzled when I didn't. "What're you doing, Mr. Hemming?"

"Well, at the moment, I'm lying on a cold concrete floor, no idea where I am, how my family is, assuming I'm a fugitive of the law now, and, oh, I have a thousand-pound animal pent up inside me that I can do nothing about. That's what I am doing, Not Francis. What're you doing?" I asked sarcastically.

"Asking you if you're ready to try beating the wolf again."

Slowly, painfully, I sat up, fixing the man with a face of anger. "I just showed you that I couldn't control him. So, you want me to try it again?"

"If at first you don't succeed." He replied.

I gently rubbed my face, regaining my composure. "How long was I out?"

"About an hour. It's not yet one A.M."

"And you want me to try again now?!"

"Do you give up so easily on all your endeavors?"

That was it, the final word.

"Alright, fine." My blood boiled. "Why not just let him run?"

"You're just going to let the wolf win, to just break out, so that it becomes accustomed to taking over whenever it has the notion to do so?"

"I've tried everything else! I can't beat this thing, he's always there in the background of my head. Like he's—"

"Like he's hunting you?"

I nodded.

"Have you ever seen how wolves hunt buffalo?"

The question struck me as odd, but he hadn't seemed one to waste time on idle fat chewing.

"Not with my own eyes, no."

"The pack encircles the herd, the bison form a defensive ring, all horns and broad skulls facing the wolf pack. While the bison hold this defense, they are safe, the wolves will leap in occasionally, trying to get the bison moving, but until the bison turn away, the wolves have no ground. It is when the prey bolt that the wolves have the advantage. Learn from the bison. Hold fast against the wolf, face him head on. He cannot hurt you Rainer, he is you, he was born when you became a werewolf. He owes his life to you, but he will try to live his life through you, if you do not hold him at bay."

"I have 'held fast' against him, Not Francis, that's why my family isn't dead, but that's not enough. I have to beat him and so far, I can't." My anger subsided as I shamefully recognized that this man was trying to help me. "I'll try, but I'm gonna' lose again, at first at least. You gonna' club me every time I fail?"

Not Francis chuckled. "This room was built specifically for this purpose, it's a gas chamber."

My look of alarm must've translated what I was preparing to say.

Not Francis lifted a hand. "It releases a gas that is not fatal, but it'll knock you out should the wolf take control. In the unconscious state the wolf will withdraw, leaving you a man, where I will wake you and you will repeat the process."

"How long does this normally take?" I asked.

"The fastest I've seen accomplished the feat the first time she attempted to harness the wolf, the longest was a week."

"A week?!"

"A week." He flatly replied.

I shook my head. "I'll probably break that record."

"Your wolf can be controlled, Rainer, you *can* do this. The earlier you learn to control it the better, though you face an uphill battle, I will not lie. The wolf has gone unchecked for a substantial amount of time. That said, the wolf already obeys you to a certain degree. Four months and the wolf hasn't claimed a human life? That's not the doing of a wild wolf. The wolf may not bow to you, but it respects you, I will say that."

"Alright." I conceded. "I'll try again. But before I do, got any tips?"

Again, Not Francis chuckled. "Every wolf is different but there is one thing that is the same. It's a battle of the mind."

"I figured that much, but what I draw on for strength never seems to be enough. No matter what I picture, what memory I–"

"Memory?" Not Francis said. "You've been trying to hold the wolf with memories? That cannot be done."

"What do you mean?" I asked.

"You're trying to use the past to fight the present. The past is over, done, dead, useless except for remembrance, and the future is uncertain. You must face the wolf in the present. Where you conjured up memories, you must conjure the wolf itself. Don't send recollections to fight the wolf, they haven't a chance, the wolf will devour them. *You* must face the wolf, Rainer Hemming, you and you alone. All the strength you need, is what you are."

I nodded wordlessly, sorting out the mass influx of information, and taking a sort of comfort in at least understanding why I had failed.

"Let's do it."

* * *

I saw the wolf in my mind's eye, a huge beast, as black as a starless sky, standing before me.

Its head was enormous, its muzzle equally terrifying. It was panting, displaying its gleaming teeth.

We stood on a plane that wasn't part of this world, a place where nothing existed but a man and a wolf. It was the first time I'd actually laid eyes on the creature, and as frightening as he was, I found comfort in the words of Not Francis.

"The wolf cannot hurt you. He is a part of you."

The wolf stood at a distance. Just as I had never seen him, he had never encountered me. He was unsure what to make of the occasion. I had never before summoned him from wherever he came. His ears were erect, alert, his snout was raised, catching my scent, confirming my identity. He knew me, that was for sure, and he was curious about this situation. He lowered his head, eyeing me warily, moving from side to side, studying me. He did not growl, his hackles weren't raised, his tail was at ease.

He was bewildered.

Slowly I took a step towards him, testing the waters. He didn't move, simply watched me.

Another step. No movement, he simply kept his head low.

I took this as a sign of submission, a sign that the wolf Not Francis claimed to respect me, had resigned himself to be mine.

I did so foolishly.

I took strides towards him, and he kept his head low.

I stopped a few yards from him, and again, Not Francis' words rang in my ears.

"He may not bow to you…"

Seemed like a good place to start.

"You are mine." I took a stern tone. "I am the master here. You will bow to me."

Not the right thing to say.

His ears laid flat, his hackles jacked up, his tail went rigid, and his bright fangs bared to me in response.

He hinged back on his rear legs just before he catapulted towards me, and for a moment I felt brief terror as his teeth sank into me, before he ripped me apart.

* * *

Not Francis observed through a narrow slot in the reinforced door as the man before him doubled over and the change began to occur. After a few seconds the wolf ripped out of the man, furious and looking for a body to shred.

Shaking his head with a chuckle, Not Francis closed the slot and hit a large yellow button, fumigating the room.

* * *

I awoke again on the floor, Not Francis standing over me, a wry smile on his face.

"Well, it's safe to say you pissed him off."

"He ate me…" I panted. "The bastard ate me. You said he couldn't hurt me."

"And here you are." Not Francis said.

"That sucked." I blew out a heavy breath.

"I believe you." He laughed.

Now *I* was pissed off.

"Not Francis, get out."

"As you wish."

This time the wolf had his head raised high, a display of dominance.

My temper and a tendency of being rash got the better of me.

"You stupid dog!" I yelled. "You think you can just eat me?!"

The wolf again tore from Rainer's body, though now the wolf didn't seem quite so agitated. Seemed it had blown off some steam.

Yellow button.

Not Francis again stood over me. "Eaten again?"

"There's a chance," I tilted my head, "that I deserved that one."

"Again?"

"Yup." I nodded.

The wolf greeted me from a sitting position, almost mockingly.

"I'll give you that one." I said.

He just looked at me, tongue hanging out lazily.

"But you will bow to me. And you're going to do it now."

Yellow button.

"Eaten?"

"Obviously." I answered

"Take a break?"

"Nope."

Yellow button.

"Again?" Not Francis asked.

"Yup."

Yellow button.

"You're sure about this?"

"If at first you don't succeed, Not Francis."

Yellow button.

"Should I ask?"

"Nope." I answered.

* * *

During this seventh attempt, Not Francis was peering through the slot when a woman joined him.

"You found him." She stated with crossed arms.

"I did." Not Francis smiled.

"How's he doing?" She asked, glimpsing over Not Francis' shoulder.

"Wolf is up six. Ah, seven."

Yellow button.

"It's black…" The woman's voice trailed off with the observation.

"Mhm." Not Francis hummed. "They say the color of the wolf reflects the soul."

"Then my wolf is certainly the wrong color." The woman said.

"I believe white suits you well, at the very least it compliments your call sign."

"Maybe you should call it quits for tonight." The woman offered. "Or is he making ground?"

Not Francis shook his head. "At times it seems that he is taking control, but then the wolf dashes the thought. This wolf isn't weakening as he should be. Each time the shift takes around five seconds. On the first attempt, he shifted in 4.2 seconds, then 4.5 the second time. The fifth attempt gave me hope, it took 5.8 seconds, but the sixth and seventh were both 4.7. This wolf is strong."

"How long has he been a wolf?"

71

"Four months." Not Francis answered.

"There's your explanation." The woman scoffed.

"But he hasn't killed anyone in that time."

Not Francis turned his attention back to the man in the room. "I believe that should be the last attempt for today. It's nearly three in the morning. You should rest."

"Just a few more tries." A voice echoed from the slot.

"So be it." Not Francis replied.

Yellow Button.

"It's fifteen after three, son."

"I've got this."

Not Francis sighed.

Yellow button.

"I'm growing rather tired, Mr. Hemming." Not Francis frowned.

"Can you make it through just a few more?"

"I suppose."

* * *

The wolf had now grown tired of my arrogance and demands for his submission. His default stance now was that of a very angry wolf, every measure his body possessed to convey that message was on display. From all the failures however, for all my insolence, he never once went on the attack right out of the gate. He always waited for me to make the first move. That was the only quarter he allowed however, and that was far from the progress that I needed.

My patience had long since left me, perhaps Not Francis was right. Maybe it was time to take a rest, let the wolf cool down, and myself. Unfortunately, while I had figured out how to reach this place, where the wolf and I alone existed, I didn't know if there was an eject button.

The only way out that I knew for certain was to get myself eaten, and I wasn't keen on revisiting that just yet.

With a sigh I sat down, and the wolf seemed to be taken aback, unfamiliar with this take on the unfolding drama. He maintained most of his assertive posture, though he did seem to soften some. He hid his fangs, and his hackles lowered, but his tail was still erect. He was still relatively upset with me.

I shook my head as I spoke, not loudly, nor demanding, simply speaking. "I'm supposed to be in control of you, and you're supposed to listen. I'm supposed to call on you when I need you, and you're supposed to answer that call. You live because of me; you owe your life to me."

I took the moment to mock Not Francis where he couldn't hear me.

"Learn from the buffalo, oohdy-doo." I leaned back on my hands and lowered my chin to my chest.

"Buffalo never had to learn to live with the wolf. Never had to deal with a wolf *inside* them. Never had to deal with being part wolf."

My head snapped up.

The wolf still stood at a distance; he wasn't the cause of my action.

"Part wolf." I stood, and every sign of aggression returned to the wolf.

"Well, seems I may've been going about this wrong. The buffalo have already taught their lesson. Face the wolf. But I've faced you as an enemy, a dog to be muzzled. I couldn't see the forest for the trees. *I* am part wolf."

I took a step towards the wolf, and he snarled, expecting more of my attacks.

"Just as you are part man." I spoke smoothly. "It's not just me anymore, is it? And it never was just you. It's not a man and an animal walking side by side."

The big black wolf raised his head high as I drew only a few yards away. Again, he put away his teeth, and his hackles softened.

"It's a man and an animal, walking as one creature."

I took the final step towards the wolf and I felt his hot breath on my face as I looked up into his eyes.

"You're not a dog to be leashed, not a tool to be used only when needed. As I require you to be there when I need you, you demand the same of me, and there will never be a time that we don't need one another, because we are one in the same."

The wolf fully relaxed, and I understood why the wolf had always allowed me to make the first move, it was waiting. Waiting for me to cross the threshold into a new view of things.

"Thank you for your patience." I looked into the wolf's green eyes, and I realized I was looking into a mirror.

For no particular reason I raised my arm to the wolf's muzzle, an action that I commanded and simultaneously did not.

The strangest thing happened.

I saw myself standing before the wolf, I was looking at myself, my human self. I was looking from the wolf's eyes.

In a motion that both I and another governed, I spread my jaws and brought them to rest on the human's arm, and I felt both.

I felt the arm between my teeth, felt it graze over my tongue. I felt the teeth against my arm, no pain, simply holding it. The hot breath on my skin, the smell of both man and wolf filled my nostrils.

"You feel this too, don't you?"

The human raised his opposite arm and laid his tiny hand across the wolf's great muzzle, then touched the coarse black fur beneath the wolf's eye.

The wolf felt the small, callused hand cross over its hide.

"Walk with me wolf, and I will walk with you."

* * *

"Do you think he fell asleep?" The woman had just returned.

"He could have, I suppose." Not Francis replied. "He hasn't moved for a while, has he?

Not Francis checked his watch.

"Wanna' gas him just in case, then we can put him to bed somewhere?"

"I'd prefer if you didn't." Came the reply.

Not Francis sighed gratefully, spent with the hours, yet happy that the endeavor had drawn to a victorious close.

"Well done, young man. This night you have taken yourself back. The wolf is no longer a hated enemy, but rather your strongest ally. Let's get some rest shall we?"

Hours of repetition mistook Not Francis' hands. He had every intention of unbolting the door. His tired hands however, guided by muscle memory, had a different plan entirely.

Yellow button.

8

The Red Moons

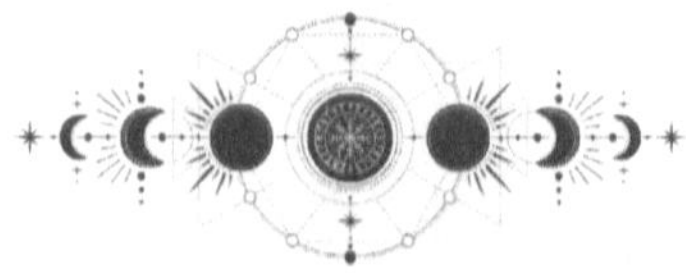

9/25
4:30 P.M.

I awoke in what seemed to be a hospital of sorts, surrounded by white walls and numerous beds.

As I sat up, I found the other beds bare, marking me as the ward's only patient.

A bit of movement drew my attention right, and as I turned, my eyes landed on a man in a trench coat. His back was to me, though I figured I knew who this was.

Sort of.

He stood alongside a desk, behind which sat a brunette nurse. She noticed me stirring and quickly nodded in my direction.

The man turned, and as he began my way I found I had assumed accurately. The man who pulled me from the precinct.

Not Francis.

Reaching my bed, he pulled up a chair and smiled. "Good evening."

"Thanks." I made no attempt at politeness, recalling my final gassing.

"How are you feeling?" He courteously asked.

"Sore." I rolled a shoulder. "Like I slept on concrete."

"You did for a short time." He smiled, offering a light chuckle that lended itself to the idea that he wasn't telling the whole story.

"Mm." I hummed. "Any particular reason for that?"

"Fatigue and repetition." Not Francis sighed. "You did keep rather late hours."

"I did it though." I smiled. "He's not going to try breaking out anymore."

"This is true," Not Francis nodded, "and I must admit, I am impressed. I didn't expect you to take the helm so quickly."

"I don't think I'd call that quick." I scoffed.

His smile faded as he shook his head. "You misunderstand, Rainer. For four months, your wolf was a creature of his own devices, loosely regulated. Yet in a matter of hours, you harness him. It's rare. Rarer yet is the fact, as I previously stated, that you hadn't claimed a human life in that time."

"Four months isn't that long." I shrugged. "Like you said, maybe he just respected me."

"There is no 'maybe' in that regard, Rainer. His respect for you is undoubtable." His brows hardened. "Keep in mind, there have been those that have succumbed to their wolves in a matter of weeks, days even."

His words certainly put a new perspective to my situation, and I cast a silent thanks to my newfound ally.

"At least we're past that part now." I nodded, offering up a small smile.

"Indeed." Not Francis nodded. "The first of your trials."

"Trials?" My brows raised.

He nodded. "To be discussed later. Now, I will tell you what you will call me."

"And I was getting fond of 'Not Francis.'" I chuckled.

"I was not." He barely shared the humor before he cleared his throat. "A-hem, my *call sign*, the only name you'll ever know me by, is Phoenix. Captain of The Citadel."

"Citadel?" I blinked, his suddenly serious demeanor telling me he was switching gears.

"This place." He raised his hands to either side. "This is The Citadel. Home of The Red Moons."

"The what?" I squinted, suddenly wondering if I was still recovering from the last gassing I took.

"You are not the only one with this affliction." Phoenix gently shook his head. "We belong to the Wolven Council, a paramilitary organization composed of the world's werewolves. The Red Moons are a piece of that organization."

"Just–" I rubbed my face, trying to keep up. "What? What is happening right now?"

"You gained control of the wolf, and now I am offering you a new place in life. A place here, with us, with The Red Moons." Phoenix spoke with an air lending itself to the belief that he was doing me a favor.

"Yeah, I got that part," I briefly paused, "but I've got no idea what that means."

The Wolven Council? There were enough werewolves to make an actual organization? Military no less? And Phoenix led a unit of it?

His words rang with pride for The Red Moons, but that didn't really mean anything to me. I understood that he was asking me to stay but, fact was, I hadn't the foggiest notion as to what that entailed.

All I knew for certain was what had set me on the path that ultimately led here. The woman that changed me. She was the reason I was at 411 Pine in the first place.

"Phoenix," I stammered, "I appreciate you inviting me to stay, but... I've got nothing to give. I don't even know what it would mean to stay."

Phoenix nodded. "It would mean taking up the mantle of humanities protector. To protect them from the things that they don't see, to keep them from winding up like you."

"You mean I would be a soldier." I stated.

"Yes." He answered bluntly. "I'm sure that if you had the choice, the events that brought you here would never have taken place. We, The Wolven Council and The Red Moons as a part of it, aim to keep that from happening. I regret to say that we failed you but, if you choose to stay, some good may come of it."

I couldn't argue against that, any of it, that very concept being what took me to 411 Pine.

Despite the wolf and I being at odds, it seemed that certain abilities of the wolf were passively gained. In my case, an extraordinary sense of smell and a boost to my ears.

I believed that I had trailed her to 411 Pine, though I never expected what had followed.

"Maybe with The Red Moons I could find her."

"If I stay," I asked, "will you help me find the woman that did this to me?"

For the first time Phoenix frowned, and I assumed it stemmed from my intentions of vengeance.

"I understand your feelings, Rainer," Phoenix started, "but revenge is a nasty business. More often than not, the hunter loses a part of themselves in the endeavor. Obviously she has proven that she can't be left to roam, but I can't say that you pursuing her would be wise. Furthermore, I can't guarantee that we would ever find her. She could be a drifter, long gone by now."

"I was changed four months ago, Phoenix." My brow furrowed. "Just two weeks ago, I picked up her scent. She's still here."

"You picked up her scent?" Phoenix's eyes narrowed, something not quite adding up in his mind.

I nodded. "My nose got sharper after the change, just figured it was a side effect of what I was."

"Perhaps." He tilted his head, though he seemed far from convinced.

"If she is still here," Phoenix pressed on, "we may be able to find her. We have been combating rogue wolves who spread this affliction here, though with each we eliminate, the harder they are to find. The question remains however, will you join us?"

I shook my head.

It was too much, much too fast.

"Phoenix I– I don't– I don't even know you, anything about you. Like how you knew I was a wolf in the first place, or how you knew I was in custody?"

"I monitor a lot of things," he shrugged, "*a lot* of things. One of which is police chatter, and when I heard they had someone coming in for questioning about 411 pine, I had to look into the matter. As for the wolf, I knew that the moment I smelled you, that's all there is to it."

I shook my head, recalling prior events. "Am I a fugitive now?"

"No." Phoenix replied. "In fact, it's most probable that you're about to be presumed dead."

"Dead?!" I nearly shouted.

Phoenix nodded. "The authorities found a burned out sedan matching the description, more importantly the plate number, of the one used in your 'kidnapping' from the station. Enough of your prints likely survived the fire, and a silver lining of your initial failure to harness the wolf was the generous amount of skin tissue you shed."

"Just on prints and skin they're going to believe I'm dead? Despite there being no corps– Wait, I wasn't in the car."

"No, no you were not," Phoenix smiled, "but there was a lot of skin, Rainer. It did not require much effort to make it look as if you were. This may have eluded you thus far, but the shift is a rather messy affair. Your human skin doesn't simply disintegrate, it falls away, often in rather sizable slabs."

I recalled my time in the gas chamber. I was in there several hours, the place should have been covered in blood and gore at the pace I kept.

"If that's the case, why wasn't the taming room a bloody mess?"

Phoenix offered up a wry smile. "When you shift, Rainer, the wolf forms beneath your skin. Your blood vessels, arteries, sinew, muscle, and bone all become the wolf's. As it grows, it tears through the skin. It's a rather unsettling thing when first witnessed, despite being largely bloodless."

"There wasn't any skin though?" I shook my head. *"Unless–"*

"The wolf ate it, Rainer." Phoenix seemed to fight the urge to chuckle.

"That– that's dis–"

"We did establish on multiple occasions that you were upsetting him."

I couldn't argue Phoenix's point, but still. The wolf literally ate me.

Pushing past the unsettling notion of my own wolf eating my skin, I still had to acknowledge there was still a lot that would be missing from the car fire.

Namely anything close to hair, teeth, and bone.

"Still doesn't excuse the lack of a body." I said.

Phoenix chuckled as he replied. "I read the article, Rainer, from the Kirkwood Tribune. The gist of it was that authorities responded to a report of a car fire off of rural route 4, thirty miles east of Kirkwood. By the time they got there the fire had mostly gone out, but there was evidence that there had been a body within during the time of the fire. Forensic personnel were called in short order and it was made a crime scene. This morning in an official release from the Kirkwood P.D. it was stated that 'numerous samples had been obtained for further analysis, but it was highly likely that this was in connection to a kidnapping at their very precinct, as the vehicle can be placed there at the time of the event.' That's all paraphrasing of course, and there was a link to that story as well, but I already knew the details of that."

"I'd assume their story didn't have all the facts." I said, round about saying I'd like an explanation for the events of the evening.

Phoenix understood. "Not long after I arrived, one of our teams took the building, moving the four present officers to one of the holding cells in the back. No one was harmed, ours or theirs, though I suspect Pierre has a rather sore throat."

"Still," I said, "there's no body to be found. How will they think I'm dead?"

"They won't need a body, Rainer." Phoenix explained. "Every cop who fancies himself a detective will put two and two together here. You were brought in with the intention of being questioned about events at 411 Pine. You never were suspected of killing anyone, but they suspected you found the body and maybe saw something they could use. They will assume that whoever did the killing somehow got wind of you being questioned and potentially knowing something. When they see the footage of the militants that stormed the place, they'll believe it was all done to take you, which we further encouraged when I drew on you. The explanation for the lack of your body will be that you were killed, then burned, or killed by burning, and then for some reason, your body was removed. Maybe it hadn't burned enough for your murderers liking. The police will find reasoning."

"I would bet you my bars though," he gestured to the two silver captain's bars on his collar, "that when the forensic results come back, you'll be pronounced dead."

His story made good sense, and while it freed me from an outlaws label, it meant something else as well.

"My family–"

"Will be notified, yes." Phoenix shrugged. "If they have the mindset though, they can net a healthy settlement in a wrongful death case."

"That's a very twisted way of finding a bright side."

"You must be able to find light in the darkness." Phoenix said as he leaned forward, slowly speaking. "Will you stay?"

"Not to sound ungrateful," I frowned, "but do I really have any other options?"

"You do, truth be known." Phoenix nodded. "You don't have to be a combatant. There are other roles in The Council that you could fill. Our communities are always in need of hands."

"Communities?" My brow raised. "As in communities of wolves?"

"Precisely." Phoenix nodded. "There are towns dotted here and there that are entirely made up of Council personnel, be that retirees, noncombatants, or enlistees on leave."

"They are fully functioning municipalities." He furthered. "Stores, banks, post offices, everything that you would expect of your typical town really, if you were to exclude the fact that every soul in the districts were wolves."

"What about people?" I asked. "Y'know, regular people?"

"Human can't live in them." He bluntly answered.

"And how exactly does that work?" I raised my hands, struggling to grasp the concept. "It'd seem pretty obvious with signs reading 'werewolves only.'"

He chuckled. "Yes, that would be obvious. It's actually quite simple though. These towns are Council owned and, by rule, landlocked by some sort of zone where no other building is permitted, whether it's national forest land or Bureau of Land Management, what have you. All the property that could be developed has already been utilized, and it never hits the public market in the event someone moves or passes away."

"But surely human's pass through from time to time." I shook my head, unable to believe that a mass grouping of wolves could go unnoticed.

"Of course they do," Phoenix nodded, "but aside from shifting in front of people, how would humans know they were amongst wolves?"

Phoenix ended here, still leaving me with his previous question.

Would I stay with The Red Moons?

If I left, if I went to one of these wolf communities, what would that entail? Be a store clerk for the rest of my life?

I looked down to my hands, recognizing what The Red Moons had already done for me.

Here, I had already achieved in a matter of hours what I couldn't do in four months. Just as with the towns, I was surrounded by wolves. I wouldn't be alone. More than that though, I wouldn't be alone in my search for her.

"I could make a difference here." I thought. *"I could do what Phoenix said, keep other people from going through what I have."*

"I'll stay." I conceded.

Phoenix grinned. "Welcome to The Red Moons."

He whistled sharply and the nurse, a slim brunette, brought over a small pile of clothing.

I observed the common clothing, and nodded.

"Get dressed and I'll introduce you to your squad. Like I said, Phoenix is my call sign. You will be needing one as well. It is your name here and the only thing you'll be known by."

Phoenix patted my shoulder as he turned towards the door. "Once you're ready, dressed and call sign figured, come down to the main floor to meet your team."

"The team of militia?" I asked.

"No." Phoenix shook his head. "There are too many local operations to risk them being recognized."

"As opposed to me, a literal dead man walking?" I said crossly.

"You're dead, Rainer. Only your friends and family will remember you now. As for the rest of the world, they never knew you existed in the first place."

With that sunny sentiment, Phoenix stepped through the door, and though his final words were far from comforting, I knew he was right.

I threw my feet from the bed and began thinking of possible names.

One was reoccurring, though I wasn't sure why.

I walked out of the infirmary, down a set of stairs and into a crude training area.

Three punching bags hung from the ceiling, and a set of weights rested near the exterior wall. Several pairs of boxing gloves lay near a large square of blue mats on the floor.

A few targets were erected on stands near the mats, featuring thick white pads adorned with broad bullseyes, several perforated by small knives.

"Are they ninja's too?"

As I stepped onto the concrete floor, four faces turned to stare at me.

I looked to Phoenix. "This is it?"

Phoenix nodded. "Your team, Alpha squad. The other two teams are out on assignment. On the far right there is Doc, not much for talk. Even though he's only twenty-four, you'd struggle to find a finer medic."

Doc nodded to me and though I'd just heard his age, he didn't look over eighteen. Platinum hair, unevenly trimmed, lay on his head, only a few shades brighter than his skin. He had a scrawny build, neither fat nor muscle dominating his body. Crystal blue eyes peered from his narrow face as he studied me. He was the only member to wear a long sleeved shirt, though still black, like that of the others and myself.

"Beside him is Knight," Phoenix continued his introductions, "your close quarters specialist. She's among the youngest operators, at seventeen years old."

A black-haired girl winked at me, her brown eyes as kind as her beaming smile. I instinctively liked her. On her left bicep, beneath the short sleeve of her shirt, I could make out part of a tattoo. It looked like the tip of a black blade, embedded in her tan skin.

Phoenix moved on. "Beside Knight is Marcus, he's your Lieutenant. That's the rank of all the squad leaders. He's a legacy child, age of twenty-two."

Marcus sported caramel brown hair that traveled down to hard brown eyes, his bangs actually covering one. His frame wasn't much bigger than Doc's, but bolstered significantly more muscle. He bore a sour expression on his face and a pair of boxing gloves on his hands. The sleeves of his t-shirt had risen, revealing that he was sporting a healthy farmers tan.

"Next to him is Frost. Alpha's weapons specialist. I haven't found a firearm she can't shoot, more importantly fix, also eighteen."

Her sharp eyes fell upon me, seizing me as my breath caught in my throat.

In that instant I was taken by her beauty, despite the fact she was wearing a sweat drenched tank top and yet another pair of sparring gloves. Flowing brown hair cascaded down in gentle waves, and I suddenly found my eyes locked on her lips. Full, gentle curves, a warm shade of pink. Her eyes, twin pools of the purest blue, commanded my attention, holding me captive, locked in their depths. A bead of sweat, sliding from her sharp brow, freed my eyes as I chased it across her flawless features. As she took efforts to slow her breaths, a few solitary strands of hair fluttered before her slightly parted lips. In the light she seemed to shimmer, the sweat glistening, adding to her already luminous sheen. The saturated shirt tightly clung to her form, hugging her breast, embracing her tight core. A tattoo held her left arm, just like Knight's, and best I could tell, they matched. A blue shield bearing a black wolf print, laid over a crossed pair of black swords.

"And you are?" She demanded more than asked, snapping me from my stupor.

"What the hell, Rainer?" I was shocked with myself. *"It's like you've never*

seen a woman before."

Hoping my admiration hadn't been obvious, I peeled my eyes from her.

"My call sign is Fenrir." I collected myself. "I'm nineteen. I– I don't really know what I'm going to be in Alpha."

"Fenrir, huh?" Knight said as she nodded, accepting the tidbit I had offered. "Know any of the lore?"

I smiled. I did know the lore. "A creature of Norse legend, a wolf of enormous size. Some stories depict him as being several stories tall and over a mile long, but in more realistic lore, he was slightly larger than a full-grown Clydesdale."

Phoenix chuckled. "Also considered the father of all werewolves."

I turned to face Phoenix, unaware of this. "Really?"

"Per wolf lore, anyway." Doc spoke. "Seems the most plausible reason, and I use that term very loosely, for the size we take in wolf form."

Marcus' eyes indicated that he wasn't overly impressed with my choice. "A bit brazen, isn't it? To just barely get a handle on your wolf and then choose a call sign like that?"

I couldn't help but notice Frost's annoyed smile with Marcus' words.

"Oh, come on, Marcus." Knight held her smile as she gently ribbed him. "Maybe he's just a big Norse fan. Doesn't mean he's gonna' act like he's some kind of badass."

"Alright then." Phoenix drew our attention. "Introductions taken care of. What can you do?" He questioned me.

"I don't really know what that means." I confessed uneasily. "I mean, I guess I'll do whatever I have to at the given moment."

"We'll see." He muttered. "You'll need training, but we're somewhat limited on ammunition at the moment. We'll have to be sparing."

With these words, my mind was suddenly put to the Challenger, and all that was in it.

"Should I bring it up? How would I explain it?" I questioned myself. *"And it hinges on whether or not Alan's ditched it. If he has then it'd be for nothing. If he hasn't though... It can't stay there."*

"I might be able to help with that." I suddenly blurted.

"What do you mean?" Phoenix asked.

I swallowed a lump of uneasiness. "There's... Well there's a car on my farm. It's been... upgraded. To the point that we might be able to use it here."

"A car?" Frost scoffed. "How's that going to help?"

"It's full of weapons and ammo for starters, and it's been reinforced. For all intents and purposes, it's a tank. Could probably rob a bank with the damn thing." I said, realizing too late how that must have sounded.

"Got ourselves a prepper here." Marcus poked a bit of fun, garnering chuckles from the squad.

Phoenix's eyes narrowed as he looked down his nose at me. "You– This car, how difficult would it be to secure?"

"I won't know until I get there." I replied. "If it's in the same place I left it, not at all."

Phoenix looked away from me, over the others, looking for something, though it almost seemed he was looking through them.

"You realize that you cannot see your family again," Phoenix suddenly looked to me, "you understand this?"

"I do." I nodded. "I only brought this up because– Well it can't stay there anyway, and we could use it."

"Very well." Phoenix's eyes remained narrow. "I will allow you to get the Challenger, but you are not going alone."

9

First Contact

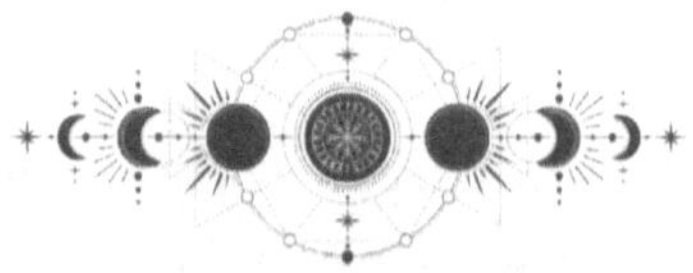

9/25
2346 Hrs.

After a short commute by black van, courtesy of an unknown driver, Frost and I began the short trek along the tree wrapped dirt road leading to the back pasture of my family's farm.

Conversation was virtually non-existent as we walked, Frost leading me by at least six feet at all times. It only took a few attempts at striking up conversation for me to gather that she wasn't in the mood for chit-chat.

As we neared the pasture, I began to grasp why her call sign was Frost.

"Which way?" She growled as we reached the border of the field, where the trees ended and the long grass began.

"Left." I sheepishly replied. "Barn is close to the other side of the field."

"Stick to the treeline, stay in the shadows. Understand?" She quietly spoke over her shoulder as she led on.

"I don't think that anyone will be here, Frost." I knew that Dad would have everyone hemmed up in the house. "No need to hide."

"You'll have to stop thinking like that." She looked back almost disdainfully. "When you think you're safe is when you're most vulnerable."

There was a time I would've doubted her words, seeing as I had roamed these hills and hollows for the past six years.

As I looked into the trees, I could foresee every creek, every deer trail, that lay within. They all knew the tread of my boots. This was, or had been, my home.

Now the killings had started again though.

I shook off a sudden chill that rolled down my skin. *I've got the wolf now. We'll be fine. Just for her peace of mind though, I'll keep it down."*

"Come on." I made a moderate attempt at keeping my voice low as my pace quickened, catching up to Frost. "It's just up the way."

"Hey!" Her eyes burned as she put a hand to my chest. "You may know these woods, but I know what goes bump in the night, okay? You go fumblin' around and you end up dead. Keep your voice down and walk like you've got a shred of sense."

"Jeez, I thought I was." I shook my head, wondering how quiet she actually wanted me to be.

I had enough mind to keep my mouth shut though, and soon enough, the barn came into view.

The Challenger was still sitting in the barn as I had hoped, and I couldn't help but feel a sense of relief as I spied the car in the bay. It would've been all too easy for it to be discovered, or, in the more likely case, Alan's conscience drive him to leave the car somewhere to be discovered.

I came to stand at the base of an oak tree with Frost, peering across the open field towards the car.

It was right there, waiting to be taken, so why was I hesitating?

"What're we waiting for?" Frost asked impatiently, shifting the straps of her backpack.

"Sorry," I said, "I just know that I'll never see this place again and I wanted to–"

"Say goodbye?" Frost said sharply. "Feel fortunate that you got this opportunity, most of us weren't allowed this luxury."

As I took in the farm for the last time, toying with the straps of my own pack, I wondered if I had done something to piss Frost off.

"Why exactly are we packing clothes around?" I asked, referring to the contents of our bags.

"Clothes don't survive the shift, Fenrir." Frost shook her head, the obviousness of the question irritating her. "We always have spares."

"Mm." I mumbled. I had figured as much, but the question was more to stretch the moment than genuine curiosity.

"It's nearly midnight." Frost growled. "Let's go already."

I sighed as I nodded. "Yeah, alright."

The chattering of voices suddenly reached my ears as Alan and Vivian appeared on the dirt road entering the field. "Oh, no."

"What're they doing here?" Frost asked, before turning to me, fury taking her blue eyes. "Did you set this up?"

"What? No." I shook my head. "I don't know what they're doing here. Maybe they're just walking."

They didn't turn around, instead making tracks towards the Challenger.

"Forget the car." I said, turning back towards the woods behind us.

"No." Frost said, her voice stern. "We'll wait, with any luck they'll leave. Phoenix sent us out with the assignment of getting the car, that's exactly what we're doing."

"Assignment?" I questioned. "This isn't some mission–"

Frost cut me with her eyes as she drove a finger into my chest. "That's exactly what this is Fenrir, a mission, and the objective is to secure that car. You'd just better pray that what's in there is worth spending our time."

"I wouldn't have said anything otherwise." I offered a weak defense. "Is the car really that big of a deal though?"

Frost sighed with aggravation. "The car is just a car, another set of wheels, the weapons and munitions are the real objective."

I thought back to what Phoenix had said, about The Red Moons being part of something larger. The Wolven Council he called it.

"If The Red Moons are part of The Wolven Council, why don't they keep The Red Moons supplied?" I asked.

"First off, we usually just call it The Council. To answer your question, that's above my rank." Frost answered bluntly. "My job is to get the mission done, every time, that's it. I'm a soldier, nothing more and nothing less."

There really wasn't anything for me to say to that. Frost was right, she was a soldier, and a damn good one if she was as consistent as she let on. She was no nonsense, and was quick on the draw to remind others of the task at hand.

Alan and Vivian continued on towards the barn, completely oblivious to the breathing shadows amongst the trees, and I started to fear that Alan was currently on his way to dispose of the car.

"Frost," I shook my head, "we're going to have to–"

"Shh!" She raised a hand and glared over her shoulder into the woods behind us.

She slowly shifted to glance around the oak tree, suddenly on edge, intently focused on the trees behind us.

"What's wrong?" I whispered.

"You don't smell that?" She quietly replied.

I followed her gaze and drew in a deep breath. I found the smell of iron, a rich metallic aroma. It wafted over us, originating somewhere further within the trees.

I knew the scent, though I was puzzled as to *why* I was smelling it.

"Blood?" I questioned as the wolf began to bristle in my core, answering my inquiry.

It *was* blood, and a lot of it.

It wasn't from our cattle, at least I didn't think so. They still should've been in the feedlots.

Goosebumps rippled up my arms as I took in another putrid breath, recalling the injury on the young heifer.

"Maybe something took a deer?" I tried to rationalize the iron curtain that wrapped around us, to no avail. *"No, the wind hasn't shifted, and we didn't smell it when we got here. The source is moving. Something... something in those trees reeks of blood."*

The wolf grew restless, stirring within. I could feel his anger, and a sudden lust for blood, the same as the last time I had lost control to him.

"Did you smell this that night? Is that why you fought me so hard?" I asked, trying to calm him and myself, failing at both.

"Frost…" I breathed as my body began to hum. The trees that I thought I knew so well suddenly became foreign to me, an unknown spookiness settling over them, reaching out to me with frigid hands.

I looked to Frost, finding that her body faintly rattled.

"Is she scared?"

The wolf inside led me to believe otherwise. I had learned the smell of fear with the horses, an unsettling bitter aroma.

This wasn't it.

This was a sharp smelling spike of adrenaline.

Frost's fight or flight response was priming up, and I was confident that flight wasn't in her repertoire.

"Frost–" I began to ask for an explanation.

"Quiet." She glanced behind us again before letting out a growl. "If we find ourselves in a fight, stay out of the way. If you can't, do not look in their eyes. You understand?"

I wordlessly nodded as she pushed off the tree, towing me into the long grass on an invisible tether.

Her pace had quickened, as had my pulse.

"What about Alan and Vivian?" I asked.

"We're getting them out of here, I'll figure the rest out later."

The night fell largely silent, eerie even. The crickets ceased to chirp, no animals called out, it was dead quiet.

I cast a cautionary glance over my shoulder, seeing nothing at the treeline, nor anything moving within the trees.

"Stay close." Frost reached out and grabbed my arm as I turned to her.

The sudden feeling of staring eyes tingled my skin as the wolf growled, leading me to once more look back to the trees.

Four figures stood at the same tree we had.

"I just looked…They weren't there, nowhere close to being there… How did they get there so fast?" My breath quivered.

"Who are they?" I asked.

"More what than who." She growled. "Just keep moving. When we get up here, get them in the car. We have to keep them safe, got it?"

"Frost–"

"Got it?!" She repeated herself.

I nodded.

We reached the barn, finding Alan and Vivian within, alongside the car.

I could hear quiet words.

"I wish he would've just left this thing alone." Alan said. "Now we've got to get rid of it before it's found."

"He thought it would help, Alan." Vivian said, eternally defending me. "He meant well. His heart was in the right place. He just didn't think it through."

They were unaware of our approach, evident as they continued looking over the car.

"What do I say?" My brain rattled. *"Do they already think I'm dead?"*

I looked once more to the trees. They were still there, unmoving, no advance or retreat.

Frost's words drove me forward.

"We have to get them out of here. We have to keep them safe."

"Alan." I gently said.

Alan went stock still, rigid.

"Rainer?" He slowly turned, his eyes wide as they met mine. "Rainer, what're you doing here?"

When he didn't say that I was dead, I knew that word hadn't yet been delivered.

I allowed myself to smile. "I could ask the pair of you the same thing."

"We were talking about you. How you were kidnapped from custody." Alan's tone turned dark, as if suspecting something foul afoot. "What's going on, Rainer?"

"Alan, I–"

"We don't have time for this." Frost said, pulling attention to herself. "The two of you need to get in the car, it's not safe here."

"What– Who are you?" Alan questioned her before turning to me. "Did she do it?"

"Alan," I pleaded, "Just–"

"Who is she, Rainer?" Vivian quietly asked, her voice teetering on the edge of suspicion.

I felt time ticking away, knowing nothing other than the fact that they were in danger.

"Dammit!" I cursed. *"They aren't supposed to be here!"*

But they were, and they wanted answers, but there was absolutely nothing I could say that they would understand or believe. All I knew was that we needed to move, *fast.*

Something had set Frost on a razor's edge, a wolf of experience. If it put her in such a state, by no means should I have been anything less than terrified, and I wasn't far off.

The night was spiraling out of control, and yet again I had no idea what was happening, only that something was very wrong and time was fleeting.

The wolf knew it too, pressing against the walls of my mind, wrestling for purchase.

"Who is she, Rainer?!" Vivian's voice rose, suspicion giving way to anger.

"It's none of your concern who she is!" I yelled as I pushed back against the wolf. "What matters is you two need to get in the car and we need to get the hell out of here!"

With my shouts, Vivian had taken her fill, unwilling to remain a moment longer.

She bolted, and as she tried to run past me, I reached out for her. I caught only the faintest bit of flannel, feeling the fabric of her shirt brush over my fingertips as her strides carried her towards the trees.

Frost could only turn and yell. "Stop!"

I had already started after Vivian, and I heard Frost's footsteps behind me.

Ahead, Vivian was nearing the wood line.

They were there, watching her.

Suddenly, though my eyes struggled to catch them move, they emerged from the darkness, becoming visible in the moonlight.

Their eyes seemed to gleam red, and I sickened with the realization that they *were* red. Dark as blood.

One of them smiled.

Their teeth, where the canines should've been, were far too long.

The wolf bristled inside of me. He knew what they were.

Vivian screamed as they came into her sight, caught between them and us, surrounded by monsters.

She tried to stop on the dew wet grass, but her shoes did little to hold traction.

She slipped, a mistake that may have very well saved her life as the closest lunged for her, missing only because of her quick drop.

The wolf hungered inside me, an immense wave of heat taking me as hatred for these creatures flooded over me.

The wolf knew what they were and somehow, he was communicating it to me, pushing their name through my mind.

I doubled over, commanding the wolf to come forth.

He was only too eager to oblige as he ferociously gripped my body. I felt my body breaking as he ripped the muscles into position, snapping the bones and wrenching them into place rather than taking the time to properly enhance them.

"We can't fight if you kill me!" My brain screamed as it became clear he was making no effort to dull the pain, too focused on completing the shift.

As quickly as the pain had come, it vanished. As I opened my eyes, I found four massive paws beneath me, moving more of their own accord than mine, rushing toward the trees.

The first to fall was a male, the very same that had made a move for Vivian. Drawing near I could see that his tangled hair did little to dull the glimmer in his bright eyes. With a hiss he turned to face me head on, bracing for a collision that wasn't destined to come.

I reared up, bringing my forepaws down onto his shoulders, my claws raking them to the bone. With a single motion, my jaws severed his head.

I turned to another, letting the head of his companion roll from my mouth, licking the sides of my muzzle as I learned the taste of their blood.

He snarled as I advanced on him, revealing his fangs. Slowly he began to retreat, keeping his hands at the ready, brandishing long nails more akin to daggers. As he continued to fall back he made sure to keep me in front of him, never giving me the opportunity to strike from the side or rear. My patience waned, moments from charging when his eyes darted to my right.

"Shit!" I cursed my obliviousness.

I turned, knowing what his actions meant, as the force of a freight liner blasted into my side. Shattered ribs screamed as I was throttled from my feet, the ground catching me with no less force.

I gasped for breath, though I found no relief as a bit of foamy blood leapt from my lips. Only then did it dawn on me that at least one of my lungs had been perforated by the broken ribs.

Before me stood a single vampire, some twenty feet away.

She was motionless in the moonlight, save her eyes, traveling over my unmoving body.

"What is she waiting for?" I gasped as I choked.

A bit of wind played at her black hair, and a moment later, it seemed that she became the wind.

My eyes didn't lie, though I was sure they did.

She was on me instantly, shouldering my bottom jaw out of the way as her fingers twisted into the fur of my throat.

A sickening laugh echoed in my ears as I felt her weight shifting, leaning in, inching closer to my throat.

"It can't end like this!" I growled. *"Alan and Vivian are still here, they aren't safe yet!"*

As if hearing my thoughts, the wolf ratcheted my ribs back into place, and with an involuntary gasp, breath burned back into my lungs.

The hands in my fur clenched as she rocketed forward, fangs intent on piercing my throat, just as I heard the guttural roar of a charging wolf.

A massive white beast leapt over me, taking the vampire in its jaws and ripping her away.

I bore witness as Frost slammed the vampire to the earth, pinning her down with a massive paw, just before tearing away everything north of the vampire's stomach in a bloody mess.

As I regained my feet, I spun wildly, trying to find my friends.

A shrill scream erupted behind me and as I turned, I found Vivian.

She lay in a crumpled heap, beneath the single remaining vampire.

Again my legs pressed onward, and the last vampire had barely turned when she received the full impact of my body ramming into her.

Bloody screams ripped from her throat as savage teeth caught her midriff. In that moment, I devoted every fiber of my aching body into shaking the life from her.

Her screams grew louder as my jaws compressed, reaching a bloody crescendo as she was cleaved in half .

With her death, all fell silent. No longer did the field echo with the sounds of battle.

The last vampire had been vanquished.

I found myself standing on four shaky legs, gasping for breath as adrenaline coursed through my veins.

"What just happened?"

I didn't have to move to know what the pasture now looked like. We had killed four vampires.

I had killed.

There was no hesitation, no thought of right or wrong. In that moment, the wolf and I galvanized our bond. He had made me brave, consuming any fear in my bones, to the point that I was so brazen as to charge headlong into a fight, despite the fact that I had been in nary one in my brief existence.

A sudden sting on my right side set the wolf on the offensive as I turned with a snarl, ready to resume the bloody fight.

Frost quickly leapt back, clear of my teeth and brandishing her own.

She had been checking my wound.

Knowing I'd mistook her gesture of concern, I ducked my head in an apologetic motion.

She seemed to accept it as she put away her fangs, her eyes traveling past me.

I turned, following her gaze to where an ashen Vivian lay.

Slowly I stepped towards her, knowing what was before me, but unable to accept.

I gently nudged her body with my muzzle, rocking her only slightly.

The life had left her body.

We had failed.

I had failed.

I looked towards the barn, towards the car that had brought us here. What would've happened if Frost and I hadn't been there?

Would the vampires have been there?

Alan was nowhere in sight, and in my heart I hoped that he had run, that he hadn't seen what took place.

In that instant, what the farm had been to me shattered, no longer a place I knew. The past laughs and happy recollections died that night, in their wake, a bloodied field. The place where I took life, and where Vivian had…

All I wanted to do was get away, to slam my eyes shut. To suddenly wake in my bed, for all of it to be a nightmare.

I knew it wouldn't be so.

Frost blasted a hot breath from her snout, drawing my attention, and as I looked to her, I found her nursing a front paw. Bright blood flowed from the pad of her foot.

"When was she hit?" I asked, wondering if she even knew. The melee had been quick, nearly as fast as the vampires themselves. It had lasted only a matter of seconds, but I knew those seconds would forever be a part of me.

I lowered my head as I looked over to my pack, laying only a few yards away.

"Let's get out of here, wolf."

I carried the pack away from the bloody grass as I felt the wolf begin to shrink away, and once more I became a man.

The tall grass of the field did enough to shield my lower half, enough that I could stand and not risk exposing myself in any case.

As I finished dressing I turned to find Frost in the distance, still in wolf form. She was looking over our battlefield, as short as the battle had been. Her eyes were steady, staring forward, taking it all in without focusing on any certain aspect.

What was she thinking?

In the moonlight I could see she wasn't a typical timber wolf. Her coat was as white as snow, as lovely an animal as she was a woman.

She finally looked away, nearly taking a step towards me when she stopped and turned back, drawing my gaze with hers.

A soft rustling of grass echoed through the night, and a lone figure stood amidst the corpses, whitewashed in the pale light.

A moment before, she had been laying on the ground, where she had fallen… where she had *died*.

Bloodied blond hair draped down, obscuring her face.

I knew this person, I knew her scent, I knew her name.

"Vivian?" I asked.

Frost took a step towards her and emitted a low growl.

"No." I shook my head.

Vivian slowly raised her head.

"Please no." I begged.

Vivian brushed the hair from her face, revealing her eyes.

"No!" I screamed, feeling as if the vampires were tearing at my heart.

The light green eyes of my past friend had vanished, murdered, their crimson imposters burning holes in my soul.

Frost hunkered down to leap, to route the final vampire, and Vivian responded with a breath that hissed through her teeth.

Vivian took only one step back before quickly turning away, vanishing into the forest with the same breathtaking speed I had witnessed earlier.

Frost seemed to start a pursuit, unwilling to yield, though she had only taken a few strides when she stopped.

As she turned back, I discovered the reasoning. Her right shoulder was bloodied, a set of gashes cut through her hide.

Just like the calf.

She started towards her pack, her eyes moving to mine as she passed me by.

Having found her pack, Frost moved to the barn, ducking inside. A moment later I heard the zipper of the pack working.

"Get in the car," Frost shortly called, "and check your wound since you don't want me to."

"Are you alright?" I called as I moved towards the barn.

"I'm fine." She quietly answered. "You?"

Raising my shirt to inspect the gouge in my side, I couldn't help but shake my head in awe.

It was already healing.

I was shocked, a wound that size should've taken weeks to heal.

Frost came into view wearing a black tank top and jeans, lacking a bra however, and I had to turn away as I observed that little was left to the imagination on such a cool evening.

Suddenly I remembered the contents of the back seat. The money, the sole reason I had kept the car.

Reaching into the cab, I started pulling duffel bags from the car, turning to heave them into the barn loft.

Frost joined me as I sent up the first.

"What're you doing?" She asked. "Is that–"

"It's nothing that we need." I continued my work.

"That doesn't answer my–" She caught my hands as I prepared to send the last bag to the loft. "Stop, Fenrir."

She gently took the bag, and I grimaced as her hands worked the zipper.

As the bills came into view, her eyes darted to mine.

"What is this?" She asked, and there was no missing the accusation in her voice.

"How can I explain this away?" My mind threatened to break, this was the last thing I needed.

"I didn't steal it." I shook my head, forsaking any quick lies that came to mind. I was done lying. "Someone did, but it wasn't me. These bags are the reason I kept the car, Frost."

I paused, giving her time to form a response. When she failed to produce one, I continued.

"My family–"

She raised her hand, quieting me. "Did you kill anyone to get it?"

"No." I shook my head. "It was in the car, when the car was left to me."

"By who?" Her voice remained low.

"I don't know who it was, I didn't really care at the time. I was just trying to help my folks and–"

"Enough." Frost picked up the final bag, and I waited for her to say to load it all back into the car, that The Red Moons needed it more.

I was surprised when she sent the last bag sailing into the loft.

She turned back to me with a face bordering on understanding. "This stays between us, Fenrir. I'm allowing this in the faith that you're being honest with me, but I'm going to look into it, and I will find the truth. So you're sure that you didn't steal it?"

I nodded. "I'm sure. Like I said, someone did steal it, but it wasn't me."

She nodded as she looked back to the trunk, and as I looked to her, namely her shoulder, I found it was all but healed, a few scratches remaining.

As she pulled the panel down, her eyes falling over the firearms, she nodded. "Hmph. These will do. Where's the ammunition?"

"Box in the bottom of the trunk." I tapped on the false bottom.

She also checked this, finding a multitude of ammo boxes.

Again she nodded, before holding out her hand. "Keys?"

I didn't bother to put up a fight on who got to drive, I didn't really feel like driving anyway.

She wordlessly slid into the driver's seat as I moved around to the passenger side and ducked into the car.

She put the car into drive, starting in the direction of the dirt road, only using a single hand, the other sitting in her lap. As I looked to it, I found it still sprung an unhealthy leak.

"Let me see your hand." I whispered blindly, trying to come to grips with the evening.

She reluctantly obeyed.

Skin tissue was reforming around the edges of her hand, though it was still bleeding in the palm.

"My side and your shoulder have already healed." I studied her wound. "Why hasn't your hand?"

"Those were from claws." She explained. "This is a bite. Their saliva prevents clotting, makes it easier to drink."

From beneath the seat I produced a first aid kit I spotted days before, and gently began dabbing the blood and dirt away with gauze. Replacing soiled pads with new several times, I sat in silent awe, observing the flesh begin to regenerate. It was healing before my eyes.

"Why do we heal so quickly?"

"Part of being a wolf, we heal pretty fast under normal conditions." Frost's demeanor hadn't changed a bit, even after a near death encounter. Something I thought she should've been happy about.

"How's your side?" She asked again. "I know the skins healed, but I could've sworn I heard something crack."

"I'm okay." My voice was little more than a murmur.

"You're sure?" She repeated.

Questions filled my head when no words escaped Frost or myself, only the sound of the engine drumming on as we continued through the trees, though I knew most of the answers.

What the hell happened here? How is this possible?

I peered down at her hand again, still not trusting my eyes, hoping that the past two weeks had been nothing but a bad dream.

I knew they weren't, and sure enough, Frost's hand was nearly healed. Fresh skin crept across her palm, finally sealing the wound.

She clenched her hand and noticed the attention I paid. "Gotta' stretch the new skin, little tough when it all comes back. A day or so, it'll be back to normal."

I nodded as I looked up to her.

Her hair, now pulled into a low ponytail, traced along the back of her slender neck.

She glanced over at me from the corner of her eye, and I looked away as I realized I'd been staring.

"Thank you for saving me, Frost." I attempted to avoid any awkwardness. "When I was pinned."

"It's fine Fenrir, you patched me up in return. We're square." Her voice sounded like she was smiling. How she could, I didn't have a clue.

"Well... Just thanks."

She abruptly changed the subject. "You okay?"

This sudden show of compassion jarred me, and as I took it in, I knew she wasn't asking about injuries anymore, not physical ones anyway. She was asking about Vivian.

"She's been–"

What could I say? That she'd been my friend for a long time? That she never knew I changed, but she was always there for me? That at the time of her death, friends were all we were, though she, and I from time to time, wanted to be more? That the final words she heard from me were in anger?

What was there to say?

I fought back tears as I leaned my head to the rest, turning my closed eyes towards the ceiling.

Tearlessly I mourned Vivian, now a creature I never would have dreamed existed. I mourned for Alan, a friend who I would never see again. Mostly though, I mourned myself, knowing all of it was on me.

That Vivian's blood, her death, was on me.

"It's not your fault, Fenrir. We did everything that we could, no one can argue that. It's a harsh lesson, but it's true. We can't save everyone, all we can do is try."

My hands moved to fists as Frost's words held me, anger and agony both fighting to escape from my heart.

"I should've been able to protect her." I growled, anger getting the best of me, all of it focused on myself.

"Fenrir–" She began to protest.

"That's not my name." I turned to the window, speaking through gritted teeth at the reflected face. "My name is Rainer."

Right then, in mourning myself, I mourned Rainer Hemming, because a part of him had died, left to lay with the creatures on that field.

For a moment Frost was quiet, not quite sure what to make of using my name. "This is what we fight, Rainer, this is *why* we fight."

"She died because of me."

"No." She gently whispered. "You are untrained and unfamiliar to this, Rainer. To protect humans, you need both of those things, and the reality is that had we not been there, both of your friends likely would've died."

"What do we protect them from, Frost?" I knew what they were, but something inside me refused to believe, had to hear it from her lips.

"We fight two things in this world, Rainer, sometimes rogue wolves, and sometimes, vampires."

"So now what?" I asked as I wiped a solitary tear from my cheek. "We have to hunt her down? So that she doesn't hurt humans?"

Frost's face twisted, conflicted, not willing me further damage, yet refusing to lie.

I had already known the answer, but still a piece of me hoped that it wouldn't be so.

"There is the chance we'll never see her again, Rainer."

That did little to relieve the pain in my heart, though I understood its intention.

As I collected myself, my breath growing steady, my burning anger smoldered into shame.

No amount of comfort from Frost would change this. No words could undo what had been done.

They couldn't bring Vivian back.

I looked to the window, refusing to let myself slip further. "Let's go home, Frost."

10

Learning of the Foe

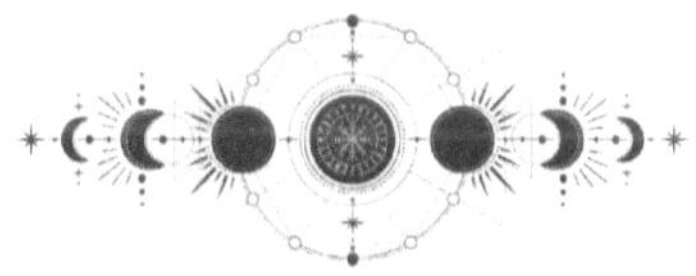

I came awake with a jolt and found Frost on her bunk, next to mine, a book in her hands.

"Nightmares?" She stole a glance, slight concern curtaining her eyes.

I groaned, feeling the tackiness of sweat clinging to my skin.

The night's rest had been anything but restful. Every time I closed my eyes, I bore witness to Vivian's death.

"I'm sure your book is a better story." I replied.

She spun her legs from the bed, leaning forward with a gentle smile. "Well, considering it's a maintenance manual for an M4, I highly doubt that."

"You're reading a maintenance manual?" I scoffed.

A devilish grin played at the corners of her mouth. "Beat's robbing banks."

Her smile warmed me, teasing that there may be something beneath her icy exterior.

I couldn't help but manage a dry chuckle.

Setting down the manual, her smile faded, much too soon. "Phoenix wants you to stop by his office."

She stood with a curt nod, banishing the warmth from her face, once more donning her cold mask.

She walked out of the only doorway in the room and I heard the falling of her boots on the descending stairs.

Delicately, mindful of any potential pain remaining from the night before, I swung my legs out of bed.

Finding no pain, not even an ache, I ventured a look at my side. The wound was completely healed, leaving only threadlike scars. I was amazed that I wasn't somewhat sore, I had sustained the injury only hours beforehand.

Looking away, I found a black trunk next to my bunk. On the lid was a loosely riveted strip of metal bearing my call sign.

I hadn't remembered seeing it when I came in, though I hadn't really paid much mind to anything when we got back.

I didn't speak to anyone, didn't want to. I wanted, needed, to be by myself. Everyone graciously seemed to accept that.

Opening the chest I found black T-shirts stacked in an orderly fashion, next to an evenly fashioned column of blue jeans.

Accompanying the jeans and shirts were several pairs of black gym shorts, and I assumed these were dual purpose, for both sleeping and exercise.

I selected a shirt and pair of jeans, just pulling from the top of each stack. Given my choices I really couldn't go wrong.

I was in the process of pulling on the shirt when a familiar voice called out to me.

"You know Fenrir, you really oughta' take better care of yourself. That's twice in the past two days you've had a near rendezvous with catastrophe. Got sprung from the clink and hit by a vamp. Any pain?"

I turned, finding Knight, black hair glistening in the light that came through a nearby window. Her smiling face was a welcome sight after both the prior night and my unrelenting dreams. I was grateful for the comfort I found in her kind eyes.

"Well, you gonna' stand there all day? C'mon let's go." She hurried me.

"Go where?" I asked as I gently tugged the creases from my shirt.

"Time to start your training." She was forced to looked up at me, as I was a whole head and a half taller than her. "Nice wheels by the way."

I mumbled as she started off ahead of me. "Thanks."

I followed her through the door, downstairs, and onto the main floor, finding myself in an open space across from the training area.

She suddenly stopped and turned around to look at me, her smile gone. "I'm sorry about your friend, Fenrir. Frost said things went south."

I nodded, attempting to dodge the subject. "Where's Phoenix? I'm supposed to talk to him."

She pointed to a small office situated beneath the infirmary.

"That's his office."

I nodded as I asked for curiosity's sake. "What did this place used to be?"

She gave a small shrug. "It was an equipment warehouse I think, somewhere along the way it was abandoned. We found it useful as a forward operating base, FOB, for our missions. That's all I know."

"Gotcha." I nodded as I looked to Phoenix's door, then again to her. "What's this training all about?"

"Everyone has to go through it. It's not really an optional class, and Frost was fairly adamant that we start ASAP."

"Mm." I nodded, wondering if it would've made a difference last night.

She gave a crooked smile. "Hey don't worry. In a few hours you collared a wolf that's been doing his own thing for four months. You can handle our training."

A set of double doors to the left of Phoenix's office opened as the rest of Alpha team walked into the main room, Frost leading the way.

She offered a curt nod, while Marcus fixed me with a rather disdainful frown. I was sure he approved of the evening's outcome about as much as I did.

Doc took a moment to nod his condolences, his sad eyes conveying that I had his sympathy.

I sighed as I looked at the still swinging double doors. "What's in there?"

"Chow hall." Knight answered.

My stomach growled in response, and I realized that my last meal had been before leaving the farm.

"Hungry?" Knight asked.

"I could eat." I said.

She chuckled. "Come on."

"But Phoenix?" I looked towards his door.

"I'm pretty sure he'll understand you eating breakfast." She said. "Now, come one. Chows pretty good here, you gotta' meet the chef anyway."

"What's his name?" I asked.

"Call sign's Cookie."

"Cookie?"

* * *

I learned "Cookie" was an obsidian skinned mountain of a man, sporting a full dark beard and mustache, built more like a heavy weight boxer than a chef.

"Morning, Knight!" He shouted from behind a long buffet style counter. His eyes shut as he yelled cheerfully, and when they opened, he noticed me. "Who's your friend?"

His voice was deep as the Marianas trench.

"Fenrir." Knight called back.

"Fenrir." He squinted his eyes as he looked to the side, then shrugged. "Nope, ain't heard that one before."

"What's on the menu chef?" Knight asked, elbowing me in the ribs and nodding towards Cookie.

Cookie pointed a spatula at Knight in jest, though his smile remained. "Now Knight, I told you before, it's Cookie or nothing, and it's eggs, bacon, n' flapjacks."

"Sounds great." I said, hoping that some food would settle my stomach, though I didn't have much faith in it. Hungry as I was, I knew the ache in my stomach was born of nerves more than emptiness.

"He speaks!" Cookie's dark eyes widened. "I'm just funnin' ya kid. Go on and find yourself a seat, n' I'll have a plate to you in a sec'."

Knight looked offended as we made our way to a long stainless steel table. "Cookie! What about me?!"

"Now, Knight," Cookie shook his head as he shoveled eggs onto a plate, "you know I always hand deliver the tray first time someone eats here. What kinda' establishment would I be runnin' if I didn'. Gotta' leave a good first impression, otherwise customers don't come back."

"Like *you* have to worry about people coming back." Knight raised a single brow as we took our seats.

That got all of us chuckling, and I found I was infinitely thankful for my companions. At the very least, they could lighten a mood.

"Yeah, I know." Cookie rounded the end of the buffet line with a plate so full I was sure it was going to crack under the load.

"But still," Cookie continued as he sat the heavy plate before me, complete with fork and knife, "most people gettin' here had a pretty rough trip. It's nice to have a hot meal.

"Now," Cookie pointed to the plate, "eat up, you look like you'll blow away in a strong breeze."

He turned to leave then spun back around.

"Sorry." He extended his hand. "I'm Cookie. Nice meetin' ya'. Fenrir, right?"

"That's it." I shook his hand, though it was more his hand swallowing mine in a vice-like grip. It was then that I observed his busted knuckles. "Have it out with the grill, Cookie?"

He chuckled. "Nah, tune up on the van. See I cook 'cause I'm good at it and, honestly enjoy it, and let me tell ya', one meal of MRE's was enough for me. My designation in the unit is actually mechanic and wheelman."

"Wheelman?" I asked.

"He's the best driver you'll ever meet." Knight said. "We need to get from point A to point B, he gets us there. On short operations he stays in the vicinity, if it's a longer affair he drops us off and comes to get us later."

I hadn't seen our driver the previous night, but if that was Cookie's role within the unit, I was fairly certain it was him.

"Saw your car out there, Fenrir." Cookie nodded out the door. "Mind if I take a look around her sometime? Love to see what's under the hood, and Phoenix'll want a radio in there eventually anyway."

"By all means." I nodded. "Might want some new plates if you're gonna' take it out for a spin though. Pretty sure it's hot."

"It is." Cookie nodded and I figured either he or Phoenix had already ran the plates through some clandestine service of theirs. "And I'll take care of that. Don't need that kind of attention. Anyhow, you enjoy your meal."

As Cookie returned to the chow line, Knight leaned over to me. "Hope you like a bit of spice. Powdered eggs are hard to stomach otherwise."

I nodded. "I'll manage."

"Good." Knight smiled as she started towards the line.

I began with a cut of pancake and found them to be extraordinarily light, fluffy and full of flavor.

The bacon didn't disappoint either, thick cuts just on the verge of crispy. I wouldn't have complained in any case, my stomach was calming, though I couldn't say if it was the food or the company.

Knight returned as I bucketed the first bunch of eggs into my mouth, and Hell met my tongue.

My eyes began watering as I realized Cookie hadn't brought me a drink.

Then I heard Knight giggling.

With a parched voice I managed, "Drink?"

Without looking at me, still giggling, she pointed her fork to the chow line.

There stood Cookie, with a glass of water and a smirk.

I nodded as I moved to retrieve it.

"Thank you." I croaked as I took the glass.

The water was mostly gone by the time I returned to the table.

The burn now bearable, I looked to Knight. "You said a *little* spice."

Then I heard Cookie, back at the bar. "Gets 'em every time, hee-hee."

"I actually said a bit." Knight snickered as she took a bite of eggs. "It'll grow on you."

I nodded as I took in another spoonful of eggs and instantly cursed myself.

* * *

After what Cookie termed a *hot* meal, I found myself in front of the door Knight had indicated as Phoenix's.

My knock was met with a quick response.

"Yes?"

I opened the door to find Phoenix sitting behind a dark wood desk with his feet propped up from a comfortable chair. "Ah, Fenrir, glad you made it through the night relatively unharmed."

I shot him a frigid glare. "Woulda' been nice to know what I was up against."

"Well, I didn't exactly plan on you being attacked. I didn't even know vampires were in that area, but now I do, and I can look into the matter." He paused for a moment, seeming to consider saying more. "I must confess I'm impressed by your results. This kind of talent isn't normal in those who are so young in the skin. Most new wolves are hesitant, scared even, of using the wolf in combat, and without proper training most aren't even capable. You're sure you've only been afflicted for four months?"

"I'm sure." I nodded as I looked to a standard hanging behind him. A red trim, black backdrop, and a single red crescent moon as the center piece.

"Is this The Red Moons insignia?" I wondered.

He stood and walked to my side of the desk, skating past several tall file cabinets. "Your injuries?"

"They're fine, Phoenix."

"Good." He looked past me to the door, as if he could see through it. "Frost told me about your friend, Fenrir. I was sorry to hear it, but it was a firsthand lesson as to what we fight, and why. Despite the obviously unfortunate outcome, you yourself are quite lucky."

"Lucky?" I asked.

"Did you ever match eyes with them?" He countered.

I suddenly remembered Frost's words. Much as I hated to admit it, I hadn't strictly adhered to the instruction. Between the anger, the desire to protect Vivian, and the sudden bloodlust, I knew I had looked at least one vampire in the eye.

"I don't know, at least one."

"In close proximity?"

I nodded as I remembered the woman who had put me down. While we hadn't stared at each other per se, we had met eyes.

"Some vampires have a very… unique skill." Phoenix said. "We call it the spike, though it has other monikers. We don't know the entirety of the effects to the victim, only that most die screaming, and the handful that have miraculously come out of it remain in a vegetative state."

"I'm sorry?" I shook my head, this acknowledgment of what I could only consider a telepathic ability taking me by surprise. "The… spike? How does that work?"

"It's in their eyes, Fenrir, that's the best The Wolven Council can detail. In the event that someone locks eyes with a vampire, it seems up to the vampire's discretion to deliver the spike. The Council held one trial, just one, trying to figure out exactly what happened during the spike, though it was unnamed at the time. They had captured a lone vampire, and a Council Captain, Cobalt, volunteered to make an attempt at receiving the attack. He was attached to all manner of sensors and medical bits. It took a while, but the vampire finally delivered. Cobalt's brain activity, heart rate, everything in his body, suddenly spiked, except respiration. He screamed the air from his lungs, and quickly fell unconscious. He never came to, though they hoped that his body would automatically begin breathing once he passed out. He didn't. It broke the automatic impulses of his body as well. In his screaming, he had suffocated himself. After that, it was officially titled the spike, for obvious reasons."

I shook my head, understanding that I was indeed lucky, yet still feeling nothing of the sort as my thoughts lingered on Vivian.

"What's to be done about my friend, Phoenix?" I asked.

He nodded, having expected the question to arise. "You already know the answer to that, Fenrir. I'm sorry, but to confirm what you suspect, yes, if she is located she must be dealt with."

I nodded. "I guess I just needed to hear it, sir."

"Sir?" He sounded a bit offended.

"Er, Phoenix."

He half chuckled. "Not really used to manners, I'm afraid that we've just outgrown them, politeness has its place, it just isn't here. Our tactics are brutal and honestly, they have to be if we're to fight this war. I've drilled that into every squad, especially yours. They are an outstanding team."

"I wouldn't know." I looked to my hands. "I haven't got the chance to work with them yet."

"I'm aware." He paused. "I'm also aware that you need some training. In saying that, I mean you no insult. Everyone does at the beginning."

"I understand." I nodded. "Will this training take place here?"

"No," Phoenix shook his head, "I'm sending Alpha team to The Farm, it's our training site. Every operator in The Red Moons has been trained and tested there, you are no exception. Your fellow squad mates will oversee your training, and I assure you they're some of the best, they'll train you well, and they'll test you harder."

"And if I fail?" I asked.

"See that you don't." He said. "Preparations have already been made and your team is on standby, they're just waiting on you."

I nodded, disappointed that I wouldn't have the opportunity to ask him many of the questions that had formed while he had spoken.

"Something else on your mind?"

"A lot of things." I replied. "A lot of questions, but I don't want to keep the others."

"They'll find ways to pass the time, Fenrir. They spend most of their time here, a few more minutes won't hurt them. If you have questions, ask them, the opportunity for chitchat is rather rare."

My mind rolled back to the spike, how little was known about it. "It just seems that a lot of mystery still exists around werewolves and vampires."

Phoenix chuckled. "Indeed, though it seems only fitting. Creatures of darkness prefer to stay hidden, even from themselves."

"Hmpf." I puffed with a half smile.

"For all of our research, entire divisions devoted to the study of both wolves and vampires, we're progressing at an alarmingly slow rate."

"Why?" I asked.

He shrugged. "It's hard to say, Fenrir, I'm a soldier, remember? I don't have all the answers. What I can tell you though, is that The Wolven Council will make a good home for you, provided you follow the directives."

That last sentence seemed to have a charge to it, as if hinting at something, though it was impossible for me to decipher its aim.

It suddenly became apparent to me that I didn't know anything about my newfound companions, or the organization I now belonged to. What were its goals?

Phoenix sensed my rattled brain and looked back to me, politely inquiring. "What?"

"Phoenix, I'm grateful that you're helping find the woman who changed me, and I have no intention of leaving, but the fact is I don't know what's really going on here. I know you and the others and I belong to The Council, but what *is* The Council?"

Phoenix nodded. "That's a fair question, one I expected sooner if I'm honest, though I suspect you were a bit shell shocked from recent events. The Wolven Council, casually referred to as simply The Council, is a vast collection of werewolves that have dedicated their lives to combating The Blood Order. Vampires. In short, Fenrir, our primary objective is to protect humanity, above all else. We fight, so that humanity can survive."

As I heard this, "protecting humanity", my mind jolted back to the previous night.

"Phoenix," My pulse quickened, "the vampires were at my family's farm."

He nodded, his eyes softening. "They're alright, Fenrir, I've verified that, and I will keep tabs on them for a while. It's rare for vampires to break into a home to feed, though it does happen. They prefer to hunt busy cities and towns, keeping to the shadows and snatching loners who venture too close."

"How have they not been discovered yet?" I asked in disbelief. "A body with only two holes in the neck would paint a pretty clear picture."

Phoenix again nodded. "Yes it would. Most of them carry knives or a firearm, any weapon really. You think of it, they've done it. After feeding, cut the throat in a way that damages the bite, put a couple rounds in the neck, jab it a few times…" Phoenix shrugged and raised his hands.

"What about the lack of blood?"

"A single vampire can't stomach the entire blood supply of a human, there's often more than enough left to leave a bloody pool."

I shook my head as my thoughts reeled, dazed at the madness I found myself wrapped in.

"Fenrir," Phoenix drew my attention, "it takes time. You can't expect it all to come without a shock, that's another reason I send my operatives to the farm. It gives them time to adjust. Do you have any more questions?"

I shook my head. "If I did, my brain blocked them out to keep me sane."

He smiled with a light chuckle. "You'll be alright, Fenrir. Everyone here has endured this trial, and you will be no different. You've already got all the drive you'll need."

"Pardon?" I asked through narrowed eyes.

"When you wonder if you can do this, Fenrir, as you will, think back on your family, because it is they that you fight for."

11

The Farm

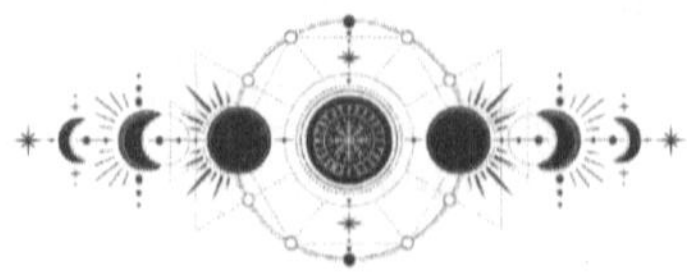

The Farm was just as it sounded, a farm. It was situated nearly forty miles east of Kirkwood on a three-hundred acre patch of dirt that grew nothing but weeds and solid oak trees.

The house was a large, albeit aged, traditional farmhouse, longer than it was wide. A black shingle roof sat atop a two-story red brick structure. It appeared that the shingles hadn't been replaced for some time, and the brick sported a healthy growth of creeping ivy. It was actually quite beautiful.

In addition to the house, a lone barn stood. Its tin roof had long ago lost its paint and was now mixed tones of brown as rust began to eat away at the metal.

The lower structure appeared to be constructed completely of wood, at least the outer shell. Long planks, bleached bright by the sun, ran up to touch the metal.

The front of the barn held a single door, wide enough to easily fit through, but lacking in terms of height. The previous owner must've been a person of smaller stature.

On the back side of the barn was a sturdy lean-to. From what I could see, it looked out over a sizable firing range, edged with tall earthen berms.

"Well," Knight smiled as she stood beside me, "what do you think?"

I nodded, having calmed down since my chat with Phoenix. "It's beautiful."

"You haven't seen anything yet." I turned to face Frost, finding her stepping out of the black cargo van that had carried us all.

The Challenger had remained at the Citadel at Phoenix's request, probably changing the plates and installing the radio Cookie had mentioned.

"There's a lake behind the house," Frost continued, "one of the best parts of The Farm."

Again, Frost floored me with her night and day attitude changes. It was amazing, she was simply able to turn it on and off, serious when she had to be, normal when it was permitted.

"If you like water." Doc said as he joined our gathering.

"You don't like water, Doc?" I asked.

"I like water as much as the next." Doc answered. "I do not like what I cannot see *in* the water."

"Like fish?" I asked again, trying to contain a chuckle.

"Like snapping turtles." Knight began to laugh. "Doc had an unfortunate encounter with one of the lake's residents."

"I managed to keep all my toes if that answers any questions, Fenrir." Doc concluded.

I couldn't help but chuckle then.

"Alpha team!" We all wheeled around to find Marcus, standing next to the van. "Let's introduce the pup to the place."

We all started towards the farmhouse and Knight moved next to me, trailing the group.

"You've been kinda' quiet since you got back, Fenrir. I know you're upset about your friend. If you need to talk, we're all here. I hope you know that."

I nodded. "Just not much to say about it, Knight… I couldn't save her."

"That is not your fault, nor is it Frost's." Doc said up ahead. "The pair of you were lucky to detect them before they attacked."

"Though none of it would've happened if the pup hadn't gone to get a car." Marcus said. "The vampires may not have even shown up, your friend would've been fine. I hope that car is worth it."

His words drove deep as any blade, cutting their way into my heart. I tightened my jaw, condemning any feelings to remain where they were.

"Marcus," Frost snarled, raising a defense on my behalf, "Phoenix approved it. He had no reason to believe there were vampires in the area. Fenrir isn't at fault."

Marcus turned around, matching hard eyes with Frost, and they both stopped only a few strides apart. For a tense moment, it seemed they were about to come to blows.

Frost raised a brow, daring Marcus to make the first move, retreat or otherwise.

"Doesn't matter anymore." Marcus growled as he turned back to the house. "What's done is done."

As Marcus stepped up to the door, withdrawing a key from a hanging lantern, Knight reached my side.

"Don't let him get to you, sometimes he forgets people have feelings."

I nodded wordlessly, shoving aside my injuries as I moved to the door, passing by an empty gun rack on the porch.

Stepping through the door, it became obvious that it had been a while since any one had visited. Dust particles floated through the air and a thin mask of the debris covered everything in the massive main room.

In this single room was the kitchen, dining room, and living room. In the back left corner a staircase ascended shortly before turning right and continuing upwards out of sight.

I assumed the bedrooms were upstairs as there were no additional doors on the bottom floor.

"Well," Frost grumbled through pursed lips, "guess the first thing would be to clean the place."

"Mhm." Knight frowned as her eyes darted around the room. "All the might of The Council and we can't get one or two people just to keep the place clean."

"Not worth it." Doc said as he placed his hands on his hips. "How often are we here? This is the first time this year and it's nearly October. Besides, The Council is unaware of this particular locale. I believe Phoenix prefers it that way. "

"Yes, worth it." Knight smiled as she argued. "*We* wouldn't have to clean it."

"Come on," Frost chuckled as she picked up a nearby broom, "it's not gonna' clean itself."

"Need a leaf blower." Knight mumbled as she drew a white rag from a kitchen drawer, tossing me one as well.

"Pup." Marcus' stern voice drew my attention. "Dining room is yours. Table and chairs, top *and* bottom."

He looked at Knight from the corner of his eye.

"Not gonna' let that go are you?" Knight smiled as she turned from the half cleaned kitchen counter. "I followed your instructions, Lieutenant."

Marcus laughed, and it was hard to believe that only moments ago he and Frost had been at odds. "You did not. I said to clean the table and chairs."

"And I did." Knight smiled as she turned back to the counter top.

"If you could overlook the two foot cobwebs hanging underneath the table." Frost chimed in as she swept.

Knight glanced over her shoulder, casting Frost a jesting glare. "No need for your input."

"I concur." Doc said from the back window, toweling away the most recent blast of cleaner. "Since in fact it was *I* that removed the aforementioned cobwebs."

"Real nice guys, gang up on the youngest." Knight feigned insult before attempting to shift the attention. "Got a new guy here ripe for the razzing."

Marcus looked from the floor to the table, and his eyes smiled mischievously.

"Nope, he's doin' alright." Marcus tried to suppress a smile as he went back to sweeping.

"What do you–" Knight stopped as she turned to me, finding that I had already knocked down the cobwebs.

She fixed me with a flat look. "Kiss ass."

"That is rather impolite," Doc turned away from his window with a smile, "picking on the new cadet."

"I–You–" She frustratedly stammered before sending her now putrid cloth at Doc's glistening window.

All eyes helplessly watched as the wet rag slapped the sparkling pane, leaving a dirty splat.

Disgust curled Doc's lips as his gaze followed the cloth, squealing down the glass.

His head followed as it fell to the floor. Only then did he look back to the window, giving it a comically quick spritz of cleaner before furiously wiping away the grime.

"And what do you say to that?" Knight bolstered a crooked smile.

"Still cleaning up after you." Doc sighed.

Laughter suddenly took the room, dissolving whatever tension was left between the team members.

As the laughter subsided and we set back to cleaning, Marcus' words weaseled into my mind despite the fact that, as far as I was concerned, all was forgiven.

As I cleaned the cherry table, I couldn't help but feel he was partially right. I found silent tears dripping onto the table top, brought forth by thoughts of Vivian.

I knew what Frost had said, and I wanted to believe her, but her words did little to dull the blade in my gut.

Phoenix had told me to think of my family when I needed reminding, and while they would help, Vivian would be my drive. If this was to be my life, as Phoenix had indicated, if my sole purpose now was to fight The Order, to fight vampires, then it would be for what they did to Vivian. To make sure it didn't happen to anyone else.

I blinked away a tear, scrubbing it into the table.

I rubbed my cheek to my sleeve, smearing the residue away from my face as I felt my resolve harden.

In that moment I cemented my mind. I would pass this training, but that wasn't enough.

I would become the best soldier in The Wolven Council. I could accept the fact that my normal life was over. I would become death to every vampire in existence.

As I finished with the table, I found I had been the only one cleaning. Everyone else had stopped, taking note of my state.

I was surprised by them though. On every face, there was no anger or disdain at my tears, even the unpredictable Marcus. Their faces held only sympathy. They knew exactly what I was going through, as if they had all gone through it themselves.

Knight threw down her cloth and walked to me wordlessly. As she got closer I could just see the shimmer of tears in her own eyes.

I was further shocked as she wrapped her arms around me and tucked her head against my chest.

"I'm alright, Knight." I smiled, warmed by her quick show of support, though a bit off put.

"Too late." Marcus' eyes softened as he looked upon her. "She can't take it. Someone goes to hurting, she gets all wound up too."

My breath caught as Frost took steps towards me, uncertain of her aim.

She laid a hand on Knight's back before looking to me with a half smile. Her eyes seemed to speak with apology on Knight's behalf, knowing that this was unusual, while also thanking me for allowing it.

Knight held me for a moment before Frost cleared her throat, tenderly addressing the youngest of the group.

"Knight, you know that boundary where it goes from sweet to awkward?"

"Mhm." Knight hummed.

"You're there." Frost smiled.

"Yeah, alright." Knight pulled away before looking up to me shyly, almost embarrassed. "Sorry."

I felt my eyes smile as I shook my head. "Nah, I needed it. Might've drowned on the table top otherwise."

Joined by laughter from the group, I tried to chuckle away my own embarrassment.

Twice in the past two days I had nearly broken down, both times in front of Frost.

"No more of that. At this rate someone will be cracking jokes about me drowning the vampires in tears."

"Well," Marcus clicked his tongue as he scanned the room, "that's about as good as it's gonna' get. You all get settled into your rooms."

The others quickly took to the stairs, leaving me still before Marcus.

"Right." He said as he leaned his broom against the wall. "Your room is the middle left. End of the hall on the right is the bathroom."

I nodded, collecting my pack and climbing the stairs as I suddenly, and just as inexplicably, wondered which room was Frost's.

The hall was somewhat narrow, though the kind lighting made it appear less so.

Reaching my designated door, I half turned as I opened it, unintentionally looking straight across into Frost's quarters, finding her transferring clothes from her pack to her top dresser drawer. In her fingers were barely existent lace bottoms.

"Is that... lingerie?"

The image of Frost in all but transparent blue bottoms suddenly jolted into my mind.

I recoiled as I felt heat flushing my face.

"Why did I look?"

I stepped into my room and closed the door, shaking my head, attempting to clear the persistent thought that quickened my pulse.

Regaining myself, I found the room quite simple, only a bed and dresser standing within.

After some cleaning, it was ready for use, and as I looked into the mirror atop the dresser I noted the lengthening stubble on my face.

"Lookin' a little scraggly, Rainer." I looked at my unkempt hair. *"Need a haircut too."*

Conversation echoing from the main room drew me back downstairs and as I returned, I found most of Alpha once more scattered about the room. Doc and Marcus were sitting at the table, while Knight rummaged through cabinets in the kitchen.

"Guuuys." Knight whined in a long breath. "There's nothing to eat in here."

"Feeling like a hunt?" Doc asked with an air of excitement.

"I was thinking more along the lines of a grocery run." Knight replied, dealing Doc's eagerness a light blow.

"If *you* bring back the produce," Doc counter-offered, seeming unwilling to capitulate just yet, "*I* will provide the protein."

Knight gently elbowed me as she nodded up stairs before raising her voice. "Who's gonna' cook?!"

"Not it!" Frost called from her bedroom.

Knight lightly giggled, as Marcus rolled his eyes.

"I'll cook. At least then I'll know it's edible."

"Awfully bold of you to assume that no one else can cook, Marcus." Doc smiled.

"I've eaten your health food, Doc." Marcus fired back. "A little salt never killed anyone."

"As a matter of fact," Doc countered, "it has."

"Sorry, Doc." Frost chuckled, making her way down the stairs. "Not feeling a zucchini boat tonight."

"Fine." Doc pouted as he teased. "Do not come crying to me when your arteries are clogged."

With that he moved to the door, seeming eager to get on with his hunt.

* * *

The rich aroma of stewing rabbit permeated the farmhouse that evening, nearly full enough to satiate hunger on its own.

"Pup," Marcus called as he stirred the pot, "give me a hand will you?"

As I drew near, I observed him gently ladling the soup into five bowls, Knight intently peering over his shoulder.

Marcus smiled. "Knight, go sit down, any closer and you'll be in the kettle."

"Then it'd be too sweet to eat." Knight smiled as she took her bowl.

I too smiled as I began transferring bowls to the table, stalling the conversation of Doc and Frost, who had already taken their seats.

As I deposited Frost's, her hand gently brushed mine as she took the bowl, the stroke of a feather, yet strong enough that I had to fight the urge to let my hand linger a moment longer.

As Marcus and I took our seats, he looked to Doc, who had already depleted a healthy portion of his meal.

"Is it safe to say you approve, Doc?" Marcus smiled as he picked up his spoon.

Doc nodded, swallowing his most recent morsel. "Definitely worth the thirty minutes of life it cost me."

Marcus chuckled to himself as he turned his attention to his bowl.

I managed a quick blessing over my soup, and as I began to eat, it struck me how natural this felt, how right. It felt like I belonged here.

* * *

As early evening wound down, each operator settled into their own devices.

For Knight, this meant bundling up in a purple blanket on the blue couch and delving into a hardback book. Her eyes quickly traveled the pages, lending that she was an avid reader.

Across the living room from Knight, Marcus and Doc played cards, each sitting in blue padded armchairs that matched the couch. A redwood coffee table stood between them, each of them holding a few cards.

Frost had taken the moment to steal a quick shower, and I had learned the concept of ladies first was alive and well with my team. Knight would go next, then it was up to us guys.

As I ran a hand through my hair, I remembered looking upon myself earlier.

"Anyone good at cutting hair?" I asked Marcus, not wanting to bother Knight.

"Knight does pretty good." Doc said, still focused on his cards, and I couldn't help but look up to his uneven hair.

Scrambling for a response that wouldn't cause injury, I rattled. "That's okay, she's busy reading."

"You mean you want a decent haircut?" Marcus' dark eyes smiled up at me.

I looked to Knight from the corner of my eye, awaiting some sort of repercussion.

"She did not hear." Doc laughed, ignoring the jab. "She is in the book."

Footfalls landed on the stairs and I felt Frost enter the room, a charge rippling through me.

Her hair lay in damp strands, still laden with moisture. While her hair had momentarily lost its body, it only accentuated hers, gently outlining the elegant curves along the nape of her neck.

"I can cut your hair, Fenrir." She offered, toweling her face before turning to Knight.

"Knight, it's–" Frost smiled as she gently kicked a decorative pillow from one end of the couch, bouncing off Knight's drawn knees.

Only then did Knight take her eyes from the book. "Hmm?" She hummed inquisitively.

Frost giggled. "Your turn."

"Already?" Knight saddened, upset she had to put the book down.

"Unless you want us to go ahead." Doc offered.

"Nope." Knight gently laid down her book and cast aside the blanket. "Following Marcus once was enough. Sheds more hair as a man than a wolf."

"Funny." Marcus spoke into his fist, eyeing his cards.

"Take a chair outside, Fenrir. I'll be along in a minute." Frost smiled.

I nodded, grabbing a chair before stepping through the door, letting in a few golden rays from the setting sun.

As I waited, my breath suddenly came short and shallow, a tinge of excitement tickling my skin, and I looked down to see fine pricks along my arms.

At the sound of the door my hands clenched the back of the chair, and I turned back to find Frost passing me by.

I watched her, trying to contain myself.

"Here's good." She gestured to a well lit spot near the corner of the house, bathed in the sun's remaining warmth.

As I sat in the chair, anxiousness pulsed through me, my body buzzing.

A flash of fabric drifted before me, and I found a towel quickly draped over my chest. It was damp, smelling of petrichor.

I turned rigid as I realized that this was the very towel she had used.

"Sorry if it's still a little wet." Frost said, still behind me.

"It's fine." I quickly replied.

"Any particular cut?" She asked politely.

"Whatever you think is best." I said, feeling the cool moisture of the towel transfer to my shirt.

My heart drummed in my ears as she stepped before me, bending down to look at my face.

"Hmm." She hummed, her eyes traveling over my face as I drank her in.

She glowed in the light, water droplets sparkling on the smooth skin of her neck.

"Alright." She spun a pair of scissors in her hand. "I think I've got it."

Once more she moved behind me, and I felt the teeth of a plastic comb moving through my hair.

"So," she quietly asked as she worked, "what do you think of the place?"

"It's nice." I started to nod, catching myself with a chuckle. "Sorry. It's nice, though I think it's more the people than the place."

"Hmm." I heard her smile as her fingers glided through my hair, a shiver coursing down my spine.

I felt a line of hair catch between her fingers, and every cut rumbled into my core as her warm hands moved.

I closed my eyes, picturing her hands as they ran through my hair, seeing it as I felt it.

It felt good, right. It was comfortable.

"Quite a head of hair you have, Fenrir." She said, pulling me from the edge of waking dreams.

"Yeah." I chuckled, feeling silly with myself. "Honestly I don't think I've ever let it get this long."

"It's not *that* bad." She laughed as I felt another cluster of hair get snipped away.

"Right." I smiled, taking another breath of her, wishing I could taste the air.

"What is wrong with me? It's a haircut."

It felt right though, all of it, like it had always been this way, like I wanted it this way.

I *did* want it this way.

I opened my eyes, frowning, suddenly feeling foolish, stupid. It was just a haircut, she was doing me a favor. So why didn't I want it to end?

"So you're religious?" Frost abruptly asked as she worked.

"Pardon?" I blew a couple clippings from my lip.

"It looked like you prayed over supper." She replied.

"Oh." I chuckled. "Yeah. We always prayed over supper. Breakfast and lunch, dinner my dad called it, were normally eaten on the run."

"Mm." She hummed. "Is it one of those pre-cut prayers? The same blessing every time?"

I smiled as I recalled a brief conversation with Mom. "No. Mom said those felt like they weren't sincere. Like it was just a motion to go through, although Dad did always make sure to mention the farmers that grew it and the hands that prepared it."

"Go to church on Sundays and all that?" Frost toiled.

"As often as we could." I smiled. "Mom and Dad made it a point not to miss it much, and I have to admit that there were some days it seemed the pastor was talking straight to me. Those were the ones that always drove home hardest."

Frost's lips lifted in a smile. "I know exactly what you mean, Fenrir."

"You're a believer then?" I asked.

"I am. Very few things am I certain of, but God is one that I am. This team, the whole of The Red Moons actually, we're all believers. We tried getting together on Sundays for a small mass, but it didn't last long. When a team was in the field, it was hard to concentrate on the message, let alone deliver the message, when we were all worried about them. So we opted for a prayer together, asking for their safe return." Her voice softened towards the end.

"Now for the hard part." The strength in her voice returned as she turned her attention back to my hair.

She knelt in front of me, looking at my bangs.

Again her eyes darted about, making imaginary cuts.

She smiled with her thoughts, putting a bit of excitement to my chest.

"Close your eyes, Fenrir." She said as she reached up.

As I closed my eyes, eagerness filled me, waiting for the moment her hands returned, a light breath escaping when they did.

Her fingers danced ever closer to my brow, and all I could think of was what her hands would feel like on my face.

What they might feel like if they pulled my face to hers.

"Alright, done." I felt Frost pull away. "Um, Fenrir? You can open your eyes now."

"Right." I replied as I opened my eyes, embarrassed once more.

"Well?" I asked.

"It looks… it looks good if I do say so myself." She gave an alluring smile. "Makes your brows stand out."

"They need a cut too?"

We both laughed, though I was willing to sacrifice every hair on my face if it meant I got to feel her hands again.

* * *

That night, after showers were taken, the team called a meeting, and I figured that it had something to do with my training.

Marcus gestured for me to have a seat at the far end of the table, away from the squad so that they were all facing me.

"I'm not going to beat around the bush with you pup." Marcus' eyes had hardened, conveying the seriousness of our meeting. "Alpha team works just fine as it is, but we're a man short. We could make use of a support man. *You* will fill that spot."

I nodded. "Alright, what would a support man do?"

"You'd be our squad support gunner, Fenrir, suppressive fire will be your role." Frost answered shortly. "Either to keep the enemy behind cover until we can flank, or to hold the enemy back until we can withdraw from the fight."

"How long is this training?" I asked. If all I had to do was learn a particular firearm, then it shouldn't be more than a few days, at most a week.

"A month." Knight said, in a business like manner.

"A month?" I repeated. "Just to learn the role of support gunner?"

"No." Doc said. "While support will be your role, all Alpha operators must learn the fundamentals. Alone we must be able to perform adequately, as a team we should be able to bring down an entire enemy installation."

It sounded rather glorified hearing it that way, but I hadn't known Doc to be arrogant.

Straight to the point, Marcus looked to me. "You're starting with Doc. He's going to teach you trauma basics. This is the easiest part of your training, but in the field it could be the most important. Part two will be with Knight."

Knight took the lead. "Close quarters and infiltration tactics. It's one week."

"You're with me for the third bit." Frost said, almost mechanically. "Firearms and support training."

"And last," Marcus drew my attention back to him, "if you make it past the others, I will show you how to use the wolf. Movements mostly and how to use it properly. The wolf is your greatest weapon, but if you don't know how to handle yourself, it's dead weight."

"All this will take a month?" I asked skeptically.

"A little less than." Doc replied. "If all goes well."

Eagerness filled me as I asked, "When do I start?"

"First thing tomorrow." Doc replied.

12

Trauma Class

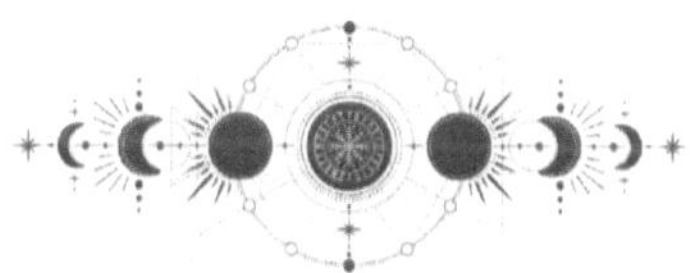

9/27

0800 Hrs.

The next morning found Doc and I at the kitchen table, the other operators either leaving the house earlier or, in Knight's case, catching a few extra Z's.

"Alright, let us begin." Doc said as he stood from the table, moving to a nearby bookcase and withdrawing a textbook.

"Are you settling well, Fenrir?" Doc calmly asked.

"It's a lot to take in, Doc, if I'm being honest with you."

"I would be concerned if you said otherwise." Doc smiled as he returned. "That is why we start with something a bit slower."

He laid the textbook down on the table, and I could see it was an anatomy book.

As he did, I noted his calmness. Everything he did was precise, calculated, no needless motions or words. He was in no rush, nor did he drag his feet.

"No," Doc said with mild humor, "I do not expect you to memorize the anatomy of the human body, but in order to provide effective first aid and trauma care, a basic understanding is needed. Starting with the locations that will result in instant or rapid death."

He went on this way, pointing at various parts of the body and explaining what happened if hit there. His tone grew a bit grave as noted that some injuries, such as a bullet to the head or heart, were obviously beyond his capability, as well as the wolf's, to mend.

Spinal injuries were a bit of a mixed bag, hinging solely on the exact nature of the injury.

Delving away from the spinal injuries, Doc's mood quickly recovered as he touched on other wounds, those that required pressure, tourniquets, or splints.

Some required a traction board or bar. He produced his monstrous bag, quickly detailing what he carried in it. Morphine auto injectors, bandages, tourniquets, splints, a small traction rig, as well as other medical instruments.

He then withdrew a small silver canister with an inch-long needle at one end, and a single button at the other. It appeared much like the morphine injector, but about half the length.

"No doubt you have heard the stories of silver being fatal to werewolves?" Doc said as he looked to me. "They are true. You get hit with a silver bullet or get cut by a silver blade, it will kill you very quickly. This," he gestured to the injector, "is Anver. Anti-silver. It prevents the silver from killing the wounded, but it must be administered quickly. Wait too long and the victim will still expire as silver drastically slows our regenerative abilities."

"What exactly does silver do to us?" I asked.

Doc nodded. "A good question."

He pointed to the illustration, specifically the right leg.

"Say you were to be shot in the right leg. Other than the obvious damage of destroyed tissue, very quickly the blood in the veins cauterizes, continuing through the arteries from the point of impact. The silver literally cooks the blood in our veins. Despite research efforts we are still uncertain why it does this. The blood within grows thicker and thicker, impeding oxygen delivery to the entire body. The body spasms, a single enormous contraction as everything stops. From this point, Fenrir, three minutes is all the time you have to receive Anver, past that amount of time, even if you receive the serum, your brain has been deprived of oxygen for more than three minutes, resulting in serious and permanent brain damage."

I gulped as he finished his explanation, the gravity of this particular matter driving home.

"Fortunately," he glanced at the injector, "The Council concocted that. An agent specifically engineered to counteract the coagulated blood. The make-up is classified of course, and I doubt that any outside of those that developed it actually know the construction. I suspect some sort of thinning agent, but aside from that, I am unsure. It does as it should, that is all I know for certain."

"And silver is common?" I asked hesitantly.

Doc nodded in return. "Unfortunately, yes. In every backpack used, we have two injectors of Anver, but I must request that you avoid silver. We do not have a very large supply, and it is rather hard to come by."

"Copy that." I said.

Doc looked to his watch; it was just pushing three in the evening.

"That'll do for today, Fenrir." He said. "Submit what I have shown you to memory. Tomorrow when we continue, I will pull the necessities from my pack and teach you how to apply them."

"That's it?" I asked. "We're done?"

"For today." Doc smiled. "You have taken in more information than you think. For now, focus on retaining it."

* * *

Supper that evening was Marcus' deep fried squirrel, which even the heart healthy Doc couldn't say no to.

Knight had been impatiently waiting since the first fuzz tail hit the batter, Doc doing what he could to keep her occupied with banter about fried zucchini, while I couldn't help but notice Frost's absence.

After dropping off her bag of squirrels, she had gone upstairs, and was yet to return.

"Should I let Frost know the food's done?" I asked.

"She has been up there a long time." Doc noted curiously.

"Probably on the phone with her boyfriend." Knight shrugged.

I hadn't considered that possibility, distracted by my infatuation with her. My heart sank with the weight of Knight's words, and I couldn't help the jealousy that tugged at me.

"Why am I jealous?"

I knew exactly why I was jealous, I had only gone to bed last night thinking about her fingers in my hair.

In the dimly set light of my mind, her hands once more found my hair, as my lips found hers. The warmth of her body against mine, blue lace at my fingertips.

The foolish dreamings of a nineteen year old.

Laughter suddenly filled the room, and as I turned to the others I feared my face had betrayed me.

"Right." Marcus shook his head as he chuckled. "Like *we* have enough time for significant others."

Knight sighed dreamily. "Makes you jealous of Slade and Edge doesn't it?"

"Who?" I asked.

"Some of the other Red Moon operators." Doc said, still smiling. "The only two in the entire unit to have a tangible partner."

"No one else is seeing anyone?" I asked in disbelief. Surely Frost's beauty drew someone's attention. "People outside the unit?"

Doc shook his head. "Humans are off limits, for obvious reasons, and the nearest Council town is two hours away."

"Doesn't keep Marcus' letters from coming in though." Knight smiled mischievously.

Marcus shook his head, annoyed. "We're just friends, Knight."

"Remember that in nine months time." Doc humorously jabbed.

Marcus sighed in resignation as he looked to me. "Had to ask, didn't you?"

"I just… find it hard to believe that no one else is dating." Sadness creased my brow. "Even outside the Red Moons. That's what we should be doing isn't it? People around our ages do that, they have boyfriends or girlfriends, they go on dates, they see a movie or–"

"We're not people though, Fenrir." Marcus nodded empathetically. "We're Council soldiers. Simply put, we don't have a lot of down time, and what we do have is usually put to use at The Citadel, or something else Council oriented. Sure you can write letters, you can make calls, but that's all you'll ever hold, and they are no replacement for the touch of another."

"So, people generally date inside their unit?" I asked.

"It is a continuous trend." Doc admitted. "We are closest to one another, our bonds forged by the fires we walk through."

"I figured that would be against regulations or something." Surprise rang in my voice.

"It's not encouraged," Marcus confirmed, "but the majority of units are like ours, full of young people. You're not gonna' stop it, The Red Moons just have a deterrent."

"Deterrent?" I repeated.

With a crooked smile Marcus shrugged.

"There are only three women in the Red Moons. One is a toddler," He lightheartedly jabbed at Knight, "one is dating a linebacker, and the other is the ice queen. The options are pretty much exhausted."

"Toddler?!" Knight looked away from her food, and I knew things were serious.

Marcus laughed under Knight's tongue lashing and I turned to Doc.

"I'll be back." I smiled as I started to stand, having observed Frost's plate next to me, still waiting for her. "I'm gonna' get Frost."

"No." Doc's words, suddenly sullen, halted me as his quiet voice took a stern edge, quieting our bickering companions.

Marcus looked at his watch, and his face shifted to match Doc's.

"Damn." He sighed, almost regretfully.

"What?" I asked excitedly.

Knight folded her hands in front of her face, signifying the total destruction of the thus far happy evening.

"What?!" I said again. "What's wrong?"

"She probably won't be down tonight, Fenrir." Marcus rubbed his brow as he turned to the stove.

"Why is that?" I asked a little softer.

"Pass the training," Knight said, "and she may tell you."

I looked down to the table, to the plate next to me.

"We should still take her food up." I looked to the others.

Doc shook his head. "She is best left alone, Fenrir."

"Why wouldn't– Is she so volatile that they–" I frowned. *"Well, I never was accused of being the brightest."*

I fully stood, scraping Frost's plate from the table as I started for the stairs.

"It's your funeral." I heard Marcus whisper, and I could only imagine him shaking his head.

Each footstep on the stairs became thunder in the sudden silence of the house.

I didn't understand. Why? They may not have made the issue known, but their demeanor had shifted enough that even an outsider like me could tell something was wrong.

Why would they just leave her?

As I stopped in front of her door, it wasn't fear that I felt, of an explosive response or otherwise. It was curiosity, questions, all of them asking why she was being left alone when it seemed that she may very well need someone.

Gently, I rapped at her door.

There wasn't an immediate response, though the quiet rustle of blankets and a soft shuffle towards the door led me to believe that she may've been in bed.

The door cracked open, just hardly, barely enough for her to look out.

"What?" She asked quietly.

"I brought your food up." I smiled, gently raising her plate.

"If I wanted it, I would've come down." She bluntly replied.

"I just–"

"Thanks, but no thanks, Fenrir." She nearly growled as the door clacked shut.

"Well, damn." I sighed as I looked down to the plate in my hand.

It almost felt wrong that I left the plate on the floor outside her door, like I was leaving food outside of a prison cell.

"At least it's there if she wants it." I turned to my own room.

* * *

That night found me lying in bed mere steps from Frost, wondering why she hadn't come to supper, why she had behaved like she had.

I didn't want to know just for the sake of knowing, I wanted to know so I could try to help, assuming that I even could. Given the opportunity though, I would've tried.

As I tried to fall asleep, guilt weighed down on me.

Although it had been short lived, I was happy, excited even, to know that Frost wasn't seeing anyone. Then for everyone to take such a grave stance regarding her, followed by the reception I'd received at her door...

There were no wishful thoughts for me that night, no phantom kisses or brushes of skin, only hopes that she was alright.

* * *

9/28

1430 Hrs.

Day two of trauma found Doc and I again at the table, and it was all I could do to pay attention, still dwelling on Frost.

My mind, never resting, continued to lend itself to asking why the events of the previous day had occurred.

Naturally, mum was the word, and though I had seen Frost out and about, an improvement over the day before, she had nothing to say on the matter.

The one potential upside to the whole ordeal was that when I had woken, the plate outside her door was gone. Of course, there was nothing to say if she had taken it or if someone had simply tidied it up.

With that, I was left to keep wondering, and attempting to keep up on Doc's lesson.

I wasn't fairing too poorly, catching the high points in any case, and it helped that most of the information was akin to common sense.

We revisited bullet wounds for a time, which found Doc again touching on silver, and how these effects, chiefly the speed at which they fully kicked in, hinged on proximity to the heart.

Injuries to the chest presented new problems for obvious reasons. Collapsed lungs, blood loss, shock, a spinal wound, all of these required more care than we could typically provide in a combat situation.

"Even with silver out of the equation, the wolf still requires a bit of time to mend these injuries." Doc said, bringing me to recall the fight at my family's farm.

Without a doubt my ribs had shattered, and with the bloody froth that jettisoned from my mouth, I was fairly certain that at least one of my lungs had collapsed.

"If these wounds take the wolf so long to heal, why—"

"Are there cases where some wolves heal faster?" I couldn't contain the question.

"What do you mean?" Doc asked politely.

"How long does it normally take for a wolf to heal these wounds? I realize that in a fight, seconds are precious, so how long are we talking?"

Doc's brow furrowed as he attempted to scrape together the best response. "There is no set guideline, Fenrir. Each wolf will heal at a different rate that is dependent on numerous factors. General health, fatigue, nutrition, the nature, severity, and complexity of the wound. Blood loss leading into shock could take the wolf upwards of twenty minutes to remedy because the wolf is tasked with repairing the wound while simultaneously replenishing blood supply. A collapsed lung may only take the wolf a few minutes to mend if it is only a single lung impacted by a standard lead round. Add broken ribs penetrating said lung, and now the wolf must address both issues and, again, we now face the prospect of a lengthy mend."

Doc once more returned to spinal wounds. "Spine injuries are the longest to heal, provided the wolf survives the current situation. If the column is only shifted, applying pressure to the cord, the wolf can return it to its natural position, but this is a painful and long endeavor. Up to a week in some documented cases. If the cord is cut, the outcome is much more uncertain. Statistically, in the event of a fully severed spinal cord, only fifteen percent are able to regain function of their body below the break, and of those fifteen percent, fewer ever regain the full range of function."

I frowned at the bleak facts that Doc laid out. It seemed that the wolf did indeed have its limitations.

My question remained however. Why had I healed so fast? Surely Frost would've questioned this as well. She obviously *heard* something crack, but maybe she didn't see the tell tale crimson foam that I coughed out.

Maybe I hadn't actually suffered a collapsed lung?

No, I knew I had. I couldn't breath, and I'd seen lung shot deer in a state similar to my own.

"So," I shook the questions from my mind, knowing no way to ask them, "if one of us were to be wounded like that, what's the best course of action?"

"Get them clear of the fight, before their adversary can finish them off." Doc grimly finished.

With a sigh I leaned back in my chair. "Guess we're more vulnerable than I thought."

Doc nodded. "There are many ways that a wolf can meet an end, some less pleasant than others. Old age has never been on the table."

My blank expression must have told Doc that my capacity, more my ability, to retain any more information was exhausted.

"Are you alright, Fenrir." Doc looked at me a bit sideways. "Even at the start of the day you were less attentive than I expected."

"I'm alright." I nodded. "Just worried about Frost I guess."

He smiled at this. "About yesterday?"

Again I nodded. "Sorry that I haven't been a stand up pupil today."

"Quite alright." He closed his books. "I will not fault your concern. Call it a day?"

"Sounds good." I nodded as I stood, stepping towards the door.

As I moved into the sunlight, I felt the faintest of breezes break over my face, carrying the smell of the earth.

I ventured around to the back of the house, finding no one in front, and as I rounded the corner I found a single figure seated alongside the lake.

She sat in a red folding camp chair, a matching bucket hat on her head and a blue fishing rod planted beside her.

As I approached, the black hair made clear that it was Knight, and my heart sank a bit. I had no opposition to seeing Knight, but the fact of the matter was that she wasn't who I sought.

"Fenrir." She smiled back as I grew nearer. "Done for the day?"

"Yeah." I nodded. "One more down."

"What was today about?" She picked up her fishing rod, lightly bobbing the tip, more playing than fishing.

"More on gunshot wounds, and special injuries." I replied flatly.

"Don't take it for granted." She advised. "You'll need it in the field, and training only gets harder from here. Sit? I've got an extra pole."

I cast a quick look around, once more looking for Frost, once more unable to find her.

"Be rude to just blow her off."

"Why not?" I sat next to her, taking up the other rod, sending the lure into the glassy waters.

"Were you looking for someone?" Knight asked as the tip of her rod dipped, making an effort to set the hook just a moment late. "Dang."

I chuckled as I sprawled out, propping myself up on an elbow. "Not really. I mean I was, but now that I think of it, I really don't know why."

"Must've been Frost." She began reeling in her lure.

"What makes you say that?" My eyes darted to her.

"Well," she sent the lure back to the water, "you just left Doc, you found me and still looked around, and for some reason, I doubt you're hunting for Marcus."

"What reason is that?" I asked.

She turned to me with a sly smile. "Call it a woman's intuition."

I smiled as I shook my head. "Yeah, I was looking for Frost. Wanted to make sure she was okay after last night."

"Mm." Knight hummed through her smile. "She's alright, Fenrir. She's out hunting. It's sweet of you to worry about her though."

I tried not to hang on her wordage too much as I toyed at my reel. "Like I said, not sure why I was looking for her. She's got all of you to talk to about things. Guess that's kind of arrogant of me, huh?"

"Not at all." Knight shook her head. "Like *I* said, it's sweet."

"Alright," I smiled, "I let it go the first time, now it seems deliberate. Why sweet?"

"You're not attracted to her?" She bluntly asked.

"I, well–" I stammered. "Jeez, kinda' put me on the spot there didn't you?"

"Kind of the point." She giggled.

I was lost on how to proceed at this point, if I clammed up, Knight had her answer anyway.

"I mean, yeah I guess so," I chuckled, "but when you say it like that–"

"It kinda' puts you on the spot?" She smiled.

"That is correct." I laughed as I observed her miss another bite. "Have you caught anything?"

"Nope." Knight smiled. "Don't really care though, I just like sitting in the sun and listening to the water."

"Fair enough." I smiled as I looked to the sky. "It is a pretty day. Wish I could've spent more of it outside."

"Oh, don't worry." Knight leaned back in her chair. "Next week you'll be in it all day. And the week after that. And the week after that."

"Good." I nodded as I absently looked down to my hands. "Hey, Knight?"

"Hmm?"

I looked up to find her eyes closed beneath the shade of her hat.

"When you asked about Frost, that's gonna' stay between us right?"

She fixed me with a single open eye as she smiled. "Don't worry. I won't tell Ol' Ironsides a thing."

"Thanks, Knight." I smiled. "Knew I liked you for a reason."

I jumped in surprise as her rod rocketed into the water, towed behind an unseen fish.

Knight barely opened her eyes as the rod came to a stop near the middle of the lake.

She smiled as she closed her eyes, returning to her leisurely state. "It can't be for my fishing skills."

"Well no one's perfect." I chuckled.

"No. I suppose not." Knight sighed as she quickly dismissed the lost tackle. "So has Doc yelled at you yet?"

"Not yet," I shook my head, "but to be honest, I don't think I've ever heard him yell. At all."

"Most of the time he doesn't." Knight nodded. "Just wait until you get to the–"

"Having any luck?" Frost's voice rang as a soft footfall crunched in the grass behind us, leading Knight and I to turn back.

A small rifle in her hand, companied with her heavy pack, indicated that at least *she* had been productive.

"Eh." Knight waved a hand. "Not really. Tried for a while and didn't do any good, so I gave up. Fenrir's not doing much better."

"Well," Frost's lips gently lifted into a smile as she looked from us to the water, "some days the fish just aren't b– Is that my fishing rod out there?"

"Oh, was that one yours?" Knight asked as if she hadn't known.

"Man," Frost shifted her weight, putting her free hand to her hip, "I really liked that pole."

"Well, you know the old saying. If you love something let it go," Knight fluttered her hand, "and if it's meant to be, it'll come back to you."

"Yeah, I'm pretty sure that's about relationships and people, Knight." I looked up to her. "Things that have the capacity of returning themselves?"

"Potato, tomato." Knight turned to her friend. "I'm sorry, Frost. I'll get you a new one."

"It's alright, Knight." Frost smiled. "It's just a pole. Come on, you guys can help me clean these quail."

"Yeah, alright." Knight stood as I began reeling in an empty line.

"So what were you gonna' say about Doc yelling?" I asked as the lure skipped over the bank.

"Hmm?" Knight replied. "Oh, never mind. You'll see."

13

Spades

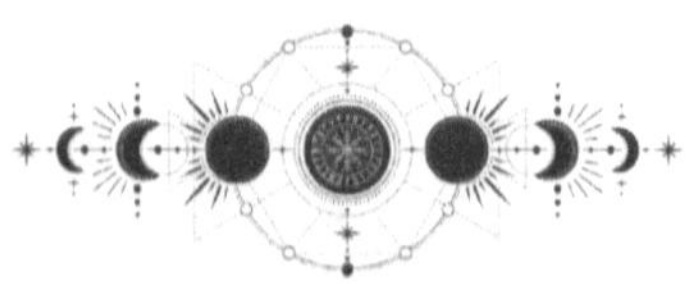

Another day of training with Doc had come and gone, mostly uneventfully. That evening, a Wednesday night, following a quick, and largely cold shower, I came downstairs to find everyone gathered round the table.

Everyone but Frost, who sat alone at the coffee table in the living room, gutting an M4.

Supper was long over, the dishes cleaned and put away.

"Fenrir," Marcus smiled as he looked to me from the head of the table, "about time."

"Didn't know I was late." I replied.

"It's Wednesday." Knight smiled as she spun around, seated at the opposite end of the table from Marcus. "Cards tonight."

"What're we playing?" I asked as I looked over to Frost, still working on her rifle.

"That is yet to be determined." Doc sighed as his eyes darted between

Knight and Marcus. "Marcus wants to play spades, Knight wants to play phase ten."

"Mm." I hummed, sliding into place between Knight and Marcus as I looked at Frost. "Been a minute since I've played either of those. Though I'm pretty sure we'd be one person over limit for spades."

"I'm good." Frost said as she thumbed the bolt of her disassembled rifle.

"That's alright, she's no good at Spades anyway." Marcus shrugged before I caught Frost shooting him a quick frown.

"Doesn't matter." Knight smiled. "We'll be playing phase ten anyway."

"We'll see." Marcus looked to Doc.

"Ready?" Doc glanced between Knight and Marcus. "Go."

They both raised a fist, chanting in unison.

"Rock, paper, scissors, shoot!"

With scissors against paper, spades was the game of the night.

"Ugh, fine." Knight rolled her eyes.

"Look on the bright side, Knight, you're on my team, so you're gonna' win." Marcus smugly smiled as he started dealing. "Said you've played before, Fenrir?"

"Yeah." I nodded.

"Good." Marcus smiled.

"It does get rather cutthroat at times." Doc warned. "Marcus is known to bag himself out to break a nil or a bid. That said, going nil is best avoided unless one is certain they can make it. Better to make a low bid than go back 200 points."

"Simple enough." I nodded. "How many points are we playing to?"

"One thousand." Marcus replied as he finished dealing.

"Lengthy game then." I said as I looked at my cards, finding a well balanced hand, though the trumps were all low value. Ace of clubs, king of hearts.

"*Two.*"

"It normally goes pretty quickly." Knight replied. "Ten hands or so normally has Marcus' team winning."

I nodded, suddenly grasping why Knight didn't really want to play spades.

"You any good, Doc?" I asked as I sorted my suits.

"I do alright." Doc replied as I heard the bolt ram home in Frost's rifle.

"Is that what you do for fun, Frost?" I asked.

"Yes," she replied shortly, "though not right now."

"O-kay then." I answered, finding myself wondering what else she liked doing.

"Bolt release is a little 'sluggish'," Knight whispered as she performed air quotes, "on her rifle."

"I said sticky, Knight." Frost replied, more occupied with her work than her words. "You just don't like the word."

"Sticky just tastes… weird." Knight scrunched her nose.

"Sticky?" I chuckled as I raised my brow. "You don't like the word 'sticky'?"

"For whatever reason," Doc brushed the hair above his ear, "Knight doesn't care for certain words."

Marcus fiendishly grinned as he looked to me. "Like M–"

"Don't you dare." Knight growled, all humor having left her eyes as she jabbed a pointed finger to Marcus.

"Alright, alright." Marcus looked at his cards, waiting for Knight's finger to fall before whispering her way. "Moist."

"Aughhh!" Knight shuddered, craning her neck. "It's even worse when you whisper it!"

Marcus chuckled before looking to me. "You guys lead the bidding, Fenrir, and no table talk when the game starts."

"Alright." I smiled before looking to Doc. "My bid's two."

"So we have five." Doc nodded before he looked to Knight as she put a pen to paper, our designated score keeper. She drew two lines on opposite sides of the page, one reading MK, the other titled DF.

"And let the games begin." Marcus smiled.

* * *

As the game went on, I found my eyes continuously drifting over to Frost, quietly toiling away at her rifle.

"Does she ever do anything but work?" I wondered. *"Surely there has to be something she enjoys doing other than soldiering. Everyone needs to recharge once in a while. Maybe that's what happened the other–"*

"Your turn, Fenrir." Knight politely chimed, drawing me back to the game.

"Right." I laid my card.

The two teams kept relatively close together in score over the course of the game, right up until Marcus took an extra trick, setting Doc and I back 50 points.

As it stood, it was looking to be the last hand with Marcus and Knight at 920 points, while Doc and I sat at 860.

Even if we took all thirteen tricks, we still wouldn't win the game, but we'd be close to it.

"Just gotta' take enough tricks to keep the game going."

Marcus smiled as he shuffled. "Gonna' have to start playing for money."

Knight rolled her eyes. "It's hard enough to play this game without also losing money, Marcus."

"That's true, I guess." Marcus held his smile. "At least it would be a guaranteed source of income."

"Feeling blow hardy tonight?" Doc calmly asked as Marcus dealt.

"Well," Marcus tipped his head, "we'd have to screw up pretty bad for us to lose now."

"Because you never mess up." Knight frowned.

"There's a reason my team always wins." Marcus grinned as he side eyed Frost. "Although I do get nervous when Frost is my partner."

I looked to Frost, finding that only her eyes had shifted to Marcus with a cold glare.

Marcus' arrogance, however lighthearted, finally irked me as it became directed at Frost, and at that exact moment, my life goal became clear.

"Don't let Marcus win."

As I looked over my hand, I had to consciously keep myself smiling. I held mostly trash.

Heavy on low value hearts, moderate count on clubs and diamonds with nothing higher than a six. Two Spades, the jack and the two.

"Unless Doc's loaded over there, we're screwed– Wait..."

"I'm going nil." I nodded.

"Guess that leaves me with four." Doc replied.

"A hail Mary, huh?" Marcus chuckled, appearing to be counting another victory. "Might as well."

"Think I'm about to bust your winning streak, Marcus." I smiled, hoping that I could pull it off.

"Oh-ho." Marcus put his elbow to the table top as he offered a toothy smile. "Confident enough to bet a week's worth of KP duty?"

I held my smile. While I wasn't keen on a week of "kitchen patrol", the chance to wipe the grin from Marcus' face was well worth the gamble.

"Bet." I nodded as I chanced a look at Frost.

Her smile vanished as her eyes darted to her rifle, having rested on me only moments before.

"Probably thinks I'm silly for taking that bet." I almost laughed.

"By your lead, Fenrir." Marcus gestured to the table.

"Here goes." I let the six of hearts fall, watching as Knight followed with the ten , then Doc with the queen. Marcus took the trick with the ace.

Point to MK.

"They'll dump their high values first, so they can try to get under me." I scanned over my cards, really only concerned about the two trumps. The two was my only buffer if spades were led. Only three cards on the table could beat the jack.

Marcus led the second hand, laying the eight of diamonds. I followed suit with the five, Knight laying the seven and Doc surprisingly taking the trick with the jack.

Point to DF.

Clubs made an appearance on the table as Doc led with the ace, Marcus dropping the queen, me the six, and Knight the two.

"Knight just dropped the two of clubs. Is she out of clubs already?"

I began to worry that spades may be broken, and the high spades ran out, before I had a chance to off load the jack.

Doc raised his eyes to me as he wordlessly slid the king of hearts onto the table before Marcus, I, and Knight respectively played the jack, five, and nine.

Point to DF.

"Think Doc's getting worried." Marcus poked as Doc dropped the ten of clubs, followed by Marcus' king.

"Nah." I smiled as I laid the five. "He knows we've got this in the bag."

"Oh, we'll get ya.'" Marcus smiled only briefly before Knight's Jack of clubs wiped it away.

"Not like that you won't." I laughed.

Point to MK.

Marcus' competitive side flared a bit as his hard eyes landed on Knight. "You just threw the two of clubs, *now* you're throwing the jack. You do know how to bust a nil, right?"

Knight rolled her eyes again. "Yes, I do. You had already taken–"

"Pardon me," Doc gently rapped the table, "but is this not the aforementioned table talk?"

Marcus fumed as he looked back to his cards. "My bad."

"Look a little worried, Marcus." I smiled.

"Not hardly." Marcus slapped the four of diamonds to the table.

"Well, biscuits." I sighed as I looked to Doc, slowly uncovering the three before I turned to Marcus. "Looks like you just can't quite get me."

"Little cocky, aren't you?" Marcus barely showed the hint of a smile, like he was enjoying the witty banter. "And biscuits?"

"Will you two play nice?" Knight asked as she lowered the ace of diamonds.

"Nonsense." Doc cast away the six. "This is infinitely more entertaining than beating Marcus at his favored game, and truth be told a reprieve from cursing is rather enjoyable."

Point to MK.

"I'm about to knock the sloppy haircuts off the both of you." Marcus' pointed finger bounced between Doc and I.

"Hey!" Knight threw away the seven of clubs, looking from Doc to Marcus. "I work hard on Doc's hair, and Fenrir's– Looks really good actually. Who–"

"Why thank you, Knight." Frost chimed in with a smile. Whether that smile was a result of the compliment or because it further deepened the hole I had just been kicked into remained to be seen.

"*You* cut his hair?!" Knight wheeled around in her chair while Doc lowered the eight of clubs.

"Where was I?" Knight asked.

"On the couch. Fenrir even knew you cut Doc's hair." Marcus answered as he dropped the king of spades, cutting off my chuckles.

"Uh-oh." Marcus sang with raised brows. "Someone's got a little higher trump than they should've gone nil with."

"Only two left that can beat the jack." I set down the four of clubs. *"Please have one of them, Doc."*

Point to MK.

"Gonna' have to cook up some four course meals next week." Marcus laid the king of diamonds.

"You like doing dishes?" I regained myself as I laid down the two.

"He's still trying to make their bid. He's going for both."

"Shit's gettin' deep." Knight lowered the queen.

"Say it is not so." Doc threw down the nine.

Point to MK.

"Let's see what you've got, Fenrir." Marcus casually tossed the eight of spades onto the table.

"Here goes the cushion." I laid down the two with a smile. "Close."

"Whoever loses," Knight dropped the Ace of spades on the table, "is gonna' hear about it for a while with all the smack going on."

I nearly shook my head. *"One left out there."*

Doc frowned as he pushed the five of spades across the table.

Point to MK.

"Wanna wrap this up, Knight?" Marcus grinned.

"If only for you to stop antagonizing." Knight gently deposited the three of clubs as she turned to me. "Now, back to the haircuts. You walked right past me, huh?"

"That's not exactly how it played out." I managed a chuckle while Doc spun the nine of clubs. "You were reading, and I didn't want to bother you."

"Don't let him lie to you, Knight." Marcus jeered as he slapped down the four of spades. "He took one look at Doc's hair and said 'Oh, no way!'"

"Fenrir," Doc calmly lowered his cards as I parted with the four of hearts, "if not for the good of the universe, then for us. Do not let this man win."

Point to MK.

"Think we've got this one in the bag, Doc." I hoped.

"Gonna' take more than rabble rousing to dethrone the king." Marcus smiled as he dropped the eight of hearts.

"Think I've got more than a fair chance with you playing like that." I mic dropped the three of hearts.

"Doc, please have the queen!"

"I'm sensing a bit of a competitive side in you, Fenrir." Knight smiled as the seven of spades rolled from her fingertips.

"It does appear that the relaxing games are only for you and I to share, Knight." Doc smiled as he released the six of spades.

Point to MK.

"Yeah it looks that– hang on." Knight looked to Marcus, holding a single card, while the rest of us held two. "Why do you only have one card, Marcus?"

Terror took Marcus' eyes as he thumbed at the card, suddenly becoming two in his hand. His eyes widened, and I could see his heart sink.

"No." Marcus cooed as he looked torn between laughing and crying.

"Whatcha got there, Lieutenant?" I smiled, having a feeling I knew what the surprise card was.

Knight gingerly laid the ten of diamonds, while Doc laid the nine of spades.

"Make it or break it, Lieutenant," I smiled, "and I don't think you're gonna' break it."

"Oh, shut up." Marcus quickly rattled as he tossed the queen of spades in disgust.

"And you still couldn't catch me!" I ribbed as I slammed down the one eyed jack.

Point MK.

"At least you won't get your bid." Marcus growled.

"About that." Doc winced as he laid down the ten of spades, unable to hold himself despite the fact that it wasn't his turn.

"Son of a–" Marcus yelled as he hurled the seven of hearts in disgust. "Save us, Knight!"

"I can't." She giggled as he let the queen of hearts fall.

"And with this," I slowly slid the two of hearts across the table, "the crown falls."

Point DF.

"Well at least you got your nine." Doc smiled. "What uh, what does your math make of that, scorekeeper?"

Knight's mouth smacked as she looked to the paper. "Marcus and I have 1010. You and Fenrir have 1100. Can't believe you've done this, Marcus."

"She was stuck to the seven!" Marcus attempted to defend himself as Doc and I laughed.

"What was that you said about four course meals?" I looked to Marcus.

He didn't reply as he sheepishly moaned.

Doc suddenly stood, spinning to look over the entirety of the room.

"The king is dead." Doc proclaimed before bowing at the waist. "Long live the king."

The entire room, Marcus included, burst into laughter at Doc's odd humor.

As my eyes drifted to Frost, I found that she too laughed, though as our eyes met, her laughter subsided. Her smile remained though, as her eyes held mine for only a moment longer before they dipped away.

14

Medic

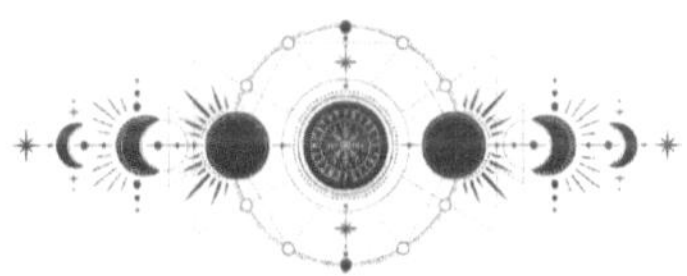

"She's bleeding out!" Doc screamed in my ear as I nearly shot from bed to ceiling.

Knight lay on the floor next to my bed, a dark stain on her right leg, femoral artery, losing blood quickly judging by the crimson puddle on the floor.

"The wolf can save her, but only if you give it time to heal her!" Doc bellowed.

"What the hell!" My brain fumbled. *"How did she– Did she intentionally hurt herself?!"*

"Fenrir!" Doc yelled.

The classwork of the past six days with Doc screamed into my head as I quickly snatched my pack, sitting on the floor by the post of my bed. Wrenching it open, I was still shaking sleep from my head as I reached through the zipper. Fishing inside the bag I found the tourniquet where it should have been, rolled tight at the top right corner. As I wrapped Knight's leg eight inches above where the wound should've been, I found there was no injury.

"What... What is this?"

It suddenly hit me.

This was a test.

"I'm hit!" I heard Marcus yell from the main room.

I was suddenly grateful that I had fallen asleep in my jeans the night before, otherwise I'd be providing first aid in boxers.

"It's silver!" Doc barked as he followed me down into the dining room.

I dropped my pack again, reaching for the Anver canisters in the bottom left pouch of the pack, and I was surprised to find a spent shotgun shell. On the side in sloppy marker, "Anver" was scrawled.

I nodded as I pushed the shell against Marcus's thigh, so the body could pick it up and quickly move it.

"Medic!" I heard Frost cry outside.

Hurrying to the door, I located Frost in the grass nearby and rushed to her, falling to my knees as I neared her.

"The muscle's pushed the broken bone out of her arm! Fix it!" Doc bellowed.

"Right, traction." My mind worked.

This was something I wasn't prepared for. Wounds like this, though I knew how to treat them, were primarily to be handled by Doc. His pack was the only one designated to hold a traction rig.

As I looked up to Doc for the first time, standing a mere foot away, I found that he was wearing his pack.

For whatever reason, instead of moving around him to get the bar, or asking him to turn around, I reached up and grabbed him by the collar.

He didn't seem to expect this, as when I pulled him towards me, he fell like a sack of bricks, landing belly to the dirt with a grunt of indignation.

With the pack now conveniently in reach, I removed the traction rig from the side of Doc's pack and set about applying it to Frost's arm.

I gave the bar a few ticks, enough to put pressure on Frost's arm, simulating use. I followed up by removing a bandage wrap from my pack and wrapping it where I assumed the wound would have been.

Once satisfactorily done Doc looked up to me. "Well done, Fenrir. You just saved most of the squad."

I sat back next to Frost, catching my breath as I looked to Doc. "Sorry about that Doc, words just weren't working at the moment."

Doc chuckled as he righted himself. "Do not apologize for saving a teammate. Though I must admit I have not yet seen that tactic deployed."

"I thought it was funny." Frost laughed as she sat up and began removing traction from herself.

"Oh yes, very humorous." Doc scoffed as he brushed himself off. "Obviously you have passed, Fenrir."

I matched his smile, knowing I was one step closer to becoming what they needed.

I was still reeling from my rough awakening and as I looked at Doc, I realized it was the first time I'd ever heard him raise his voice.

In all of the class work he had been calm, cool. In testing I found he flipped to the other end of the spectrum.

"That concludes your medical training." Doc said as the rest of the team joined us.

"Now it's my turn." Knight smiled. "Tomorrow that is."

"Off for the rest of the day?" I asked.

"I think you earned that much." Marcus chuckled. "Since Doc just scared the hell out of you."

"Think I got him back for that." I chuckled as I glanced up to him.

"Indeed." Doc smiled.

15

Grocery Run

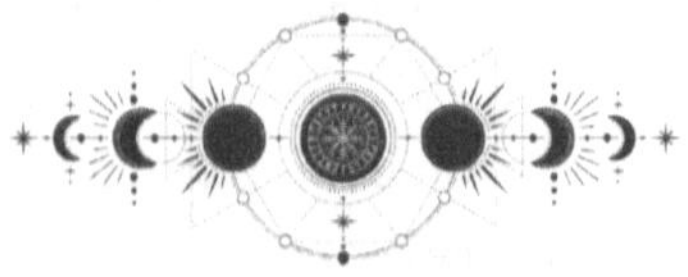

10/02
0730 Hrs.

I opened my eyes, capitalizing on a Saturday off by getting a bit more shuteye.

"One week down. Three to go." I smiled as I sat up. *"If the rest are anything like this, I'm golden."*

I yawned as I pulled on my clothes, fully expecting to enjoy the day off.

Opening my door, I heard the low thump of bass from Frost's closed door, followed by a set of electric strings.

"Huh." I smiled, surprised more than anything. *"Hadn't figured her for a metal fan, though it does seem to be her preferred element."*

I recognized the song as I started towards the stairs, unable to help timing my steps to the beat.

"At least she's got good taste." I chuckled to myself, looking forward to wasting my day throwing a fishing line in the lake.

Making my way down stairs however, the hope of a lazy day was quickly banished.

"Fenrir." Marcus smiled up from his book, Of Mice and Men, at the kitchen table. "Good job on the test today."

His congratulations caught me off guard, as unexpected as it was welcomed.

"Thanks, Marc–"

"As celebration, I'm giving you your first mission. You and Frost, as the late risers, won the award of going grocery shopping."

At the mention of late risers, I took a moment to look around the main room, finding only Marcus and myself.

As trivial a thing as grocery shopping was, I didn't want to bother Frost. Not if she was doing something she actually enjoyed doing, and certainly not after the last time I had knocked at her door.

"Could I go with Knight or Doc?" I asked.

"Doc's running his laps around the lake," Marcus looked back to his book, absentmindedly pointing through the back wall before thumbing over his shoulder, "and Knight is making preparations for your training with her. So you and Frost are shopping."

"Copy that." I replied.

"Good." Marcus nodded. "List is on the fridge. Get Frost and get gone."

"Alright." I frowned as I stepped to the refrigerator, plucking the decently sized list from beneath a magnet.

"Sure Frost is gonna' love this." I started up the stairs as I crammed the list in my pocket. *"Twice now sent on a collection run with the rookie."*

The music, now Skillet, still boomed from her room, and with my knock the band fell silent, the ensuing quiet nearly deafening.

"Yeah?" Frost called through the door.

"Hey," I shook my head, almost embarrassed for bothering her again, "Marcus wants you and I to go and get groceries."

Her door opened, finding her in more relaxed attire than I'd generally seen.

A black spaghetti strap tank top, coupled with form fitting shorts, put my pulse on high as I made a very conscious effort to look only at her eyes.

"Are you serious?" She tilted her head, sending a cluster of brown bangs across her face.

"Afraid so." I nodded.

With a sigh she looked back into her room. "Fine, give me a sec' and I'll be down. He give you a list?"

"Yeah." I looked down the hall, fighting my eyes.

"That will be your responsibility then." She noted. "You'll get the reaming if you lose it."

In reaction I put a hand to the pocket of my jeans, feeling the crinkle beneath the denim.

* * *

"You do realize that we'll have to go to Davenport, right?" Frost looked to Marcus as she joined us downstairs after changing into a black hoodie and jeans. "Can't really drag Fenrir around Kirkwood."

"Or you could go to Oakstone." Marcus nodded, still perusing the pages of Lennie and George. "That's why the list is longer, their supercenter is a little larger than Kirkwood's."

"So long as you know." Frost replied as she took the van keys from a hook on the wall. "Let's go, Co-Pilot."

As I followed her out into the morning I couldn't help but look forward to the day.

No, I didn't really want to bother her earlier, but since Marcus demanded it, I was pretty well clear of fault. If she was mad at anyone, it'd be him.

More than that though, I wasn't opposed to spending time with her, and the half hour drive to Oakstone, forty-five to Davenport, didn't seem long enough.

She was probably the one member of the team I knew the least about, though she certainly knew the most about me. Our mission to retrieve the Challenger made sure of that.

"Maybe this will help that. Maybe she'll open up a little bit." I optimistically smiled as I watched her step into the cab of the black van.

My smile remained as I climbed into the maroon passenger seat, its pristine state matching the rest of the old square body van's interior.

It was clear that this van meant a good deal to Cookie. It was near mint, delicately maintained and fresh. No doubt with the aid of the various cleaning supplies in a red milk crate behind Frost's seat.

"You like grocery shopping?" Frost cast an annoyed glance my way before looking to the windshield, sliding the key into the ignition.

"Not particularly." I chuckled. "Just a nice day."

"It *was* a nice day," Frost shook her head, "until you knocked on my door again."

"Dang." I looked out my window, unsure how to follow her short reply, or if I should even make an attempt.

Suddenly the prospect of a lengthy drive no longer appealed to me.

Frost sighed as she rolled the key, only for the van to emit a sharp click.

Frost shook her head. "Of course the battery would be dead."

I nearly smiled. At least I could state the good news of not having to go shopping, meaning she could get back to her music and whatever she would rather be doing.

"Guess no shopping then." I managed to keep my face straight.

"Also no leaving at all in the event we need to." She frowned at me.

"Guess I screwed up there too." I frowned as I weakly waved towards the front of the vehicle. "Pop the top."

I stepped from the van as the hood released, and I quickly propped it on its stand. It didn't take long to locate the battery, finding the sticker saying that it was only a few months old.

"Are you a mechanic now?" Frost grumbled as she stepped from the cab.

"Not leaking or swelled." I looked over the battery, testing the cables. *"They're tight, and they're not corroded. Probably not the battery."*

"Do you know what you're doing?" Frost asked bluntly.

"Got a hammer?" I asked.

"A hammer?" Frost repeated skeptically.

"Yeah." I nodded. "You know, claw on one side, flat spot on the other, you hit things with it?"

Seemingly amused with my smartass wordcraft, Frost smiled with a single raised brow. "Yeah, I've got a hammer, Fenrir, want me to tell you where to put it?"

"Think I already know that answer." I chuckled. "Where is it? The hammer, obviously."

"Back of the van." Frost's eyes smiled for just a moment before she nodded towards the back. "Cookie keeps a small tool bag in there."

"What exactly are you planning on doing with the hammer, Fenrir." Frost asked as we stepped to the back of the van.

"Well," I opened the door, finding the hammer, "I figured I'd hit something with it."

Again she smiled, this time letting out the faintest giggle as she closed the door. "Alright, smart aleck."

"At least I made you smile." I twirled the hammer as I stepped to the passenger side of the van.

She was quiet as I slid under the vehicle, and as I located the starter, I hoped I hadn't upset her. Standing near my legs, she was in a prime position for retaliation.

"So, I feel like I should tell you," Frost's voice echoed a warning, "that if you hurt Cookie's van, he's gonna' hurt you."

"I'm not gonna' hurt his van." I smiled as I tapped the hammer to the starter. "Mind hitting the key?"

She didn't reply as her boots crunched on the gravel, ending as she stepped up into the cab.

The motor whirred to life above my head, and I couldn't help but smile as I pulled myself out from under the van.

"Starter's going out." I moved to Frost's window.

"Why wouldn't it be?" Frost frowned as she nodded. "Can you fix it?"

"No," I answered, "but if we get a new one, I can replace it."

"Better let Marcus know." Frost replied. "I forgot to get the credit card from him anyway."

"M'Kay." I held the handle of the hammer out to Frost.

She took it without a word, spinning round and dropping it out of view as I started towards the house.

"Hey, Marcus?" I poked my head in.

"You're still here?" He didn't turn away from the book.

"Starter's bad on the van." I answered. "Needs replaced. Frost said to tell you, and to also get the credit card."

"I see." Marcus closed his book, digging a wallet from his back pocket. "Which also reminds me."

He produced a credit card, named for one "James Bleakley" and then held out a few bills.

As I took them, I found that they were hundred dollar bills, five of them. "What's this for?"

"The card is for your groceries and the starter," Marcus flopped his wallet on the table before returning to his book, "and the money is an advance on your pay."

"We get paid?"

"Did you think you were working for charity?" Marcus calmly asked.

"I just didn't think– Why am I getting an advance?"

"Phoenix seems to believe that you'll do just fine with the training and become a Red Moon and so authorized half a paycheck to go to you now."

"That was nice of him." I tucked the bills into my pocket.

"It was." Marcus sounded like he was starting to get annoyed. "Now please go, I'm really trying to read this book, and I fear that any further interference will result in a good pelting *with* said book."

"Copy that." I ducked from the door.

* * *

"Ready?" I smiled as I looked over to Frost from the passenger seat.

"I suppose." She pulled the van into gear, getting us underway.

The expression in her eyes made clear that she was still less than enthused to go shopping, though it seemed like she was in slightly better spirits.

"Let's see if I can help that along." I reached for the radio dial. *"92.7 I think?"*

Bumping up the volume, the heavier rock tones of Metallica thumped through the speakers.

"Unforgiven." I smiled as I tried to find a happy volume for the van's aged speakers. *"Hard to beat that."*

A semblance of a smile took Frost's eyes as she glanced at me.

"Are you doing this hoping to improve my mood?" She smiled as her eyes returned to the road.

"Is it working?" I offered a crooked grin, finding I had flawlessly set the volume, still able to hold conversation.

"A bit." Her smile held as she looked to the driver's side mirror, tracking our departure from the farm. "So, where'd you learn mechanics?"

"The farm." I answered. "My farm that is. Dad and I took care of all the vehicles and equipment."

"That said," I chuckled, "I'm far from a mechanic. Just learned the simple stuff."

"Like how to swing a hammer?" Her voice bobbed, as if holding in amusement.

"Come on, you can do better than that." I set my mind to make her laugh, to keep her smiling at least.

"Oh for sure." I nodded. "Learned a good wrench'll do the trick too."

Her full lips slightly parted as a giggle echoed in the cab.

"I'll take that I guess." I smiled, happy that I seemed to be doing something to make it less of an inconvenience, though I still felt bad about it.

"Sorry for pulling you away from your day off." My smile lessened as I looked to the window.

Without words, simply in a soft sigh, I heard a bit of regret.

"It's not your fault, Fenrir, I'm well aware of that." Her voice smoothed. "Sorry that I was a little salty about it. For the record, it was because we had to go shopping in the first place, not because it was with you."

I caught myself, fighting to keep from jerking around to face her.

"She's just clarifying." I inwardly laughed at myself. *"So there's no hurt feelings."*

"Thanks." I smiled over to her. "So, what do we call each other out here?

I mean, it'd be kind of odd to throw call signs around."

"Just call me as you normally do." She answered. "The call signs are already in place to protect our identities, and it's not unusual for people to have nicknames."

"So," I tried to wrap my brain around that concept, "if the call signs are used to protect our identity, why don't we just use them in the field and call each other by name?"

She frowned, only slightly. "If all we know each other by is a call sign, then it's a lot harder to give up information if we're captured."

I recoiled a bit, surprised at my own ignorance. If we knew each other's actual names, we could, willingly or coerced, give each other up. Assumedly this was a measure to keep our families safe, to safeguard any weaknesses we had left in the world.

"I hadn't thought of it that way." I looked from the window at the passing farmland.

"Wouldn't expect you to." Frost bluntly replied with a shrug. "You're new, Fenrir, it's just one of the things you learn."

I nodded, grateful for her somewhat gently delivered response. Yet I was painfully aware of a violation of this statute.

"I told you my name, Frost." I looked down to my jeans. "Sorry about that, I guess."

"I know," she smiled over to me, putting a spark to my chest, "and I don't hold that against you, either."

Timidly, I matched her smile, knowing that being professional as she was, she had probably already scrubbed away that foul up.

She wasn't alone in trying to forget the aspects of that night, though I figured she would be much more successful than I was.

The radio opened up the first few ticks of a song, and Frost started to nod along to the beat.

Any weakness left my smile as I looked to the window, attempting to rid her of any self-consciousness.

"Let your hair down, Frost." My chest warmed, happy that she at least felt comfortable enough with me to enjoy her music.

"You must have earned at least that much."

As the words started, I heard Frost begin to join with a hushed voice.

She was doing really well considering she was singing under her breath.

I knew the song, though I hadn't heard it over the airwaves in quite some time.

It wasn't as heavy riffed as Skillet, though it shared the notion of second chances, at another shot in life, eloquently put by the vocalist's words.

"...came out of the darkness with a bullet in my hand, I've got one more shot at livin'."

The song suddenly changed as I heard it again, for what might as well have been the first time.

A message hung from the chords, and it was resonating within Frost.

It left me wondering.

"What's your story, Frost?"

I was contemplating asking, though I couldn't bring myself to speak as the heavier tones landed, and I could feel that this song meant something special to her.

I smiled, happy to leave well enough alone as I looked over rolling fields.

My farm crept back into mind, the mention of dad and spent evenings covered in oil leading me to question if they were okay.

The music gently fell away, not quite at the end of the song.

I turned back, finding Frost's hand on the volume.

"What's up?" I asked.

She offered a glimmer of a pretty smile, a sense of knowing in her eyes. "Was about to ask you that."

"Nothing." I shook my head, plastering on a smile.

"Don't give me that, Fenrir." She looked back to the window. "Talk to me."

"I was just thinking, Frost." A true smile took my lips. "No reason not to enjoy the music."

"Well, what about your kind of music?" She gestured to the dials.

"All you'd have to do is turn it back up." I looked over to her. "You've got pretty good taste in music."

"Appears you do too." Her eyes smiled. "Seriously though, if you need to talk–"

I shook my head. "Really just trying to focus on my training."

"It's a decent trip to town, Fenrir." She glanced over. "If you've got questions, lay 'em on me. I'll answer to the best of my ability."

"Well," I tilted my head, "with Doc, I learned what to do for us, like if we're hit by silver. Obviously silver is something of a kryptonite for us, but is that all? Are there other 'special' things out there?"

"Not to my knowledge." She answered. "That said, silver is just one of the ways we could go. A lot of what would kill a human will still kill us."

"What about vampires?" I asked as my mind raced to the opposite end of the spectrum. "Like a wooden stake to the heart, sunlight, garlic, silver?"

The smile returned to Frost's lips as she giggled.

"Oh, yeah," humor rang in her voice, "those are right up there with the crucibles and magic wands."

I couldn't help but laugh along. "Well how should I know?"

"I know." She chuckled. "The stake to the heart thing, yeah it'll work, but it's not so much to do with the wooden stake and more about something stuck in their heart."

"Okay, that's fair." I smiled. "The rest are no good?"

"A big enough crucible could make a good bludgeon," she replied lightheartedly, "and I suppose you could choke one to death with a clove of garlic."

"Alright, alright." I laughed. "How about sunlight?"

"That'll kill 'em." She nodded. "Cooks 'em from the inside out. Ashes and all."

"That's pretty wild." I shook my head.

"Well they are night creatures for a reason, Fenrir." She replied.

"Will any sunlight do?" I asked.

"*Direct* sunlight." She emphasized. "Only if the light touches their skin. Covered up, they're free to move just like us, and to kill them, they've got to have either a large amount of skin showing or something vulnerable, like their head or chest. Even with that, it still takes a hot minute for the light to do its work. If just a little bit of skin gets hit, it'll hurt sure, but it's not a death sentence."

"Mm." I nodded, absorbing the information before a wry smile took my face. "They sleep in coffins, right?"

"Good Lord." She pressed her hand to her forehead with a laugh. "Are you serious?"

"No!" I chuckled. "I figured they just slept upside down."

"Well that's accurate." Frost said matter-of-factly.

"What? Really?"

"No!" She laughed, a smile beaming across her face, putting dimples to her reddening cheeks.

The breath nearly left me as I witnessed the beauty she tried to keep tucked away.

"For real though," she regained herself, though I was grateful that the dimples remained, "if we ever tackle a cauldron, you'll find they sleep in beds just like everyone else."

"A cauldron?" I asked.

"Three or more vamps." She answered. "Also a term for a group of bats."

"Did not know that." I looked to her. "Though that seems to be a recurring theme this morning."

"That's why I told you to ask, Fenrir." She smiled. "Anymore?"

"Only about a million." I smiled.

"More than that if I can put a spin on them that makes you smile."

"Sounds about right." She nodded. "Go ahead."

I felt my cheeks warm as I got the feeling that she was enjoying this. Why I wasn't sure, but I sure wasn't going to stop and ask.

"What's old for a wolf?" I asked. "Doc said something about old age."

I intentionally left out the bit about wolves not typically perishing from advanced years.

"That's a valid question." She nodded. "We age, just extremely slowly thanks to the regen abilities of the wolf. If you see a wolf that looks like he's ninety, he's probably several hundred years old. Vampires are another matter altogether. Best we can tell is that they're immune to disease and the effects of old age. Never seen one who looks over forty, and that was a fit and fighting forty mind you. Fortunately, they're not entirely invulnerable."

I nodded, thinking that Phoenix was the oldest looking wolf I'd met, and he didn't appear over his mid forties.

"Have you ever seen wolves that look that old?" I asked.

"A few." She nodded again. "Not out in the field obviously. They live out retirement in the Council towns, doing what old folks do. Watering gardens, reading the mail, watching TV. There aren't many of them though. Wolves aren't normally given the opportunity to die of old age. If they've lived that long, they either weren't fighters, or they were some of the best fighters. It's a goal to die of old age."

I smiled, ignoring the unmistakable gravity of the statement. "Any of those towns around here?"

"One, about two and half hours northeast." She replied. "Marcatia, I think the name is? Anyhow, we've gone up there a few times on R&R. They've got stuff to do as far as unwinding goes. A mall, restaurants, theater, a couple libraries and outdoor stores. It's a nice little spot. Little as in twenty-thousand people."

My eyes widened. "That's not little."

"Not big either." She smiled. "The big ones are set up in the suburbs of major cities. Pop's are pushing fifty to sixty-thousand."

"How many wolves are there?!" I raised my brows.

"There's a handful of us." She chuckled. "You realize that there are eight billion people in the world right?"

"Yeah, but with numbers like that, wolf populations would be–"

"In the millions?" She smiled. "Yeah, just like vampires."

I leaned back in my seat, earning another laugh from Frost's lips.

"And people have no idea what's out there?" I whispered, more to myself than Frost.

"Oh, I'm sure some do." She answered. "Survivors or witnesses, but I'd wager they fall into the same category as those that believe birds are extinct and all birds are now government drones."

"You're saying they're not?" I rattled, quickly regaining my composure.

"Every *single* bird?!" She shot back with a giggle.

We both broke into laughter as I looked upon her anew, finding that I sat next to a woman that I had never encountered before. An intriguing woman who absolutely captivated me.

I was loving every second of it, and it seemed I wasn't alone in that.

That or she was simply thoroughly amused with my misconceptions.

In either case, I was happy to be given the chance to see her like this.

Hitting city limits, a more serious question took my mind.

"Moving away from feathered drones." I chuckled. "Is there some kind of protocol for working this close to humans?"

"Not really." Frost replied. "I mean, don't wolf out, but other than that no."

"Okay." I nodded. "Just didn't know if there was a set scenario or something like that."

"Mm." She smiled before shooting me a side eye, her voice taking a joking edge. "Like a role play kind of thing?"

"Sure." I nodded. "You know, like if I was supposed to–"

The suggestion of her voice struck me as my face warmed.

"Not quite what I was implying." I knew I was red, but I dared to fire back. "That does raise the question of if *you're* into that kind of thing, though."

She mischievously smiled, the lifted corners of her mouth quickening my heart.

"Perhaps." Her eyes teased, a subtle spark in her sapphire eyes arcing to me. "You?"

"If you are, by all means."

"Perhaps." I shrugged with a smile, my face and body burning despite the fact that my virginity was very much intact.

It was with relative ease though that Frost led my mind to places far from purity.

I found myself wondering if she really was into things like that, what her kinks might be. I distinctly recalled when I had glanced into her room.

I started to laugh, unable to contain myself. "That took an unexpected turn."

"What?" She joined. "Did I make you uncomfortable?"

"No." I shook my head. "Just caught me off guard."

"Really?" She giggled as we pulled into a supermarket parking lot. "I mean I was just joking, but the way you answered, I would've assumed you'd had conversations like that before."

"In all honesty," I replied as she situated the van between two sedans, "no I haven't."

"Oh bullcrap." She smiled as she freed her seat belt. "That was way too easy for you not to have done it before."

"It was, wasn't it?" I had to agree.

"Guess it's just easy talking to you." I smiled, instantly regretting it when her smile lessened.

She didn't look angry, not upset at all actually, simply turning neutral.

"What's wrong?" I asked.

"Nothings wrong." She answered. "Just getting my game face on."

Just like that, it was clear that all fun and games had ended, as once more we found ourselves essentially on a mission.

"How can you do that?" I wondered, uncertain if I should be envious of her professionalism, or feel sorry that she felt the critical need to be this way.

"When was the last time you allowed yourself to really relax, Frost?"

"Can I see the list?" She asked.

I nodded, pulling the folded paper from my pocket.

"Alright." She tore the page down the middle. "This half is yours."

I looked to the paper, finding the edible portion of the list, leaving her with toiletries.

"We'll meet up at the registers." Frost said as she stepped from the van. "Try not to take too long, alright."

"My list is *twice* as long as yours." I laughed as I closed my door.

"Not at all by design." Frost chuckled, leading the way into the supermarket.

"Of course not." I smiled as we both picked our carts.

"Maybe she hasn't gone full Ice Queen?" I allowed myself to hope.

"See you in a bit." She pulled left, leaving me in front of a monstrosity of a food section.

"Yeah." I looked to the first item on my list. *"What in blue blazes is Ezekiel bread?"*

I raised a brow as I looked to the next item down the line.

"Bell peppers." I looked to the nearby produce racks. *"Yeah, let's start with that."*

* * *

A half hour later, every bit of it spent searching for items I was certain Doc had added, I finally made it to the registers.

Much to my surprise, there was no sign of Frost.

"There's no way she got lost looking for razors." I shook my head as I laid my forearms on the cart.

The aisles of the toiletries section all let out directly in front of me, albeit a fair distance off.

As I waited, watching for her to appear, I took a moment just to look at the people passing me by.

Occasionally they'd cast a glance my way, simply being aware. None of them knew what was only a few feet away.

"How can all of this be a secret?" I looked down into my cart. *"How can humanity not know about us?"*

"I was not!" The slightly raised voice of a man caught my ear as a younger couple approached.

Both were red in the face, though I suspected for different reasons.

"Cayden, don't lie." A short blond scolded her dark haired partner. "You were staring at her butt!"

"No I wasn't, Bre!" He shook his head. "I was looking at the shelf next to her."

"Alright, fine," she retorted as they passed me by, "what was on the shelf."

"Mascara." He replied matter of factly.

"Cayde, the mascara was right in front of us. *I* was looking at the mascara."

"Bre, I–" He fell silent as she broke away from him, leaving him standing a few feet behind me. "Damn."

"What're the odds?" I nearly chuckled as I started towards the toiletries, passing by the floral section at the front of the store.

I started looking down the makeup aisles as I passed them, eventually finding the mascara, and Frost on the other side, halfway down the aisle.

She didn't notice me, intently looking over the black palette of eyeshadow in her hands, filled with an assortment of glittering colors.

"Not once have I seen you wear eye shadow." I smiled, trying not to acknowledge that her jeans definitely fit well. *"You're too busy being a soldier to do anything more than the basics."*

Gold lettering flashed my way as she closed the palette before returning it to the shelf.

"Summer Shimmer."

I smiled as I pulled my cart away, refusing to disrupt her moment of normalcy.

Turning round, I found a spinning rack of sunglasses. I smiled as I stepped up to the rack, sure that this would suffice in making her think she hadn't been noticed.

I heard the wheels of a cart begin rolling, and I fixed my attention on a pair of red lensed glasses.

Her cart rolled next to mine, continuing until she was shoulder to shoulder with me.

"Thought we were gonna' meet at the checkout?" She asked politely.

"I know." I smiled. "I got done and didn't see you up there, so I figured I'd see if you needed help. Obviously I got distracted."

"Obviously." She replied, maintaining her neutrality.

"Come on." I begged, hoping to hear her laugh again, to see her smile, to witness the spark in her eyes. *"Show me the life in you, Frost."*

I put the glasses on, turning to face her.

"What d'you think?" I asked as the tag bobbled on my nose.

A glimmer of a smile showed through, a tease just enough to burn my chest.

"I think," she stared at me before looking to the rack, "you should put those back, and we should get going."

"Yeah, okay." I chuckled as I returned the glasses, content with the meager results of my games as I spun my cart around. "Let's go."

Side by side, we started towards the registers, and I hated the frown that crossed my lips as I felt her phase back into her mission state.

Abruptly my heart, having thundered only moments before, yearning to bring out what waited behind her shields, ached at her dual existence.

I wasn't so dense as to try and believe our lives as wolves were meant to be peaceful things. Less than twenty-four hours into what had become my new life I learned that I was to be a soldier.

But there had to be periods of peace, didn't there?

A time to recharge, to repair.

Watching Frost though, it was hard to believe that her times of peace were anything more than fleeting moments.

"What I know about you couldn't fill a thimble, Frost," I looked over to her, *"but I know there has to be more beneath what you show the world. And I want to see it."*

As we passed the flowers, I noticed Frost's eyes fasten onto a bouquet, a vibrant and stunning arrangement of black and blue petaled roses.

It stood apart from the other arrangements to the left and right, sunnier shades of orange and yellow standing against the overpoweringly beautiful dark tones.

I looked to the tag as I passed the flowers.

"Midnight Supremes."

A shriek rang out, the happy cry of a young child, and as I looked from the flowers, I found a mother, looking a few years older than myself, pushing a cart. A golden band held the left ring finger of her alabaster hand.

She looked tired, strands of auburn hair pulled from her otherwise neat ponytail.

The vocal child, a pudgy little fellow, sat in the basket jabbering away at his exhausted mother. Another youngster, a little girl, held her mother's free hand, toddling along, her red pigtails bouncing with every tiny step she took. In her hand was a dolly in a blue dress.

As her mother continued tugging her along, the doll fell from the child's grasp, barely touching the floor before Frost's hands left her cart.

"Mommy!" The child cried as her mother looked back, finding Frost scoop the doll from the floor, wiping away a speck or two of dirt.

"Here you go." Frost crouched, holding the toy out. "She's got a pretty dress."

The child didn't reply as she pulled the doll in for a hug, though the smile of the mother spoke volumes of thanks.

I couldn't help the smile as Frost stood, smiling herself as the family departed us. It wasn't to last though, my smile fading.

Just like the young couple, just like every other soul that passed by us, they had no idea what waited beyond the boundaries of their lights.

When it had first been said to me, that we fought for humanity, the concept hadn't been lost on me.

Seeing them here though, putting faces to the notion, toddling babies and exhausted mothers, it landed with undeniable weight.

"You ready?" Frost asked as she stepped back to her cart.

"Yeah." I nodded as I looked back, earning a smile from the blue eyed baby boy in the basket. "That was really sweet, Frost."

"Well what was I supposed to do?" She smiled as she pulled me along on an ethereal tether. "Just leave her doll on the floor?"

"I didn't mean that as a bad thing, Frost." I smiled. "It's nice to see that side of you."

"What's that supposed to mean?" She turned to me with a raised brow.

"Well," I raised my eyes, "the team does call you the 'Ice Queen'."

"What can I say?" She shrugged. "I'm not perfect."

"I beg to differ."

"I wouldn't say that." I replied. "That was a perfectly normal thing to do."

"As if anything about us is normal." She puffed under her breath.

"Part of us is." I smiled. "We're still human."

Her smile absolutely vanished, though she didn't offer a reason.

"Come on." Her hushed reply came. "We've still gotta' get that starter."

***

The starter secured, we started the drive back towards The Farm, and I could no longer ignore the fact that Frost's mood had rapidly deteriorated following my 'human' remark.

I hadn't meant it as a bad thing, I was trying to pay her a compliment without being overly obvious.

Looking over at her, I found her eyes devoid of any remaining current. *"What have I done?"*

"Frost," I quietly said, "you good?"

She sighed, remaining silent for a moment before she nodded.

"I'm alright, Finn." She replied.

"Did she shorten my call sign?" I curiously noted.

Pushing away the why, I took the opportunity to revisit her own words, only a little more sensitively.

"Please don't give me that, Frost." I leaned forward, looking to her eyes. "You were okay until I said something about being human. Did I upset you with that?"

"It's just..." She shook her head. "We're not, Finn."

"How's that?" I gently asked.

She frowned. "We're wolves, Fenrir. We aren't human anymore. Humans are too weak to do what we have to. They can't stop a vampire, or a rogue wolf, they couldn't do anything but die."

"Yeah we can do a lot, but I feel like what we do is in part because we are human." I looked at the windshield. "If we weren't, we'd be like the fairy tales that you hear about werewolves. Mindless killers. If we weren't part human, we wouldn't care what happened to them. We wouldn't care about anything, and I definitely care. About a lot of things. A lot of people. My family for instance, for the people I'm with now, about you. If it wasn't for the human part of us, I don't think any of that would matter. We'd just be dogs on a leash. Being human is what allows us to make the right choices, like you picking up that little girl's doll. If you were nothing but wolf, you wouldn't have cared."

"Are you saying that animals never do nice things?" She calmly asked.

"No," I shook my head, "they frequently do. A good dog typically cares about its owner, but that generally boils down to how the dog was raised and trained. Humans have the God given ability of freedom of choice, to choose between right and wrong, and we still have that, at least I do. And I feel like you do too."

"Sometimes it's hard to believe that God has anything to do with us." Frost nearly whispered. "We're just as much beasts of the night as vampires are."

"I think God has everything to do with us, Frost, just like all people." I smiled. "We are part animal, and if we don't control it we could cause a lot of damage, but in controlling it, we, The Red Moons, The Council, we use it to protect others. We made and keep on making the choice to defend people. How could God not see that?

"And I know that, technically yes, we are monsters, but so are some humans. We can't always control what happens to us," I managed a smile as I recounted my recent days, "but we still have the ability to take an absolutely crap hand that was dealt to us and make something good of it if we decide to. What happens to us doesn't define us, what we choose to do afterwards, I think that does."

She didn't offer a response as we started out into the country, and I feared that I may have absolutely destroyed the joy from the first part of the day.

"In all honesty, I was just trying to give you a compliment."

"I know, Finn." She shortly answered. "And thank you for that."

She remained silent after that, and as I watched the fields roll by, I felt myself torn apart.

I knew what she was saying. That being human wasn't without its weakness, while the wolf offered nothing but strength.

It seemed that she had come to cling to the wolf, and all the strength it provided, perhaps going so far as to try and cast her humanity aside.

If that was her aim though, I hated to break it to her that she had sorely missed her mark. I had witnessed her compassion, numerous times now.

With Knight, with the child, with myself, though she largely managed to maintain her icy wall most of the time.

I knew that I'd never be able to do that, finding myself trapped, living in what I was certain was a realm between wolf and human.

I knew the strength the wolf offered, but I also recognized the strength of humans.

In my heart, two worlds collided, and I felt that I belonged to both, unable to refuse either of their callings, not that I wanted to.

I was proud to be human, and was quickly growing to say the same of being a wolf.

I felt that acknowledging both, still holding the human side close, wasn't a downfall. Wasn't it possible to keep and utilize the best qualities of both? The wolf mustering strength and fortitude that humans never could, while being human kept the true nature of the wolf suppressed.

"You may not realize it, Frost." I glanced over. *"Or maybe you do, and are just trying to ignore it, but you're still very much human. And it's in those moments, where you let that side of you shine, when you lay down your shields, that I think I might really fall for you one day."*

* * *

1420 Hrs.

The ride back seemed infinitely longer than the ride out, conversation being scarce to say the least, and there was no denying that I had certainly upset the felicity of the outing.

Wordlessly, Frost and I had unloaded the groceries, delivering them to the kitchen, where Knight and Doc had assembled to tidy them away.

I frowned as Frost carried the last two sacks to the door, leaving me alone with the van and the impending starter change.

"Probably sentenced her to another evening of barricading herself in her room." I hammered at myself as I took a socket set from the back of the van.

As I put the socket to the first starter bolt I shook my head.

"Maybe I overstepped." I spun the ratchet. *"I did bring God into it. 'God's with me, so who could stand against me.' I hope that she didn't take it that way."*

"Damn." I swore. *"Forgot the solenoid cable. Get your head right, Rainer."*

Gravel crunched near my feet as I lowered the worn out starter. I braced, waiting for someone to ask me what I had done to put Frost in such a state.

"Most likely Knight." I sighed. *"She won't be happy with me at all."*

"How's it going down there, Finn?"

I was surprised to hear Frost's voice.

"Getting there." I smiled, happy she had taken the time to check on me.

"Need any help?" She asked, sending me a shock wave of whiplash seeing as the drive back had consisted of, well, nothing.

"Plenty of room for another set of hands." I quoted my dad.

No sooner had I said the words than she slid in next to me, pressing her shoulder to mine, effortlessly sending a rumble of thunder down my spine.

"What do you need me to do?" She asked, looking up at the void left by the old starter.

I reached over, straining to steady myself, taking the new starter in my hands. "I'll hold it in place, you start the bolts. See the holes?"

"Mhm." She hummed as she lifted the bolts, examining each of them. "Any particular order?"

"Nope." I shook my head as I put the new starter in place. "Just get 'em started and then you can tighten 'em down."

"Okay." She nodded, reaching up.

As she spun in the top bolt, her hand rested over mine, and with each brush of our skin, the charge in my veins grew stronger.

"What is she doing here?" I smiled, unwilling to believe she had come out here just to help me. *"Maybe she just wants to see how it's done?"*

"Thinking about picking up mechanic work?" I asked as she moved to the second bolt.

"Seems like it's good stuff to know." She replied. "And it seems like you know your way around a bit of it."

"Especially if it consists of hammer work." I smiled over to her.

She let out a quiet giggle, and I couldn't hold myself any longer.

"Frost." I reached up, taking her hand down from the final bolt.

A bit of alarm showed in her eyes as they flashed to me, and my throat clenched as, even in the shade, I saw flecks of bright blue scattered throughout her eyes.

Tiny shards of ice floating in cerulean oceans.

"We didn't talk much on the way back." My eyes held hers as they softened, watching as they slowly moved to my shoulders before venturing back up. "I'm sorry that I upset you. I was just saying what I felt. I wasn't trying to push anything on you or come off as an–"

"Finn," she let out the first breath of a chuckle, and in the mild darkness around us, I swore I saw her cheeks redden, "you didn't upset me, at all. You just… gave me food for thought. It's been a long time since anyone's done that. Even longer since I thought about being human, partly anyway."

"Well," I looked back up to the undercarriage, "I will try not to do that in the future."

"Fenrir," She drew my eyes back, locking them to her's, "that's not what I'm saying. Don't stop doing that. Keep being you."

Breathlessly I looked at her, every fiber of my body rattling with energy, yet at a total loss for what to do with it.

She smiled. "So you gonna' show me what to do next?"

"Right." I cleared my throat, picking up the ratchet. "Just snug them down first, then put the gas to 'em."

"Okay." She raised the tool, quickly snugging the bolts. "How tight does it need to be?"

"Well," I tilted my head, "I'm sure there are torque specs for this, but I don't have a clue what those might be, so we're just gonna' do it this way."

I reached up, placing my hand over hers on the handle, careful to put most of the pressure where my fingertips met the ratchet so I didn't hurt her hand.

"Pull." I nodded.

The socket slightly spun before I felt the bolt properly sink home.

"That's it." I nodded as I lowered my hand, vainly trying to ignore the electricity that danced across my palm. "Think you got it?"

She nodded as she hit the second.

"Will you check this one too?" She asked, keeping her hand on the ratchet.

"She has to know." I smirked. "Sure."

Hand in hand, we checked each bolt, and by the end of it I was certain that I was charged enough to jump-start the van myself.

"What about this one?" She flicked a dangling cable.

"That's the solenoid cable." I nodded, pointing to its home. "This one requires a bit less strength. The solenoid's partially ceramic, so it'll break if you go too hard."

"M'kay." She situated the cable and raised the ratchet after I changed the socket. "How tight is too tight?"

"Snug it down." I nodded.

A couple quick clicks had the cable secured in place.

"A little more." I smiled. "Don't be scared of it, just be careful."

"Want to give me a hand here, Finn?" She asked.

"So that if it breaks it's not just your fault?" I chuckled.

"Yes." She smiled.

"Alright." Once more I put my hand on hers, taking full hold, knowing that I wouldn't pull hard enough to hurt her.

The socket barely moved, seating the nut and ending the best starter change I'd ever done in my life.

"Well, that's it." I lowered my hands. "You just changed a starter."

"Not too bad." She nodded at her handiwork. "Thanks, Finn."

"You could've figured it out." I smiled. "Kinda' like the nickname I've recently acquired."

"It was actually an accident the first time it came out like that. Then I just kept saying it." She smiled, though it seemed a nervous kind of smile.

"If you don't want me to–"

"No." I smiled. "Caught me off guard again, but it's growin' on me pretty quick."

"Hard to say if it's because it's a little warmer than a call sign, or if it's because you gave it to me."

"Okay." She smiled as she shimmied from beneath the van. "Hope you're hungry by the way."

"Oh?" I followed her into the daylight.

"Yeah," she brandished another beautiful smile, "Doc's working on the first meal for Marcus' kitchen duty."

"Sounds good to me." I chuckled.

* * *

As my head hit the pillow, I still felt the charge rippling through me.

"This has to mean something." I smiled as I raised my hands, tensing the fingers that only hours before had taken Frost's. *"The fact that she asked me to. She knew what she was doing after the first time, she didn't need my hand to know she was doing it right."*

My hands fell to the bed as I smiled at the ceiling.

"Maybe she didn't need a helping hand." I finally allowed myself to hope. *"Maybe she just needed **my** hand."*

16

CQC Intro

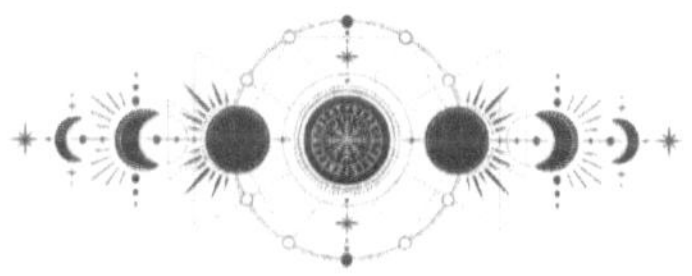

Week two started, leaving me with Knight on close quarters combat and infiltration tactics.

Despite having slept only a few hours, it seemed the energy imparted by Frost was still alive and well.

"Ready, Fenrir?" Knight smiled in the main room of the farmhouse.

"As ready as I can be." I said, further joyed that week two found me with Knight.

Her and I had hit it off pretty effortlessly, but with her sunny disposition, I didn't see how anyone couldn't.

"Good." She said. "We'll be starting with close quarters combat, then we'll move on to infiltration tactics."

I looked to the table behind her and saw a narrow black box, its lid firmly latched.

Knight followed my gaze and chuckled. "We'll get there, Fenrir."

"Sorry." I nodded. "Just eager I guess."

"Good." She smiled. "That means it matters to you whether you pass or fail."

With the mention of that particular outcome, I became aware of a question that I probably should've asked much sooner.

"What happens if you fail, Knight?"

"I don't know, Fenrir." She shrugged. "None of us do. The failures simply go away. As soon as Phoenix learns of it, they're picked up by another team and that's the last we see of them."

"I wonder if they end up in one of those wolf towns?" I thought back to my last conversation with Phoenix.

"It's a possibility," Knight said, "but there are a lot of other places in The Council they could go. Places other than a combat unit that are still military oriented, desk jobs and what not."

I nodded, trying to push from mind any thought that I could fail the training, despite the fact that it was a very real possibility.

Knight saw this and made an attempt to encourage me.

"Fenrir," she locked her eyes with mine, "you are not going to fail, alright? You are leaps and bounds ahead of the failed cadets already in the fact that you've seen combat and survived. Hell, you did more than survive, you made kills. You faced vamps when you had zero training and killed two of them, that's more than some who passed the training can say. And we all acknowledge that fact, we credit you for it. If you can kill vampires without knowing anything about combat, then you can pass this piddly training course of ours." Her beaming smile returned.

I couldn't help but smile. "Thank you, Knight."

"It's nothing." She said. "Alright, back to training."

That day I learned the knife every Alpha operator carried, a typical hunting knife.

A polished black handle with a silver pommel and hand guard, and a six-inch stainless blade. The cutting edge glistened below a generous fuller.

"Nothing fancy." Knight said. "No tanto blade, no powder coating, this knife has one job, to keep you alive when you're on top of your enemy and can't shift."

Moving on, she taught me a few methods for holding a knife. The "Ice Pick Grip" that was featured in nearly every movie in creation. I also learned that against an experienced adversary, this was a terrible choice of grip.

There was the "RGEO" hold, Reverse Grip Edge Out, where the blade protruded from the bottom of a closed fist, much like the ice pick grip, but the blade was flipped around. In this fashion the blade acted as an extension of a closed fist, and in a punch attack the blade followed the blow with a sideways slice.

Knight noted this was her preferred hold.

Knight then proceeded to cover the "Hammer Grip", which finds the blade forward of the fist, making it ideal for quick stabs and jabs.

She went on to say that there were a multitude of other ways to hold a knife, but these were the ones selected by the squad, though she didn't really elaborate on the reasoning.

Soon after, I learned that Knight was the only member of Alpha to utilize throwing knives, six-inch knives of solid steel.

"Ever tried your hand at throwing?" Knight asked.

"No." I shook my head. "The idea always seemed a little backwards to me. I mean, you have a knife, then you throw it, knife gone." I chuckled.

Knight nodded. "I understand, and that would make sense if we only had the one knife. We carry six throwers in addition to our standard. For all intents and purposes, you should never find yourself needing a blade."

"Why is it you're the only one to carry the throwing knives, Knight?" I asked.

"I'm the only one with the patience to become proficient with them." She said with a grin. "After training it's up to you whether or not you want them."

"Guess we'll just have to see how good I am with 'em."

"Let's get to it then." She turned her attention to the mysterious black box I had seen.

As she opened it, I found six more throwing knives matching her own, along with a black vest, adorned with various pouches, holsters, and sheaths.

"This is your combat vest." Knight removed the vest from the box. "It'll hold everything you need downrange, including your knives."

As I took the vest in my hands, I found six small sheaths, three on either side, on the portion of the vest that would cover my ribs, clear of the pouches and holsters on the front.

On the left shoulder was a larger sheath, undoubtedly for my hunting knife, positioned so that the handle would lay against my chest.

"The sheaths are situated so that they'll be out of the way, but easy enough to get to when you need them." Knight nodded. "Go ahead and put it on."

"We pull throwing knives from our sides?" I asked. "It doesn't take too much time?"

Knight shook her head. "Keep in mind that you probably won't be deploying these in an active engagement situation. Ideally the enemy wouldn't even know you were there. These lend themselves to stealthy infiltration operations."

"Hmm." I nodded as I donned the vest, taking only a few moments to tighten it where necessary. "Seems like a good enough fit. We ready to throw then?"

"Whenever you are."

* * *

I found that throwing knives were definitely not my cup of tea, not at the start anyway.

Knight attempted to teach me the "military half spin" which found the thrower holding the blade vertically, the cutting edge towards them.

"With this throw the blade should make a half rotation before reaching the target." Knight explained. "Maximum range is about twenty feet, twenty-five or thirty if you practice enough."

This specificity from her was unexpected. While she was normally carefree, now in her element, she was just as precise as the instruments she deployed.

"We'll start here." Knight stopped about six feet in front of our target, named Scarecrow.

He was an oddly constructed fellow. He had no legs, only a post holding up a burlap sack of straw with no arms and sporting a vastly oversized head.

"Just focus on the basics for now." She said. "Then we'll work on your speed."

"And the basics are?" I asked.

"The pointy end goes into the target." She smiled.

"Right, got it." I pulled my first throwing knife, my fingers pinching the base of the blade, near the hilt.

"Send it." Knight spoke from behind me.

So I did. The knife flew true, driving straight into Scarecrow's head. Except it was the wrong end of the knife. It would have been perfect had it not been the pommel making the blow.

I frowned as the knife fell to the ground.

"Know what you did wrong?" Knight asked.

"Other than just giving him a headache?" I asked with a chuckle.

"Pull another knife." She scoffed at the poor joke.

As I did she came round to my side.

"So you held it here." She put my hand where it had previously been. "This would be good for twenty feet or so, a slower rotation. At this distance, you'll want to choke down on the blade, around the tip. It puts a faster turn to the blade."

"Your form was good." Knight offered up a bit of praise. "Just need to work on the grip."

As I reached for the next knife, finding its handle, it occurred to me that deploying these knives may take longer than needed in order to catch an enemy by surprise.

"So," I asked as I spun the blade around, using both hands to avoid slicing myself open, "how exactly do you deploy these quickly when the blades are held in the sheath, and the blade needs to be in your hand to be thrown?"

"Seems like it takes a bit of time." I said before pulling back my arm and sending another blade at Scarecrow. A solid connection, the blade stuck in the right side of his chest.

"Good hit." Knight nodded as she passed me by on her way to Scarecrow. "Bad location."

"You want to hit either the heart, the neck, or the head." She said as she wrenched the blade from the straw man. "Good Lord! Good force on the throw though, had it buried to the hilt."

"To answer your question though," Knight returned, handing me the knife, "it's the same reason that I'm the only one to carry throwing knives."

She turned to face Scarecrow, allowing me to observe her technique from the side.

Her eyes focused, selecting her mark on the target. "Watch my hand."

Her fingertips played at the handle of a knife for only a moment before it was ripped from its socket. An elegant roll of her fingers followed, finding the blade in her hand and her index finger on the hilt of the knife, setting the choke. A lightning fast draw to her shoulder, her muscles tensing, priming up for the throw that sent the blade straight into Scarecrow's head, centered in one of the two black dots that represented eyes.

Whereas it took me several seconds to prepare for the throw, she had drawn and delivered in less than one.

"Yeah, you might still be the only one to use throwing knives." I lifted my slack jaw.

"Just give it an honest try, that's all we ask." Knight smiled to me.

"So the heart or head? I'm assuming the eyes to be precise?" I asked as I attempted her fanciful flip, scoring a healthy knick in my finger before the knife fell to the earth.

"Damn." I wiped the blood on my pants.

"That'll happen," Knight chuckled, "and yes, eyes, neck or heart. Though if you put enough force to it, you'll punch through the skull. We do this because it results in rapid or instantaneous death. The entire point of the knife is to be silent. If you score a bad hit, the element of surprise is lost anyway."

"Makes sense." I nodded as I retrieved my bloodied knife from the ground.

"I'm going to do this." I set my mind as I looked to the knife, taking a moment to observe the blade in my hand. *"It's nothing but metal. It goes where I tell it to, it has no free will. It makes no mistakes, the only shortcomings are mine. So let's fix that."*

Again I attempted the flip, this time avoiding a cut as I managed to miss the knife altogether.

"Biscuits." I growled.

"Why don't you just focus on the throwing?" Knight asked, though obviously amused.

"No." I shook my head. "If I'm gonna' carry them, I need to know how to do this."

"Fair enough." Knight smiled as I picked up the knife again.

The day was full of ups and downs. For every time that I successfully flipped the blade, I dropped it thrice. Once having a rudimentary grasp on the flip, the problems started on my wind up.

More than once I threw the blade back over my shoulder, much to Knight's humor.

*"Maybe I **should've** just focused on the throwing."* I shook my head.

"You're actually doing really well, Fenrir." Knight consoled. "If you need to, slow down and master the motions until you get to the throw. Then you can put your back into it."

"Copy that." I sighed.

Slowly, very slowly in fact, but surely, I got better with the techniques. Dropping the knife less and less while delivering more and more hits to the desired targets.

As I fell into habit, the rest of the day, and half of the next, grew easier and by midday of the second I was consistently drilling my targets at twenty feet. As I repeated the motions, I found the endeavor somewhat therapeutic, and also encouraging.

My hands seemed to find their rhythm as I threw, consistently scoring decent hits as my mind began to wander. It didn't travel far though, only as far as Frost might be, curious to what she was doing at the time.

"Probably cleaning a gun. Maybe jamming out or wishing she had bought that makeup. What else does she like to do? Boxing perhaps?"

I recalled that when I'd first met her, when she'd first commanded my attention. Shimmering beneath a light dose of sweat, her hands wrapped in boxing gloves.

"Seems the blades have taken to you nicely." Knight's brows rose as I called back my absent mind. "If you can keep your focus like that, you'll be a nail driver."

I chuckled, observing my last four throwers buried in the Scarecrow's right eye. "Thing is, I wasn't even focused on throwing."

"Well, whatever you were thinking about, keep thinking about it."

"No problem there." I nearly chuckled as one of Knight's past references came to mind. *"Ol' Ironsides."*

Much like her call sign, that particular moniker lent Frost an air of fortitude. Yet, while Frost had the ability to be cold, I was quickly growing to favor the idea that there was a much warmer side of her.

Frost seemed to be tender with Knight, like when she had hugged me, and then there was the shopping trip, and the events after. While the day had held its shares of downs, it contained what I could consider nothing else than a high note on a scale previously unknown.

"So why do you call Frost 'Ol' Ironsides'?" I suddenly asked.

"That explains it." Knight smiled.

"What?"

"Why your aim's so good." Knight wryly smiled. "Thinkin' about stickin' something somewhere else?"

"Ugh, Knight, come on." I shook my head as she giggled. "But if I was, it'd probably be somewhere mois–"

"Ah, ah." Knight raised her hand. "I started it, you won it, I surrender."

"Seriously though." I laughed. "Why do you call her that?"

"Cause she's just as tough as that name suggests, Fenrir. Though I guess it really didn't kick in until she shut Marcus down."

"Shut Marcus down?" I asked.

"Well," Knight tilted her head side to side, "I don't know, maybe a year ago, Marcus just kind of… noticed her, I guess. He took a slow approach, trying to find out what she liked and all that. Naturally he was nearly glued to Edge and me at the hip, digging for information. When he finally worked up the nerve to ask her, you know, asking if he could take her out to dinner, and how attractive he found her, she just said, pretty bluntly I might add, that 'The feeling is not mutual.'"

"Jeez." I chuckled, suddenly feeling sorry for the guy. "Just like that?"

"To the letter." Knight nodded.

"Dang." I cocked my head. "That's pretty rough. At least he tried I guess."

"Which is more than I can say for you right now." Knight replied. "You haven't asked me to tell you a single thing that she likes."

"Because I pay attention." I smiled as I sent another knife. "I may not know a ton of her favorite things, or any of them for a matter of fact. But I know some things that she likes."

"Well, whatever you do, don't make a big deal out of it." Knight advised. "While I've never seen her in a relationship, we've spent hours talking about it. She doesn't go for showy stuff. 'Grandstanding' she calls it. Frost doesn't care about what the rest of the world sees or knows about her relationship. It's about what she knows to present *in* the relationship. There's no attention seeker in Frost, none of this 'look at this diamond so and such bought for me' or 'he spent this much money on me'. That stuff actually upsets her pretty bad, because at that point they're seeking validation from someone that doesn't even matter. That's not to say that she doesn't want nice things, but they can be small, things that are special to her and her other.

"I've never seen her in love, Fenrir," Knight continued, "but I've got the feeling that when she does, she loves hard. Think you could handle that?"

I suppressed a laugh. "I'm not so brazen as to say that she's gonna' fall in love with me, Knight. I'm a greenhorn after all, and she is my superior. Now I'm finding out that Marcus missed his shot, and he's not what I'd call an ugly guy. Doesn't exactly boost my confidence."

"So what're you gonna' do?" Knight asked. "We've already established that you find her attractive. Are you just gonna' sit on it?"

"I'd call her more than simply attractive." I smiled, thinking on the latter portion of Knight's inquiry. "I don't know what I'm going to do, Knight. I don't want to 'sit on it' but I don't really know how to make that next step. From friends to couple… There's a line drawn there for a reason, sometimes pursuing the second ruins the first."

"You miss one hundred percent of the shots you don't take." Knight smiled. "Just, take it slow. You said you know some of the things she likes. Wouldn't be a terrible place to start."

"Yeah but, all those things are just things that she appears to like. I want to know something that she would love. Something…" I struggled for words. "Something that might mean next to nothing to everyone else, and might not even be that expensive or flashy, but would mean the world to her."

Knight paused, looking over me for a quiet moment.

"What?" I smiled.

"Just thinking." Knight shook her head before smiling up to me. "I think I know."

"That was fast." I chuckled. "What is it?"

"A snowflake." Knight replied.

"A what?" My smile flattened.

"Everytime I go to Oakstone with her, she always makes a point to stop by the jewelry counter and look at this one little silver necklace with a snowflake on it. It's got a diamond center, and little blue crystals at the tips of the arms. I don't even like snowflakes, and I think it's pretty cute."

I frowned. "If it's silver–"

"It's stainless steel." Knight smiled. "Same as this."

From beneath her shirt, Knight drew a silver chain, a small like colored cross hanging from it.

"I see." I nodded. "Do you really think she'd like it that much?"

"I do, Fenrir." Knight grinned. "I'm fairly certain that her love of snow was also a contributing factor when she chose her call sign."

"Alright then." I smiled as I sent a blade into Scarecrow's heart. "Thank you, Knight."

"Her birthdays in January by the way. The twenty-seventh."

"Didn't really wanna' wait that long." I chuckled.

"Christmas is just around the corner." Knight offered a suggestion.

"Still three months." I smiled.

"It'll be here before you know it." Knight shook her head with a grin. "I want to see her open it. It's the least I deserve for all the help I've given."

"Fine." I smiled as I sighed, conceding to Knight's request. "I'll hold off on the necklace."

"Still oughta' buy it soon. They'll sell quick this time of year."

"That's a good idea." I nodded. "When's the next grocery run?"

"Probably after your next test."

"So three days-ish?"

"Round about." Knight nodded. "I'll go with you. It'd suck if you got the wrong one."

"Yes it would." I laughed for only a moment, before quieting down, grateful for the quality of company I found myself in. "Seriously, thank you, Knight."

"It's no problem." She smiled. "To be honest, I'm doing it for Frost just as much as I am for you."

"Not that." I smiled. "Just, thanks for being who you are. You're pretty special."

"Oh, well I already knew that." Knight chided, all thought of throwing knives gone as her mind went back to Frost and I. "I'm rooting for you guys, Fenrir."

"Really?" I asked.

It meant a lot that she did, more than I could put to words, but I couldn't help but feel a bit conflicted.

"What about her and Marcus?"

"Being a little vague there." Knight smiled. "Her and Marcus as in do I think they'd be a good couple, or are you asking if there would be hard feelings?"

"Both I guess." I shrugged.

"As a couple, no, I don't think they'd work. Marcus has a healthy ego that Frost would be only too happy to deflate when it needed done. Speaking of though, you probably scored yourself some brownie points with spades the other night." Knight laughed before continuing.

"As far as hard feelings go, I think you're clear of that. Marcus seems to believe that she'll never care for anyone as much as she does being a soldier or her guns, and she seems to be content with him believing that. I don't think he'd be mad at you either, in case you were worried. After it all played out, I think he realized that they're better off being teammates as opposed to an item. Two very domineering personalities."

"Are you saying I'm a pushover?" I put my hands on my sides as I turned to her.

"No, you're not a pushover." Knight giggled. "You're mellow. Most of the time anyway. I've seen you talk smack, but that's not who you are. You're not cocky, or arrogant, and that's why you and Frost would be so good.

"She's not cocky either, just confident," Knight tilted her head, "and a *little* headstrong from time to time. She's come to lean on that 'Ice Queen' label Marcus put to her, though it's mostly only to him. She's pretty easy going with Doc, and between Frost, Edge, and me, well it's like three sisters running around. You though, I think you've got a chance, Fenrir. Sometimes, not always, but sometimes, I see how she is around you, and it's almost like you walked right past her walls."

"What d'you mean?" I asked.

"I heard a little bit about your shopping trip." Knight smiled. "What you said. The talk about being human and all. I think she needed to hear it, and she definitely wasn't upset talking about it. Sometimes, I think she forgets. She needs someone who reminds her of that. That she still is human. You did. I think you're good for her."

A smile took my lips. "I appreciate your confidence, Knight, but I think that it's a little early to be using present tense regarding us."

"I don't think so. Even if you don't make it to being a couple, you're still gonna' be there to remind her. She'll remember every time she sees you." Knight put a quick elbow to my ribs. "So long as you stay as sweet as you are."

"Well what can I say," I looked at Scarecrow, now thoroughly a pin cushion, "you're rubbing off on me Knight, sweetness, knife skills, and all."

A little color reddened her cheeks as she smiled at me. "Always quick to pay a compliment."

She took in a breath, her gaze traveling to Scarecrow as her mindset seemed to settle back on the task at hand. "Doing pretty good, Fenrir."

"A good teacher helps." I smiled as my stomach growled.

"I agree." Knight laughed. "On both counts. Let's get some lunch."

17

CQC Proper

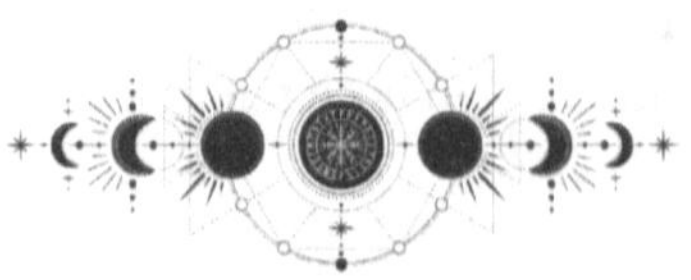

10/04
1205 Hrs.

"I think we're ready to move on to the next portion of our work." Knight said after a quick chow. "You've proven quite adequate with throwing knives."

I shook my head. "I don't know, Knight. I still throw oddballs now and then. I think that a bit more practice here would be a good idea."

"Consider it homework then." Knight smiled. "Keep practicing. Try to throw an hour a day for the rest of your training, and keep it up when we get back to The Citadel. You do that, and I'd bet money that you'd be driving nails at thirty feet. And mind you, I don't gamble."

Her praise, however sincere and appreciated, did little to silence the notion that I was just now starting to get a solid grasp on throwing knives. To set it down so soon seemed counter intuitive, but it didn't really seem like I had a choice. Rather than continue now, I had earned an after hours assignment.

"So what're we on to now?" I asked.

"The only thing left *to* do." Knight said. "We fight."

"Pardon?" I fixed her with a raised brow.

"Mhm." She nodded. "It's time that we move to hand to hand combat. Best way to learn how to use our knife is to put it to work."

"Surely you don't mean our actual knives?" Alarm rang in my voice.

"No, no," Knight said, "the margin for error is too narrow. We'll use these."

She produced two replicas of our hunting knives, though upon inspection I found them to be a sort of semi-rigid high density foam.

"This is one of the most important pieces of our kit, Fenrir. You have to learn how to use your knife and use it well." She said, lacking a smile, conveying the seriousness of her words.

"How do you judge that?" I asked.

"You have to be able to beat me." She replied.

* * *

We stood a short distance apart on the grass in front of the farmhouse, and as Knight rolled her shoulders she spoke.

"Don't expect to win the first few times, Fenrir, I won't go easy on you, none of our enemies will. With time you'll get better, it's just like throwing knives alright? Don't get discouraged."

"Okay." I said with no lack of uncertainty.

As I shook myself out, I was growing more appreciative of Knights demeanor. It seemed she was the *real* support role here. Sure, her squad role was infiltrator, but she looked to uplift other's spirits, refusing to let a single member get down on themselves.

"Ready?" She asked.

I nodded. "I'm ready."

She drew herself in, bringing her hands close to her face, holding the blade RGEO style while dancing on the balls of her feet.

I mimicked her and within three seconds, I was dead.

She swept up to me and drove the blade into my ribs. Mid charge she had changed her grip to the hammer hold.

"Huh." I took a step back.

She smiled. "That's what I lead with Fenrir, every time, because it teaches the most important lesson in close quarters: stay mobile."

"I see your point." I said as she returned to her previous position.

"See whatcha' did there." Knight chuckled.

I laughed. "Didn't really mean it that way."

"Alright, again." Knight drew up again.

This time I slowly approached, drew up as she was, both of us holding the knife in the punch fashion. I didn't hold it this way because she did, it simply felt right in my hand.

As I drew nearer, we began a sort of spiral dance, each waiting for the other to attack.

My eyes were fixed on her blade, waiting for her to move.

Once her patience had been exhausted, she rushed me, like I knew she would.

Suddenly my feet froze beneath me, without rhyme or reason, and I found her blade pressed to my throat.

"Do I need to explain the most important lesson again?" She giggled.

"No." I laughed."I've got it. Stay mobile."

We resumed our original stances, and once again began our spiral.

My feet obeyed me as we moved, inside to outside, one foot then the next. Everything was functioning as it should.

Then she moved, and again my feet froze.

She didn't even put the blade to me, simply stopped, and her hands fell.

"What's wrong, Fenrir? You're locking up when I move in on you."

"I don't know." I shook my head. "Everything is fine until the second you charge in. Then my feet just stop."

Her narrowed eyes and slow breath told me that she was processing the situation.

"Fenrir, I can't teach you to attack until you know how to defend. You haven't moved your arms once, to strike or attempt to block me."

"Use my arms, got it." I nodded.

"*And* your legs." Knight pointed to my feet. "Stay mobile."

I nodded as a knot of anxiety firmly rooted itself in my gut. "Got it."

I most certainly did not.

* * *

1500 Hrs.

The end of the second day for hand to hand combat witnessed me yet again having no luck in besting Knight, despite all the advice and encouraging words she provided.

We even took the time to practice "in the air" drills, where it was just her and I standing side by side, jabbing, slashing, and countering without having a tangible target.

I did fine with those exercises, but every time we squared up and she moved, every single one, I froze, my feet laid in stone.

Her words and my high hopes had carried me through the failures initially, but not anymore. I was inconsolably doubting myself now, made worse by the belief that she was too.

How could she not? And who could blame her?

With the wave of a hand, Knight called the cease fire, bringing the day's trials to an end.

"That's it for today, Fenrir." She said softly.

Her words did more than halt our training, I felt they were the nails in my coffin.

Tomorrow was testing day.

It had to be, as the fifth and final day was reserved solely for infiltration tactics. That said, I was nowhere close to being ready to match her, let alone beat her in combat.

Failure stared me in the eye, a mere week and some odd days into training. I had carried knives my entire life, if only pocket knives. I knew the absolute basics, don't touch the sharp side. I had never been in a knife fight, but I had always assumed that should the instance ever come up, I wouldn't just stand there and let myself get filleted.

Thankfully the situation never did arise, otherwise it was hard to imagine that I'd be anything other than a tenant in the county morgue.

As I looked to Knight, I knew that if I were to have any chance tomorrow, our training couldn't end yet. "Knight–"

"Fenrir." A calm yet commanding voice lifted my eyes to the farm house, to Frost, a rifle in her hand. It was larger than the rifle she'd held only days ago, more suited for deer or elk. Over her shoulder I spotted a framepack, though it was suited for someone with a larger stature than hers.

"Yeah?" I whispered.

"It's your turn to get supper." She looked to Knight. "Go ahead and get some rest, Knight. Make sure you're ready for tomorrow."

"Sure." Knight said defeatedly as she left us, her head hung low.

She knew as well as I that I didn't have a snowball's chance in Hell at beating her in the morning.

"Not much point in going after big game, Frost." I said dismissively. "I'm going to fail."

"With an attitude like that you will." She replied sternly before holding the rifle out to me.

As I took the walnut stocked rifle, I shook my head. "I'm just trying to be realistic, Frost. I haven't beat her yet and with tomorrow being the–"

"Talk while we walk." She turned, leading me away from the house.

"Frost," I gently caught her arm, all fancies and daydreams laid to rest as I faced the prospect of failure, "I can't beat her. There's no point in doing this when you all are going to go back to The Citadel and I'm…Well I won't."

"Are you officially tapping out then?" She asked bluntly. "The training's too hard for you?"

"No, I'm not tapping out. I don't want to fail–"

"Then don't," she softly said as she gently put a hand to mine, "and get out of this mindset that says you've already failed."

I frowned as I looked to her hand, resting on mine, before looking up to her face. She was smiling.

"How can you be smiling right now?" I asked in disbelief. "I'm on the verge of losing everything I want, and you're smiling."

"Because you're not the first to think that you're not going to make the cut. Every operator that's worth a damn questions it." She tenderly freed her arm from my hand. "Now come on, the deer are in the valleys this time of day, but they won't be for long. If we don't move soon we'll miss our chance."

"Alright." I gave in. "Lead on I guess."

As we entered the woods, I realized how much I really did want this.

Frost, the fixation of my thoughts over the past days, had just offered me encouragement and I had felt nothing, even when she had placed her hand on my own.

"So what seems to be the issue, Fenrir? Why are you struggling?" She asked a short way into the trees.

"I don't know." I shook my head. "All's well until she steps in on me. Then I freeze, my brain just loses all ability to direct my feet, and every time I end up with that stupid foam knife against me."

"Hmm." She hummed. "Is there some past trauma in your life involving a knife? I don't mean to pry, I'm just trying to help."

"I know," I nodded, "but no. I've never had a bad experience with a knife, well if you don't count the number of stabs and cuts I've taken over the last two days."

"So it's something else then." Frost deduced. "If we can figure out the problem, we can–"

"Frost," I quieted her, "why are you doing this?"

In the short time I'd known her, I had never witnessed her be *that* unnecessarily cold. Certainly not to the point of earning Marcus' "Ice Queen" label, but she seemed straight laced enough that she wouldn't go out of her way to help a rookie that was floundering either.

As my question landed on her, she stopped, slowly turning to face me.

"I'm doing this for the good of the team, Fenrir," her voice softened into little more than a murmur, "and I'm doing it for you."

"I–" I felt an unmistakable heat rush to my cheeks, "I don't understand,

Frost."

"Do you remember what Marcus said about Alpha squad doing just fine? That wasn't entirely true. To say we get by would've been a more fitting appraisal. We need you to pass this training, and I *want* you to pass."

"Why?" I asked.

"Because I've already seen you do the things that we do, even if they were things that you shouldn't have been able to. You harnessed your wolf in hours, Fenrir, and hours later you deployed your wolf in a way that rivals our own. If I didn't know better I'd say that you've used the wolf before. It came naturally to you. Using the wolf in combat is a skill that most people have to develop, just like everything else."

"Do I need to remind you that a vampire rolled me that same night?" I said skeptically.

"You had no idea what you were fighting, Fenrir. You didn't know how they move, or the speed at which they do. You didn't have a clue. So, no, I don't hold that against you. And even after that night, you chose to stay. You had the opportunity to leave, Fenrir, you could've left this all behind and went and lived in one of the Council towns as a mechanic. You could've led something of a normal life, met a girl, had kids, all of that. You didn't choose that though. You chose us, and I'm choosing you."

There was a brief pause in her words, and the momentary silence only served to drive her final words, three that set my heart to tapping, into my core.

"I'm not going to just let you fail, Fenrir." She resumed. "You're gonna' have to work for it, but if you don't quit us, I won't quit you."

"I–" Words briefly failed me. "Thank you, Frost."

"Now," she smiled as she turned, "back to the task at hand. What do you think the problem is?"

I looked down to the rifle in my hands, still unable to pinpoint the root of my lead feet.

"I don't know, Frost. I'm taking it seriously. I just can't keep my feet moving, or any part of me for that matter. I just lock up."

"Not much for me to work with there, Finn." She sighed. "Acting like that, freezing up, it's normally because of something you've experienced. It's like people who've been a victim or close witness to gun violence, sometimes they can't cope, and they become extremely uncomfortable around firearms, to the point that if one is fired they do the same thing you're doing."

"It's not that." I shook my head, aggravated that I could only say what wasn't the cause of my shortcomings.

"I'll think on it." Frost said as the wind shifted, washing over us, bringing with it the heavy odor of iron.

"Frost, stop." I took a knee, quickly scanning the trees. "I smell–"

"Blood?" She smiled down at me. "As you should. Means Doc's made a kill. Come on."

"Doc's hunting too?" I asked as I stood.

"He's the only one that was." She smiled. "Had you cycled the bolt on that rifle, you likely would've had several more questions."

As I racked open the rifle, I found the chamber bare, and the internal magazine empty.

"What was this all for then?" I asked as Frost continued on, following the scent. "For show?"

"That's exactly what it was." Frost turned back. "I couldn't let anyone, *especially* Marcus, think that I was trying to help you. Goes against my call sign. Not to mention it kind of goes against the rules of our training."

With those words, I realized just how far off Marcus' understanding of Frost really was.

"Then why are you doing this?!" I asked again, the situation still not adding up in my mind.

"Because, Fenrir," she looked to me once more as her voice softened, "as much as you need us, we need you even more."

As she said this, her eyes trailed to mine, softening as her voice had, and as we held each other's gaze, I found a warmth in her eyes that I hadn't seen in the light of day.

She was putting her neck on the line for *me*. I hadn't asked for her help, and she was honestly the last I would've expected it from.

"So," I tried in vain to evade the sudden onset of feelings, "Doc was out here actually hunting, giving you the chance to try and address the problem. Is he aware, or is he in the dark too?"

"I've already said that I couldn't let anyone know." She quietly replied as she turned into the wind.

I couldn't help but feel like, simply judging by her demeanor, this wasn't something Knight wouldn't have a hand in. She was always quick to help.

"Why are we keeping Knight out of the loop?" I asked. "This seems like something she'd be a part of."

Frost shook her head, though I could see she was smiling. "Knight is the kindest, most sweet and caring person I've ever known, Fenrir, but when it comes to training, she's a professional. She knows she can't take it easy on you, can't give you a single false hope or victory. If she does, then she's setting you up for failure should you ever need the skills that you were supposed to learn. She would rather you fail honestly than pass in a lie and wind up dead."

I nodded in understanding, though Frost's words led me to question if what she was doing would be counted in that same category.

"And how is that different from what you're doing now, Frost?"

"I'm not giving you fake wins, Fenrir." She countered. "I'm simply trying to help you weed out the problem."

"Well, Knight tried the same thing, asked some of the same questions, and you can see how that turned out."

"Yes, yes I can." Frost stopped, looking down into a shallow draw, finding Doc kneeling beside a collapsed Whitetail doe, a compound bow not far from him.

"Evening." Doc called to us on our way down.

"Hey, Doc." I smiled as we neared.

"I was unaware that you two were hunting as well." Doc smiled. "Might have stayed at the house otherwise, beat a couple more bucks out of Marcus over the poker table."

"More hands to cover to more ground." Frost quickly replied before I could make a sound. "Seems you've had good luck though."

Doc nodded. "With her, we should be set for another week."

"Well," Frost shrugged, "seeing as you've done the hard part, why not let Fenrir and I do the rest."

"You will get no argument from me." Doc chuckled as he sat next to his bow. "Please make sure to save the heart and liver though, I made efforts to take a double lung shot."

"Of course." Frost replied before looking to me. "Go ahead and gut her. You have rope, Doc?"

"Always." Doc replied as he removed his own framepack, opening one the larger storage compartments along its side. "Also have bags for the organs, Fenrir."

As Frost took the rope and moved away, I stepped to the doe, hunting knife in hand.

As I set about field dressing the deer, making sure to deliver the desired innards to Doc, my thoughts returned to the impending test.

"What am I going to do?" I muscled through the pelvic bone. *"It's bad enough that I'm on the cusp of being sent away and now—"*

"Making pretty short work of that, Fenrir." Frost said as I looked up to her.

"Done it a time or two, and also a lot of cattle." I replied as I lifted the doe's upper body, spilling her entrails to the earth.

Frost stepped to, making narrow incisions between the tendon and bone on the doe's hind legs, quickly running the rope through the holes.

"Hoist her up," Frost nodded to a nearby branch she'd thrown the rope over, "and we'll get the hide off. You take one side, I'll do the other."

"Sounds good." I nodded as I stepped under the branch, quickly lifting the doe from the ground.

"So did you grow up on a cattle farm, or were you a ranch hand?" Doc asked as Frost and I set to work skinning the doe.

"Grew up on, well sort of." I replied, not really wanting to delve into my family. I had enough going on as it was.

"Sort of?" Doc asked.

"For the past six years I lived on a cattle farm." I replied shortly. "Spent every day doing something with 'em. Rounding them up, feeding them, chasing 'em back in the fence when they got out."

"Mm." Doc nodded. "Grew your own beef then?"

I nodded. "Sure did. Dad preferred it that way, so he knew what went into the cattle, and so into us when we ate th–"

"Watch it!" Frost called as I saw a glint of steel, her blade flipping over the doe's spine before falling towards my hands.

I jerked away, the knife skating past my fingertips as it fell to the ground.

Clear and away from the deer I looked over to Frost, seizing the opportunity to give her a hard time. "Have I done something to upset you, Frost, or do I just need to keep an eye out for flying cutlery from here on out?"

"I did warn you." Frost huffed as she retrieved her knife. "Accidents happen."

"Don't leave, Doc." I looked over to him with a grin, momentarily forgetting the former overtone of the evening. "Might have to throw some stitches here in a while."

"Alright smart ass." I heard Frost smile. "Just keep talkin', I'll remember it for next week."

"What's next week?" I asked as we got back to skinning the doe, my mood sombering.

"You're with me on weapons training." She replied.

"Provided I can pass tomorrow." I said somewhat bleakly.

"Oh, I think you will." Frost replied. "At least now."

"What's that mean?" I asked.

"You'll see." She smiled as the doe's hide fell to the earth.

18

Starlit Rendezvous

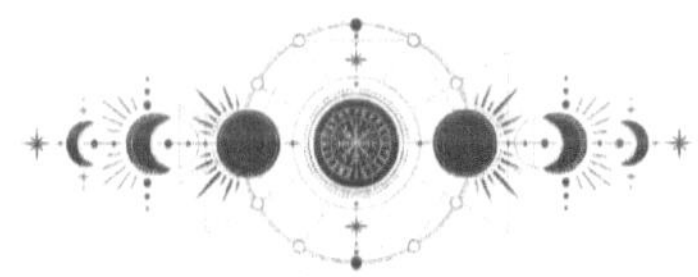

The farmhouse had fallen silent hours ago, the operators of Alpha squad having retired to their rooms. Observing the hour, I hoped they were all asleep.

I lowered my socked feet to the floor and looked to the corner post of my bed, where my vest waited.

Nearly two full days I had challenged Knight with the hunting knife, and in that time I had been receiving nothing but a stomping, failing to claim a single victory.

I had but a few short hours left to get the knife right in order to keep with the course criteria.

Knight had told me that the blades took time, and I didn't really take my shortcomings to heart until I saw the concern in her eyes. She was beginning to consider the possibility that I may not pass.

Frustration creased my brow as I shook my head. I hadn't expected my training to be easy, but I had maintained the hope that I would at least be getting better.

What was I doing wrong? I kept my eyes on Knight, always. I was ready to evade at the faintest twitch of her muscle, but every time she made her assault, I froze.

She told me to use my arms, and the few times I had, the result was me flailing around, providing little contest for her.

Was I overthinking it? Stuck in my head, too focused on my feet or hands? What was going on?

Maybe I just needed an easier adversary?

This in mind, I pulled on my vest and tenderly picked up my boots, taking care to ensure that the heels didn't clack together.

The door knob briskly rattled as I took it in my hand, and for a brief moment I remained still, listening for any indication that I had woken my companions.

When the chatty door knob went unanswered, I opened the door and gingerly stepped into the hall.

I was careful in returning the door to its home, and was relieved when it obeyed my silent command to be quiet.

Fortunately the front door of the farmhouse proved well oiled, and as I stepped out into the moonlight I allowed myself to breathe easily.

As I pulled on my boots, my mind raced over the areas I knew for fact needed attention.

Footwork, if I remained stationary I'd never stand a chance.

My arms needed to come into play, it wouldn't be enough to simply evade Knight.

Eventually, regardless of whether or not I was moving, Knight would draw in close enough to tag me, and when she did, if I didn't manage to "kill" her first, it would do me well to have the ability to guard myself.

Of course I had no knowledge as to whether my attacks were even existent. Knight was on me so quickly that I'd never gotten a chance to make a strike. So that too, needed to be addressed.

"So, that leaves just about everything." I didn't know whether to laugh or

cry.

I made my way to our sparring grounds, and my gaze fell upon Scarecrow.

A stuffed torso, giant head. It couldn't advance, it couldn't retreat, it possessed no capacity to attack me.

"This is a complete waste of my time." I sighed. "Why the hell can't I get this?"

I ran a hand through my hair as I paced before the dummy.

"It's not that hard. She moves, you move. If I could just make it past the first three seconds maybe–"

My hands fell as I grew quiet.

"This is pointless." I looked towards the lake as my feet carried me accordingly, heading towards the dock. *"Did I really expect to help myself sparring with a scarecrow?"*

The boards of the dock chirped under my boots, continuing on until there wasn't another solid step to be taken.

I let myself down onto the rough timbers, flat on my back, my eyes tracing the embers above.

Millions of lights, fireflies eternally trapped in the heavens, shimmered down at me, each with a story that might never be known, despite their strongest wishes.

"I know the feeling." I thought.

Would my story be akin to theirs? Lost in the dark aether? Having all the potential, all the will, but none of the ability?

"Tomorrow will te–"

A blue star caught my eye, the only star whose name I knew.

"It's Rigel." Vivian had said one night.

"It's the brightest star in Orion." She continued.

"I'd say it's the brightest one up there." Alan nodded, crinkling the grass he lay upon.

"Blue stars are supposed to be the brightest." Vivian replied.

"I didn't know it had a name." I said. "I've looked at it a lot. It's the only star I can consistently find."

"What?" Alan propped himself up on an elbow to look over at me. "You can't find the *north* star? It's baked right in!"

"Not as easily as I can find that one." I chuckled. "That's why I made it my favorite star."

"Good thing you don't want to be an astronomer." Alan chortled as he let himself back down into the grass.

"Didn't know you knew words that big, Alan." I smiled.

"At least I can find the frickin' north star."

I smiled in the recollection beneath Rigel, happy that, come what may, I had the memories.

My smile faded as I felt the heavy weight of nostalgia, knowing that I'd never have the chance to create more of those moments. All that remained was memory.

"I miss you guys." I frowned as I looked back over what were becoming hazy days, only to be remembered. Summers spent between the three of us, sometimes four with Kathryn, but always three. Exploring the hills, the streams, the whole world at our feet. Everyday we found adventure lining the trails, always on the search for an unknown corner of my home. Laughter hung on the breeze as the seasons changed, and for a time they were all that changed.

Until I did.

Then everything else followed suit.

I let out a heavy sigh as I stared up at Rigel. It was the same star, still my favorite, though much had changed beneath its light since those nights of looking up.

The road that led me here was first set foot upon beneath Rigel. I had learned of vampires, and killed them, in its light. Under its gaze, Vivian had died.

For everything that had changed though, it was still the same. Just as bright, just as blue as those nights where three friends pointed up at it.

"Fenrir?" A voice called, giving me a start as I sat erect, quickly looking back.

Only a few strides away, having never made a sound as she traversed the boards, was Frost.

"What are you doing out here, Fenrir?" She softly asked, as if raising her voice would shatter the calm of the night.

"Just… looking at the stars." I answered quietly as I looked back to Rigel. "Well, I guess just one to be honest."

"Which one?" She sat next to me, much to my surprise.

There were no chastising words, no reminders of the looming test. For the moment, it seemed she was indulging me in my irresponsibility.

"Rigel." I pointed. "The blue one in Orion."

"I see it." She said. "Are you partial to that particular star?"

I smiled as I nodded. "Favorite star. I've always been able to find it. Probably because it's blue. We spent a lot of time looking at it on the farm."

"We?" She asked.

"Me, Alan, and…" My voice trailed off.

"Her?" She quietly said.

I nodded. "Yeah."

"You were close?"

"Yeah, all three of us were. Most summer days we were together, and most of the nights. Camped a lot, if you could call it that. We'd take an evening and set the hammocks on some back piece of the farm, light a fire, and cook a small supper. Once the fire died down, we'd spend most of the night looking at the sky. Talked about everything and nothing. Most nights we'd fall asleep in the grass, really didn't need to bring the ha–"

"I meant you and her, Fenrir." Frost politely clarified.

"Oh, yeah, we were close. She was my best friend," I cleared my throat, "but so was Alan."

"Just friends?" She toed the line of prying.

"Yeah, just friends." I allowed the questioning. "Before the change we might've been closer."

"That's not true." I frowned. "We *were* closer before I changed. Afterwards… Afterwards I started to pull away. From everyone. It seemed like the best way to keep them safe."

"Seems like it worked." She replied. "It kept them safe."

"Did it though?" I asked softly.

"I didn't mean–" Frost must've realized the error in her words. "I'm sorry, Finn."

"It is what it is." I let out a heavy breath. "I can't change it. No one can."

I turned to look at Frost. "I'm sorry I never thanked you for helping me through that night."

"You thanked me." She nodded. "I wasn't just going to let that thing kill–"

"Not that, Frost." I managed a weak smile. "After the fight."

"Oh." She looked to the water, seemingly caught off guard. "You don't have to thank me for that, Fenrir."

"You didn't have to try to help me through it either." I smiled. "I'm happy you did though."

Her cheeks flushed as she stared at the water, though I saw a bit of a smile pull at her lips, a simple and subtle change that put wing beats in my stomach.

No sooner than it appeared however, did her smile vanish, turning into a sorrowful grimace.

"Why do you do this to yourself, Fenrir?" She whispered.

"Do what?" I matched her tone.

"Keep looking back on them, on your old life? It only brings you pain."

"How can I not? If and when I pass this training, it will be them I fight to keep safe, that I fight for. For those babies we saw at the supermarket, for their mother." In speaking the words, I felt my resolve harden. "I've failed once already, I won't fail again."

"What happened to the guy that thought he had already failed?" Frost quietly asked.

I thought for a moment before answering, looking back to Rigel's light, a small smile creeping across my face.

"He just needed to remember."

Frost sighed as she stood, and I couldn't help but notice a beaming smile on her face.

"Come with me." She breathed.

"Where to?" I asked as I stood.

"Where could we be going, it's the middle of the night?"

"Do you trust me, Finn?" She asked as she smiled at me.

She had to know that I did.

"Of course I do, Frost."

"Then come on." She turned away as she led me towards the trees east of the farm house.

The butterflies in my stomach morphed into a hurricane as my mind took flight.

"Where are we going? What are we doing?"

"Frost," I chased her through the trees, "could you clue me in on this?"

"This?" She chuckled. "It's you, Fenrir."

"What about me?" I ducked under a branch. "My training?"

"Kinda' the lack of." She replied as we came to a stop on a wide trail that led deeper into the trees. "I've watched you time and time again. You start out drawn up well, a good grip on your knife, feet moving, all the basics. Then Knight takes a step and you turn to stone."

I looked to the ground as she took a few more strides ahead.

"We've been over this, Frost. I don't know why I'm locking up. I'm ready every single time, but when she moves I just stand there. I just stand there and watch her slam that stupid fake knife against me."

"We're going to try something a little different tonight." She said over her shoulder, pressing onward. "Unless the mopey guy has made it back around?"

"No!" I nearly shouted. "Frost, I want this, okay? I want to be an Alpha operator, I want to do something about vampires, to be strong enough to protect people so they don't end up–"

"Like your friend." Frost came to a stop, finding her in the middle of a small clearing.

"Yeah." I replied quietly.

"You said that looking back, remembering them, that was your fuel." She spoke with her back to me. "That you would fight for them, to keep them safe."

I looked up through the dwindling canopy, finding Rigel had followed us through the trees.

"Yeah." I looked back to her. "Look, Frost, if you have any advice, I'll take it."

"Just one." I caught a flash of steel in Frost's hand, just before she spun round to me. "Prove it!"

I saw the glint of a blade careening towards my chest, and my body found its drive as I stepped right only a moment too late.

A dull sting on my arm told me I had been hit, but the lack of trickling blood indicated that it was only a scratch.

I didn't have time to take stock of my injury though, nor did I have the few seconds needed to shout her name.

My body buzzed with adrenaline as she began her assault anew.

Her blade was lightning, a sudden bolt screaming in my direction, ending occasionally with searing thunder when she made connection.

I was struck by the absolute difference in her fighting style compared to Knight's.

Knight was smooth, fluid, dare say graceful in her movements, from the spiral dance to the attack.

Not Frost. She was naught but fury. Her attacks were aimed to one end, overwhelming the foe with brute force and rapid succession.

Amid the storm, my feet fell into rhythm, moving me from side to side, back when necessary.

I was dancing with the tempest, with Frost.

I was doing it.

Something within told me to take a step forward. As I did, I found her burning blue eyes rivaled even Rigel's light.

She made a final lunge, a final bolt cast towards my chest.

It's hard to say who was more surprised when I caught her wrists, though the shock was certainly hers as I allowed her to push me backwards.

In that instant, time fractured, slowing to a crawl.

My back kissed the earth as I put a foot to her stomach, ever so gently lifting her feet from the ground just enough to throw her off balance.

She continued over me, turning loose of the knife as she needed her hands to facilitate her rolling recovery.

We both rose to our feet, and it was only then I noticed that the pair of us were spent, drenched in sweat, panting for breath.

The knife had changed hands, from hers to mine, though I was far from happy following the bombardment.

"Not so hard, now is it?" She let out a heavy breath.

"Little different when I'm fighting for my life." I replied.

"And there's your problem, Finn." Frost suddenly smiled as she produced a mock hunting knife. "You're not threatened by this, you're not taking it seriously. You might be consciously trying to, but your brain's not. Not like just now."

"Frost, just now, you could've killed me." I shook my head.

"With that?" She pointed to my hand.

I looked down my hand, finding no razor edged weapon in my clutch, but rather a butter knife, fresh from the kitchen drawer.

"It's in your head, Fenrir." Frost smiled.

"Frost," I stammered, "I– How did you figure it out?"

"You remember skinning the doe?" Her smile grew.

I narrowed my eyes as I shook my head. "Skinning the d–"

The knife she dropped. It was directly over my hands.

"You didn't lose your grip on that knife, did you?" I nearly smiled as I shook my head.

"No, I did." She held her grin. "Just wasn't an accident. It was all I needed to see though. Something in you, your brain, *you* generally, is not taking the replica's seriously."

"Well, at least we know why now." I conceded with a small smile. "But that still leaves us without a fix for tomorrow, Detective. We won't fight with real steel."

"And that is where I say I've done all I can for you. The rest is up to you. You've got to find a way to convince yourself that you're fighting for your life. Can you do that?"

"How can I trick myself into thinking I'm fighting for my life, when I know

damn well that I'm not?"

I felt the wolf move, a brief vision flashing into my mind's eye.

"Well that's not a good plan." I shook my head.

"You alright, Fenrir?" Frost asked. "Did I startle you that bad?"

"No." I raised a hand. "I'm good."

"Good." Frost nodded. "Better get to bed then, Knight will be expecting you bright and early for the exam."

"How's that go?" I asked.

"You'll challenge her three times. Best of three is the victor."

"Any warm up beforehand?" I asked.

"What do you think?" Frost tilted her head. "You've run yourself down to the wire here, Fenrir. I just hope that you can get yourself straight."

I half smiled as I shook my head. "Thank you, Frost."

"You realize you just thanked me for chiseling on you with a butter knife right?" She smiled.

Under her smile I couldn't help but scoff. It still didn't make sense to me, the help I was receiving. She had given me reasons, but I still didn't buy it. Just because someone was good with the wolf? For the good of the team? I was far from talented in any single portion of our skills.

"I don't understand this." I whispered as I shook my head. "You said it goes against all these things, yet you're still helping me. The first mission you and I went on, you said you were a soldier, whose job was to get the job done, every time. That doesn't sound like someone who'd break orders to save a helpless greenhorn."

"You're not helpless, Fenrir." She shook her head as her tone softened. "You just hit a wall. I've already told you that you have some degree of skill, natural abilities that, by all rights, you shouldn't. Not only does it make you valuable, it also makes you easier to train because it's easier to focus on problem areas. That alone makes you a cadet worth putting time into."

I was still far from sold on this regurgitation of what she'd said previously.

"So, just because I can use the wolf decently?"

"Partly, yes." She replied.

"And the rest?" I asked.

She hesitated, not entirely willing to go on.

"We all swore to fight for humanity, Fenrir, everyone in The Council, some of us never having seen what it is we'll actually fight. You have." She whispered. "You've seen vampires and you've killed them. More than that though, I know that you're telling the truth when you say that you'll fight to keep them safe. This I know, because I've seen you do it. And you have already witnessed and come to grips with the fact that can't keep them all safe."

I was quiet, her soft words resonating as she continued.

"Despite that, just like I said earlier, you chose to stay, knowing what combat is, nearly being killed and losing one of your friends, you chose to stay with The Red Moons. As far as I'm concerned, Fenrir, you earned your place with us when you made that choice. You chose to stay and fight for your friends, so that they are kept safe from our world." She shook her head as she looked at me with a smile. "You're already a soldier, Fenrir. And I believe you've got a good heart. Those two things in unison are pretty rare in our particular line of work and,"

She briefly paused, though her smile remained, "if I'm entirely honest, I'd like to see you stick around."

In awe, I smiled at her, careful so that the following words echoed my wonder, so they couldn't be mistaken for criticism.

"How do you still have your call sign when you act like this?" I gently praised.

Her cheeks reddened as she smiled, turning away from me as she chuckled. "Because my default stance *is* Frost, and largely, that is who I am. I'm strong because the others need to see strength, but I'm not numb to death, Fenrir, and I can see when one of us is hurting, just like Knight. She just has to act on it. "

"Well, it suits her." I laughed. "Don't worry, your secret's safe with me."

"I know." She smiled as she started towards the house. "Seriously though, you should get to bed. You show up like a zombie and start knocking Knight around, they'll be sure to ask questions."

"Probably right." We stepped from the trees. "If it comes up though, I'll just tell 'em I spent the night fighting Scarecrow."

"You honestly think they'll buy that?" She giggled.

"Probably." I shrugged. "Heck, I almost did. "

"Are you serious?" Her footsteps stopped.

"I said *almost*." I laughed. "Guess we're even now."

"What?" Frost raised a brow.

"Well, you owed me one for teaching you how to fix the van, right?"

"Oh," Frost almost seemed surprised, just before she smiled, "yeah, I guess so."

* * *

0800 Hrs.

Knight again stood before me. She hadn't yet drawn her weapon, and I could tell from the look in her eyes that she was genuinely worried about the outcome of her examination.

So was I.

I hadn't slept a bit, I was too nervous, too scared to sleep. If I failed this, my newfound purpose would never see the light of day.

Frost's words rang in my head, that I didn't see the replicas as a threat, and I knew she was right.

In the darkness of our early morning duel, I was fighting for my life, or so I had thought.

Today, in the light of the sun, I had to regain that mindset.

I had to get my head wrapped around that, to push my brain into the state of fight or flight. Of survival.

All those times that Knight and I had sparred, not once had I experienced an adrenaline drop like Frost brought on.

In my questioning the night before, I had only found two options that might elicit the appropriate reaction.

I couldn't argue that they were certainly viable ways to force it, and though I didn't have enough shots at this to be choosy, I really didn't like the second option.

The rest of Alpha convened around us, eager to see how I would fare, well aware of my lack of progress.

Knight looked to them, as if silently asking their approval to begin.

Marcus nodded, and Knight responded in kind before looking at me.

"You ready for this, Fenrir?"

I nodded as we each took hold of our knives.

It started as it always had, the spiral dance, closing the distance.

My eyes were fixed on her knife, as always.

I stared at it, trying to force the adrenaline.

Nothing.

"Dammit." I thought. *"I wouldn't be opposed to a little help here, wolf."*

She dove in, and I felt a brief spark, a subtle thing that barely registered. Not nearly enough for me to attempt an evasion.

I stared at the knife as it plunged towards me.

"Come on, come on!" I vainly begged. *"Come on, move!"*

I felt the blade shove into my stomach and I heard the disappointment in Knight's sigh.

She had just given up on me.

"You have to win from here." Knight whispered, now fully expecting for me to fail.

I looked to the bystanders, to Frost.

She nodded to me, making a low fist that perfectly displayed her silent thoughts.

"Get it together, you can do this."

"Come on, she believes in you, get yourself right, take it seriously!"

As I returned to the starting position, I knew that if I failed, even once more, I was done.

"This is it." I thought, straining to evoke the desired response from my body. *"If I fail again, there's no hope of avenging Vivian."*

Nothing, no rush of energy, no stirring of anything.

"If I fail, I'll never find the woman that did this to me."

Useless. Little more than a resting heartbeat.

"If I fail, I have to leave, and all this will have been for nothing."

Futile. My breath remained calm, unhurried.

"I'll have to leave Frost."

My heart lurched as my breath seized. The wolf stirred, ruthlessly crashing through whatever borders had been erected.

My veins scorched as flames coursed through me, the heat of the wolf.

I felt him creep to my core, unfurling from wherever he dwelt. It seemed the notion of leaving here, no, not here, of leaving Frost, was something he wouldn't idly allow. His ferocious energy flowed to my hands, to my feet, and every space between, setting me aflame.

He would fight beside me.

"Alright wolf, let's see what we've got."

Knight nodded again, signaling our start, and as she drew herself up, knife in a RGEO grip, my body shuddered, the wolf pushing a spike of adrenaline.

"Is there a reason for that smirk, Fenrir?" Knight asked with understandable aggravation.

I shook my head as I cleared my face, unsure myself as to why I had been smiling as we resumed our dance.

My body tensed as the wolf rolled his shoulders, as if this was something he was familiar with, like it had been only a brief time since he had last seen this sort of fight.

A curious tingle took my fingertips as I rolled the blade to a hammer hold, my other arm brought up close, ready to defend.

Knight's blade suddenly switched hands, from right to left, an instant before she rushed in with a quick jab I was surely meant to evade.

The wolf had a different idea.

I stepped in on her, her blade gliding past my vest.

Shock glistened in Knight's eyes as I caught her throat with the back of my arm, quickly wrapping it around her neck and rocking her backwards, giving me her chest.

In a few short seconds, I had secured my first victory, fulfilled as I flipped the blade in my fingers, driving it to the base of her throat.

As I relaxed, helping her stand upright, her fiery eyes fell upon me.

"Seems you've found your fight." She growled as a small smile played at the corners of her mouth. "Aggro... Very well."

"Might have overdone it a bit, wolf." I cautioned. *"Maybe rein it in."*

Knight turned away, heading back to her starting post, shedding her vest.

"Oh dear." Doc's voice rang with concern.

"Draw up, Fenrir!" Knight roared and I got the impression that I had royally screwed up.

I had barely readied myself for the final round when Knight began the assault.

She was lightning, a mirage, jolting from side to side, impossible to predict, rapidly closing.

In a blur her knife shot out, aimed for my chest, only narrowly missing as she allowed her momentum to carry her on.

Before I could wheel around to face her, I felt an arm take my throat from behind, just as the blade came from the right, screaming towards my chest.

Evasion was impossible, this I knew as I brought up a hand to catch her wrist, keeping the knife at bay, but just barely.

My right hand alone began to falter, and as I brought up my left to assist, I knew that I had to get out of this hold, *fast.*

"I have her arm, her body's behind me... I don't want to do this."

In a sickening moment, I felt the wolf smile.

I threw my right shoulder forward, putting my strength into her arm as I arched my back, dragging her over the top of me with every intention of slamming her to the ground. Surprise had left her, proven as she fluidly rolled upon impact, quickly righting herself and rebounding.

A flurry of jabs and slashes kept my feet moving, and I realized, much to the wolf's pleasure, that Knight was furious.

I managed to evade a sudden stab, only to have my feet swept from beneath me.

My breath leapt from my lips as I slammed to the ground. I only just opened my eyes to find Knight standing over me, her knife quickly falling.

"Shit!"

I rolled right, feeling the blade graze my arm before it hit the dirt.

"Not a killing blow, I'm still in the fight!"

Digging for whatever purchase I could secure, I swung my leg, taking both of hers as she crashed to the ground.

Not for long though, both of us hurrying to regain our feet before the other.

I beat her by mere heartbeats, but my advantage was nullified as she launched into me, putting a boot to the center of my combat vest.

As I staggered back, she smiled through heavy breaths. "Come on, Aggro, or was that just beginner's luck? Am I going too hard on you?"

My veins blistered as the wolf snarled, sending an inferno to my core, taking the insult very personally.

"I've gotta' end this quick." I panted. *"The wolf's gonna' kill her."*

As if privy to my thoughts, she lunged, a quick jab towards center mass.

Again I watched her blade blazing towards me as time began to still.

"Not yet. Too soon and she'll dodge it."

Three inches away, and that was being generous.

"Not yet."

Two-ish?

My knife fell from my hand as I took both of her wrists, guiding her knife up towards my shoulder as I fell back to the ground.

I felt the coarse foam burn against my collar bone as I put a boot to her stomach, flipping her over me.

I heard the breath leave her as she clattered to earth, giving the split second I needed.

My hand miraculously found my knife, and with a final heave, I guided the blade to her chest.

She let out a heavy breath as I relaxed, the wolf suddenly retreating, taking his energy with him.

"Good fight, Fenrir." Knight exhaled before reaching over, putting a few pats to my head.

I rested my head on my arm as I chuckled, hoping that she wasn't still upset with me.

"Are we good?" I asked as I looked over to her.

She waved a hand dismissively. "Of course we are. You surprised me, that's all. Not totally uncommon for hands to get thrown."

"You guys gonna' get up?" Marcus came to stand over us with a smile. "Or do I need to call Doc over?"

"Oh, shut up." Knight smiled as she took his hand, hauling herself to her feet.

"Your turn, pup." Marcus grinned as he extended his hand.

As he pulled me from the dirt he delivered a hearty smack to my shoulder. "Good job."

"Thanks, Lieutenant." I nodded.

"Had us a little worried." He raised a brow. "Happy you got yourself sorted."

"Yeah I know. Sorry about that." I turned to Knight."Is there still enough time for Infiltration tactics?"

"Psshh." She waved a hand. "That can be taken care of pretty easily. We've the better part of two days still and we can work on it through the rest of your training if we need to. Most of it's just book learning. Lots of diagrams and pictures. This was the big one, Fenrir. I didn't…You *really* had me worried."

"You didn't think I'd fail did you?" I laughed.

"I…" Knight slowly nodded, "was beginning to wonder."

"I believe all of us were." Doc chuckled as he crossed his arms. "Knight was beside herself yesterday evening. Pray tell, Fenrir, what events took place between yesterday and today?"

My eyes widened ever so slightly as I looked over the group, careful not to look straight to Frost.

"Great, I gotta' say it."

"I spent most of the night," I mumbled, "fighting Scarecrow."

"What?!" Knight looked to me with wounded eyes.

"Ha!" Marcus clapped his hands as he laughed. "Bag o' straw's a better teacher than Knight!"

I raised a hand as I prepared to speak a defense on Knight's behalf. "Now that's not what I–"

"Let it go, Fenrir." Knight growled. "It won't help."

"I'm sorry, Knight." I managed a smile teased frown, trying to hide my humor with the situation while Marcus continued chuckling.

"You couldn't just tell a fib and make something up?" Knight sighed as she shook her head.

"Well what else could I say?" I smiled. "That last night my own personal angel taught me to knife fight?"

"I guess that's true." She shrugged. "If you'd said something like that they never would've believed you."

"Right?" I chuckled as I cast Frost a sly glance.

Her eyes met mine for only a moment before she looked to the ground, though the morning light did nothing to hide her rosy cheeks, nor to diminish her dazzling smile.

* * *

Infiltration tactics were just as Knight had said, mostly book work. Occasionally she and I would work through the motions so that I had a better grasp of a certain concept, but for the most part it was straight forward. Various lessons, ranging from methods of killing an enemy with the knife in a manner that preserved the uniform to the intricacies of trap making filled my final hours with her.

I learned that infiltration operations were best left to a small strike team, three or four operators, as they could move quickly and not draw much attention.

There was no written exam, nor was there any official field practice for the infiltration portion, it seemed the focus of the week had been to grasp the knives, which I had barely managed.

"When we get back to The Citadel, we'll continue to practice, and it won't just be me there. You can take on any of us, and it helps, everyone has a different style, different speed, different stance. You'll continue to grow more effective. Plus you've gotta' learn how to fight without making eye contact."

"Do what?" My voice raised.

Knight nodded. "We just cover the basics, get you squared away to the point you can fight wolves. Against vampires, well you know about the Spike right?"

I nodded, recollecting Phoenix's words.

"We try to avoid fighting them in close quarters, ten feet or less, and we *really* try to just shoot them, but if you were in a tight proximity fight with a vampire, you want to avoid eye contact."

"Is that how you fought me, Knight?" I asked quietly.

She nodded. "You've gotta' make it a habit. I try to focus on the neck, it keeps my eyes from theirs and it's a prime target."

"Wouldn't it make sense to practice that here?" I asked.

"It would, but we try not to overwhelm the cadets. Just learning the knife is, as you yourself have witnessed, sometimes a struggle."

"That's fair I guess." I nodded.

Week two came to a close, ending in success, and I had earned the right to carry the vest I had worn during training, as well as the skill to use any one of the knives the sheaths contained.

The start of week three was upon me, Frost's week.

At the mere thought of spending an entire week with Frost my heart quickened, and an armada of butterflies took flight in my stomach.

It was then that I came to the conclusion that there truly was something there, something I hadn't felt yet in my brief existence.

It felt silly, immature, to label it a crush, something left for children.

It seemed so much more than that. I wanted to be near her. I could feel her enter a room, the faint bristle of excitement letting me know she was near.

I craved the building charge, and the thunderous release in the moment our skin met.

Yet, there was still the fact that she was a seasoned soldier, and I was a rookie.

Then again, she did go against her own chosen call sign and the regulations of training to help me.

"Hey, Knight." Marcus drew our attention from the kitchen table, where we had spent the last half hour mostly chit-chatting.

"Yeah, L.T.?" Knight answered.

"You're on for the grocery run tonight," Marcus' eyes spoke apology, "sorry it's a little late in the evening. Pick a sidekick and get going."

Excitement rushed over me, eager to make good on Knight and I's agreement.

"I'll go." I blurted, barely keeping my voice down. "Just in case the van acts up again."

Marcus nodded approvingly, ignorant to my true motives. "Good on you, Fenrir. Please hurry home, I can't sleep until you're all here and accounted for."

"Why's that?" I asked.

"You're all my responsibility and your safety is my priority." Marcus smiled warmly. "Wherever we are, you guys are mine to take care of."

I smiled, this being the closest thing to acceptance I had seen out of Marcus. It may not have meant anything to him, but it spoke volumes to me.

"Well, get going." Marcus smiled. "Get back safe."

"We'll hurry." Knight smiled over to me as she stood, fully aware of my intentions.

As I followed her to the door, it was all I could do to keep myself together, nearly passing her by on the way to the van.

"Slow down, Fenrir." Knight giggled. "Don't wanna' make it obvious."

"Sorry." I slowed my strides. "Just a bit excited."

"You don't say?" Knight giggled.

19

The 249

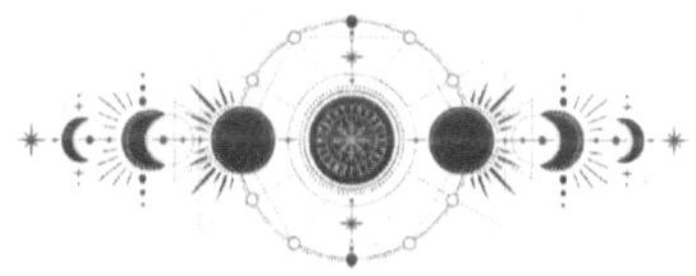

10/08
0500 Hrs.

My eyes flew open, though I didn't know why. From the back of my mind, a soft creak resonated from memory.

"Did I hear that? Or was I dreaming? Is someone in the room with me?" My pulse quickened. *"No. I would've heard the door."*

"Was that you wolf?" I asked pointlessly, knowing well that he couldn't answer.

A single halfhearted tap landed on my door, the unmistakable sound of a knuckle put to timber. None followed however, and in the unbroken silence, I questioned if the house was simply talking as it settled.

Another creak, perceived as thunder as I strained my ears, sang under the door as my feet landed, quickly opening the door.

Now wide awake, I found Frost, half threshold into her own bedroom across the hall.

"Frost?" Her name was the only question needed.

She was dressed as if she was about to deploy on a mission. A black vest, loaded with magazines and equipment, laid over her jacket.

"Are you leaving?" I asked, finding my voice a little deeper than normal, sleep still holding my throat.

"Hm?" She raised a single brow before realizing how the situation looked. "No, this is for your training."

"My training?" I looked down to my watch. "You realize it's just after 0500?"

"I know." She said. "I meant to tell you yesterday, this week starts earlier, and runs later."

"Is that why you were creepin' on my door?" I smiled, taking advantage of my husky voice.

"I was going to let it slide this morning," she chuckled, "since you and Knight were out a bit late, but seeing as you're up, let's get to it."

I nodded. "Alright, where to?"

"Get yourself ready and meet me downstairs." She started away from me. "Bring your vest and pack."

* * *

A few minutes later I joined Frost at the kitchen table, finding a cup of coffee in her hands, another at the end of the table.

"Coffee break already?" I grinned as I sat next to her.

"I figured I owed you that much, given the time." She smiled over to me. "And my day doesn't start until I've had a cup of coffee."

"Caffeine junky, huh?" I poked.

"Nope." She inhaled the steam from her cup. "More of a coffee connoisseur, even though I'm alone in that profession here. There's cream in the fridge if you'd like."

"Nah." I looked down into the pitch contained in my mug. "Black is good with me."

"Ugh." She shivered as she joked. "Uncultured savage."

"Just got used to it." I shrugged. "Most of the time it was grab a cup of joe on the way out the door. No time to spruce it up."

"Oh, great." She rolled her eyes. "*Another* problem for me to fix."

"You haven't got a clue." I smiled before taking a sip of my coffee.

"Speaking of," her voice lowered, "good job yesterday, Fenrir."

I raised my brows as I set the mug down. "Don't know if I'd say 'good' job. Think I dealt Knight's feelings a pretty solid hit."

"Surprised me too." Frost admitted. "I know that I helped you the other night, but you were still a far cry from being a knife fighter. Then you come out swinging like that? What happened?"

"Well," I tilted my head, "I had hoped that sacrificing my cushion in the first round would do what I needed, push my brain into some kind of fight for life mode."

"Looks like it worked." She said before putting her lips to the rim of the mug.

"Never thought I'd be jealous of ceramic."

"No, it didn't." I shook my head, both in response to her and to clear my mind. "It didn't do anything."

"It had to do something." Frost replied skeptically. "Otherwise you wouldn't be here right now."

"It wasn't losing the buffer that pushed me over the edge. When we squared up for the second round, I thought of all that I stood to lose if I failed. That's what did it."

"And what did you stand to lose?" Frost asked, drawing my eyes to her, once more captivating me.

"Why does she do this to me?" The butterflies in my stomach raged. *"What makes **her** do this to me?"*

"Everything." I whispered as I tore my eyes from hers. "All the progress I've made, all the work you guys, *you*, have put into me. All the hopes, the intentions. Think what really sent it home was the thought of losing all of you. I've gotten pretty fond of ya' these past few weeks."

"Well," Frost smiled, "it doesn't hurt that you fell into place so easily. You get along with everyone, which let's be honest, in terms of Knight and Doc, I don't know anyone they don't get along with. Knight loves people and so long as you're not reckless, you'll never have issues with Doc."

"And where do I stand with you?" I nearly left the sentence at that as I realized it sounded exactly as I meant it.

"And Marcus?" I quickly added.

"Marcus is a wild card." Frost leaned back in her chair. "But, he isn't yelling at you every five minutes, so I'd say he doesn't hate you."

"And you?" It seemed safe enough to ask now.

"We're good." She smiled at me through narrowed eyes. "After this course of training though, that may change."

"Guess I'll have to make sure I don't upset you then." I smiled before finishing off my cup.

"It's not me that'll have the ax to grind." She chuckled. "It'll be a miracle if you don't come out hating me."

"Don't think that's possible. Or am I about to get the full 'Ice Queen' experience?"

"Probably will." She chuckled as she set down her empty mug. "But it won't be my attitude that leads you to hate me."

"Then what?" I laughed.

"You'll see." She took her mug and my own to the sink. "Rather quickly as a matter of fact. Come on."

She reached for the door. "Our training will start in the barn."

"The barn?" I nearly laughed.

"That's right," she spoke over her shoulder, "and after that it's into the woods."

"No desk work on this one then?" I asked as I caught up to her.

"There is, but we're not to that point yet."

"Copy that." I nodded.

As we stepped into the barn Frost reached over and flipped a switch, casting light over the space.

It was what one would expect of a barn, open floor space towards the door, the back half filled with square bales of hay.

I couldn't help but notice the center was stacked oddly. All the other bales were stacked at length, only the ends visible. The bales in the center were positioned so that the top, the bit where the twine was, faced outward.

"Am I stacking hay for you today?" I smiled.

"No." She answered shortly, and I could feel her demeanor shifting. "Pull out the center row of bales, two deep."

"So I'm *un*stacking bales today." I set about my task.

"If it takes you much longer," she shot a bit of smart ass, "then yes it'll be all day."

As I pulled off the first bale in the second set, I discovered the top of a metal door. Removing the rest revealed a keypad next to the door.

"Very secret agent." I remarked as I stood aside, allowing her to pass me in the narrow corridor I had opened.

She didn't reply as she pushed a series of numbers, being rewarded with a mechanical clink.

I took a step forward as I anticipated her opening the door. She caught me off guard as she spun around, and I found that her demeanor wasn't the only thing that had changed. She had hit the switch in her control center, going from easy going and coffee drinking to full metal jacket.

"All bullshittery stops at this point, Fenrir." Her blue eyes, soft only moments before, had become steel. "We're going to be working with hot weapons, and if you get stupid, people get hurt. I want your brain on point and on target. Copy?"

"Copy." I replied.

The butterflies I had felt the night before, that had prevailed into the morning, had just been ruthlessly incinerated.

"Good." She nodded as she turned round, putting her hand to the door.

As she opened it, the room filled with white light, illuminating a modestly stocked armory.

Several assault rifles hung on the wall, accompanying a meager selection of sidearms, and a handful of shotguns.

Beneath them were several wooden ammo boxes.

"Not much for a squad to work with, let alone a squad support gunner."

"Over here, Fenrir." Frost called my attention to a single stainless steel table, a pristine machine gun atop it, resting on its bipod.

"This will be yours." She looked at the machine gun. "The M249, or SAW, Squad Automatic Weapon. 5.56 by 45 millimeter cartridge fed by a two-hundred round M27 disintegrating belt from a detachable ammo box. Open bolt operation, seventeen pounds dry, twenty-two loaded. This particular rig has a barrel length of 18.3 inches. Effective range of 700-hundred meters. Cyclic rate of fire 850 rounds per minute. In a pinch it will accept standard STANAG mag's like our M4's. Iron sights, bipod, two point sling, adjustable stock, and a quick-change barrel, of which you'll carry one spare. Get all that?"

"Uh…" I stammered. "Not to bring up the aforementioned bullshittery but, I don't have the capacity to retain that rapid volley of information and numbers you just spewed at me."

She nearly smiled, breathing the faintest bit of life into my crippled butterflies.

"You'll pick it up." She nodded, getting a handle on her composure. "As squad support gunner you will be responsible for the majority of suppressive fire, be that so we can make a retreat in which case you will take rearguard, or so that we can flank the enemy position. In any scenario you need to be capable of laying down accurate fire. Rounds that don't impact near hostiles will do little to keep them in cover."

"Copy that." I nodded. "So range time?"

She shook her head. "No. Before I put the 249 in your hands, you're going to learn to move with it. Twenty-two pounds may not sound like much, and for a wolf it really isn't, but in addition to your vest and your pack, you're going to feel awkward and bulky moving around. Set your pack on the table."

She bent down beneath the table, returning with four square pouches. "These are for your ammo boxes."

She slid two across the table to me. "I'm putting one on either side of your pack. I trust you can put the other two on your vest?"

"I'll manage." I chuckled as I set my pack down, turning my attention to the webbing on my vest, lacing the straps on the pouches through the material.

"You'll also be needing a sidearm." Frost spoke as she worked. "Pick one from the wall. Tell me which one, *do not* touch them."

I looked to the wall as I finished up with my vest.

Of the selection of handguns on the wall, I recognized only one.

"The 1911 available?" I nodded to the dated model.

".45 ACP. Large round, little slow, but makes up for it in knock down power." She looked up to me. "Over compensating for something?"

"Hey!" I chuckled. "Thought the bullshittery was supposed to stop at the door."

"Only for you, Fenrir." She grinned. "I *know* what I'm doing."

"You're right." I frowned through a bruised ego. "I may not like you after this."

"You haven't seen anything yet." She bounced her brows.

"So what now? I just run around with the 249?" I gestured to the SAW.

"Not with this one." She puffed. "You'll use these."

Again she bent down under the table.

I quickly jerked my eyes away as the slimmest glimmer of blue lace appeared over the top of her jeans.

"Maybe I won't hate you." I breathed.

"What?" She craned to look at me.

"A-hem. Nothing." I smiled. "Just something in my throat."

"Mhm." She eyed me as she stood up. "You'll use these for the time."

My smile died as she set another 249 on the table, identical to mine, that is if mine was encrusted in a film of rust.

"What... happened?" I poked a brown flake from the barrel.

"It's just a retired rig. Old and worn out with a warped barrel that someone overheated. I could try to rebuild it but between the cost and time of doing that, it's better suited for training at this point. Rather you smack the barrel or snap the sights off this than a good unit."

"Makes sense." I couldn't help but feel sorry for the old war horse.

"And you'll be needing this." She slapped an equally disgusting 1911 down on the table.

"Another retiree?" I asked.

"Yup." She produced a thigh holster from beneath the table. "Pulled it out of a mud pit a while back. Who knows how long it's been there."

"Oof." I shook my head as I strapped the holster to my leg. "Ready now?"

"Almost." She looked to the ammunition crates. "Grab five belt boxes out of the top one."

I nodded, following the command, though upon opening the wooden crate, I couldn't help but tilt my head in curiosity.

There were five belt boxes, but the belts held odd looking rounds. They were standard brass, the tips were… different though.

"Are they supposed to be blue?" I spoke aloud.

She sighed. "Happens even to the best sometimes."

I turned to find her grinning, eyes narrowed, clearly enjoying herself. *"This is not fair, not even close!"*

I bit my tongue as I looked back to the boxes. "I'll take that as a yes."

"It's simulation ammunition." She chuckled. "As close as you can get to the weight of a standard round."

"While making sure that the rookie doesn't get live rounds." I nodded as I returned with the stack of boxes.

"They're still hot." She said as she slid two boxes into the pouches on my pack. "Just shoot paint instead of lead."

"Tactical paintball." I said as I picked up a box, somewhat struggling to get it into the pouch.

"Having trouble there, Fenrir?" She chided as she hooked an ammo box to the rusty 249.

"Just, focus on what you're doing." I rattled as I managed to seat the last box. "There."

"Now you're ready." She smiled. "Hope you don't mind getting dirty."

* * *

I'm not sure what I expected when she talked about me getting dirty, but it wasn't this.

For this piece of training Frost had taken me, with pack, vest, and 249, into the woods behind the farmhouse.

"This is the gauntlet." Frost stopped at the head of an obstacle course.

I could make out two logs over the path before it veered out of view.

"This piece is all about learning to move with your gear, Fenrir. Don't worry about trying to move with the 249 in your hands, just keep it slung–" She looked over to me. "Yeah, that's not gonna' work."

"What?" I asked.

I had the 249 slung over my shoulder, the barrel pointed to the sky.

"Let me show you." She stepped behind me, taking the 249 from my back, talking as she adjusted things, tingles taking my skin every time she touched me. "Put the sling over your left shoulder, under your right arm. Keep the 249 in front of you."

She stepped back around to my left side, just behind the barrel of the derelict LMG.

"Now, spin the sling and the SAW, so that it's resting on your back." She walked me through the motions. "Now, make sure there's just enough slack in the sling that you can shoulder it when you bring it back around."

Again I followed the command, putting the stock to my shoulder, making sure to keep my finger away from the trigger.

"It'll do." She nodded. "And thank you for showing me you're not a complete idiot."

"I do know some things." I gave her a flat look.

"Well common sense doesn't always prevail." She replied. "Some people try to fight straw dummies to improve their hand to hand skills."

"I didn't do that." I cocked my head as I looked to the course. "So am I running for time?"

"No." Frost replied. "Though it would reflect well on you to hustle. If you're going to be any sort of an effective squad support gunner, you need to be in good condition."

"I feel like I'm in decent shape."

"Well we're about to find out." She smiled.

"We?" I looked over to her. "You running it with me?"

"No. I'll be up there." She pointed to a metal shack at the top of a nearby hill. "From there I'll be able to see you. We've got speakers wired up through the course, so I'll be in touch."

"Okay." I nodded, taking a moment to observe what I could of the gauntlet, which wasn't much.

"Well, go!" She pointed.

Pack and all I took off into the trees following the trail. Twenty yards in I faced the first obstacle, a log three feet off the ground.

I crossed over it with the grace of a hippo. Although the gear wasn't particularly heavy, Frost was right, it was still awkward.

Moving on I hadn't made it ten yards before I was at the next log, higher than the first, too high to jump.

I moved to duck beneath it, catching my pack and nearly pulling myself from my own feet.

I swore as I hunkered lower, clunkily shambling my way under.

"Yeah, sorry about the logs." Frost called over the speakers. "Storm took 'em down, and we haven't got them cleaned up yet. On second thought though, I think I'm gonna' add 'em to the course."

"This isn't even part of the actual obstacle course!" I puffed as I ran onward, right into a waist deep mud pit.

"*Now* you're there." Frost's voice echoed through the trees.

"Yup, figured that." I slogged through the muck, leading to the first true test.

A narrow wooden ramp stood before me, leading up to a fifteen foot wall.

"Up the ramp, jump to the wall, down the other side!" Frost roared as The Ice Queen came out.

Slippery boots did next to nothing to hold the ramp, and after what seemed an eternity of ice skating I made it to the wall, hauling myself up and over.

Letting myself go, I watched the short distance to the ground disappear into a muddy splash that painted my body and face.

"Ooh," Frost's voice winced, "yeah, shouldn't have been looking down."

"No shit!" I wiped the mud from my eyes.

I looked ahead to a wooden box frame, two ropes dangling from it, each with an odd metal sleeve just below the framework.

A shorter ramp than before led up the ropes, and as I neared them I found another soupy concoction between me and the far side.

"Don't miss the rope!" I jumped.

I didn't miss the rope.

It disconnected in the sleeve.

For a split second all I felt was sickening free fall before I broke the soup's surface, resulting in a putrid brown tsunami.

"Down he goes ladies and gentlemen." I barely heard through the mud. "Come on, you've still got two to go. Cookie could run this faster than you!"

The next obstacle was straight forward enough, another wooden frame, boards running across it with a lot of air space between, making a long strided ladder wall.

"This one's not so bad." I let myself down on the far side before turning to face the final obstacle.

Another wooden frame, this one holding a net of heavy rope.

"Last one." I sprinted towards the grid work.

* * *

Fenrir's hands had just hit the net when heavy footsteps drew Frost's eyes.

"Lieutenant." She nodded professionally as Marcus stepped into the small room.

"Frost." Marcus' voice mirrored hers as he stepped up to the window. "How's our cadet doing?"

"It's his first run if that tells you anything."

"Mm." Marcus grunted. "So, terrible?"

"Actually, no." Frost replied in aggravation. "He's not setting speed records, but he isn't stopping either. He's got good stamina, even for all his slipping and sliding and extra weight."

"Fairly fit then?" Marcus raised a brow.

"Appears to be." Frost nodded.

"Good, saves us a bit of work." Marcus replied as he looked down to a small control panel, and the buttons thereon, arranged on either side of an illustration of the course. "Have you hit him with one of these yet?"

"Not yet." Frost replied shortly.

"May I?" Marcus grinned, seeing Fenrir halfway up the networking.

"Of course."

With a crack, two blasts of earth, accompanied by white plumes of compressed air, blanketed the area.

As the clap faded away, quiet curses could be heard from the course.

"I don't see him." Marcus smiled as he craned his neck. "Though I didn't hear him splat. What d'you think?"

"It's not like it's gonna' hurt him." Frost shook her head as she tried to look through the dust. "Probably just scared the hell out of him."

As the dust and fumes settled, Fenrir became clear, hung by a leg, upside down in the net.

"Ah, there he is." Marcus chuckled as he moved for the door. "C'mon, let's go get him down."

"No." Frost stared from the viewport. "Give him a minute, see if he can get himself free."

"Very well." Marcus nodded as he slowly turned round to face her. "I was going to bring it up later... I spoke with Phoenix this morning."

"Oh?" Frost said with notable curiosity. "Did you call him or–"

"He called." Marcus answered. "Bravo and Delta have a location."

"Are we being pulled back?" Frost's voice hummed with anticipation.

"No." Marcus shook his head. "They'll be able to handle it. Should be home before we are."

"So we just keep on training?" Frost asked with a notable degree of disappointment.

"That's honestly what I came to speak with you about, Frost." Marcus looked from the window to the flailing Fenrir, still upside down. "I want your opinion. You've seen him in wolf form, what he can do. In the event we have to deploy– Could he go without my training and the final–"

"No." Frost shook her head. "Absolutely not."

"Bit of a strong response." Marcus crossed his arms as he leaned against the wall. "Unless I'm mistaken, you yourself said that he made two kills, and didn't fare too terribly in combat. He's passed Doc and Knight, and so long as he handles the SAW alright, I don't see why–"

"I also said he nearly got himself killed, Marcus." Frost countered. "Besides, then you'll see what he can do yourself."

"Alright, I'll put him through his paces." Marcus nodded. "But this will be his last full week. We may not even have that much time, if something goes–"

"I understand, Marcus." Frost hummed.

"If there's time, do you think I should throw down my own gauntlet?"

"No." Frost shook her head. "He's past fighting cardboard dummies."

"You're sure?"

"You don't understand Marcus." Frost turned to him, taking her eyes from Fenrir for the first time. "I've seen people move well with the wolf, but it took them time, even me. There's a learning curve, right hand becomes front right paw. How many cadets have you seen eat dirt because they tried to run with only their back legs? You'll see."

"Frost," Marcus shook his head, "if he moves and reacts half as well as you make it sound then there's nothing more we can do for him. We don't do combat training as wolves and aside from my gauntlet and the dummies, all we have is the basic movement routine. I really don't know what you want from me here.

"Honestly, it sounds like he lied." Marcus nearly growled as Fenrir pulled himself upright, fighting to retrieve his leg from the ropes. "He's used the wolf before."

"I don't think that's the case, Marcus. I was there when he tamed the wolf, unless he was putting on one hell of a show, but even then, Phoenix is a hard man to deceive.

"For that reason," Frost turned back to the obstacle course, "I don't think Fenrir lied, but if it wasn't for that, I'd be sure he was."

Fenrir finally freed his leg, righting himself on the net before shooting a pissy glare towards the observation deck.

"Plenty of fire in this one." Marcus chuckled.

"Mhm." Frost agreed as Fenrir's feet landed on the far side of the net, marking his completion of the obstacle course. "I'll have him run the obstacle course a few more times. Then we'll hit the range."

"He has fired a gun before, right?" Marcus asked.

"He will have after today." Frost smiled.

"Frost." He gently spoke.

"Yes, Lieutenant?" Frost caught the change in Marcus' tone.

"Keep Bravo and Delta's operation under wraps, okay. No one knows but you and I."

"Then why tell me?"

"You know why, Frost." Marcus half smiled. "I've always told you that I see you as my second, someone to lead the group should any–"

"And I've always told you, find someone else." Frost coldly replied. "I've got no interest in leading the team, Marcus.

"Back to the front!" Frost yelled from the deck as she pointed. "There's a path that runs next to the course, use it. No obstacles on it, so there's no reason not to haul ass. Go!"

* * *

1000 Hrs.

"Head to the front, hold there!" Frost's voice echoed through the trees.

I panted as I booked it back towards the starting point for the umpteenth time.

My legs burned from fighting the muck and ropes and I felt myself starting to wear down. Even though this was just my first day of going at it, I figured I would have fared a little better, I felt like I was in good shape in any case. I couldn't deny that I certainly felt the gun in my hands now, and the thousand rounds was definitely heavier. Of course I was packing an extra thirty pounds of debris, so that didn't help in the slightest.

With a sick chuckle I realized that this was the most fun I'd had in training, even though fun wasn't the purpose. I was playing in slop, eating mud, loaded like a pack mule and getting screamed at, but I was loving it.

"Would I feel like this if it wasn't Frost?"

I knew the answer to that.

No way.

I was, after all, playing in slop, eating mud, loaded like a pack mule and getting screamed at.

But, with Frost, I cherished every time her voice called my name.

As I neared the starting point, I found Frost waiting patiently.

"Run it again?" I huffed as I came to a stop.

"No, that'll be enough for today." She frowned. "Today you familiarized yourself with the course. Next four days you'll be on it plenty. We're moving on."

"So *now* I get to shoot?" I asked.

"Not like *that*, you don't." She nearly laughed as she shook her head. "You're a gun's worst nightmare right now."

As I looked down on myself, I had to admit she was right. I was a mess of mud, sand, and rope fibers.

"Y'know, this wouldn't be nearly as bad if it wasn't for your trick rope thing." I slung mud from my fingertips.

"That's one of the course's best lessons." She smiled as she turned. "C'mon."

"What lesson is that?" I allowed myself to be towed along.

"Don't always trust what you see, and always have enough steam to make it to the far side without help."

"Is that lesson for the course or a life lesson?" I asked.

"Both." She smiled as she stopped near the farm house, stooping over to pick up a water hose.

"Time to clean up." She fiendishly grinned.

"You're enjoying this aren't you?" I chuckled as I put my muddy hands to my equally muddy hips.

"You're not?" She turned the valve on the hose spigot, the only thing sparing me being the nozzle at the hose end.

"That largely depends on how warm that water is." I pointed to the water hose. "Not overly fond of cold water."

"I didn't think it'd worry you too much. We already know from your choice of sidearm that you're lacking somewhere." She replied.

"Wish you'd give–"

She hit me with the water, and I nearly locked up as I learned it was far from warm.

"Je–" My breath left me as I laughed, raising a hand to shield myself. "Frost, it's too cold!"

"Oh, don't be a baby, Finn." She failed to suppress her laugh as she made sure to drench me entirely.

It took nearly five minutes of icy hell to blast away all the filth I had acquired.

"That'll do I guess." Frost finally laid down the hose. "Ready?"

"Not really." I wrung water from my shirt.

"You'll dry." She nodded as she started for the barn. "Come on, times a'wasting."

There I stood, dripping wet, having been screamed at, pelted with insults, dirt, and whatever else came out of those blast tubes, all by *this* woman, and yet I couldn't pry my eyes from her as she walked away.

The confidence in her stride, the spark in her eyes when she teased, the smile she offered when she knew it was working. It was impossible to say which was the core cause, but every one of them, and many more simple gestures, only led me to admire her all the more.

"What is wrong with me?" I asked as I twisted another dose of water from my shirt.

Again I looked up to her, still unaware that I wasn't following.

Finally she noticed my absence, turning to fix me with something between a scowl and smile.

"Are you with me, Fenrir?"

"Don't think I have a choice in the matter anymore." I murmured as I started towards her.

"What's that mumbles?"

"Nothing." I smiled as I drew closer to her.

"Weren't talking shit were you?" She smiled.

"What? No, why would I? You've been nothing but friendly since the crack of five this morning." I chuckled.

"Now I *know* you were talking smack." She grinned as she threw a half hearted kick at my foot.

"Hey!" I stepped aside. "All bullshittery–"

"Oh, shut up." She smiled over to me, holding my eyes just long enough for me to think that her heart might have been hammering as hard as mine.

"C-hem." She quickly looked away, her face turning serious. "We're moving to the firing range now. I'll give you a quick rundown on the operations, and then we'll see what you can do. Have you used a firearm before?"

"Yeah but nothing like the 249." I shook my head.

"At least you recognize that." She nodded. "Range rules are pretty straight forward. One: Do nothing without the call from the Range Master, that's me."

"Figured that much." I nodded.

"Two: Barrel Discipline. Keep the barrel down range at all times. Three: Don't be an idiot."

"Easy enough." I replied.

After a short stop at the barn to collect the 249 and ammunition we made our way to the range.

It was little more than a flat swath of earth forty yards wide and two hundred yards long, edged with tall earthen berms. Wooden cutouts dotted the range here and there, all at different ranges, each with a fresh black and white bullseye stapled upon it.

"Home sweet home." Frost smiled as she set the 249 down on its bipod. "Alright, get down there behind it, stock to your shoulder."

No sooner had the stock met my arm than she started going over the gun, expecting me to keep pace.

It was all my hands could do to keep up as she rattled off various directions, though I managed to perform satisfactorily.

"That'll do." Frost nodded as she set an ammo box down, speaking as she worked. "That was a five point safety inspection. Now when you start firing, I'll be just left of you, acting as a belt handler. Anything goes wrong, misfire, jam, squib round, anything, just let it lay on its bipod and I'll show you how to fix it."

"Copy that." I nodded.

Frost looked down to her watch, leading me to look to my own, finding it approaching 1100.

"Break for lunch real quick?" Frost asked. "Half hour?"

I smiled, though it was for much more than a chance to eat. "Sure."

"Probably get into some dry clothes while you're at it." Frost suggested.

"Yeah," I smiled, "definitely."

"Even better."

As we started towards the house, Knight stepped from the door, right on schedule.

"Frost," Knight smiled as her eyes darted to me, "got a minute?"

"I– Yeah, I guess. What's up?"

"Where did you get that blue fishing pole?"

"Knight," Frost chuckled, "it's really not–"

Quickly as I could, I shucked my boots at the door, making hurried steps up the stairs to my room.

I was half naked by the time I made it into my room, in a hurry to drop the wet clothes and pull on a fresh set.

Belly flopping onto my bed, I scooped a palette of Summer Shimmer eye shadow and a vase of Midnight Supreme roses from the floor, right where Knight said they'd be.

"Thanks, Knight." I smiled as I peeked into the hall, finding it empty.

Knight was still keeping her busy.

Opening her door, I looked down to the nightstand on the far side of Frost's bed, conveniently out of sight from the hall.

"Perfect." I smiled, gently lowering the vase, propping the palette up against it.

"This will probably be where you find out how she feels, Fenrir." I recalled Knight's words as I closed Frost's bedroom door.

"What do you mean?" I asked as we drove back to the farm.

"She's gonna' know it's from you, goober." Knight said straight faced. "She's gonna' know that you saw her with that makeup and the flowers. The two items together are going to point straight to you."

"Yeah?" I chuckled. "And?"

"She may not respond well to this. In fact she may be pissed that you even bought these things. She also may not be happy that you went into her room to drop them off."

I had to admit that Knight was right. "I see your point."

"Once you drop them off, you're pretty well on your own." Knight said. "For better or worse."

"What if she *isn't* upset?" I asked, daring to be hopeful. "What would she do then?"

"I don't know, Fenrir." Knight smiled as she raised her brows and shook her head. "It'd be uncharted waters that I've never seen anyone tread before."

"Suddenly you are not as helpful as you were before." I nervously laughed.

"I just want you to be aware." Knight joined my laughter. "Hopefully, if it does upset her, she doesn't set you out in front of the team."

"Is that something she'd do?!" My nervousness bordered anxiety.

"I don't know, Fenrir!" Knight laughed.

"Oh my gosh." I chuckled as I looked to the ceiling, a strange high taking hold of me, the sensation of going out on a limb, praying it didn't break.

"Well," I thought as I started down the stairs, *"here's to finding out."*

Leaning against the kitchen counter, Frost looked up to me, her gaze holding me as I stepped to the landing.

"Thought I was going to have to come look for you." Frost said with an air of annoyance.

"Still got twenty-ish minutes." I nervously looked at my watch.

"Make it ten." Frost said rather bluntly. "You need to get some range time."

* * *

1130 Hrs.

"Here." Frost slung a pack of ear plugs my way as I once more nestled in behind the 249. "It's pretty loud."

"Thanks." I nodded as I tore open the package.

"Load a belt." Frost spoke as she came to lay on my left side.

With the clack of closing the cover I nodded. "Loaded."

"Now, three bursts of fire on the closest target, seventy-five yards." She said.

I racked back the bolt as I took in a breath. With the squeeze of the trigger, the gun set to drumming against my shoulder, the target shuddering while dust and chunks of earth kicked out of the back berm.

To my surprise, as the machine gun chewed through the rounds, I found I enjoyed it, more than I figured I would.

"Cease fire!" Frost screamed in my ear.

As the gun fell silent and I set it down, I turned to find her frowning. "Bursts, Rambo."

She pulled up a set of binoculars. "Well you chewed the target up decently, at least for the first half of your salvo."

"Here, let me show you." She set down her field glasses before stretching in front of me, placing her arm over mine. As her hand landed on mine and commenced short sequences of fire, I couldn't help but believe my heart was rattling faster than the 249.

"That's what I'm looking for." She withdrew. "I want the burst to be three to five seconds long. It maintains accuracy, and you have a chance to reassess your aim every three to five seconds."

"Alright then." I breathed. "Bursts."

So I carried on, a short volley, check my aim, repeat. For the most part, Frost was silent, there yet not entirely present.

I didn't mind too terribly though. Truth be told, I was having a good time just putting rounds down range.

Only once did I get carried away and let loose a lengthy sequence of fire, which Frost was quick to address.

"Do I seriously need to hold your hand on this, Fenrir?" She frowned.

"Only if you want to." I grinned.

It seemed that she hadn't expected that particular quip, though I was sure she wasn't upset as the corners of her mouth gently lifted.

"Continue firing, Fenrir." Her eyes, hovering over now rosy cheeks, slowly moved from me.

She didn't say much after that, and I worried that I may have come on a little too strong.

Coupled with the uncertainty of how my gifts would be received, the rest of the day passed almost too quickly for my liking.

"That's enough for today, Fenrir." She said as the sun began to sink below the trees.

"Already?" I forced a smile. While I was thoroughly enjoying my evening of plinking away, I was also rather anxious pending her inevitable discovery.

"Still got to clean it." Frost nodded as she led me back to the barn. "That's part of your job. Maintaining the 249. Cleaning a firearm is tedious, but when we're down range on a mission, we need to be able to trust our equipment."

I couldn't argue with that, a squad support gunner without a gun wasn't much good.

We made our way back into the armory, where Frost gestured to the table. "Set it up here, and I'll show you how to take it apart."

The bipod had barely touched the table top as she set to work on it, lifting the cover and feed tray, popping pins loose at the stock, gutting the unit and separating the pieces. The barrel, gas tube, bipod, they were all stripped away.

In what I'm certain was less than a minute, the 249 had gone from a functioning platform to a carefully laid out array of components.

"Oil and rags are on that shelf back there." Frost nodded as she wiped a bit of powder residue from her hands. "Grab one of the brushes too."

As I retrieved the supplies, I couldn't help but wonder how she, at eighteen years old, had come to be what she now was. Not even so much what had led her to The Council, but what had led her to her role in the team.

A weapons specialist?

I dwelled on this as we started wiping down the individual pieces of the 249, and I still couldn't wrap my head around it.

Phoenix spoke like this was something she had already possessed when she came to The Council. If so, what world did she come from? And if not, why choose this?

She was good at it, no doubt about that. In the time it took for me to satisfactorily clean the barrel, she had already scoured ninety percent of what remained.

"Alright." She set down the grip assembly. "Put it back together."

"Uh, about that." I rested my knuckles on the table as I looked up to her. "I may need an assist."

"Think I can help you there, Finn." She smiled before she began walking me through the intricacies.

"She's using my nickname. Might be a good sign." I struggled to hope.

It took me quite a time longer than her, but after a few minutes, and a couple pinched fingers, the 249 returned to its original state.

"Now," she smiled up at me, "we're done for the day. Think you can do it by yourself next time around?"

"We'll see, I guess." I chuckled as previous questions lingered on my mind.

"If you don't mind me asking, how did you end up doing this?"

She seemed a little taken aback with this, and before my eyes, I watched her walls raise. "As in?"

"A weapons specialist." I waved at the 249. "Just doesn't seem like something a standard eighteen year old woman knows."

"What about any of us is standard?" She scoffed.

"Well that's fair." I smiled. "You don't have to answer, I was just–"

"No, it's fine." She smiled, almost apologetically. "I just… misunderstood.

When I came to The Red Moons, I didn't know any of this stuff. I just picked up a field manual one day and started reading. On the third or fourth read through, I dissected an M4 and put it back together. It caught Phoenix's eye and next thing I knew, he and I were reading manuals together and then tinkering around with different weapons. It kind of became a hobby for the pair of us. One of us would have a shit day, and that was what we'd do. The other would inevitably show up and start helping, and before you knew it, we were talking about whatever happened that day. I think he was just impressed that I stuck with it, and after a while, he made that my role in the team, said that when I was working with weapons it seemed like I was in my element."

She paused for a moment before looking up to me. "He's a good man, Fenrir. You've dumb lucked your way into a good home."

I nodded. "It sounds like it. Good to know we've got a good guy leading us."

"Yeah." Frost warmly smiled. "He's like a dad to a lot of us, especially Knight."

"Why's that?" I asked.

Frost folded her lips as she smiled, knowing that she may have said too much. "It's not really my place to say, Fenrir."

"I understand." I nodded. "I'm sorry if it came off like I was prying. I was just curious."

"It's okay." She held her smile as she nodded. "Have to ask though, since you seemed to carefully pick your wording, were you implying that *I* am just standard?"

Heat rushed to my cheeks as I grappled for a response that wouldn't say too much.

"I– Eh– What I meant was–" I could see her amusement rising as I fumbled.

"No." I sighed as I chuckled.

"You do have a way with words, Fenrir." Frost giggled.

"Oh I'm blessed." I raised my brows as I shook my head. "You should see what happens when someone puts me on the spot."

By day's end, I was quite comfortable with the 249. I was fairly confident that had it not been for the ball of nerves in my stomach, I would've enjoyed Frost's company even more than I had.

As I laid down that night, having left the others downstairs, I patiently waited for the sound of Frost's door.

Worst case scenario, I'd know very quickly if I had upset her.

"If I did, maybe I could play it off as a thank you for her helping me with the knife?"

It felt like hours that I laid there, though my watch seemed determined to show that it had barely been forty-five minutes.

Eventually, after several heart pounding sequences that found footsteps passing by her door, I heard Frost's door open.

"Maybe I shouldn't have left them on the nightstand?" My mind raced. *"If she's with anyone other than Knight– No that wouldn't be, no one goes into her room, except her and occasionally Knight."*

I shook my head as I heard her door shut.

"Well," I flipped over to my stomach, *"she's not breaking down my door. Maybe that means she isn't–"*

A single footstep landed outside my door, clenching my throat, holding the air in my lungs as I waited for her to throw the door open.

"Shit! What do I do?!" My brain screamed as I succumbed to my anxiety.

There was no knock, no turning of the door handle, and for a moment more I held my breath.

"What is she doing?" My thoughts slowed.

No assault began, on the door or on myself, and I heard her once more return to her room.

"Is she not angry?" I might've smiled, had it not been that mere seconds before I felt like a child, terrified of the potential beast that hungered just outside my door.

My mind had breathed life to Knight's warning, and I had done little to resist it, as I had become certain Knight had been correct.

It appeared that she wasn't mad.

Either that, or she wasn't so heated that it couldn't wait until later.

"Stop that." I told myself, mildly frustrated that I had let myself be taken like this.

Knight had also said, during our time together, that it seemed like I had already made it past some of Frost's walls.

"Why didn't I dwell on that, instead of how it might turn sour?" I frowned, knowing full and well why I hadn't, because I was hesitant, fearful even, of hoping for something more between us. Even though it was first and foremost in my mind.

"Alright." I took a breath as I thought. *"Don't get ahead of yourself. I've gotta' kill the uncertainty, give her a chance to make her thoughts known."*

We'd be mostly alone all week, but I was unsure if she'd bring it up once we got to work. She was too professional to bring up personal matters during business hours.

"Coffee." I nodded. *"She likes to start her day with coffee."*

I looked to my watch, setting an alarm for 0415.

"Should give her plenty of time to address it if she chooses to."

An unpleasant image of receiving a bath of scalding hot coffee flashed into my head.

"Nah." I shook my head. *"That would be pretty unhinged. She wouldn't do that."*

I rolled to my back, staring at the ceiling.

"Would she?"

20

All About Perspective

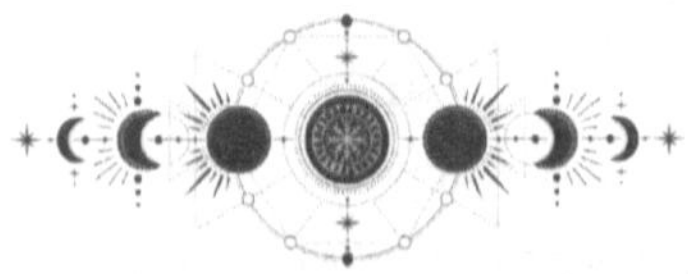

10/09
0425 Hrs.

Anxiously I waited by the huffing coffee pot, my eyes fixed on the stairs while the subtle pitter patter of coffee filling the urn dominated the quiet room.

I tallied every heartbeat that drummed in my ears, a heavy thrum that seemed to be counting down what could very well amount to be a doomsday clock. Again, my head was falling victim to itself.

With this sense of near panic, I was forced to admit that what I felt for her was well past the stage of attraction or the trivial beginnings of feelings. It was becoming clear that whatever grew in me, whatever name it was to be called, was just as equally important as me passing the training.

To me anyway.

Above my head, in the hall, footfalls landed, starting towards the stairs.

"At least I'll know soon." My eyes remained on the stairs only a moment longer as I shook my head.

"I can't just be staring at the stairs! It'll be weird!"

I spun round, quickly pulling a mug from the cupboard and setting it on the counter.

"Should I pull one down for her too?!" My mind raced as I tried not to laugh at my shaky hands.

"My Lord, I'm a mess." I further fought the urge to chuckle as I recalled something Alan frequently said when frazzled.

"I don't know what to do with my hands!"

The footsteps paused on the stairs for a moment, and I assumed she had eyed me standing by the coffee pot.

"Let her make the first move." I tried to collect myself, fighting my bound chest, each and every breath a struggle.

"Are you trying to bribe me, Fenrir?" She asked.

"That is... not what I expected?"

"I'm sorry?" I looked over my shoulder, finding her appearing somewhat amused.

"Well, it would just make perfect sense." She teasingly smiled. "The obstacle course kicking you 'round too hard?"

I smiled. *"Of course. I hadn't even thought about it like this. Of course that's how she'd take it."*

"It was more of a thank you, Frost." I whispered. "For doing what you did."

"Oh." The teasing portion of her smile faded, though the corners of her mouth remained raised, held up by something a little sweeter, daresay heartfelt.

"You didn't have to do that, Fenrir." Her eyes fell to the floor.

"No, I didn't." I smiled as her eyes slowly rose to mine. "Neither did you. Thank you."

Frost let a burst of air carry a light chuckle from her throat as she looked past me. "Is the coffee part of the thank you as well?"

"No." I shook my head, retaining my smile. "That's just something nice for you."

"Think it's all pretty nice, Finn." Her cheeks began to redden.

"Well at least I know I'm doing something right." I reached up to the cabinet, brave enough now to get her a cup.

As I filled her cup, leaving enough room for whatever creamer she may want, I smiled in relief. Finally, my heart was calm, yet the energy humming within was stronger than it had been in recent memory, without a doubt stronger than it had *ever* been.

"I guess I've got my answer." My lungs took in a deep breath, feeling as if it was the first breath I'd ever taken.

"Here." I held her cup out. "Made sure to leave room for your goodies."

"Thanks." She smiled, her fingertips resting on mine just a moment longer than necessary.

"So," she turned to the refrigerator, selecting a bottle of cream, "you saw all that when we were at the store that day? The eye shadow and the flowers?"

I nodded as I lifted my cup from the counter. "Yeah."

"You didn't say anything about it, and you didn't come down the aisle?"

"Frost..." I struggled for words, noting the recurring trend that seemed to predominantly occur in proximity to her. "I didn't want to bother you. Didn't want to impose."

"Mm." She nodded as she took a seat at the table. "How did you know about the flowers, though? I didn't even pick them up."

"I just noticed that they caught your eye." I smiled as I shrugged. "I just catch little things like that sometimes."

"And you got them, despite never having seen me with flowers and, I'm pretty sure, never having seen me wearing eye shadow." Frost said, striking me a pretty look akin to intrigue.

"Yeah, that did occur to me but, hey you know, one day you might want to go into town and look a little fancy." I laughed as I started to fumble. "I don't know, Frost, I just wanted to say thank you with a little more than just saying, well, thank you."

Her giggles at my botched attempt only served to keep my laughter going, and as she quieted down, her eyes met mine, something sincere shining within the blue pools.

"You're very welcome, Finn." She smiled. "I'm happy that you're still hanging in."

"Me too." I whispered as my chest thumped.

"So," I cleared my throat before taking a sip from my cup, "same thing today?"

"Kind of." Frost smiled down at her own cup. "I'm going to keep you on the obstacle course this morning, til about 1100, then we'll break for a quick lunch. Yesterday was just an introduction to the 249 and the trail. From this point on, until we leave, you'll start your days at the course."

"Is Marcus going to be up to meet me on the obstacle course at 0600 next week?" I asked.

"I had considered that," the humor returned to Frost's voice, "but now that I see you're going to be making coffee, well I can't pass that up."

"Just because of the coffee, right?" I cast a glance her way.

"That and the sheer entertainment of watching you fall in the mud." She grinned.

"Thanks." I chuckled. "So, what comes after me running the trail every morning?"

"For the rest of this week," Frost answered, "you and I will be on the range, firing and cleaning."

"That's it?" I asked.

"That's it." She nodded.

"I expected some kind of test." I shrugged. "Every other week has had one."

"The test is coming," Frost smiled, "make no mistake there. It's just... different."

"Different how?" I asked.

"Guess you'll just have to stick around and find out." She grinned.

"Alright." I sighed. "So what're we working on at the range?"

"Everything." She replied matter of factly.

"Anything in particular you want me to work on?" I asked.

"A few things." Frost nodded. "As you're now familiar with, the 249 takes a moment to reload, swapping boxes and feeding the belt, etcetera. In a firefight those moments can be crucial. I want you to get faster on your reloads. That said, don't foul up the system and make the reload longer than it has to be."

"Communication is key here." She continued. "When you've gotta' reload, call it out. The same for if you have a misfire or if you're displacing. This let's everyone know that you're out of the fight, however briefly it may be, so that they can put additional fire downrange until you're back online."

"Reloading, misfire, displacing." I said. "Got it."

Just as I feared, the following days with Frost blazed past.

Every one of them opened with me trudging along through the obstacle course, religiously collecting mud for Frost to blast off of me.

The time afterwards became filled with putting rounds downrange with the 249.

I continued to learn how to effectively and accurately utilize the weapon, as well as how to move with it in mock 'firefight' scenarios Frost has posted up on the range.

Metal drums became cover for me to bounce between, ensuring that I called out that I was displacing before putting rounds on this target or that pile of sandbags.

Barrel discipline was one of her most referenced concepts, and I wondered if someone in previous training had nearly shot her.

On my last trail run for Frost, after a particularly grueling jog through the mire, I had to admit that I was disappointed that Frost and I's time was coming to an end.

"Still wouldn't mind if the water was warmer though!" I fought not to caterwaul as the icy water hit me. *"It's colder than normal!"*

The frigid water broke over my shirt, and as I looked away in efforts to remain semi-dry, I wondered if this was a humorous send off of Frost's making.

I prepared to make my accusation as I began to open my eyes, and from the edge of my sight, through narrow corridors, I found Frost's eyes lingering on me, a smile tugging at her lips.

I steeled myself, the cold water suddenly unnoticed as my chest tightened under the intensity of her gaze.

I tried to keep my breaths calm, letting her eyes devour me as her teeth teased her bottom lip, flares igniting in my core.

In her fascination, the hose's aim began to fall down my chest, diving towards more sensitive regions.

I smiled as I looked at her. "Hey, easy there!"

In an act of instinct, she recoiled, caught in her pleasure, the water leaping from my belt to my face.

"Frost!" I roared through my laughter, taking in a healthy bit of water.

The hose fell away, finding the pair of us laughing, myself partially drowned.

"We need to talk about your barrel discipline." I chuckled as I shook the water from my hair.

* * *

At the end of week three, I was as close as I could get to a full-fledged squad support gunner, though it was a bitter-sweet affair.

It had been my favorite week so far, and it didn't take much thought to conclude that it was simply because I had spent it with Frost.

I was still unsure why the test had been delayed, to be taken at a later date. It didn't quite make sense not to take the test while it was all fresh in my head.

Maybe that was the point though? To see what I retained after time away from the 249?

"Well, Fenrir," Frost smiled, "that's good enough for Alpha squad. Just remember, you'll still be running the course in the mornings. You'll have the 249 clean before your training with Marcus."

"Is it really gonna' hurt that thing to miss a bath or two?" I laughed. "Can't get much worse."

"Clean-ish then." She smiled as she growled.

"Yeah alright." I said before looking to her from the corner of my eye.

"Marcus gonna' hose me down after I make my runs?"

An ember took Frost's eyes, just before she turned away. "I guess I can help you out from time to time. Just because you make coffee."

"And you enjoy drowning me with the water hose." I laughed.

"That too." She smiled.

* * *

Later that evening, after supper and customary congratulations, I realized that the end was certainly in sight, and rapidly approaching, though it still felt so far from me.

As I absentmindedly put away the final dinner plate, Frost's aforementioned test lingered on my mind, though it wasn't far from company.

Next week was the final hurdle, a week to be overseen by Marcus, who had, as of yet, failed to say much about my progress, for better or worse.

Was this his normal way? Did he normally just… exist?

My mind pushed past the impending time with Marcus, on to what waited for me on the other side.

I smiled as I pushed through the door, into the starry night, a cool breeze gently tugging at my shirt.

Pine floated on the wind. I closed my eyes as I took in a lung full of evergreen.

It smelled like home, the stands of pine, the thickets of cedar.

I opened my eyes, locking onto Rigel.

"Almost there." I smiled.

21

Final Trials

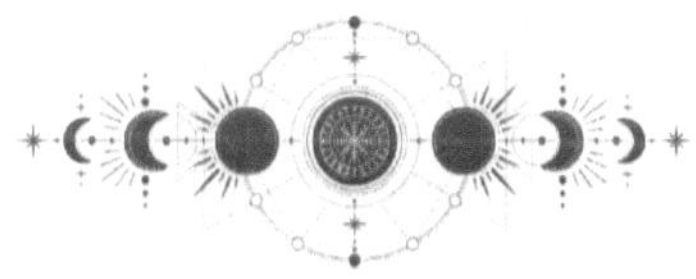

10/14
0800 Hrs.

With no lack of apprehension I stood before the final member of Alpha team.

Marcus had remained unchanged since I had first met him, unchanged as in unpredictable.

In one instant he was calm, and in the next he was quick to snap, without any measure of explanation.

I hadn't yet mustered the nerve to ask the others about this. I was, obviously, new to things. Perhaps Marcus was simply establishing the pecking order.

In that regard however it made little sense to be so inconsistent in temperament when he knew I at least understood he was the squad leader.

"Look tired, pup." He said.

"I'm good." I shook myself in the morning sun.

"Good." Marcus softly grumbled. "This portion of your training focuses on the wolf. Simply the basics; movements, reactions, attacks and withdrawals. Pass my courses, listen to my words, and you will be an Alpha operator."

I nodded, waiting to receive further instruction. If the opening days with Frost were any sign of things to come, I wasn't wiggling a toe without Marcus giving the all clear.

"Before we start," Marcus sniffed, "there are a few things to discuss."

"Okay." I nodded.

"Frost and I have spoken a bit about you and your wolf. At current, she's the only one who has seen you use the wolf. She said that when you encountered the vampires at your family farm, you didn't hesitate to shift, and upon completing the transformation you began engagement."

"That's accurate." I replied.

"So you're familiar with moving as the wolf then?" Marcus asked.

"I… guess. I mean, isn't everyone?"

"Not at your stage, Fenrir. If you move as Frost claims you do, well, in that case you've saved me quite a bit of work."

"Move as Frost claims I do?" I repeated him. "I don't understand Marcus, I just move. Is that normally an issue?"

"Yes." Marcus bluntly answered. "It normally takes the better part of a day just for cadets to figure out how to walk properly."

"I can manage that." I smiled.

"I'd be inclined to believe so, otherwise you'd be dead. Do as I ask anyway." Marcus nodded.

"So, do we spar as wolves now?" I asked.

Marcus shook his head. "Do you remember what Knight said when you asked her about training with real knives? How the margin for error was too slim? Imagine a pair of thousand-pound wolves going at it tooth and claw. We never engage one another as wolves, someone would die."

I nodded, picturing the unfortunate outcome of such training.

"Scarecrow will be your opponent." Marcus said. "You won't be landing attacks, this is simply for me to gauge your abilities with the wolf. How you move. I need to know if you actually possess the skills Frost claims you to, or if you were just extremely lucky."

"I understand."

"Good. Let's go."

* * *

0830 Hrs.

Once again, I squared up to Scarecrow, though now it seemed terribly unfair.

A straw man pitted against a giant wolf.

Marcus and I had walked to Knight's training area as men, and upon reaching it, Marcus instructed me to stand in front of Scarecrow and turn. Once I had done that, I was to await further instruction.

And so, there I was, waiting, not taking a step, barely taking a breath it seemed.

"Alright, Fenrir," Marcus spoke from behind me, "this should be an easy one. Turn around to face me."

"What is this?" I thought as I spun round in place, finding more than just Marcus standing behind me.

The entire squad was present, much like they had been when I had taken the final with Knight.

Marcus nodded, and much as he tried to hide it, I caught the faintest bit of surprise in his eyes.

"Good." Marcus said. "Now walk to me, slowly. If you fall on me, I'll kick your ass."

Once more I complied, cautiously approaching Marcus.

When I came to stop before him, he nodded again.

He smiled ever so slightly. "Alright, when you turn back to Scarecrow, charge him. Lunge to his right, jump away, then lunge to his left. Jump back once more before circling round behind him. I'll repeat this as you do it. Go!"

I wheeled around on my hind legs, and charged towards the helpless bag of straw.

259

"Lunge right!" Marcus yelled.

"The 'to do' list wasn't that long!" My thoughts roared as I moved through the motions, deaf to Marcus's commands.

I lunged right and quickly leapt back before lunging to Scarecrow's left and retreating once more.

"Circle round!"

"I know!" I laughed.

In a quick dash I passed by Scarecrow before sinking my front claws into the earth, whipping my hindquarters around, effectively flanking my opponent.

"That's enough." Marcus waved me over. "Your flanking maneuver was a bit flashy don't you think?"

With a short huff I offered my reply.

I was glad to see Marcus found the humor in my response as he chuckled. "Seems Frost was honest. You move just fine. My gauntlet would be a waste of time for you."

He looked to his watch and looked back to the squad. "Can I call it? Or should I have him do some more?"

"See if he knows 'Roll Over' or not?" Knight snickered.

"Rather impolite of you, Knight." Doc smiled as he shook his head.

Marcus looked back to me. "Well, that's that. Go get some clothes on, and I'll meet you back at the farm house."

∗ ∗ ∗

1000 Hrs.

"Well, Fenrir." Marcus alone stood before me in the farmhouse. "I'm pleased to say that you've made it past every operator Alpha squad has to offer. Though you muddled the line on Knight a bit. Had us all a bit concerned."

"I know." I nodded. "Just had to wrap my mind around a few things."

"We're all glad you did, especially Knight. She would've been devastated had you failed."

"Nobody has ever failed with her before?" I asked.

"Not one she's taken a liking to." Marcus explained. "She warmed up to you rather quickly, which she normally does, but when they begin to falter with her, she doesn't normally take it so hard. Typically, she sees it as they are failing her. This time, you could see in her eyes that she felt she had failed you. But no matter, you passed and saved us having to put her back together."

"So that's it?" I asked. "I'm an Alpha operator now?"

"Not yet, Fenrir." Marcus said, "Tomorrow? Perhaps. There is one piece of training, one of the most important, that I am about to give you. The wolf is your greatest weapon, but it is also your greatest weakness."

"What do you mean?" I struggled to grasp the seemingly contradictory concept.

"As a wolf, you have the brute strength and raw speed that allows us to do what we do, but with it comes an enormous risk. Not only of discovery, but an extreme personal risk to *you*. The wolves are huge, Fenrir, this you know, and as such, make very easy targets. Very rarely do we utilize the wolf because of that risk. It's much harder to hit a human sized target behind cover than it is to hit a wolf charging you head on. Firearms are our primary tool of engagement, the wolf is our last hope. Do you understand?" Marcus asked.

I nodded, having never thought of that, though it was alarmingly obvious.

"Take the rest of the day off, Fenrir. You've earned it."

I should've known that there was a catch.

* * *

10/15

The next morning, the same as I had for days now, I awoke at 0415.

"The last day." I smiled to myself as I pulled on my clothes.

"Wonder what Marcus has cooked up for me today?" I pulled my vest from the bedpost as I headed for the door.

The hall was quiet, as it normally was at that time of morning, and I started once more towards the stairs, en route to make Frost's morning pot of coffee.

As I descended the stairs, I was surprised to find Doc seated at the kitchen table, a black duffel bag upon it.

"Trouble sleeping this morning?" I politely asked. "Give me a few minutes and I'll have a pot of coffee–"

"Do not bother this morning." Doc said as my hand landed on the pot.

I smiled. "Well, not to be rude, but I normally put on a pot before my morning–"

"You are not running this morning." Doc said as he looked at the bag.

"Oh?" I took my hand from the pot. "Why is that?"

"Open the bag, Fenrir." Doc replied.

Wordlessly I stepped to the table, opening the bag to find an array of equipment, some of which I hadn't yet used.

"What is all this?" I started laying the contents on the table.

A radio and its holster. A long wire with a small button on it beneath two ear pieces, connected to a looped strap with two small discs on it. Dummy knives, three belt boxes of the blue tipped ammunition, as well as two magazines for the 1911. Safety glasses, and a black ball cap.

"This is what you need for your final, Fenrir." Doc shortly replied.

"This is what Marcus meant with his 'tomorrow' comment." I sighed as I looked down at the equipment.

"Get yourself sorted." Doc sniffed. "Then we will link up with the others."

Most of the equipment was self explanatory. The knives were to replace their steel counterparts, the radio and its holster fit comfortably just forward of being directly beneath my left arm, the strap however was an oddity.

"What exactly is this thing?" I asked as I lifted the contraption.

"A laryngophone." Doc answered as if I'd know what that was.

"A what?" I said.

"It is a mic band that fits on your throat." Doc smiled as he gestured to his neck, the rig already in place. "It is wired into the radio cable and your ear pieces. When you wish to speak, press the push to talk button, and the transponders, the discs, will pick up the vibrations of your throat."

"Push the button. Got it." I fumbled with the strap, attempting to get it situated on my throat.

"I find the push to talk button is best placed near the center of your chest." Doc advised.

As I fixed the small black pod to the left side of the vests zipper, I looked up to Doc. "How do I look?"

There was a trace of regret in Doc's eyes as he nodded, managing a gentle smile.

"You look–" He let out a subtle sigh. "You look like an Alpha operator."

"Isn't that a good thing?" I smiled, curious with his demeanor.

"It is." He quietly answered, leaving unspoken whatever was on his mind. "Come on, we should collect our weapons."

Stepping out, I found the gun rack next to the front door was no longer empty, now home to two firearms, one of them a 249.

The second weapon, the longer of the pair, was something of a peculiarity, out of place with its wooden furniture next to its largely composite sibling.

There was nothing fancy about it, appearing rather dated as a matter of fact. A wooden stock that transitioned into a wooden forearm, broken only by the magazine well.

Atop the rifle, the only modern touch on the unit, was a small red dot scope, maybe three or four times magnification.

Looking upon the rack, a cold knot wrapped my heart, and as I put a hand to my chest, I felt the rapid drum of fear.

"What am I scared of?" I swallowed uneasiness. *"The test?"*

"No." I shook my head. *"It's what hangs on the test, and what's on the other side of it."*

I wrung my hands as I looked to the 249, still waiting in the rack.

I knew how to use it, the functions and handling. As far as operations went, I knew what I was doing, courtesy of Frost's thoroughness.

In terms of practical use however, I was far from experienced, and to hear the term "Final", as in final exam, well it didn't seem that mistakes would be encouraged.

"Surely they don't expect me to ace this right out of the gate?" I thought. *"How can they? I've never–"*

"Are you alright, Fenrir?" Doc asked as his eyes fell upon me.

"Mhm." I nodded. "Why do you ask?"

"If you strangle your hands much more, I fear you may cut off circulation." Doc chuckled.

I looked down to my sweaty hands before wiping the moisture away on my pants. "Just a bit nervous I guess. I don't want everyone to expect me to be good at this right away, and I don't want to let anyone down."

"You would only disappoint us if you gave up, Fenrir, and that said, I do not foresee us being disappointed. You have overcome too much to start quitting now."

"Thanks, Doc." I smiled.

"No thanks needed." Doc picked up his ancient rifle, giving it a once over. "Just stating what is evident."

"Not to change the subject, but why is it that you use something that looks like it came out of the Great War?"

"The M14?" Doc smiled. "It is not *that* dated, Fenrir. Granted it did enter service during the Korean conflict, and saw use in Vietnam, but to say–"

"You know what I meant." I laughed.

"I know." Doc seemed to travel away as he looked at his reflection on the action of the rifle. "Just felt right when I first picked it up. Wood and steel. It is simple, yet lethal."

"That's all it needs to be I guess." I couldn't help but notice Doc's state. "Are *you*–"

"Doc, Fenrir, you have a copy?" Marcus' voice called through the earpieces.

I tapped the button on my chest. "Go ahead, Marcus."

"Fenrir." Marcus' voice crackled. "Here's the sitrep. Another squad was dispatched to rendezvous with us before we make the final push on a fortified position. We have reached the RV, but the incoming squad has sustained damage en route. The support team is taking accurate fire and we don't have a medic. We need you two here stat."

"Copy that." I replied. "Where are you?"

"Not sure." Marcus replied as gunfire rattled, echoing to the house. "You've got ten minutes."

The radio fell silent.

"Well, okay." I looked to Doc. "You catch all that?"

"Every word." Doc nodded. "You take point, support gunner."

I nodded, starting in the direction of the rifle reports.

The wind blew into our faces, carrying with it the unmistakable smack of gunpowder, drifting out of the forest.

"Got a heading." I nodded as I picked up the pace, well aware of how quickly ten minutes could run out.

As we broke the tree line, Doc called out to me.

"We are well ahead of our deadline, Fenrir. We are moving towards a firefight, we should proceed with care."

"Right." I slowed my steps as I hunkered lower to the earth.

"When you move, stay low, make yourself a harder target." I heard Frost's words, spoken as I had moved between cover on the range.

"Keep your eyes and barrel up, in case you need to put rounds out."

Two hundred yards deeper into the trees, I found us creeping up on an assortment of trash. Old barrels, tires, and culvert pipes lay scattered amongst two rows of rough plywood houses, all featuring doors and windows, yet lacking roofs.

I came to a stop fifty yards shy of the debris and buildings, crouching among the undergrowth, taking a moment to survey the area and try to find the squad.

Between the two rows of houses was a single vehicle, a battered old red pick up, which looked to have been on the makeshift street for a while.

Dry rotted tires, reduced to ribbons, loosely clung to the rims, and the metal of the truck seemed to be more rust than anything.

"Marcus," I whispered as I hit the button, "we're here. Where are you guys?"

"Across the street." Marcus' answer came over the radio. "Think you're clear to move to the vehicle. We've pushed back the opposition force, get Doc up there to tend the wounded. I counted one survivor in the bed of the truck."

"Copy." I nodded to Doc. "Ready?"

"Awaiting your word." Doc pulled the stock of his rifle to his shoulder.

I nodded as I eyed a short length of sizable concrete culvert, standing near chest height, that offered cover from the rest of the street.

An end of the culvert was butted up to the corner of the nearest house, providing defilade from further down the street.

Set up there, call him forward. I thought as my feet carried me to the pipe.

Resting the 249 on the culvert, I found the street deserted. It was dotted only by the occasional impact crater, and doused in splotches of paint from past firefights.

I slowly waved my left hand, calling Doc forward as I scanned every window, every doorway for potential threats.

Doc's body thumped against the culvert as he joined me.

"Any sign of the squad?" He asked.

I shook my head, keeping the 249 sucked into my shoulder.

"Get the man in the truck, and get back here to me." I whispered.

If he stayed at the truck and we started taking fire, there wasn't a whole lot I could do for him aside from suppressing fire. If he returned, we could make a dip back into the vegetation, or flip into the building.

By my math, and extremely lacking combat experience, more options were better than less.

"Go." I nodded.

He pushed off the pipe, covering the distance to the truck in short order.

The street, its houses and the surrounding foliage all remained silent as Doc slung his rifle on his shoulder.

From the corner of my eye I watched as he reached into the back of the truck, roughly pulling a still form up over his shoulders.

I was surprised to find it wasn't one of ours, rather a full body mannequin, painted bloody across its chest. Across its forehead, someone had taken the time to write, "BOB" in bold red letters.

Doc had barely turned from the vehicle as an explosion ripped the street behind the tailgate, forcing him down as the truck began taking fire from a nearby window.

"Well biscuits." My heart pumped as adrenaline dropped into my veins.

"Stay there!" I yelled as I spun the 249, finding a broad shouldered silhouette firing at the truck from a house across the street.

A quick burst from the 249 pushed the shooter back into cover as the culvert began taking hits from a neighboring house.

"Doc, you good?" I yelled as I turned the 249 to fire.

"I am. Can I make it?" Doc called. "I cannot treat his wounds here!"

"How am I supposed to make that call?" My brain scrambled. *"I don't know how many are out there, or where the rest of our squad is."*

"I'll do what I can, Doc!" I hollered back, the 249 rattling against my shoulder as my heart pounded in my ears.

"Moving in five!"

Two more shadows skirted past the windows of the second house across the street.

"Doc, wait!" I cried. "Two more–"

It was too late, Doc had already broken from the truck.

Two rifles swung from the building, one from a window, the other at the door.

"I can't hit them both at the same time!" I pulled the trigger, sending paint streaking across the building, starting at the window and working towards the door, though not quickly enough.

I saw the muzzle flashes moments before I heard the sickening smack of impact on flesh.

With a clatter the mannequin slid next to me, its shoulders just past the culvert as the incoming fire intensified.

All three shooters now stood in full view, though there was nothing I could do as I dropped behind the culvert that was taking an absolute pelting.

Reaching over, I took BOB by the shoulders and wrenched him behind the culvert, moments before the leaf litter where he laid began kicking up with neon paint.

"Doc!" I peered around the culvert, finding him laying only a few feet away, still wide out in the open. On his shoulder and calf, two bright green splotches of paint mottled his clothes.

"I'm hit!" He yelled.

"I got you!" I yelled as I leaned from around the pipe, taking hold of his pack and dragging him behind the culvert.

Doc's feet had just cleared the pipe when another explosion let loose, much closer than the first. A streak of metal blew past the end of the culvert, mere inches from Doc's legs, and as it landed in a cloud of earth and dust I realized it was the truck door.

My wide eyes hung on the mangled door. *"They blew up the truck?!"*

"Fenrir!" Doc cried. "It's silver!"

"Anver, now!" My head screamed as more explosions sent earth over us.

"He's got three minutes, I've probably burned most of that!" I fished a mock canister of Anver from Doc's pack and quickly pressed it to his thigh.

"Anver's in!" I yelled as I peeked over the culvert, finding the three shooters still where I'd last seen them.

"The bone is sticking out of my calf, Fenrir!"

"Traction." I dropped back to Doc's pack, pulling the rig and setting it up on him as a bit more dirt peppered us.

"Wound is still bleeding pretty bad, Fenrir!" Doc panted.

"Tourniquet."

I reached into the pack for the tourniquet, where it should've been.

I couldn't find it.

"Everything has a spot in this pack!" I rummaged through the pack, fighting back a round of panic. *"Where is it!"*

"Fenrir!" Doc yelled.

"Hold still!" I yelled as my hands took his belt buckle, ripping his belt from his waist before hurriedly wrapping it around his leg.

"I'm good!" Doc nodded, satisfied with the round of care.

I turned back to the 249, bolting up over the culvert and laying a field of fire across the buildings, forcing the shooters back into cover.

"Where is our squad supposed to be?" I shouted to Doc.

"I'm going to have to reload eventually." I tried to wrap my head around this test. *"What's the goal? What am I supposed to do with a busted medic and a dummy?"*

I spun the barrel to another shooter as they stepped into a doorway, sending a quick salvo their way. It was cut short though, as an unfamiliar clack vibrated the 249.

I swore under my breath as I observed the belt still had plenty of ammunition to feed. "Misfire!"

I dropped behind the pipe, attempting to free the jam.

"Fenrir, we have to move!" Doc nodded to an open window.

"Go!" I replied only a moment before my ears picked up on rapidly approaching footsteps.

"Go now!" I yelled, looking up in time to see Knight clear the end of the culvert.

"They heard my callout!" My mind deafened me as Knight rushed me, knife in hand.

The 249 caught itself on the sling as I fell backwards, my hand flying to the 1911, not completely clearing the holster before the barrel spoke death. Sort of.

A bright blue spot of paint appeared on her chest as she crumpled into the leaves.

"Fenrir, help!" Doc's voice rang through the window.

"You've got a gun!" I raised the 1911 as I moved to the window, vaulting through the opening only for a boot to blast the pistol from my hand, pinching the hell out of my thumb in the process.

As the pistol tumbled to the earthen floor I turned to face Frost, finding her in mid swing, knife held in the movie famous ice pick grip.

"It's already too close to counter, if I catch her arm, the tip's still gonna' be in my shoulder!"

For a split second, time froze, I froze, knowing that I couldn't halt this attack as my brain screamed for me to do something, anything.

The wolf roared from his void, blasting into my hands as he batted the knife to the side, redirecting rather than stopping.

He wasn't through though, not yet. He put my shoulder to Frost's groin, wrapping my arm around the back of her knees and barreling her over.

"Wolf, easy!" I barked as I rolled away from her, drawing my own knife. *"I've got this. Let go!"*

He was reluctant to obey, drawing back, but just barely, remaining present.

As Frost righted herself, nothing but rage glistened in her eyes.

"Dammit!" I frowned.

As if back in the sparring ring, Frost started to spiral, and had it not been for the wolf, I would've done the same.

He seized my legs, delving straight in as Frost let out with a jab that skated under my left arm.

My arm clamped down on hers, helplessly trapping it as I pushed my blade to her chest while hooking her legs with mine, sending her over backwards once more.

"Wolf, stop!" I roared. *"You're going to hurt her!"*

I couldn't let that happen.

As she fell, the wolf retreated, allowing me to wrap my arm around her, catching her as midriff as we fell together.

My shoulder took the brunt of the fall, and despite feeling her eyes locked onto me, I did everything in my power not to look at her.

"Really hope that doesn't come back to bite me." I thought as I pulled myself clear, bringing the 249 back to my hands.

With a rack of the action, the 249 spat out the fouled casing.

"Doc!" I shouted as I raised the 249 to the front of the house, towards two windows and an open doorframe. "We can't stay here, we're too open!"

"I have to stabilize BOB!" Doc answered as Frost picked herself up, shooting me a look before slipping from the doorway. "He will die if we try to move again."

"Copy that!" I frowned as Marcus leaned out of his window across the street, being quickly greeted by a burst from the 249.

As I rested the 249 on a window sill a loud pop echoed down the street, followed by a cloud of thick gray smoke.

"Fenrir." Frost's voice came over the ear piece. "You need to lay down suppressive fire until Doc has stabilized the survivor and your squad arrives. Do not let them flank. Your squad will be up there shortly."

"Great." I sighed as I resumed firing.

A near hit exploded on the sill next to my hand, showering me with crimson paint.

A target emerged from cover and in a stroke of luck I scored a hit on their leg.

I was surprised when they didn't fall, rather they started walking my way. I found it to be Knight, her submachine gun raised over her head, quickly moving our way.

Darting through the doorway, she joined me in returning fire. "Doing good, Fenrir!" She smiled as she began firing at her had-been allies.

"This is how my squad arrives." I nodded.

"Kind of a cheap one you pulled on me earlier." Knight commented as she pulled a series of shots.

"Well," I tilted my head in a short lull of firing, "you did bring a knife to a gunfight."

Next, I hit Marcus, a square shot to the stomach, and he too started making his way to us.

"One left."

Frost.

"BOB can move!" Doc called from the back of the room. "We need to go!"

"Where to?!" I yelled.

"Back to the tree line!" Marcus looked from the side window Doc and I had entered through. "It's done when we exfil!"

"Almost there!" I smiled.

"Let me get set outside." I nodded to Marcus. "I'll cover your retreat!"

"Go!"

I returned to the culvert, sending rounds Frost's way, finding a single opponent much more manageable. She was spending most of her time in cover, only occasionally poking out.

"Fenrir, we're all out." Knight yelled.

"Copy that!" I replied over the gunfire. "I'll keep you covered to the tree li–"

The 249 fell silent, the bolt finding nothing more to send to the chamber.

I looked down to find the ammo box emptied.

"Reloading!" I cried, expecting the squad to pick up covering fire, though I found none.

I looked back to them, finding them all stationary behind me as the ground began to rumble.

"Now what!" I looked over the pipe, finding that Frost had changed into the wolf, a white beast rapidly charging my position.

"Shit!" I fumbled with the replacement box.

"No good, not enough time to reload!"

I looked up to find her nearly on top of me.

"Pistol's still in the house! Knives are useless! I have to shift!" I let down the 249.

"Alright wolf!" I called to him as Marcus' words rang in my ears, pushed forward by the wolf.

"We never engage one another as wolves, someone would die."

The wolf had received the true lesson.

Frost's front legs locked, screaming to a stop only inches away, close enough that I could feel her breath on my face, see the blue crystals in her eyes.

"Fenrir!" Marcus yelled, returning to his typical self, following the previous day's uncharacteristic attitude. "You just got yourself killed! Why didn't you turn?!"

I turned to him with a smile. "Someone would die, Lieutenant."

I knew that this was the right thing to say as his smile matched my own.

Knight socked my arm. "Knife to a gun fight?! You could've at least got me with a thrower!"

"What can I say?" I snickered. "Hand went down instead of up."

Marcus chuckled as he nodded Frost away, sending her back to her building.

"Good job on the suppressive fire," Marcus said as he turned to me, "and on your callouts."

"Speaking of." I raised a finger as I stepped back into Doc and I's house, retrieving my foul round from the floor.

As I rejoined the others, Frost having returned while I was inside, I confirmed what my eyes had told me when the round was cleared.

The primer was missing from the casing.

"Did you do this?" I looked to Frost.

"Of course." She smiled, the burning fire I had witnessed now gone from her eyes.

"How did you know I would use this particular box of ammunition?" I chuckled.

"Oh, it didn't matter which you chose." She grinned. "Every hundredth round in all three boxes was junk."

"Ah." I tossed the round aside. "Well, that makes sense."

"Most importantly, one of the key concerns of this test," Marcus said, calling my attention back, "we know that you would sooner take injury than hurt one of us."

The four of them incorporated me into a circle, and as Marcus looked around the others, he received a nod from each.

"Fenrir," he half smiled, "welcome to the Red Moons, Alpha squad."

"So now that the boring part's over," Knight suddenly erupted, "let's have some fun."

"Past few minutes have been pretty exciting for me, Knight." I said, earning an all-around chuckle from the squad.

From my squad.

22

Closing Words

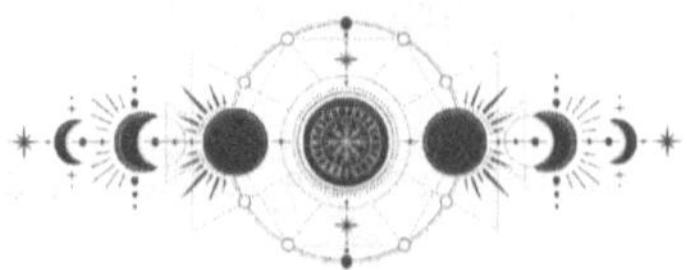

That evening, we found ourselves at the lake behind the farmhouse.

I took a seat on the beach as the others, even the turtle skittish Doc, took to the water, and I couldn't help but notice that he was the only one wearing a shirt, still clad in long sleeves.

As they splashed around, finally unwinding from training, I once more observed the tattoo I'd seen my first day with The Red Moons.

On the left arm of every operator laid the blue shield, the shape of a medieval knight's, over laid by a black paw print, behind which a pair of black swords were crossed.

Of course, I couldn't see Doc's arm, but it only stood to reason that his arm bore the ink as well.

I briefly wondered if this was the squads insignia. Having seen the standard in Phoenix's office though, I was inclined to believe that it was the emblem of The Wolven Council.

My eyes drifted from the tattoos, back to the squad as a whole, still enjoying themselves in the lake.

The water looked nice enough, and inviting as it was, I was honestly enjoying the first bit of time I had to myself that I didn't want to use sleeping.

More than anything, I was just enjoying sitting on the sand.

I was enjoying thinking about the farm.

My absence in the water was noticed however, and it was Frost, water dripping from a vibrant blue two-piece, that approached me.

I fixed my eyes on the sky as she moved closer, fearing that if I looked, I'd stare.

It was the most skin I'd seen of her, and the top of the bikini seemed to be struggling to hold her in.

She stood next to me, following my gaze to the sun, unaware that my pulse had quickened.

"You alright, Fenrir?" She asked.

I nodded. "Just reminds me of evenings on the farm, *my* farm."

Frost was quiet for a moment, searching for a response.

"You know why you can't go back right?" She asked, almost tenderly. "Why you can't contact them?"

"I do." I said, noting the plethora of reasons. "By this time, they believe I'm dead, and it's not safe. For them or for me. They can't know what I am."

"None can."

"Alan does, and he knows for certain I'm still among the living." I said. "What's the protocol on that, Frost?"

Again, Frost was silent.

"Frost?" I said.

"Only you and I are aware of Alan's knowledge, Finn." She said as she turned away, hiding her face, but not before I saw shame bite at her.

"What could she be ashamed of? Of Alan's knowledge, or of keeping it secret?"

Knight and Frost exchanged words at the water's edge before Knight started my way.

She as well wore a two-piece, black, though a bit more conservative than Frosts.

Whereas Frost had stood next to me, Knight sat.

"Thought your head was gonna' pop when she walked up to you just now." Knight giggled.

I chuckled. "Was it that obvious?"

"If you pay attention, which I do." Knight elbowed me as she smiled. "Seems that she didn't mind the presents."

"No." I smiled. "No she didn't."

Knight's eyes widened as she grinned. "Well c'mon, make with the details."

"Nothing happened." I laughed. "Really. She thought it was a bribe. I told her it was more of a thank you. I did manage to get a blush out of her though, of course I don't know if that's anything special. She's done that a few times."

"I'd definitely say it's something special, Fenrir." Knight looked to the water, to Frost, drawing my eyes along, though I tried not to stare.

"What makes you say that?" I asked.

"She doesn't blush, Fenrir." Knight giggled at my ignorance. "Not usually. She doesn't show much emotion. For some reason though, she does with you."

"Hm." I shortly hummed. "I'd like to believe that it's something between us, but I'm–"

"Not that brazen?" Knight raised a brow. "Yeah, I've heard you say that once or twice now. Thing is, when it's a recurring thing, I don't think it's brazen, Finn."

"She told you?!" I jerked to look at Knight.

"She did." Knight giggled again. "I told you, we're like sisters, Fenrir. It appears that you're growing pretty dear to her, and your *catch* today didn't hurt."

"Yup. Knew it'd come back to haunt me." I shook my head.

"It was hardly a catch." I chuckled. "She still fell. I just landed harder than her."

"Well, she appreciated it. Said you broke out some new moves on her too." Knight leaned over, brows raised. "Been studying with Scarecrow again?"

"Not gonna' let that go are you?" I scratched the tip of my nose.

"Well it came from somewhere." Knight quieted herself. "She was fairly confident that it wasn't something she taught you."

"All that talk about keeping it hush-hush." I shook my head as I smiled. "She really does tell you everything."

"Mhm." Knight smiled. "She, and Edge, are the closest thing to sisters I have here, and I couldn't love them any more if they really were."

"Well I don't know about Edge, but *she,*" I nodded towards Frost, "is pretty great."

"Mhm." Knight gently shouldered me. "Think you ruffled her feathers a bit with my exam though, throwing your first round."

"If I did," I smiled, "she never really let on. Unless that was what the shenanigans on the obstacle course were all about. In any case, if she was sore with me, she got me back the week after, and every morning since."

"Doesn't seem to have disagreed with you though." Knight looked at my arms, then my stomach. "Not hittin' on you or anything, but I don't recall that six pack being quiet so… *defined,* shall we say?"

I chuckled at her observation. "Yeah, I noticed that too."

"So did Frost." Knight rattled, humor and humility both gripping at me as I recalled that most eventful shower with the water hose.

"Yes, yes she did."

"Maybe when we get back, you guys could go into Davenport? You don't have to call it a date." Knight ribbed.

With a grin I shook my head, and my eyes returned to Frost, and my eyes hung on her arm, on the tattoo, how the blue stood in gentle contrast to her skin.

"What do the tattoos mean, Knight?" I asked as I turned to her, nodding to the ink on her own arm.

Knight's face sombered at my words, at the question loaded with unknown weight.

"It's the mark of The Wolven Council." Knight replied. "It signifies what we belong to, what we are, and who we are."

"We belong to The Wolven Council, we are wolves, but... who we are? Aren't we simply Council?"

"What do you mean, 'who we are'?"

"We of The Wolven Council are the fine line that keeps humans safe." Knight looked up as she recited the lines. "The swords that vanquish their enemies, the shields that guard them."

"Is that something you had to memorize?" I asked.

"It used to be." Knight giggled as she looked to the water. "Isn't that the cheesiest thing you've ever heard?"

"It's pretty bad." I laughed.

"But it's ours." Knight sighed. "Just don't have to memorize it anymore."

"I suppose it could've been worse." I nodded as I looked back to the water. "Don't know how, but–"

"Uh-oh." Knight cut me off, drawing my attention.

I found the smile had returned to her face and following her pointed finger, I saw why.

Marcus, mischievous grin and all, carefully waded behind Doc, caught unawares in mid-conversation with Frost.

"Turtle!" Marcus yelled as he goosed Doc with his foot.

"Aaiiee!" Doc caterwauled as he began high stepping towards the beach.

Only when Doc reached the sand did he take notice of everyone's uncontrollable laughter.

In good nature Doc too began to laugh. He pointed to Marcus as he walked back into the water. "For this sir, you must die."

With the most speed I'd ever witnessed Doc exhibit, he lunged onto Marcus, pushing him below the waves.

Again, we all laughed.

Marcus reappeared, still rolling with laughter until he saw me sitting on the beach, bone dry.

"Pup!" He pointed to me, then to the water. "Get in."

Knight leaned over to me. "I'd do it. If he has to come and get you it's not gonna' be pretty."

"I can beat him." I whispered.

Knight chuckled. "Not a chance. He's strong as an ox."

"Frost beat him." I said, remembering Marcus and her sparring.

"Because Marcus pulls punches. He'll never hit you with all he's got. He loves his team too much to hurt us."

"Nah." I said as Marcus emerged from the water.

"Better get going." Knight sang.

"Seriously?" I asked as Marcus suddenly sprinted towards me.

"Aw crap!" I sprang from the sand, running onto the short dock. "I'm going, I'm going!"

Marcus turned on a dime in pursuit.

I turned to face him and was forcefully, though somehow still gently, tackled off the dock into the lake.

Marcus turned loose of me once I was thoroughly in the water and as I surfaced, I fixed him with a flat look. "Alright, I'm in the water, and now I'm getting out."

As I pulled myself from the waves, I found Frost had joined Knight, both smiling at me as Knight shook her head.

"I told you." She raised her brows.

"Yes, yes you did." I shook the water from my hair.

"Hey, hey!" Knight protested. "We know you're a wolf, but don't be a shit about it!"

"Knight," I did my best to sound offended, "that's very hurtful."

"Can't blame her for telling the truth." Frost shot me a chiding smile.

"I was perfectly content just sitting in the sand until Mar–"

"Ah, something's got me!" A scream erupted from the water.

Expecting Doc to be flying out of the surf, I was surprised to find Marcus now fleeing, favoring his right butt cheek as something trailed just beneath his wake.

"Oh, dang." I chuckled. "Think he found Doc's turtle."

As Marcus' feet hit the sand, a blue fishing pole leapt out of the waves, tethered to him via a hook in his posterior.

"What the heck man?!" Marcus spouted as he stopped. "A little help here!"

"Not it." I ducked my head, doing a terrible job at suppressing my snickers.

"Hey, that's my pole!" Frost's jaw dropped.

"See," Knight shrugged with a smile, "like I said. If it's meant to be, it'll come back."

Realizing he'd get no aid from any of us, Marcus frantically looked to Doc.

"Medic!"

* * *

An hour later found Marcus manning a grill while the rest of us sat around a nearby fire ring.

The enticing aroma of searing meat wafted through the air, competing with the pleasant smell of the small fire.

"Whatcha' cookin'?" Knight asked as she craned her neck towards the grill.

"Well, we've got bratwurst, hamburgers, and a few steaks. Got some veggie burgers too."

"Really?" Doc almost seemed interested in the last item.

"Pfft. No." Marcus chuckled as he reached into a cooler, pulling out a glass bottle.

"Gonna' put that on your butt?" Knight giggled.

"Upper thigh." Marcus smiled as he twisted off the cap, taking a swig before looking to us. "Beer's cold!"

Knight wasted no time in moving to the cooler. "Anybody else?" She asked.

"Everybody drinks at least one." Marcus said. "Not every day a cadet becomes an operator."

Knight returned and distributed the drinks.

As I took the icy bottle, I looked to the grill and the beer, then to Doc.

"Is this heart healthy?" I asked.

"Everybody needs to cut loose from time to time. Strictly Medicinal." Doc said as he tipped back his bottle.

"To Fenrir!" Knight somewhat raised her bottle in a small toast. "Who completed the training faster than any of us."

Everyone raised their bottles, even Frost.

After taking a sip I looked to Knight. "Pardon?"

"It's true." Marcus said from the grill. "With Bravo and Delta in the field, we were all that was left as far as a response team, and we were a support gunner short. It all worked out though, your capabilities with the wolf saving us quite a bit of time."

I nodded as I remembered what I'd been told nearly a month ago, that Alpha squad could use a support gunner.

"What happened to your previous support gunner?" I asked.

Silence fell over the group and I instantly regretted my words.

"I'm sorry–" I stammered.

"No, it's fine. It's right for you to know." Frost said as she swirled her bottle. "Earlier this year, in the spring, orders came down that a group of vampires had set up shop at an old two story farmstead out in the country. Mission was simple: kill 'em."

"Something went wrong?" I asked.

"Not a thing." Doc said. "Until a perimeter patrol came back around while we were inside the house. We had not expected a patrol in the middle of the day."

"They started pouring rounds into the buildings, we were all pinned down. All except Preach. He had done exactly as he was supposed to and set up overwatch at a nearby tree line. Patrol never knew he was there until he started shooting. He got all of them, but he caught a silver round in the process. By the time I got to him, it was too late, the silver had done its job."

"You did what you could, Doc." Knight said comfortingly. "Besides, you single handedly saved us that day, or have you forgotten?"

Doc shook his head solemnly. "I will never forget."

"What happened?" I asked.

"One of the vamps on the inside," Marcus answered, "woke up as we were dealing with the others and pulled a grenade, tried to kamikaze us. Doc was on his way back from finding Preach, but suddenly he runs in and dropkicks the guy right out a second story window. Vamp hadn't hit the ground before the grenade went off in his hands. Couple more seconds and we all would've met God that day, not just Preach."

Frost looked to me, returning to my question. "You've got big boots to fill, Fenrir."

I nodded. "How long had Preach been with you guys?"

"He joined after me." Marcus said from the grill, "And I've been here four years. So, figure three, three and a half years."

"You've been with The Council for four years?"

"No," Marcus replied, "I've been with The Council since I can remember."

"You were born into it?"

"In a way. I come from a long line of Council soldiers, pure blooded wolves. My siblings, a sister and two brothers are pure bloods as well, and hold somewhat high posts in The Council. I, however, am the spawn of my mother's unfaithfulness, and though she's a wolf, my legitimate father is a human. For whatever cruel reason, the wolf passed over me. When the time came that I should've been growing into the wolf, nothing happened. The man I knew, and still know as my father only learned of my mother's treachery then. He was kind though, forgiving my mother, and shielding her from the Council with his high status of Field Commander. However, it wouldn't do for one of his sons not to be a wolf. He changed me, but it really didn't matter. My half siblings found out that I wasn't a pureblood and that was it. I don't recall a day after that where I wasn't tormented by my older siblings for being a bastard child. Younger brother was always good to me though, but I'm fairly certain that had he been older than me, he would've joined in. Anyhow, when the day came for me to begin my training with the Council, I excelled in every single course. After training I learned that I had actually out-performed each of my pureblooded siblings, but it didn't make a difference. I wasn't like them. My father saw to it that they were taken care of, being put in positions simply based on who and what they were. He then informed me that I would have to start at the bottom of the ranks, nothing would be handed to me. And so, I busted my ass every damned day, until Phoenix reached out to me. He was putting together a new team and word of my results had gotten to him. After seeing what I could do, he gave me some additional training, the training that you've received, Fenrir. After that, more recruits began showing up. Those that passed joined the unit, eventually we got enough bodies to form individual squads. And here we are."

"Doesn't really seem right." I said. "That you have to start at square one when your siblings are automatically put up on a pedestal."

"It's a good life lesson." Marcus said. "Life's not fair, and to be honest I'm grateful that I have to start at the bottom. I'm ten times the soldier my brothers and sister are, and whenever I reach their rank, I'll make sure they know it." Marcus pulled the last steak from the grill.

As we all stood to grab plates and chow, I looked to Knight.

"How long have you been with The Council?" I asked.

"Before you," Knight stabbed a steak and transferred it to her plate, "my brother Slade and I were the newest arrivals."

"Your brother's a wolf too?"

"Yup. He's the wolf who changed me." She stated.

"You say that like Slade did it intentionally." Doc said.

Knight ignored the remark and carried on. "I grew up a few hours north of here, surrounded by children, there were five of us. My brother Jesse was the youngest, the twins Jackie and Marie were between Jesse and me, and my brother Slade is the oldest."

I felt a knot form in my gut as I sensed this tale wouldn't end well for Knight's family.

"Mom and dad worked constantly, but seven mouths, that's a lot to feed, especially on their salaries. Slade was only trying to help put food on the table when he took to the streets with some guys he met in high school. They made their money mugging people for the money in their wallets. It didn't take long for Slade to say that this wasn't the way he wanted to help his family. By then it was too late though, he knew everyone in the gang and they feared he'd turn them in. They turned out to be wolves and somehow he wound up bitten."

"At least they didn't kill him." I said.

"If you ask Slade, he'll tell you he wishes they would have. After being bit, the gang figured they had him in a bind, stuck running with them. It backfired though, he killed them, all of them. He himself was only eighteen at the time. Of course, none of our family knew anything about it, the wolf or the gang. Anyhow, he never learned to control the wolf, but he had learned what it felt like when it wanted out, so every once in a while, he'd just take off out of the blue. He was nineteen by now, and I was seventeen, and one day when he took off, I followed him. He walked along the road for what seemed like hours until he was outside of city limits and well out of view of anybody passing by. And then I watched him change. Almost immediately the wolf caught my scent, and there was nowhere for me to go. I was certain he was going to eat me when his teeth sank into my leg. Somehow, in that moment, he beat the hell out of the wolf inside of him, and took control, but not before I had been infected."

"How did you wind up here?" I asked.

"By being sloppy." Knight answered. "We knew we couldn't go home, the fact that Slade hadn't killed one of us was nothing short of incredible, but two wolves in the house? There was no way. We were homeless for a while, and slowly I gained control of the wolf, but not before we'd left a string of dead livestock behind us. Phoenix and the Red Moons tracked us down, and for a moment, Slade and I knew they were going to kill us. We never expected Phoenix to offer us a home. He made it very clear the only reason we were given the option was because we hadn't killed any humans, only a band of rogue wolves."

"That was good of him." I said. "To take you in."

"Yeah," Knight agreed, "Phoenix became like a second dad to me, to us, but Slade hates himself for it. He feels like it's his fault that we had to leave home, even though he was only trying to help."

"I remember when you two showed up." Doc said after he swallowed a bit of steak. "It was not too long after I joined the Red Moons."

I looked to Doc and waited for his story.

He continued eating though and when I looked at Knight, she smiled.

"Hey Doc," Knight said, "I think Fenrir is waiting for you to continue."

Doc looked up to me as if he had no idea he had taken my interest.

"Well." He said. "My story is pretty simple. My father was, if you can imagine, a doctor, working for himself in a private practice. My mother handled the paperwork side of things, and I, as the sole child, was set up to go through med school and join in the family practice. Everything was going well in school, good grades, stellar attendance, etcetera. When time for clinicals came it was only right that I work with my father. One day a young man comes in complaining of growths in his mouth, father asks me to make initial observations. I carried on as I should have and began by looking into the young man's mouth. Father suspected an infection and upon my inspection I found that at the back of the man's lower jaw, were two large glands. I was somewhat perturbed by this as there are no glands known to be where these were. I feel his jaw, exterior mind you, and he tells me he feels no pain, nor has he felt any, he simply noticed them, and they gave him cause for alarm. Father then advised me to take a tongue depressor, which he called a spatula, and gently touch one of these glands. Father suspected as I did, that a bit of puss would emerge from the gland. Instead, what leaked out was a thick pinkish substance. Father requested I repeat this on the other gland, and my fingers grew careless. When I bumped the other gland, it apparently caused the young man some discomfort as he clamped down. Unfortunately, my right index finger was between his teeth. I had, obviously unknown to myself, just been infected with lycanthropy. Fast forward a few weeks and I wake one morning to find myself in Phoenix's taming unit. I believe you are acquainted with it."

"I know the one." I smiled as I looked to Frost.

She raised her eyes to mine and puffed, "Pass."

"That leaves you pup." Marcus said.

"It's a doozie." I said.

"Well," Knight smiled, "Phoenix didn't kill you, so it's safe to assume you didn't kill any humans."

"That's true." I nodded. "It's been a little over five months back now. A friend, by the name of Alan, and I were at a bar in Kirkwood, The Buried Hatchet. Eighteen to enter, twenty-one to drink, you know, but no one really paid super close attention. We had done this several times and found out that this one particular booth in the back corner blocked most of the view from the bartenders. So long as you ordered a soda every once in a while, no one was the wiser. Moving on, every other time Alan got a drink, he'd slip it to me, and before long I was pretty much tanked. That's where most of the memory cuts out. I remember the music, there was a live band that night, light bars going nuts, the works, and somewhere in there was a woman. A blonde. Next morning, I wake up, I feel hungover. No surprise there. It wasn't until a time later that I found out that something wasn't right.

"When the wolf came out, I had no control over it. And like your brother Slade," I looked to Knight, "I figured out the warning signs of the wolf. Then, about two months ago, my dad, well the man I consider my dad, I'm adopted, sent me into Kirkwood for some fencing and I came across a scent that I somehow knew was a wolf, and it struck me as familiar. I knew right then that the scent belonged to the person who had changed me, that's the only reason their scent would be familiar, right? Nothing came of it that day.

A while passed by. I was in Kirkwood again, and again I caught that scent. I couldn't hold it any longer. I was furious because of what I was, that I was constantly worried about hurting someone, especially my family, adopted or not. All I could think about was finding this woman and making her pay. So that night, I snuck out of the house and made my way into town, it was only fifteen or so miles. I picked up the scent right away, and it led me to a house. She wasn't there. There was a corpse inside, in pieces mostly, along with a very unconscious cop, so I didn't hang around." I nearly chuckled. "I picked the scent up again and followed it to an apartment and again, I thought I had found nothing but bodies. No woman, and the scent trail ended there. Then this guy, I assume the guy that killed the others, held me at gunpoint and told me to drive this car that was there. He had me drive him to a bar out in the sticks. He got out, then as he was leaving, he stopped and kind of growled over his shoulder that it was up to me, but I should probably get rid of the car. I didn't, it's the car that Frost and I went to get. Pretty soon the police were asking for me, just for questioning, they didn't even know about the car. I was in an interrogation room when I met Phoenix, though at the moment he was going by the name Francis. You know the rest."

Everyone was quiet for a moment, taking in what I had said. They had heard each other's stories numerous times; this was the first they'd learned of mine.

I waited for someone to crack with, so you killed a bunch of people and got away with it, or, so you're basically a thief, you stole the car.

Knight was the first to speak. "At least you got a car out of it."

I smiled in disbelief. "You never say a cross word do you."

Marcus shook his head as he chewed a bite of steak. "Four siblings have blessed her with an eternally cheerful disposition. You'd swear she craps rainbows."

A sudden ringing caught us all off guard, and Marcus quickly dug into his pocket. He produced a cell phone and brought it up to his face.

"Go for Marcus." He said. "Yeah, he actually passed just this morning. We're just– What?"

Marcus threw his paper plate into the fire.

"Now?" He asked. "Sir, no one's rested up, we need a minute to– I understand. Yes sir."

Marcus hung up before turning to us. "Load up, we're going home."

23

Briefing

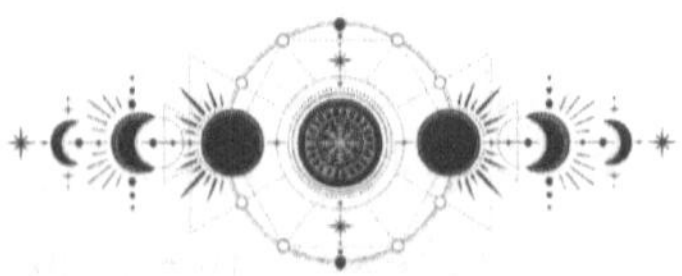

1900 found Alpha team standing at attention in Phoenix's office.

"I apologize for cutting your evening short, congratulations by the way, Fenrir," Phoenix nodded, "but we've run out of time. Bravo and Delta teams haven't made contact yet, and we can wait no longer. Alpha team will be deployed at 0000."

"What're the orders, sir?" Marcus asked.

"Bravo and Delta were deployed to deal with a compound of rogue wolves that Council brass has designated as a danger to humans. As they have yet to make contact, I can only assume that they failed to achieve their objective. Orders are fairly simple on this one, Alpha. Recover any of our survivors, and clear the compound of rogue wolves."

"What's the estimated opposition?" Marcus asked.

"I don't know, Marcus. There have been no scouting runs against the compound, and it's not a high enough priority to justify displacing other assets to investigate."

Marcus sighed as he nodded. "Understood, sir."

"Good." Phoenix nodded. "Collect your gear and standby. Everyone is dismissed, except you, Fenrir."

The squad spun on their heels wordlessly, leaving me alone before the captain.

The door had barely shut behind the team before Phoenix began speaking.

"Again, congratulations." He started. "From my understanding you fared well for the majority of your training."

I nodded, recalling my near failure with Knight. "Thank you, sir."

"I hadn't intended on sending you out so soon but the situation requires it. Are you confident that you are ready?" Phoenix asked.

"I am." I nodded. "I'm ready."

"I hope you are." Phoenix's face conveyed that he had some concerns. "Before you go on assignment however, there are some things you'll be needing."

"And that is?" I asked.

"This, for one thing." He tossed me a black bracelet.

Catching it, I found it was a rubber band of sorts, roughly an inch wide and irregularly thick. It was plain except for a blacked-out tag that contained only my call sign and a short serial number: 13244.

"Is this The Council's take on dog tags?"

He nodded. "It's a high strength polymer that will expand to remain in place in the event you turn, though you will find it's not tight enough to cut off circulation. It'll stay firm around your wrist, and it's rated for around forty-five changes. That said, it should last you a good long while."

I pulled on the bracelet, finding the fit comfortably snug. "I didn't notice anyone else wearing one during my training."

Phoenix shrugged. "They are only required on missions. Here or as in your case, training, they are optional."

I nodded. "And the second thing?"

He grinned. "The mark of a wolf."

"And that is?" I asked.

"A symbol that will be a part of you until the day you die, The Wolven Council insignia." Phoenix's expression radiated with pride as he looked at a tattoo set up in the corner.

"You do the work yourself?"

"That's correct." Phoenix smiled.

* * *

I rolled the shirt sleeve down over my left bicep as Phoenix put away his instruments. Staring at my arm, he seemed deep in thought, and I assumed it was about the upcoming operation. Running potential scenarios and outcomes through his mind.

"You're ready." He said shortly, though a bit absently.

I nodded toward the door as I stood from the chair. "Am I okay to go?"

Phoenix frowned, only slightly before looking me in the eye. "Are you?"

I felt confusion creep across my face. "What do you mean?"

"I mean," Phoenix's tone lowered, "are you okay to go on this mission?"

I nodded. "I passed the training. Preparing for this was the whole point of that, so I don't feel like I have much of a choice."

"Yes, you do." He replied. "If you're not ready and you go anyway, you'll be putting not only yourself but also Alpha in greater danger."

"I'm ready, Phoenix." I nodded. "I'm going with them."

With a deciding breath, as if evaluating it for himself, he gave a conceding nod. "Very well. We, Alpha and I, are counting on you to uphold that. You will take lives tonight, do you understand that?"

I had never doubted that Phoenix cared for his operators, but it seemed now that he cared more than he let on.

"I do, Captain." I nodded.

Phoenix offered only a nod towards the door as he moved back behind his desk. "Send Marcus in."

I quickly nodded as I took the door handle. "Yes sir."

Alpha team had apparently been waiting just outside the door. As I walked out of the office I found myself in the middle of the squad. They were tense, it was clear upon their faces.

"Phoenix wants to see you, Marcus." I looked to our Lieutenant.

Marcus nodded and walked into the office, closing the door behind him.

"Well let's see it, Fenrir." Knight nodded as she pushed away from the wall she leaned on, smiling as always, though perhaps a bit anxious. "He's given you the mark."

Knight quickly stepped forward, gently lifting my sleeve. Upon seeing my mark her eyes narrowed, finding something she hadn't anticipated.

The others saw her face as I did, simultaneously echoing.

"What?"

Frost moved to see, then stopped, just as Knight had. She stared at my arm, her blue eyes fixed on a dark green shield centered on my bicep. In the center of the shield was the black paw print of a wolf. An equally shaded pair of swords were crossed behind the print.

Frost's eyes continued to hold my mark, while Knight looked down to her left arm, finding blue and black, not the faintest shade of green.

Doc's eyes narrowed. "What does this mean?"

"I–" Frost fell silent. "Mmph."

At that moment Marcus burst through the door, his face brighter than fire, his gaze burning everything before him as he walked by the group.

Through the door, Phoenix stood on the other side of his desk, wordless as he watched Marcus leave.

"Let's move, Alpha." Marcus grumbled as he continued towards the main doors, never casting a look back.

Knight shook her head as she walked by. "Lovely."

It was the first time I hadn't seen her make light of a situation, and I couldn't deny the worry that knotted my stomach.

I had no proof, but I was fairly certain my mark had something to do with the situation.

I didn't know what my mark meant, but if it was the reason Marcus was in such a foul mood, I'd sooner cut it from my flesh.

Our lives depended on working well together.

Frost's life depended on it.

I felt a gentle buzz on the back of my neck, little more than a tickle, and I knew she was near.

"Riding with me?" I quietly asked over my shoulder, slightly worried that she might be angry too.

"Seems a better alternative to riding with Marcus." She frowned.

24

The Raid

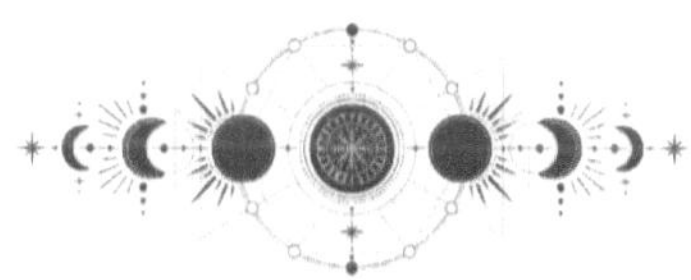

10/16

0100 Hrs.

The warehouse we knew as The Citadel sat in the heart of a forest, a good ten miles from the nearest city, Kirkwood.

Now I watched in the rear-view mirror as it became swallowed by the trees.

Frost sat in the passenger seat, deathly quiet, staring through the windshield.

Without showing obvious concern I casually asked. "Do you think Marcus is upset because of my mark?"

"Probably." She quietly responded. "I would assume so, simply because that's literally the only thing that's taken place."

"Do you know what it means?" I asked.

She cast me a glance from the corner of her eye.

"She doesn't know." I frowned.

"In any case, Marcus is our lieutenant." I said confidently. "He knows that we count on him to get us home."

"Yes he does, Fenrir," she quietly replied, "but he is notoriously hot headed. I'm not worried about us getting home, I'm worried about this having an impact on the foundation of the squad afterwards. If we can't sort this out, Alpha team will suffer as a whole."

"Then I'll have to make sure we can sort it out." I nodded. "I'm going to stay with Alpha team, nothing is taking me from you." I said, suddenly realizing the spoken words.

"You guys I mean." I mounted a quick recovery.

"Think before you talk!" I cursed myself.

"I knew what you meant." She nodded.

"No, you don't, but I wish you did."

I felt bad, like I had done something wrong, though I knew I hadn't. If anyone knew what the mark meant, they weren't saying, though it probably wouldn't change anything if they did.

Again Frost softly spoke, regret pulling at her voice. "Best advice I can give you right now is to give Marcus a wide berth until he's cooled down. Let's just get this op done, with all of us going home, and we'll sort it out ourselves."

I nodded. "Deal."

My first outing with the team was shaping up to be a rocky operation, not good considering we hadn't even started yet.

* * *

0130 Hrs.

The small compound was surrounded by hills on all sides, giving a look as if the camp had been laid in a geographical bowl.

Crouching on the northern hilltop, we could observe from a bird's eye view the entire layout of the settlement.

There were five buildings below us, accessible by a single dirt road. A fire was burning on the outskirts of the buildings, but other than that everything was silent, motionless.

I was nervous, wound tight between the operation and the volatile Marcus. I checked my gear anxiously, my fingers toying at the 249's exposed ammunition.

There was no life below, and no sound other than the crackling fire. The place was dead.

"Fenrir, get over here!" Marcus loudly whispered.

I remained low as I approached the others, making sure I crouched across from Marcus, taking Frost's words into consideration.

Marcus nodded as he began issuing orders. "Knight, Doc, pull some quick recon, see if you can find our operators."

The pair nodded before creeping to the ring, leaving Marcus with Frost and I.

"We're keeping this by the books." Marcus continued. "Quick, clean, and quiet. We'll get our operatives out first, after that, we'll move to the eastern ridge. Once we've got cover, I'll call you, Fenrir. You let off a few rounds and that'll draw them to target you, but we'll have them in a crossfire, shouldn't be too many places they can hide that we can't hit."

I nodded, holding the 249 close.

"In the event that we get into trouble, the pair of you will cover our retreat, got it?" Marcus finished.

"Solid copy." Frost nodded.

Marcus nodded as he looked between our faces a frown tugging at his lips. "We'll see you soon."

Marcus turned, joining Doc and Knight, the latter pointing to something below. Short words and a quick nod passed between them before the trio started towards the settlement, quickly vanishing from sight.

For a moment, Frost and I were both silent, only accompanied by the gentle whispers of drawn breaths.

Frost softly cleared her throat, and when she spoke, her voice betrayed her concern. "You okay?"

"Yeah," I nodded, " just worried about the team."

Frost nodded. "And others."

"What do you mean?" I asked.

"My best friend, Edge, she's part of Delta."

"If she's in there, I'm sure they'll find her, Frost." I attempted to comfort her.

"Yeah." She whispered as she shook her head, effectively shrugging away my efforts. "Come on, let's get set up."

I nodded as I slowly dropped to my stomach, setting the bipod down on the 249, roughly figuring the range at 150 yards.

The grass softly crunched as Frost lay prone next to me, her rifle before her.

As I peered down into the compound, I could no longer see the others.

"They're in." I said as I tugged at my vest, laying out a spare box of ammunition.

I started to settle down as I breathed her in, loosing a flutter in my stomach as a chill rippled down my spine.

I grasped for conversation, simply wanting to hear Frost's voice, wanting to feel the comfort it so frequently provided. "How long do you think they'll be?"

She paused a moment, processing the question. "It's hard to say. They should be avoiding loud combat. Knight will lead the way, clearing any sentries, but only those that don't move away. They'll try to avoid dropping bodies unless they have to."

Frost shook her head, her brow creased.

"What?" I asked quietly.

"We've never pulled a rescue op before, we've run some simulations before, but never actually put it to use."

"At least you've had practice." I tried to encourage her.

"That's not it." She said. "These operations are tricky, success and failure both being likely outcomes."

"What do you mean?"

"There are three ways we've found to go about it. One, you get the prisoners out first, which involves sneaking into the enemy camp, putting the rescuers in close proximity to the enemy. Number two, you set up a crossfire or surprise attack so you can knock out the enemy personnel and then save the captives. Three is to actively clear the compound while you search for the POW's. All have their downsides, the first scenario is obvious, the second concept has you starting a firefight without knowing where the captives are, potentially hitting them. The third risks bringing the entire installation down on top of you. Success is to secure as many captives as possible, even if it's only one, while losing no rescuers. Failure is to lose the rescuers and not save anyone. If we get one out and lose one of our team, it becomes a trade off, which is the same as a failure."

"What I'm hearing is that there's no good way to go about this." I said.

"That's not entirely true. Odds increase greatly with valid intel and recon, but without..." she frowned, "it's nearly always a failure. If we had suppressors and more ammo, I'd feel better but–"

Frost was cut off by a sudden scream from within the bowels of the compound. Shouting and more cries followed.

My eyes darted side to side, catching movement here and there, unable to ascertain whether they were friend or foe.

Two of the buildings splintered as explosives detonated, and gunfire erupted from everywhere, scorching rounds flying through the night sky.

"Going hot!" I yelled as I pulled the 249 to my shoulder.

As I peered through the sights, I found Alpha squad break from the buildings, rapidly climbing the hill, back up to us.

"They didn't make it to our guys."

Laying next to me, Frost pulled a shot, and I found the target just in time to see his chest rupture.

A pursuing group rounded the corner, and had just enough time to raise their rifles as I squeezed the trigger.

The 249 shook as it roared to life, though the recoil went unnoticed as I watched the entire party fall to the ground, bloody mist serving as a solid hit indicator.

Checking the progress of my team, I found them slowly making ground. Doc was leaning on Knight, the left side of his shirt dyed a shiny crimson.

For a human, what Knight was accomplishing was unfathomed, a woman of her small frame effectively dragging another body up a hill. Yet she was accomplishing this without showing the least amount of strain, testaments of the wolf.

"Doc's hit!" I called to Frost, shouting to be heard over the battle.

I looked down again, this time finding Marcus, also bearing a payload. A body lay across his back, in military fashion. To add to his precarious situation, he'd taken a shot to the meat of his left leg, appearing to have missed the bone, but slowing him down.

Three men appeared from the corner of the building behind Marcus and started firing, quickly being answered by a volley of rounds from the 249.

"Frost," I cried, "help Marcus!"

She never looked away from the scope.

"We can't!" She put a hand to her chest. "Cookie get the van up here! Fenrir we stay here, they need the covering fire–"

The rest of what she said escaped my ears; I had already slung the 249 on my shoulder, already departed for my companion below, quickly closing the distance as I sped to Marcus.

As I neared him I could see the man he carried had a hand raised, back towards the compound.

As I reached them I could scarcely hear the man's soft voice. "We can't leave them…"

"He's not the only survivor." I looked up to a Dantean vision as fire ravaged the compound. *"We can't stay, we've got too many wounded…"*

Amid airborne earth and debris I nearly drug the soldier from Marcus' back, pulling one of his arms over my neck. "Let's go, Lieutenant!"

Dirt showered us as we ran, numerous close calls as rounds slammed into the soft earth.

The ridge was nearly in reach, coercing my legs to push all the harder. "C'mon L.T. We're almost there!"

Amid the firing I heard a squelching of flesh, accompanied by a loud clack. The air thickened with Marcus' screams, and instantly my burden grew heavier, the unsuspected weight dragging me to my knees.

A flurry of curses rang in my ear and I turned, finding Marcus clutching his left leg.

The three of us were caught without cover, rounds still plummeting towards us.

"Get him out of here!" Marcus called as he drew his sidearm.

I hesitated, unwilling to leave him.

"Go!" He roared.

I cursed as I followed the order, leaving Marcus behind as I towed the soldier up the hill, Cookie meeting me as I crested the ridge.

"I got him, Fenrir!" He lifted the soldier from me, starting towards the van as I turned back to the compound.

I found Marcus had managed to move only a few yards, and had it not been for Knight and Frost's covering fire, he wouldn't have made that.

I broke cover once more, pulling the 249 into my hands as Marcus cast his pistol aside, his ammunition spent.

"I've got you, L.T!" I yelled as I slid beside him.

"What the hell are–" his eyes darted to the compound, "Fenrir!"

I turned back to find a charging gray wolf bearing down on us, a gleam of rage in its eyes.

As I fell to earth, I jerked the trigger, the 249 rattling against my side.

Bloody holes appeared on the gray's face and throat, moments before it collapsed before us.

"At least we've got cover now." I said as I righted myself, looking to Marcus.

"Only until the wolf fades!" Marcus screamed. "What the hell are you doing?!"

"Fenrir!" Frost cried from the ridge, drawing my eyes. "Get out of there!"

I nodded as I looked to Marcus. "Ready?"

He frowned, offering up a silent nod as the wolf's carcass began to shudder, the beast ebbing away.

Pulling him over my shoulders, we started the final climb, rushing back into the storm.

I felt a light slap against my side, the infuriating burn coupled with the trickling sensation across my ribs negating any need to look.

I was hit.

As my feet fell upon the hilltop, a round punched into my right bicep, narrowly missing Marcus' head.

"Fenrir!" Frost screamed as Cookie pulled Marcus from me.

"I'm fine." I growled as heat began to radiate from my torn arm, blood pouring off my fingertips.

"Get to the car!" I pointed, slinging blood.

She nodded, hurrying to the Challenger, rolling the engine over as the van sped past.

"I'm in." I slammed the door. "Go!"

The words had no sooner left me than she smashed the accelerator, quickly shooting us out onto the gravel country road.

I groaned as the fire in my arm grew hotter, spreading into my chest. I felt the warm wet trickle of blood as it flowed from the wound.

An agonizing moment later, my arm ceased to bleed, but it didn't feel right, not like the work of the wolf.

It was something else.

My vision blurred, briefly returning to normal only to haze again. My stomach churned, a feeling of nausea overtaking me.

My temples pounded, assaulted by a sledgehammer. A frigid cold grasped my body, replaced in the next instant by a wave hot as the sun, drawing sweat to my brow.

I began to shiver, though my body was blistering hot.

"Frost–" I winced.

She looked over to me and her jaw dropped, her eyes growing wide, fear deep inside of them, transferring to me.

Moments later every muscle in my body spasmed in unison, my entire body locking up, clenching together, rendering me lame, unable to move.

All I could do was scream. My legs were locked straight, pressed into the floorboard, lifting me from the seat. My sides erupted in massive stitches that grew less painful only to surge back with new strength. My arms followed to turn rigid, continuing into my fingers, hardening tight into my palms. The binding muscles grew more painful, more severe.

My lungs burned, begging for a breath that I couldn't draw in.

Once more my vision blurred, a flashing of lights and shapes, before a curtain of darkness fell on me.

25

Silver

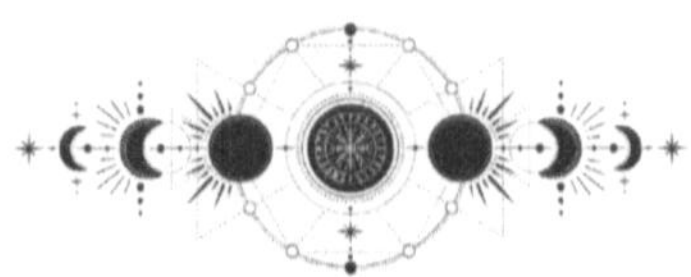

I came to in the infirmary, in a state similar to the previous instance I had woken there.

My body was stiff as steel, and unbearably sore.

With substantial effort I looked to my left. Doc was there, the head of his bed elevated. His eyes were closed, but I knew he was alive as he drew steady breaths. His blond hair was stained where it had been matted with mud and blood. But he was alive.

I couldn't see past Doc but I knew there were more beds on the other side of him, and I assumed they were in use. Maybe Marcus and the man we saved.

I looked up to the ceiling, wondering how I got there.

Last I remembered, I was running Marcus out, it got hazy after that, ending with Frost's panicked eyes.

"What happened out there? What went wrong? Everything had been quiet,

then it wasn't."

I sighed and thought about the man we'd rescued, whether or not he had lived or if we had been too late. I was pulled away from thoughts as I felt my feet falling asleep, that annoying needle-like sensation.

I wiggled my toes, shaking away the pins as I attempted to move, turning rigid as I found a hand in my own.

I glanced to my right, finding Frost's head laid upon my bed, her hand going under the blanket where it held mine. Her hair flowed down onto the bed, her back gently rising and falling as she slept.

"Why are you here, Frost?" My heart tugged. *"Why is your hand..."*

Why did she stay by me? When she could've rested much better elsewhere, why was her head laid next to me?

Was she just worried about me or...

I allowed myself to enjoy the notion that she was holding my hand because she cared about me, more than mere Friendship would allow, the way that I *knew* I cared for her.

When the exact moment had been, I wasn't certain, but I knew that in the course of my training, the testing, the laughs, the meals, everything that took place, I had started to care for her. I wanted her, and I wanted her to want me.

My free hand balled into a fist, my head fighting my heart, one knowing that she didn't feel the same, the other believing she had to, otherwise she wouldn't be where she was.

I glanced to the bed on my right and recognized Knight's figure.

Her face was a mess of dried blood, though her expression told me she wasn't in pain. She was simply sleeping.

Beside her, his back to me, was Phoenix.

He was sitting up, as if awake, but as he remained unmoving, I wondered if he too was asleep or simply resting his eyes.

I tried to speak, and at the faintest strain I felt shards of glass pierce my throat.

I looked down to Frost, knowing that she could wake him, but I found myself unable to stir her.

I couldn't.

If I woke her, she would take her hand from mine.

Again I looked to the man beside me.

"Phoenix." My voice ground painfully.

"Hmm?" He slowly swiveled in his chair to face me.

Upon meeting my eyes, a look of relief crossed his typically stern, worn face.

"Fenrir," he sighed, "I didn't expect you to wake so soon. How do you feel?"

I tried to reply to his question in vain, my sandy throat lending little help.

He saw my effort and raised a hand. "A thumbs up or down will suffice."

I wasn't doing it to be a smart ass, I was doing it to be honest. I laid my hand flat in the air and tilted it side to side.

"Could be better, could be worse."

He smiled, then cleared his throat. "A-hem." He reached down onto a stand close by and picked up a hand mirror that had laid next to a bottle of water. "Take a look at yourself."

I took the mirror and held it in front of my face, shocked that it managed to hold together. Even though I could only see my face, I had a pretty good idea of what the rest of me looked like.

Every visible vessel was a dark blue, an intricate map etched under my skin.

I pulled my left arm from beneath the sheet, finding it the same, the peculiar veins continuing on until they spider webbed into my hand.

"What's happened to me?"

Phoenix pulled away the small mirror, speaking as he did. "Fenrir, do you know what this is?"

I shook my head, suddenly hoping that I wouldn't die, and if not, that my condition wouldn't be permanent.

"It's silver, Fenrir, this is what it does." He reached into a small metal pan with a pair of forceps, proceeding to reveal a small crumpled silver slug.

"Is that *the* bullet?" I managed.

Phoenix nodded.

"No pass through?" I whispered hoarsely.

"Apparently not." Phoenix nodded, a bit puzzled with this. "Though it should've been. It didn't contact bone. A faulty round perhaps? Maybe too great a range for this small of a caliber. It's hard to be certain."

He quietly returned the projectile to the pan, so as not to wake the others, before taking the water from the nearby table.

He unscrewed the cap, and held the bottle out to me. "Drink."

I gratefully accepted the bottle, bringing it to my parched lips and savoring the taste as it began to flow. I managed to drink most of it despite the fact it was room temperature, making it slightly warmer than I'd preferred.

But it felt good on a cotton tongue and cracked throat.

"Is this permanent?" My voice returned as I handed the bottle back to Phoenix.

"No. This stage is referred to as silver shock. The Anver that Frost administered will reverse it, it's just a somewhat long process, likely the better part of a day. You'll have a scar around the point of impact however, silver burn. A small radius of the veins will never return to their normal color."

I nodded as I looked over to Knight. "What happened to her?"

Phoenix crossed his arms over his chest as he glanced at her. "She's exhausted. Her and Cookie got the others up here while Frost saw to you. Not a drop of that blood is her's, best I can tell."

Phoenix's words brought relief, and as I looked down to Frost, I was grateful that the ladies of Alpha had escaped injury.

"Anyone else get hit with silver?" I asked.

Phoenix shook his head. "Curiously, no. Best I can deduce is that the defenders initially sought to simply repel the attack. Clearly someone decided that avenue wasn't working."

"That would explain the wolf." I nodded.

"What wolf?" Phoenix asked.

"After Marcus was hit the last time, a wolf charged us. I guess he didn't see the 249, or thought he was faster than my draw."

"I see." Phoenix looked away from me for a moment, seeming to be in thought.

"How long have we been back?" I asked groggily.

Phoenix quickly looked at his watch before answering. "Several hours, it's nearly 0600. By the look of things, I doubt anyone will wake before 1200, and even that may be wishful thinking."

I felt as if I'd slept for days, it was nearly impossible to believe it had only been a few hours, but I knew Phoenix wasn't lying.

"How are the others?" I asked. "Doc and Marcus. They got hit too."

Phoenix nodded his head. "Doc caught two slugs, but they missed his vitals. He'll be alright."

"And Marcus?" I asked.

Phoenix looked over Doc, to where I assumed Marcus lay. "He'll live, though he'll be bedridden for a while, 'til the bone puts itself back together."

He looked down at me and shook his head. "What happened, Fenrir?"

"I'm wondering that myself." I admitted. "Frost and I were set up on the ridge, in case the op went sideways. It was quiet, there was no alarm, no lone shot that set it all off. It just started, everything went south all at once. The fact that Alpha didn't lose any operators is a miracle. Hard to believe that we actually saved one of ours."

"Ghost." Phoenix said. "His call sign is Ghost, Delta's infiltrator."

*"He said **is**, not **was**."* I nearly smiled. *"It wasn't for nothing."*

"Is he okay?" I asked.

Phoenix nodded. "I'm inclined to think so. He's alive in any case, though he appears to be severely dehydrated. Much longer and he would've perished."

His voice trailed off and he looked toward the two nurses seated at a desk near the door. One was thin, with brown eyes and brown hair, while the other, blond haired and green eyed, bolstered a larger stature.

Phoenix gently called. "Rachel."

The thin brunette's eyes traveled up to Phoenix as he pointed a thumb to me, and I watched as she nodded her head then looked back to her books.

"You're clear, Fenrir. You can go whenever you please. If you'll excuse me, I've got some things to attend to."

"Before you go." I cleared my throat. "Can you do something for me sir?"

He tilted his head. "That depends on what you're asking."

"Melt down that slug and coat my knife in it."

"Feeling vengeful are we?" He frowned, making it clear that he wasn't particularly fond of the notion.

I shook my head. "Leveling the playing field."

He stared at me for a moment, gears turning, before conceding with a nod. "I'll do it for you, Fenrir."

"Thank you." I nodded to him as he turned to leave.

Slowly I looked down to Frost, knowing that I'd have to free my hand of hers if I was going to move.

I had to confess that I wanted nothing more than to stay there, our hands embraced.

I laid my head back on the pillows as my eyes closed, content just being able to feel the slightest bit of her skin.

Her palm was gently callused, hardened through training and battle. My thumb softly scrolled over the back of her hand, finding the smoothest of silk, something I had tried not to dwell on during our starter change.

Subtly moving, I found her fingers, slender, ending with a gently curved fingernail that just extended past her fingertips.

I lightly smiled, drawing her hand in my mind, finding it just as beautiful as the rest of her.

"Fenrir?" She whispered softly, as I felt her head slowly lift from my bed, though her hand remained.

My heart seized, knowing I'd been caught, calming as I realized she may think I was still asleep.

"She knows, she has to know."

I felt a soft pressure slowly return to my bed as she once more laid her head down.

In one instant I developed my own understanding of guilty pleasure. I didn't want her hand to pull away, though I cursed myself for deceiving her.

"She's worried about you, Rainer!" My heart turned against me. *"And you're just gonna let her worry and get shit for sleep so you can hold her hand?!"*

I pouted against myself, hating that I was right.

"It's time."

"Frost?" I softly whispered as I opened my eyes, finding her rise from the bed once more.

As she looked to me, a smile crossed her face, and I found myself smiling as well when her hand made no effort to retreat.

"Hey." She whispered, and I couldn't help but squeeze her hand.

"Oh!" She pulled her hand from mine, surprised, lowering her eyes as her cheeks flushed with color.

"Sorry about that." She chuckled.

"Don't apologize." I cooly said. "I appreciate you staying, and there are a lot worse ways to wake up than having someone next to you holding your hand, just so you're not alone."

She looked down again, smiling this time, brushing a bit of hair behind her ear before looking up to me. "I'm happy that you're okay."

"Me too, though I have you to thank yet again for that, since you're the one that hit me with Anver." I carefully sat up, the sheet rolling from me, as I found my shirt gone and six inches of gauze wrapped around my torso, an ugly brown stain on my left side.

"I forgot about that one." I said as I gingerly put my hand to the wound, finding no pain, but a certain tension, taut new skin.

"Bullet traced your ribs, laid you open pretty good." Frost said as her eyes fell from my naked chest to the bandage.

For a moment I searched for my shirt, finding several pieces of it on the floor next to my boots.

It had been cut from me.

I quickly reached down to my thigh, making sure my bottom half was still covered. With an air of relief, I found my jeans were still in place, allowing me to swing my legs from the bed.

I stood, though a little uneasily and Frost reached out, steadying me.

"Thanks." I looked down, finding the left leg of my jeans had been cut away at the knee. With the absence of denim, I could see one more bloodied bandage around my calf.

"I never even felt that one."

"I was gonna try to get to bed." I chuckled.

"Need help getting there?" Frost asked, setting thunder in my chest as I reached down, claiming my boots.

"Well, I guess I could play it up a little bit."

"Yeah." I nodded. "Probably not a bad idea."

She nodded as she pressed herself to my right side. "Hold onto me."

"Only if you say I don't have to let go."

Slowly I raised my arm, unfortunately having to rest it on her shoulder, though my hand begged to stop as it skated past her waist.

She put a hand flat on the bandage over my stomach, while the other wrapped around me, finding its place upon the naked skin of my upper ribs, between the bandage and my chest.

An arc bolted between her hands, filling my already tense core with searing energy, feeling as if her fingerprints were branding my skin.

"You cruel thing, can't you feel what you're doing to me?"

"Ready?" She quietly asked.

I nodded, trying to contain myself. "We'll have to take it a little slow, legs still bothering me a bit."

"I'm sure that's not the only thing." Frost warmly smiled at me as we slowly descended the stairs leaving the infirmary. "You got pretty beat up, Finn."

"I'll be alright, Frost." I nodded as we started towards the crew quarters. "Thanks to you."

She held her smile, only briefly, falling away as we started up the stairs to the bunk room.

"She's thinking about the people still in that compound. About Edge, about Slade, about anyone else still captive there."

"If you need anything," Frost quietly spoke as she helped me to my bunk, "I'll be right next to you."

"Thanks." I nodded, slowly letting myself down onto my bed, trying to be gentle with my wounds and fresh skin.

Eventually I managed to fully lay down on my bunk, fully as in dangling my legs to one side of the bed. Frost had offered assistance if I needed, but I sure wasn't about to ask her to help me shed my tattered jeans for a pair of basketball shorts.

As comfortable as I could get, I stared at the ceiling, sleep being the last thing on my mind.

I thought of Slade, Knight's brother, and Edge, a girl very dear to Frost and Knight.

"Are they the only two left?"

My mind was imprisoned with the captive operatives, and as I looked over, I couldn't deny I envied Frost's exhaustion.

She had closed her eyes, and fallen asleep nearly immediately, failing to make any sound other than soft breaths.

I shook my head after what seemed hours of wondering. I knew sleep wasn't going to happen as I looked at my watch. It was 0900, still early in the day.

I sat up, attempting to be quiet for Frost's sake. I had already woken her once.

As I came out of bed, I noticed my arms and hands were mostly clear of the blue veins, except around the wound. It looked as Phoenix said it would, a small circle of blue veins forever scarring me.

I looked away from myself, my mind once more going to the operatives.

"What's going to happen to them?"

I needed to speak to Phoenix, I wanted to know what the plan was. I wanted to know when we were going back.

As quietly as I could manage, I pulled a fresh shirt and a pair of jeans from my trunk. My leg seemed more up to task since I had last tried to use it, and I found the trip to the bathroom at the back of the quarters wasn't too arduous.

Getting dressed, however, was a slightly different matter.

The jeans I got away with fairly easily, the shirt on the other hand, ended up sending fiery bolts across my ribs. More than once I had to pause, half hung up in my sleeve, to let the pain subside.

Finally clothed, I made my way down to Phoenix's door, hopeful that he had a plan ready and was just waiting for us to recover.

I rapped the door several times, and was surprised by the near instant response. "It's open."

I slipped through the door, pulling it behind me as Phoenix looked up from his desk, fixing me with a light smile. "I see you're still awake. Everything alright?"

I nodded.

"What can I do for you?"

"I needed to ask you something."

"Very well, but first." He produced my knife, my entire vest in fact. "As you asked."

I nodded as my hand took the vest, drawing the hunting knife from its sheath and observing the blade. "Thank you, Phoenix."

He nodded his welcome.

"I suppose you're here to ask about your mark." He assumed inaccurately, the mark was honestly far from being front and center in my mind, though I wasn't going to stop him.

"The Council added an agent to the ink we use for the mark, an agent that upon reaching a certain type of blood, will turn green as a marker."

"Evidently that's my blood type." I said. "Is it a problem?"

"No." Phoenix said. "The marker appears only in the presence of a pure wolf's blood. You are a pure blooded werewolf, Fenrir."

It took a moment to dawn on me, but when it did, things rapidly came into focus.

"That was it, why Marcus was so mad. Phoenix had just told him that I was a pureblood–" I recalled Marcus' story. *"And then Marcus equated me to his siblings...."*

Suddenly, I couldn't blame Marcus for being angry.

Phoenix's words pulled me from my moment of clairvoyance. "Your instincts are sharper, your reflexes faster. It explains your efficiency as a wolf in combat. I can only assume that to be the reason you and your wolf are so in tune. You are the strongest type of wolf on this planet, Fenrir."

"Simply because I'm pure blooded."

Phoenix nodded. "You weren't bitten and changed; it was simply in your body, waiting."

"Waiting?" I questioned.

"Yes, waiting to be activated, for lack of a better term."

The look he received must have told him he was performing the equivalent of talking to a very dense brick wall.

He took another try at the situation. "There are two common ways pure bloods can activate, Fenrir. One is by coming of age, the age typically being in the fourteen to fifteen range, towards the latest times of puberty. I suspect this is not the case with you, seeing you're as old as you are and you didn't change until after the night with that woman you spoke about, which is the second way it can be activated."

"Being around women?" I scoffed

"No," he shook his head, "an outside source sparks the wolf, normally the presence of another wolf. In light of you being a pureblood, what makes you believe this woman changed you?"

"The wolf, Phoenix. The wolf has been pointing me to her ever since I changed. I may not hate her anymore, but I still want to find her."

"It's going to be hard to do that, Fenrir. I've looked into Kirkwood, and none of the signs of a rogue wolf are present."

I frowned, disappointed with this development, or lack thereof. "I understand."

Phoenix seemed to sense this as he continued. "In the event she changes someone there's a chance we'll have a lead on her, but that's only if she wants to change them, or has poor control."

"How's that?"

"If you're human and are bitten by a werewolf, there is no one hundred percent chance that you yourself are now a wolf. It simply depends on the wolf's motives. As a werewolf, you can decide whether or not your victims become wolves. When a werewolf bites, it may or may not release toxins that are in two glands on your lower jaw. If the wolf doesn't release the toxins then the human remains human, if the wolf does release the toxins then the human becomes infected, and eventually moves on to being a wolf. These new "half bloods" if you will, are referred to as tainted, impure."

"I see." I nodded while feeling my face. "I didn't know about those."

Phoenix shook his head. "You may not have them in human form, some wolves have them at all times, others are present only in wolf form, it just depends on the individual."

"And how exactly does this toxin convert its hosts?"

"Well, like I said Fenrir, in your case it was in your blood but not active, but in both cases, pure and tainted, the toxin resides in the bloodstream. It has the exact traits of a typical red blood cell with the exception of one thing, it acts, in a roundabout way, like a virus, and as such the body reacts to defend itself. White blood cells are sent to destroy it. But as the white cells attack it, it absorbs them, pulling them in, then converts them inside of itself. After so long the original toxin bursts, and when it does, every cell it absorbed, now toxins, are dispersed. The cycle repeats until all the cells are converted to toxin cells that still carry out the functions of red and white blood cells. The situation is somewhat different for a pureblood, the toxins were always there, unforeign. Your body used them from the time you came to exist. All that had to happen was for them to awaken, and reveal what you truly were."

"I see."

"Now," he sighed as a light smile crossed his face, "have all of your questions been answered?"

I shook my head, my single question had gone without being asked. "What's to come of the settlement, more precisely our operators?"

Phoenix eyed me suspiciously. "Why?"

I took a deep breath. "I'd like to go back in. To get Bravo and Delta out of there."

"With who, Fenrir? Just you, Frost and Knight. No." He shook his head. "I nearly lost Alpha trying to get them the first time. I share your sentiment, and admire your loyalty to people you don't even know, but we can't go back. Alpha will be out of commission for several days, licking their wounds, and I don't even know–"

"So we're just going to leave them behind?" I frowned.

His eyes hardened as they fell upon me, as if trying to decide whether or not I was questioning his authority, then took a deep breath. "They are no longer your concern, Fenrir, nor were they ever, as you are neither their lieutenant nor their captain."

I began to protest. "Phoenix they–"

"You're dismissed, Fenrir." He pointed to the door. "Show yourself out."

I stood wordlessly and turned to the door, anger burning in me while common sense told me to leave it alone.

Outside the office was deathly quiet, devoid of the bustle of my teammates, either asleep or wounded.

I looked to the main door, beyond which waited the Challenger. The thought of leaving right then settled over me as I thought of what I could do on my own. I wasn't so bold as to think that I could take the compound alone, but the truth was, I wouldn't be.

I had my wolf, the strength he lent me, driving away fear, leaving me brave. I hadn't thought of it at the time, but I had tasted true combat, experienced it through every sense. The taste of sulfur lingered on my tongue, and my nose still stung with the acidic odor of paunch, when an enemy had been gutshot. The cacophony of gunfire hung in my ears, the cries of the wounded, the squelch of bloody impact. Through all of it, I hadn't known fear, though I knew I should've.

"You did this, didn't you wolf?"

I felt a stirring within myself, the wolf moving around, just before a throbbing pain took hold of my left arm, just below the elbow.

Pressing a thumb to it, in what seemed the point of origin, I found a small knot beneath the tissue.

I shook my head, assuming a torn muscle or some such.

I released my arm as I paced around the garage, trying to think of ways to sway Phoenix as thoughts of the captive operators hung over me.

"Slade. Edge."

That's all I knew them by, empty call signs, but I knew they were much more than that.

Knight's brother.

Frost's and Knight's closest friend.

I turned back to Phoenix's office, knowing what he had told me but, even more so, what was right.

He had to let me go back, even if it was *only* me. Keep the others, Frost, here, safe.

Let me go.

"If I die, then we lose one. Ghost could take my place. I can't just leave them."

And I hated Phoenix for possessing the capacity that he could.

I was within reach of the door and was extending my hand when I heard Phoenix on the other side.

"Commander, you don't understand, I'm not asking you to send a unit to attack a stronghold. I'm asking you to send a unit to mop up what's left and free my men! The reports from my unit indicate that they very nearly broke the enemy's battle line, and the operative we recovered assured me that my men are still alive!"

"What reports? Unless the others said something, I had just told him–"

"Commander, they were worn down enough to break out the silver and start shifting, you know as well as I what those events typically signify."

Phoenix was quiet for a moment.

"Yes ma'am, I understand, Commander." The fire had left Phoenix's voice. "Yes, a precision strike should be sufficient, low yield, so it could be passed off as a gas explosion or something along those lines."

There was a brief pause before Phoenix spoke again. "Two days? That soon?"

Another pause.

"Yes, three. Three good soldiers are going to be lost, but we've always known you can't win a war without that. It's just the cost."

Silently I cursed his remark.

"That would be appreciated, Commander, we're certainly running low. I'll arrange for one of mine to pick it up."

"No, I'm afraid he's bedridden. Round shattered his leg. My weapons specialist will be there, she goes by Frost. I understand, 1100 hours. Thank you, Commander."

"Where are you sending Frost? And after what?"

I assumed ammunition or Anver, perhaps both, though it honestly didn't matter. My only concern was that Frost was going alone.

"She's going on a supply run, nothing more, calm down."

In any case we needed the supplies, but it was of little consequence in comparison to the outcome of the settlement, and with it the operators.

Two days.

As I returned to the living quarters, lying down on my bunk, I stared at the ceiling, trying to formulate a plan.

Step one: Get there.

Step two: Don't die.

"Well that's a great plan." I ridiculed myself.

I remembered Frost's words at the compound, about ammunition and suppressors. I still had plenty of rounds for the 249, but without a suppressor I'd only draw attention to myself.

Phoenix seemed to believe that we had depleted their numbers, but I was uncertain what qualified as depleted. How many were left? Fifteen? Thirty?

I closed my eyes, hoping to rest, knowing I wouldn't as the gravity of my intentions set it.

Disobeying the order of "no further attempt on the compound" would certainly land me on the shit list. I didn't know if AWOL was a thing with The Council or not, but I was about to find out.

"If I don't get our operatives, I probably shouldn't come back at all."

I looked over to Frost, and the mere consideration of not returning set my heart to an angry skip.

"Better get the operators then."

As I watched her sleep, my chest burned as whatever had been smoldering in my core only grew brighter, hotter.

"I'll bring them home, Frost. For you."

26

A Rogue Op

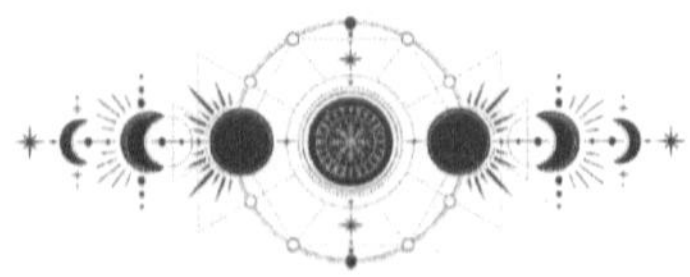

10/16
2300 Hrs.

The living quarters were still largely abandoned at the late hour, though I suspected I knew why.

Marcus and Ghost were probably still bedridden, Doc potentially tending them, with Knight very likely remaining simply in case she was needed.

With the exception of Frost carrying herself from bed to the bathroom once, I hadn't seen a soul in the quarters all day, which honestly didn't bother me that bad.

The day had mostly passed with me sitting at the single table in the bunk room, cooking up plans.

"Is it better to free the operators first? Or should I deal with the remaining soldiers first? How am I even to free the operators? Are there so few guards that I can deal with them?"

By day's end, I had accomplished little more than collecting my gear from the infirmary, going so far as to leave my bandages on since the one I had tried to remove still held back a bit of blood.

"Guess the silver really does push back the wolf's regen. Of course I also did get hit three times."

As far as planning went, all I had really managed to do was make a rough outline in my mind, branching into different outlines at each expected issue.

Whatever happened though, there was only one way to begin, and that was with the Challenger.

And not until I attempted to leave did I find the keys missing.

For a moment I feared that Phoenix had secured the keys to all the vehicles to prevent this very occurrence, though I couldn't very well ask him.

Frost had been the last to drive it. If Phoenix didn't have the keys, she did, and if she didn't, then I had my answer.

As I knelt at the edge of her bed, I couldn't help the upward curl at the corners of my mouth.

She had tossed a bit since last I had seen her, making a mess of her hair in the process, lending her a bit of bed hair cuteness.

"Focus." I quieted my mind. *"Get the keys!"*

Despite us being the only two in the darkened bunk room, I still made efforts to keep my voice down.

"Frost."

Still in sleep she let out a smokey moan, more than enough to set a shiver over my skin.

"Frost." I gently put my hand on her arm, cool skin beneath my fingers as I brushed her with my thumb.

Her eyes began to open, a small lift at the left corner of her mouth, though terribly short lived as she noticed me, only a breath away, her arm in my grasp.

She recoiled away as her eyes widened with alarm, turning slightly acidic as they fixed me.

I hurriedly brought a finger to my lips, hoping she wouldn't wake the whole building.

Whether through conscious effort or an automatic response to the gesture, her voice was hushed, though it was fairly obvious I had upset her.

"What are you doing, Fenrir?!" Accusation hung in her eyes as she pressed the blanket down on either side of her, enveloping her in bedding.

It hadn't occurred to me how this may have looked, though her response raised questions of its own.

Sadly this wasn't the time.

"Do you have my keys?" I suppressed a chuckle born of the notion that she may have thought I was trying to join her in bed.

She seemed taken aback with this, and when she replied, the edge had left her tone. "Why?"

I didn't want to answer that honestly, the less she knew, the safer she was from Phoenix's wrath when he found me gone, and her welfare was a fast growing concern of mine.

"Why do you need your keys, Fenrir?" She repeated.

The words of my adoptive mother suddenly echoed in my ears.

"Honesty is the foundation of a relationship, be that friendship or something more, do not betray trust, it is much harder to regain than it is to lose."

I felt only warmth as I reflected on her words.

"Thanks mom."

"I'm going back to the compound, I'm going to get our people out."

"Phoenix is sending us back in?" She sat erect, visual excitement rippling over her.

I lowered my gaze. "He didn't approve of this. In fact, he made it very clear I was *not* going."

Frost's eyes cast off any sign of excitement and grew hard as she realized my intent. "I see."

"Frost, I just need my keys."

"No." A subtle down curve took the corners of her mouth. "First off, you're asking me to help you disobey a direct order, incriminating myself in the process. Second, you have approximately one botched mission under your belt."

"I'll figure it out as I go." I stood. "But I don't have much time."

Her eyes flashed with anger at my insistence. "No, you're going to wind up getting yourself killed, Fenrir."

"Then at least I'll die trying to save our team, instead of doing nothing and letting an airstrike kill them."

"What?" Shocked injury took her eyes.

I frowned. "I heard Phoenix talking to a commander. He was asking for another unit to move on the compound and save our operators. She refused, even though Phoenix seemed to believe that we had nearly broken them. The call ended with them talking about a precision strike to destroy the settlement."

Edge's name scrawled itself across Frost's mind only for a moment, quickly displaced by the thought of her near sister in Alpha team.

"Knight–"

"I know." I nodded. "She's part of the reason I have to do this. Her brother, and Edge. I'm going to bring them back, I just need my keys. I'll take it from there."

Her voice became whisps as her eyes took to mine. "Why are you doing this, Fenrir? You don't owe any of us anything. You've only just finished training, and you don't even know the operators in Bravo and Delta... Last I heard, you joined the Red Moons with the intention of finding the wolf who changed you."

"I still intend to do so, but there's more to it than that now. The vampires at my family's farm... I made my mind up the day I started training with all of you. That I was going to become one of the best vampire killers The Council has ever seen, and if I have to kill a few rogue wolves to get closer to that goal then so be it. Another fact of the matter, Frost, is I do owe you. I owe Phoenix my freedom, I owe you my life, on numerous counts, and it's the same with Knight. And as my team, I owe it to all of you to try."

"You're full of surprises, aren't you?" She fixed me with suddenly tender eyes, and even in the darkness of the room, their vibrant blue threatened to seize me, pulling my mind to things far from captive friends.

"Just give me the keys, Frost." I smiled. "I can do this myself."

A scoff escaped her beautiful throat. "So you can leave the car somewhere to be spotted and tip them off? No, we'll ditch the car about a half mile out, and hoof it in from there."

I tilted my head. "We?"

"I'm not letting you go in alone, Fenrir."

Flattered as I was that she wanted to go with me, I knew she couldn't, comforted knowing that she had other tasks that would keep her from harm's reach.

"This isn't up for debate. Tomorrow at 1100 hours you're making a pick up. I don't know what, and I don't know where, but Phoenix set it up with the Commander. Probably ammo and Anver if I had to take a stab at it."

She rolled her eyes. "Great. You'll be fighting while I'm running errands."

I was grateful she hadn't said something more along the lines of "You'll be dying…" It seemed she did possess at least a modicum of confidence in me.

"And what are you gonna' do about getting back?"

That scenario I *had* thought of.

"There was a truck at the compound, provided it wasn't scrapped last night, we'll use it. If we can't, then we'll figure something else out. If we have to walk we will. The getting back isn't nearly as pressing as the getting out."

"I understand." She started to leave the blanket, then suddenly stopped. Her eyes subtly darted to her covered legs before looking up to me.

Was she naked? An image of blue lace suddenly returned to me, leaving me fighting fiendish curls that played at my lips.

She made no further attempt to move. "I'll meet you at the car."

With a nod, I turned to the door. I may have been playful, but I was careful not to push too far.

The door had barely cracked when I found Phoenix pacing the garage floor, a phone to his face.

The door gently closed, leaving me with Frost once again.

"Fenrir?!" My name quietly rang out.

Again my finger went to my lips as I turned, finding her still in bed as I nodded to the door. "Phoenix. He's on the phone."

Again I pressed the door, just enough so that I could see him.

"Get dressed." I whispered.

"How do you know I'm not?" She retorted.

I sent her a mischievous smile, accompanied by a single raised brow. "Get out of bed then."

Her brow flattened, not so much as to say she was angry, but enough to prove her displeasure with my accuracy.

"Turn around," she twirled a finger, "and tell me you won't look."

"That's an awfully tall order." I spun around.

The silence of the room only amplified the rustling of blankets, the gentle tap of feet landing on the floor.

"Not to state the obvious here, Frost, but you do realize that as wolves, we've seen a bit of each other when we do our shifting."

"That's different!" She hissed. "Just... look at the wall!"

"Different how?" I wondered. *"Ah well, whatever you want, Frost."*

Making good on her orders, my eyes locked onto the head of a nail in the wall, though quickly admitting their hunger for more exhilarating views.

She had to be watching me, had to feel the energy bleeding from me.

I wanted to look, each sound painting a portrait in my mind.

A soft scratch, as denim jeans were pulled from the floor.

My eyes ventured from the nail, though not far.

The chatter of a belt buckle, and the purr of a single elegant leg sliding into place.

A solid thud hit the stairs, jerking my eyes to the door, leaving me unintentionally breaking my word to Frost as I saw her from the edge of my sight.

The jeans were still around her legs, creamy skin disappearing beneath harsh blue denim, and above...

Not blue.

Black semi transparent cloth clung to her, only mildly darkening her pale skin, though still obscuring what lay beneath. The fabric ended just shy of her right hip, replaced by a crisscross of intricate bands.

Somehow, despite the dark room, sparkles danced from a blue jeweled star.

"Rainer!"

I turned away, every ounce of the wolf's strength battling to contain the groan that ached to escape me, both at my failure and yet, strange as it was to admit, also my success.

Fire gnawed at my skin, my core, and lower yet.

A belt growled behind me, a soft metallic tick ringing out. "Alright, I'm ready."

"Me too." I hoarsely replied as I cleared my throat.

Frost tilted her head as she drew in a breath. "I don't think you are, Fenrir."

"What do you mean?" I asked.

"Did you shower today?"

"No." I shook my head. "Wounds were still bleeding when I changed my clothes. I've still got the bandages on."

"Silver." She nodded. "You need to get that blood off of you, Finn."

"Don't really have a lot of time here, Frost." I insisted.

"There's no point in trying this at all if you're gonna' get busted six hundred yards away." She countered. "Get those bandages off."

I frowned.

I had struggled enough getting my clothes on, and even though that had been hours ago, every once in a while my ribs would still send a tinge rocketing to my brain.

I lifted my shirt, trying to ignore the sudden scream from my ribs, though Frost caught what I could only assume was my pained expression.

"That bad?" She asked.

I shook my head. "New skin."

"Mm." She nodded as I pulled a throwing knife from my vest by the bed.

The bandage on my leg came off easy enough, and I was happy to see that the scar tissue had fully formed, now free of pain.

"This one though..."

I raised my hands to the wrap on my torso.

I had just put the tip of the knife beneath the material when Frost shook her head.

"Stop for a minute will you?" She said. "Before you disembowel yourself." She opened her footlocker, retrieving a pair of blunted trauma scissors.

"Thanks." I held out my hand.

"I've got it, Finn." She stood, stepping to my side, and I felt cool steel and hands play against my back.

A bit of pressure fell away with the bandage, and as Frost pulled the soiled wrap from me, I winced away from a sudden stab in my side.

"Fenrir," Frost sighed, "you can't go out like this. You're not healed yet. The silver may not be killing you, but it doesn't look like it's done with you yet. Your wolf has done what it can with multiple injuries and silver but–"

"Frost," I turned to face her, "I'm going back."

"Fenrir…" She shook her head. "Let me see your side."

"Frost," I protested, "I'll be o–"

"Do it, Fenrir." She demanded.

I leaned back on my bed, doing what I could to raise my left arm so she could do her inspection.

I was fairly certain I knew what it looked like, a scar that ran across my side, nothing exciting.

"It's healed on the outside." Frost said. "I'm going to put my hand on your side, Fenrir."

"Wh–" I was cut short as her cool hand landed on my ribs. With a minuscule amount of pressure, Frost pushed the air from my lungs, a mixture of equal parts pain and pleasure.

"Hurt's right there?" She asked.

"A little." I answered.

"Like I said, the round traced your ribs. I'd be willing to bet that whichever rib it ran probably has some damage. Troughed, a fracture maybe, not fully broken."

"Frost, I'll be fine." I stood, returning my shirt without too much fuss.

"See? It'll be patched before you ever drop me off."

"You still smell a bit like blood." She frowned.

"A little's okay." I rolled my shoulders. "Whole place is gonna' smell like blood after last night. So long as I'm not reeking."

"No." She quietly replied as she shook her head. "Most of it came off with the bandages."

"Good enough then." I nodded, well aware of time ticking away. "Let's go."

* * *

The ride away from The Citadel started quietly, leaving me to face the grim prospect that I had made for myself.

The outlines in my head jumbled, a mess of anticipation swelling in my chest.

I wasn't scared, I was ready.

Frost must've caught my slow exhale, trying to steady myself behind the wheel.

"Are you sure about this, Fenrir?" She asked, seeming to ignore the fact that I was still healing. "You don't have to do this, no one expects it of you."

"I'm sure." I stared through the windshield.

"What're you trying to prove?"

From the edge of my sight, I saw her glance to me.

"I'm not trying to prove anything to anyone. I don't know why Frost, but I can't leave them. I realize I don't know them, but you all do, you care for them, and I care for you, so–"

"You care for them."

I nodded, my tongue refusing to say the rest of my reason for returning.

"Beneath the desire I feel for you, Frost, this damned lust and whatever else, I care about you, more than anyone I've ever met, and I won't let you lose someone you love."

I knew that losing Slade would be no different to Knight, but my heart wasn't pining for Knight.

As I looked over the treetops, the stars above sparkled, bright white, oranges, reds…

"And there's Rigel." I smiled. *"Not the only blue star I've seen tonight."*

My sudden chuckle drew Frost's attention, and without knowing the matter, she too chuckled.

"What?"

"Just… looking at the stars." I looked back to the road, centering my mind. The time for any sort of game had passed.

"Rigel, right?" She asked quietly. "Thinking of your family again?"

I nodded, a short breath purging from my lungs. "Not the one I left behind though."

"Tonight, I'm fighting for another family." I nearly shook my head, knowing that my own thoughts were inaccurate. *"Tonight I'm fighting for you, Frost."*

She didn't say anything, offering only a quick nod, though in the close quarters of the car, the energy radiating from her spoke volumes.

It wasn't the collected energy that I had grown accustomed to feeling from her, quite the opposite in fact.

She was a wound spring, primed up, waiting for the trigger to flip.

Numerous times before, over the days and weeks spent together, I wished that I had taken a place in her mind. Now, all I wanted was for her not to worry about me.

I knew she would though, and not without just reasoning. There was no doubt that what I was preparing to attempt bordered on suicide, and had firmly established itself as a poor idea.

I had to try though.

I tried to tell myself that even if it wasn't for Frost, I still would've made this effort, because three more lives still hung in the balance.

Three more lives that mattered dearly to my friends, to my family. To let them slip away without trying, it wasn't something I could do.

Those words were nothing but pretty lies however. At the root of it all, here and in every parallel plane of existence, there wasn't one where I didn't love Frost.

Without fully turning, my eyes rested on her.

She had been there when I shattered at the farm, torn apart when I first witnessed the world of the wolf and vampire rip through the veil into the world of humanity. The night Vivian died.

In her warm words I had taken comfort, and the first seeds of feelings had been sown, buried amongst the questions to the answers I sought.

At the farm, in the time we spent together, mostly our time alone, the seeds had sprouted, nurtured by kind smiles, and kinder deeds.

I remembered our time shopping together, the rare tenderness she gave the little girl, also to me. I cherished that memory even more than our time beneath the van. I wasn't sure why, but seeing her with that little girl, I couldn't help the warmth I felt in recollection.

Then there was my week with Knight, and all of its shortcomings. When everyone else had all but given up on me, losing even Knight, Frost didn't.

Because of her, I managed to keep myself alive one more week, the week spent with her.

In that time I learned a little more about her, though so much of her remained unknown to me, refusing to talk about her past, even when everyone else openly shared theirs.

And then the raid happened.

Aside from the fact that she alone had saved my life, she stayed at my side, when a bed was only a few steps away.

It was growing harder to believe that I was the only one that felt these things, yet I still refused to give myself that much hope.

It wasn't the vulnerability that scared me. It was the fear that, if I were to ever make it known, that I might lose her altogether.

Pulling to the side of the road, I killed the headlights.

"We're about a half mile out." I looked over, finding her brow creased, her pretty lips twisted into a frown. "Frost?"

"I heard you, Finn." Her soft voice replied.

"Is she worried?"

Of course she was, one man, the rookie of Alpha, trying to do something the whole team couldn't.

"You don't have to worry about me, Frost." I took a shot at the issue.

"Yes I do, number one you're new, and number two…" She paused, shaking her head. "Just be careful, alright?"

I nodded as I reached for the door handle.

"Fenrir." Frost grabbed my arm, the sudden collision startling me, and as I turned back, I found her staring at me. "Make sure you get back alive."

For the first time since our drive began, despite knowing the unpleasantries ahead, I frowned.

"Frost." I couldn't meet her eyes. "I won't make promises to someone if I don't know I can keep them."

"Don't promise someone, promise *me*." She breathed.

The air once more left my lungs as I fought not to get ahead of myself, though even harder I fought the urge to press my lips to hers, despite the fact that I hadn't kissed a girl in my life.

How could she do this? In one instant seem angry, and the next set my heart to taps.

"Say it, Fenrir."

Swallowing a lump of desire, I raised my eyes to hers, drinking in the dark pools.

"I'll come back to you, Frost." I managed a smile. "I promise."

Without warning her arms wrapped around my neck, pulling herself against me and pressing her face into my neck.

I started to speak, only to smile as I put my arms around her.

No words broke the silence, none needed to be said.

I saw this for what it was, a declaration of caring about each other, to what degree didn't matter, only making a fact that we did care.

My heart didn't speed up as I breathed her in, and the spark that had passed between us in previous days no longer held its volatile charge.

Where her hands held me radiated only a soft current as our hearts fell into rhythm.

"Don't be scared, Frost." I whispered.

She leaned back, only slightly as her eyes moved to mine, dazzling me once more with the brightness in her blue eyes.

She smiled as her eyes fell, only for a moment, before they returned.

"I can't not be scared, Finn." She rested her face on my shoulder. "For you. For them. For…"

"I'm coming back to you, Frost." I took her arms, gently pushing her back as I lowered my face to hers. "I promise."

Her lips gently parted, and her breath caught, as if she was about to say something, though she remained silent.

I smiled. "Tell me when I get back?"

She didn't say anything, giving only a small smile and a quick nod.

As I stepped from the car, turning towards the darkness, my facade fell.

"If I get back."

27

Drawing Blood

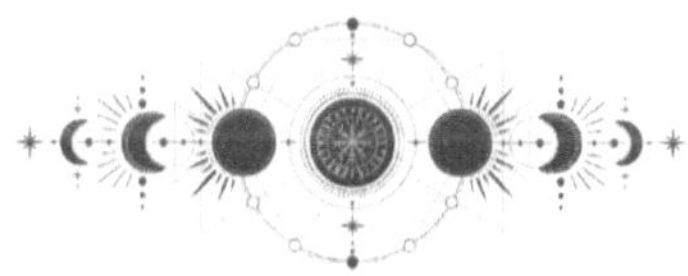

Ten minutes later, I lay on the earth, looking down into the settlement alongside the 249, doing everything in my power to push Frost from mind.

It wasn't the recollection of being only a breath away from her naked body, as pleasing a thought as that was.

It was the promise. It hung in my ears, her soft repeating voice.

"Promise me."

What did she mean by that? I tried not to lose myself in her words, grappling for what they truly meant.

The overly optimistic voice in me said that she had to care for me, while its realistic counterpart insisted that it was simply to say be careful, and make it back.

Before I could go back though, I had some friends to spring from the clink.

Amazingly, the red pick up seemed to be intact, potentially solving our issue on getting back home, but that was still a ways off at best.

Amid the cluster of buildings, only two looked as if they were still functional, the other three badly damaged, ready to fall in on themselves.

They could serve as cover, but it was a risk, they were far too damaged, just entering the structure could bring it down.

I found what I could only assume to be the cells on the opposite side of the compound, one of the two remaining buildings. It was the only building made of concrete while the others, surviving and ruins, were all of wooden construction.

"If I was going to hold a wolf, I wouldn't trust wooden walls."

That had to be the cells.

"Frost, I'm here." I pressed the button on my chest.

"You made good time." Her voice called back.

"I had a lot of cardio training." I noted with a smile. "The truck looks good. We'll try for that."

"Good luck, Fenrir." She paused. "Remember your promise."

There was no mistaking the concern in her voice.

"I'll see you soon." I said.

"Make sure you do." Her voice was hushed.

A fire suddenly came to life in the compound, illuminating five men. Four stood around the flame, the fifth having taken a knee to light the blaze.

I drew up the 249, bunched up like they were, I could bring them down quickly. I could hardly believe it would be this easy.

The fifth man stood as I peered through the sights, finding that he dwarfed the others, six foot six at a minimum.

"What if there are more that I don't see?"

I lowered the 249, erring on the side of caution. Surely more than five men held this post.

The big man seemed in charge of this group, the others all looking at him. The firelight danced in his short blond hair, upon his weathered face. He wasn't necessarily old, but he was certainly the oldest of the bunch.

Looking upon the rest of them, I gauged them to be around my age, each of average build.

"Alright." The big man's voice boomed, though he wasn't shouting. "Just got off the horn with Whitedeer. Our dead and wounded got to him a few hours ago, no better or worse than last we saw them. No additional casualties." He translated. "He's still trying to put together a support team, but they'll still be a day or two at best. Care package is still en route, no changes. That's all I've really got for you, men. Whitedeer said the mission stands: Hold the post. On the bright side, I don't think the team that hit us last night will try again very soon, they took some knocks as well."

"Not without giving some." One of the younger men, a red head, crossed his arms, and I noted the rifle slung over his shoulder. "They killed a lot of our friends."

"And we killed a lot of theirs before that, didn't we?" Hunter sniffed, concluding the matter. "A few more nights men, then we're out of the woods. Whitedeer agreed that we're all due some R&R, soft sheets and warm food."

"Why can't we just leave now? Forget the prisoners and just go?" Another man asked, his face obscured beneath the hood of a trench coat. "They'll still be here when the support shows up."

"Think you've forgotten something, Hammel." Hunter said. "She won't make it."

"She?"

Were they talking about Edge?

"We've done what we can, if she's not gonna' make it, she's not gonna' make it. We can't help that."

"It's our job to try though, isn't it. What she knows could be important."

They had to be talking about Edge.

"What have you done to her?"

"Jordan," Hunter spoke again, "you drew the short straw tonight. You've got the security room, I want your eyes on the cameras at all times until you get relieved, got it?"

I assumed he got the reaction he wanted as he continued. "Good, Nellis, you're on perimeter detail. Irving, Hammel, the two of you will be the reliefs tonight."

There was a brief pause as the tall blond scanned over his crew. "Dismissed."

The mention of cameras caught me off guard, I hadn't seen any in the compound, though in that same regard I hadn't been looking.

That left a question however.

If they had cameras, how had Alpha managed to get inside their perimeter? Unless Bravo and Delta knocked some out when they attacked? That would explain having one man watching the cameras and one actively patrolling.

They had blind spots.

The initial attack must've killed some of the cameras, it was the only plausible reasoning for Alpha making it in without getting massacred.

Little did Bravo and Delta know, but they had cleared some of the obstacles before me, a shred of luck considering I hadn't thought of cameras.

Despite that luck though, a cold knot of fear began to swell within me, something I hadn't yet known, even when facing failure at the farm.

Five men stood against me, any one of which could end me.

Greater than that, the fear of dying, was the fear of breaking my promise, of never seeing Frost again.

Anxiety washed over me, rushing my breaths, knowing that if I failed, the operatives I'd come to rescue would die prisoners, all efforts in vain as a bombing run wiped them and everything in the settlement from existence.

"This is it." My mind whirled. *"This is where I either solidify my place in The Red Moons, or I join those that have already fallen."*

There could be no error, no mistake on my part, it had to be flawless, down to the smallest sound or scent. There was no one for me to call on if I got in a jam and furthermore, I was the last chance the operators had.

The odds weren't particularly in my favor though, there were still five able bodied men between me and the operatives.

Divide and conquer would be the name of the game, starting with taking their eyes.

The security building, and the patrolling Nellis.

A simple process of elimination pointed me to the security office, furthered by a solitary soldier stepping inside.

Another soldier, who I took to be Nellis, moved towards the cell block with his rifle, while the reliefs laid bedrolls near the crackling fire, preparing to turn in until their shift.

That left the big man, the one in charge, roaming around.

As I observed, I noted the amount of time the big guy spent on his phone, probably supposed to check in every so often with command.

"Whose name did he say? Whitedeer?"

I made a note to ask Phoenix when… if… I got back, and that would be after whatever repercussions I faced.

I couldn't dwell on it now though. I had more pressing issues, the men before me, and the new threat of cameras.

As I scanned the area, I saw a small black brick attached to the security house, a tiny red light displaying that the camera was still active. It was trained on the door into the building, so that whoever was inside could look upon their visitors.

Looking over the burned-out buildings I saw the charred remains of more cameras, directed at the road, though damaged beyond function.

An hour more I watched the compound, the movements of the soldiers.

Nellis made the same circuit around the compound, endlessly going round and round, never deviating from his original route.

Hunter was less predictable, but he seemed to keep to the interior of the compound, always within sight of the fire, keeping eye on the reliefs, who seemed rather restless.

Quiet banter passed between the two of them, too quiet for even the ears of the wolf to make out.

That they would rather sleep on the ground than in one of the damaged buildings only cemented my suspicions that they were beyond use, but they did offer me a means to deal with Nellis.

Numerous times on his course, Nellis broke line of sight with the others at the fire, walking wide around the out buildings, where only the melted cameras watched over him.

None of his friends could see him there, none could cover him.

His absence would eventually be noticed though, leaving me with only one course.

Once it started, even if silent, it had to be quick, over before the other four thought to muster a response.

"Should've just shot all of them when I had the chance."

I knew it was better I hadn't though, there could've been more somewhere out of sight.

Now I knew that there were only five, and that they were expecting reinforcements inside of forty-eight hours, as well as this 'care package' business.

Nellis passed before me once again, and I rose from my stomach, slowly moving down the grade, starting a timer on my watch to track Nellis.

As I moved towards the compound, my fear only grew, my breath growing shaky and shallow as my hands set to trembling.

"Why is this happening? I've been in fights before, I've made kills. In the firefight, and with the vampires at my farm. What's happening to me?"

My mind reeled as I desperately tried to steady myself, struggling against my fleeting courage.

"In the firefight, I had my team, and I was too worried about them for anything else to sink in. With the vampires, I had my friends and Frost, as well as–"

My thoughts slowed. *"I had you, wolf. I know it was you that made me brave then, with the vampires, but why aren't you–"*

"I had let you take hold then, to face the vampires with me... You blocked fear from me."

It was the only thing that made sense.

"Wolf. I need your help, we've walked together in the days since we met one another face to face, and it seems that you've just been riding shotgun, letting me carry us for the most part, but I need you at the wheel now. I need you to keep me steady, keep me strong. If you have to take a hold, so be it, I'll give you as much as you need. We have to do this, wolf, we have to save our friends that are stuck in this place. We have to get back to Frost. Make me brave, make me a

soldier, shield me from fear."

A harsh growl resonated in me, and in terror I felt the wolf's reply form words in my mind.

"I will kill it."

Moving towards the compound, I felt warmth lay over me, the wolf embracing me.

My eyes, already able to pierce the darkness due to the wolf, suddenly grew sharper, penetrating the shadow of shadows.

What I had thought to be extraordinary ears suddenly felt deaf as the wolf took hold. A bird twitched in a distant nest, a spider's legs tapped on a blade of grass.

My nose filled with the aroma of smoke from the burnt buildings, the sulfuric notes of spent cartridges, the iron of bloodied earth.

My muscles tensed, tightened, as I drew up, casting off any semblance of a shiver as I turned rigid. Every step was controlled with predatory precision, every move smooth, gentle, yet quick.

My body was that of a man, but I was the wolf.

The wolf's growl had told me that he would kill my fear.

He had done much more than that, he had devoured it.

"Teach me, wolf. Guide me through this."

I felt him agree as a peculiar hunger awoke, knowing that blood was soon to be shed.

He seemed eager to begin.

It became easy to understand how men fell victim to their wolves as my body buzzed with energy, the wolf's power surging through me.

Creeping into position, I found the sensation of the wolf's gifts were not unlike the euphoria that Frost instilled in me. A rich intoxication as my senses were overwhelmed, yet achieving the absolute peak of awareness.

The timer on my watch showed five minutes had passed as I shed my pack and the 249. They weren't needed here.

I smiled, though it wasn't completely me, as I drew the hunting knife from its sheath, tightly gripped in a hammer hold.

Grass softly crunched nearby, Nellis' pace remaining consistent, growing ever louder. The eagerness of the wolf swelled, restlessly waiting as adrenaline thundered through me.

The footsteps grew nearer still as Nellis continued his approach.

The air swirled with the thick aroma of battle, yet I could smell the oil on his rifle.

The crackling of the fire dominated the quiet night, but I could hear his steady breath.

A footstep just around the corner; I held my breath as my body drew up, preparing for the lunge.

A shadow of a man stepped away from the building, his rifle still slung over his shoulder. It wouldn't have done him any good anyway.

In arms reach, the knife wins.

The slightest grunt of surprise left Nellis' throat as I swept his legs from beneath him, driving the knife into the back of his neck and smashing him to the earth as his body began to tremble in its death throes.

That was it.

In an instant, the existence of Nellis ended.

In less than a second, with only the slightest bit of resistance, the knife had glided through the skin, the tip working its way between the vertebrae, severing the spinal cord.

If Nellis had any luck at all, he was dead before his face slammed to the ground.

Looking down on the shell that once contained soul and spirit, I felt a tug of guilt, not for ending this young man's life, but because I *didn't* feel guilty. I had potentially killed others in the first raid, and I had certainly routed vampires in the past, but this man, Nellis, was the first man I had ever taken with the knife. How could I feel... calm? Was this the wolf as well?

"There's no time for this, he'll be missed." A piece of my brain fired.

Working quickly, I freed Nellis of his rifle and trench coat, careful to keep the latter from the blood that was quickly spreading through the grass.

A radio hung on his belt, a valuable find, lending me the ability to listen in on the remaining rogues. I turned the volume down as I put it on my side, just loud enough for me to hear.

The last secured piece, which the plan hinged on, was the trench coat, though it could hardly be considered anything more than rags.

A rough patch of embroidery work on the right sleeve drug across my fingers and as I turned my eyes to it I found a black shield, much like that of my mark. Emblazoned upon it, was a familiar symbol, though one I couldn't quite place

It was a red cross, plain and simple, but above the typical horizontal bar was another, though a bit shorter.

"Do the Rogues have units?"

The wolf pushed the question from mind, pressing on with what he had been summoned for.

As I pulled the coat over my clothes, finding it an adequate fit, the wolf drove my mind forward, already moving to the next objective.

While sharing the reins with the wolf, privy to his thoughts, his plan moving forward, I realized that his skill exponentially exceeded my own, his planning, his cunning.

He was a warrior.

"What are you wolf? Who are you?" I repeated the question I had asked only days before. *"Does this have to do with being a pureblood?"*

With a few clicks, the timer on my watch was reset, once more for ten minutes.

We were certain that in that amount of time, Nellis would be missed by Hunter's ever watchful eye.

Taking a step towards the rifle, I felt a lump in the coat, and reaching into the pocket I found a single hand grenade.

One of Knight's lessons rang in my mind and I knew I could make use of it.

Once more I looked down to Nellis' lifeless mass. There was no point in hiding him, the following sequence of events would unfold faster than he would be discovered.

Shouldering the rifle and raising my hood, I turned towards my next target, the security center.

Slowly I stepped from one shadow to another as voices reached my heightened ears. "Hey Hunter, you know Irving still hasn't heard about Razgryz?"

There was a brief lull before Hunter's voice replied. "You guys want a ghost story *now*?"

"It's not a ghost story Hunter, it's a legend, part of werewolf heritage."

"Same thing." Hunter replied.

"That's not true, legends are…well legends, they all have some sort of origin story, ghost stories are for kids."

"Well, it is a piece of our lore in any case." Hunter said. "I'm surprised you haven't heard it yet to be honest."

There was a brief pause before Hunter's voice resumed. "She's called a demon, and also an angel, and many have debated which she really is, but her name is certain. It is that of a Valkyrie, Razgryz, and she is the most powerful werewolf the earth has ever known. Her name is a rendition of Radgridr, in English, council-truce."

"Ramble away, Hunter, forget about your perimeter man for a while."

I swung around the corner of the security hut, below the onlooking camera, happy to see a door.

"She is called on occasion," Hunter's voice carried through the door, staticky, relayed through a speaker within , "the demon of the northern forests. Her ferocity in combat was second to none, she alone chose who would live and die on the battlefield."

I scarcely listened as I looked away from the door, hiding my face from the camera as I tested the doorknob.

Locked.

I gave a few light raps, and heard steps within, Jordan moving to the door.

The knife once more returned to my hand.

"Razgyrz is rumored to take a host in times of war, though she doesn't concern herself with the wars that solely belong to man. If she chooses a host, it is a war that wolves have a part in. She chooses her host by the heart in their chest, one who holds the heart of a warrior."

The door creaked open as I looked upon yet another youthful face. Surprise flashed across his brown eyes as I shoved a hand to his mouth, while the other thrust the blade through his windpipe.

His jugular tore open as I ripped the blade free of his throat, painting the nearest wall and the right side of my face a glistening crimson.

Just as with Nellis, I drove Jordan to the floor, though I didn't care to keep him from the murky pool that grew beneath.

The light in his eyes faded just as quickly as I figured Nellis' had, a nearly identical wound of opposite entry and exit.

As I stood, the wolf brought my left hand to my face, dragging the back of my thumb through the blood and across my mouth, cleaning it with a quick swipe of my tongue.

The chatter paused as I stepped over the body, turning my attention to the contents of the one room structure.

A single desk, cluttered with various papers, sat against the far wall beneath six camera monitors, of which only three functioned. One was focused on the door, while the second displayed the inner perimeter of the compound, where Hunter and the others rested. The third looked out over the road.

I began rummaging through the documents atop the desk, mostly finding logs and reports, largely useless to me.

As my hands grazed a taller stack of parchment, the shine of hard plastic caught my eye and brushing away paper blankets, I found a black laptop.

"Sometimes she chooses a kind hearted warrior." Hunter continued the story, momentarily drawing my gaze back to the monitor, finding the remaining three still at the fire.

"But sometimes she chooses a cold heart, one that will kill mercilessly. Regardless of the sort, wherever she ventures, shadows follow, bringing forward a tide of death and destruction, leaving behind crumbling cities and broken lands."

I didn't expect much when I opened the laptop, and as predicted it requested a password. Having reached the limits of my tech-savvy abilities,

I lifted a note that had been clenched between the screen and keyboard.

A short memo had been scrawled across the paper, either in haste or in terrible penmanship.

"Shipment 0800 Hrs. 200# Mixed Ag. Rounds, 100# Anver."

The contents of the supply package?

"Ag. Rounds?" My brain worked, recalling a science class that felt like it had taken place a lifetime ago. *"Silver. Two hundred pounds of silver ammo, one hundred of Anver."*

My eyes fell to a pack resting against the desk, a name embroidered across it.

"Creech."

"Must've been Jordan's."

"What must be known of Razgryz however, is though she is a valkyrie, she doesn't stand with the Aesir."

My ears piqued. *"A valkyrie that stands against the Aesir?"*

"Aesir?" A voice asked.

"The old Norse deities." Hunter answered. "Odin, Tyr, Thor, Baldr. The famous ones you always hear about."

"I thought valkyries were the ones that chose which dead went to Valhalla?" A different voice asked.

"Hunter's telling new pieces." I smiled. *"Fine by me, stay busy."*

"Generally, yes," Hunter continued, "amongst other things, but not Razgryz. She was something else."

"Like a fallen valkyrie?"

"Perhaps." Hunter replied. "She stood with what the Aesir despised."

"And that was?"

"Those that the Aesir had cast out, banished." Hunter shortly answered. "Those that threatened what the Aesir so desperately strived to achieve, order. She stood with the bringers of chaos, the jotnar.

"Somewhere along the way," the whispers of chaos continued, "humanity fell into her charge, be that an act of sympathy for what the Aesir would throw away, no one is certain, and there is nothing documented, only that she will do whatever she can to protect them, and that is what she calls her host to do. To stand guard of the humans, to shield them from the afflicted of the world."

A voice chimed, "You mean–"

"I mean creatures like us, wolves and vampires. She, the outcast valkyrie that chose chaos over order, must now stand to protect humanity, to keep the chaos at bay, and she is not alone. She took a handful of others with her into the shadows. The father of all wolves and his children, as well as the midgard serpent, and the fallen queen, amongst others. All outcasts taken into her care."

"To face them, two rose from the void between creation and evolution… The vampire lords. There are no formally accepted records of these beings, one moment never having existed, the very next arriving with the strength rivaling that of the Aesir themselves. They are physical and ethereal, water and wind, dead, yet very much alive." Hunter stopped.

"Do you believe in these spirits, Hunter?"

Hunter nearly laughed. "I'm a soldier, I believe in flesh and blood. In what I can kill with my teeth and my rifle. I'm just telling the legend you asked for."

"You've never said much about the other two, Hunter. Like their names or well, anything." A voice noted.

"Not much to be said of them honestly. They are nameless immortals, at least according to the lore. If someone did know their names, it was never cataloged. While most every piece of old wolf text references Razgryz, there is no real written history of the vampire lords, origins or otherwise. They're referred to only as specters, echoes in the dark." Hunter ended.

Having finished a present for the next to visit the building, I turned to leave, nearly passing through the door before I noticed a set of keys dangling from a nail in the frame.

I reached up, claiming what I assumed could only be the cell keys.

"Well, that's thirty minutes I'll never get back." Someone poked sarcastically.

"Shut up, Irving." Another snarled, not Hunter, one of the other grunts.

"Hey, Nellis." Hunter chuckled over the radio.

The following five seconds ticked by painfully slowly as I realized I had taken far too long in my searching of the security house.

"Nellis?" Hunter repeated, though in his voice was a hint of concern. "Jordan, have you seen Nellis make his rounds?"

I knew that the lack of response from both would set a match to the powder as I stepped from the building, amazed at the wolf's ability to remain silent as I quickly started back towards Nellis' body, towards the 249 and cover.

Rapid footsteps reached my ears, two sets moving in tandem, racing towards the security building.

Frantically I let out towards the ragged building, cursing the rifle and Jordan's pack as they thundered against my back, hoping that the noise would go unnoticed and that the laptop within the pack wouldn't be damaged.

"Hammel, Irving! Stop!" Hunter roared in the distance.

I didn't dare look back as I neared the building and the cover it offered, from both searching eyes and the blast.

"Nearly there!"

Orange light flooded over me with a cannon's clap as they hit the tripwire, and the shuddering earth nearly robbed me of my feet, saved only by the sure footed wolf as I stumbled.

A cry of pain was barely audible over the roaring furnace that had been the security room.

"Hunter!" The crying voice pierced the night.

"Irving, where are you?!" Hunter roared.

"By the security hut." Irving groaned, his voice cracking with tears.

"Can you move?!" Hunter calmly asked.

"I don't– there's a piece of metal in me!" Irving's voice turned shrill.

"I'm coming!" Hunter shouted.

Heavy footsteps, moving fast, fell on the grass near the burning security hut followed by more yells.

"Irving, where are you?!"

"Over here!"

For a time, only the flames spoke, crackling as they ate, then the shouts started up a little further away.

"What the hell happened Irving?! Hey, don't even think about closin' your eyes! Come on, stand up son!"

Hunter must've managed to get Irving to his feet, and incoming footsteps announced they were drawing near.

Two strong foot falls accompanied by an off pattern shuffle.

Irving was seriously wounded, only able to walk with Hunter's assistance.

His words slurred as he spoke to his companion pleadingly. "Hunter, just go. I'm not… gon' make it."

The fresh aroma of blood was rich with iron, more than just a small piece of shrapnel would merit. Irving was bleeding out.

Hunter harshly replied. "I ain't leaving you here, Irving. Just keep your feet moving, it's not far to the truck. The wolf will patch you up, you hear me? But you gotta' hold on, give the wolf time."

"What about… the shipment? We're s'posed to be here." Irving murmured.

"Forget the shipment."

"The pris'ners?" Irving gasped.

"Don't worry about them. *We* are leaving. Just a bit further."

For a brief moment, I considered letting them leave, just slipping around the corner and letting them go.

I knew I couldn't do that though. The blood of Bravo and Delta had been shed here, as well as Alpha's, even my own.

There would be no forgiveness for that.

I lowered the pack and rifle, opting for the 249 as I circled round the building, flanking Hunter and the injured Irving.

Two shots is all it would take. Hunter first, back of the head, and the second to hasten Irving's passing. It didn't feel cowardly, the concept of shooting two men in the back. I had the advantage, the best means of keeping my promise.

I rounded the corner to see Hunter and Irving still on their way to the truck.

I raised the 249, fixing the sights on the base of Hunter's skull as Irving collapsed.

"Irving!" Hunter roared as he rolled Irving to his back. "Irving!"

Hunter shook the young man's shoulders for only a few moments before hanging his head.

"Dammit!" Hunter slammed his fist to the ground with a solid thud.

Again I took aim as a cool breeze kissed the back of my neck.

Hunter stiffened, having caught my scent, and slowly he stood before turning to face me.

"Well done, Council. You've killed four men who were little more than students." He turned his hands out as he squared up with me. Only then did I see the pistol on his side, though he didn't reach for it.

"Bullshit." I replied. "You killed most of two units and held the others captive. That's not what students do."

"Doesn't matter what you think." Hunter shook his head. "At least have the decency to end this right, Council."

"How's that?" I asked, my finger moved to the trigger.

"By tooth and claw." His face lowered, the challenge silently declared between our locked eyes.

I smiled.

The *wolf* smiled.

I lowered the gun and Hunter grimly nodded. "Perhaps The Council still possesses a few good men."

Hunter led me in the shift by only a few seconds, but it gave him a definitive edge. Had he taken the opportunity, he could've ended the duel before it had even started.

In equal parts wonder and criticism, I was shocked that he hadn't taken a step towards me.

Not until I had fully shifted.

In a few bounds he was on top of me, his enormous jaws hurtling towards my throat. I reared away, barely getting clear of his gleaming white teeth. Missing my throat, Hunter took the next target, clamping down on my front leg, fangs raking it to the paw as I continued away from him.

Pain surged along the furrows carved by his teeth only momentarily before disappearing in a storm of adrenaline.

Scoring the initial strike, Hunter didn't fail to quickly launch another.

He charged head on, his jaws wide open. I readied myself to lunge to the side.

In a stroke of luck he tucked his head down in an effort to ram me, to knock me from my feet.

He was blind to my evasion, and when my teeth embedded in his neck I felt victory in my jaws.

He shook wildly and suddenly I found my ribs against the crown of his skull as I was slammed into the nearest building.

I felt the true strength of his frame as I was lifted from my feet, crushed between him and the wall.

With a ragged shake he freed his neck of my teeth as my body screamed under the pressure.

A bristle of fur brushed my tongue, and I clamped down, being rewarded with a wounded yelp.

Blood filled my mouth, rich, full of iron. The wolf smiled as it took in the crimson water.

I was still between the wall and the crown of Hunter's skull, and I heard the few remaining boards in the wall creaking.

With renewed vigor I tore at the bit of flesh in my teeth, determined to tear it from his body if it was the last thing I ever did.

It had the desired effect, as Hunter harshly pulled himself free, dropping me to earth in the process.

Breathlessly I watched as Hunter pulled back and shook his head, blood flowing liberally from a ravaged left ear.

The taste of blood lingered in my mouth, my fangs now stained crimson, and within, the bloodlust of the wolf ran strong.

Hunter shook off the injury, growling lowly, staring at me, though not moving, waiting for me to rise to my feet.

I was beginning to do just that when the wolf commanded me to stay down.

Hunter took a step towards me, testing me, then another.

When I made no effort at movement he leaned back, loading his rear legs.

He came at me like a freight train, jaws set wide. I was defenseless, laying on my side, and in a split second he had covered much of the distance between us.

I could feel the ground shake as he thundered towards me, jaws set for my torso.

The wolf responded, greeting Hunter with a strong hind paw, slashing across his face. The razors tore three gashes from below his ear to the tip of his snout, and in a blast of adrenaline my jaws swung to compress on his throat, ripping away fur and flesh as he continued over me.

Hunter was carried forward by sheer momentum, colliding with the wall, shattering under the force of impact. Hunter's back legs dug at the earth and no sooner had the air entered my lungs than I had to force it out in an attempt to escape the slashing talons that scored gashes in my flank.

The move had only taken me a few yards away, but it proved enough to get me clear.

I spun round, prepared to face the wolf once more, only to find him gone.

The wolf had left Hunter, leaving the legs of a man protruding from a massive crater in the side of the house, largely still save an occasional twitch.

A drowning cough rattled from the broken man, and as I took strides towards the as of yet unmoving legs, I returned to my human stature.

The wolf maintained his hold, in case he was needed again in short order.

As I drew near my eyes fell upon what little was left of Hunter's face, covered in deep scores and gouges.

His ear was hardly recognizable as an ear, mostly tattered and torn away, complementing the bloody gashes across his face.

But those wounds were not what had done him in.

In the final attack, his throat had been torn open, revealing all manners of vessel and artery. On the right side of his neck, blood gently rippled, more so with every heartbeat.

He watched me approach, though only his eyes moved. Blood stained his lips and chin, and as he spoke more crimson spittle rose from his throat, cracking his once strong voice.

He looked to the sky, choking through words. "A good fight."

I nodded, no words seeking to escape me as I followed his gaze, both of us looking to the impending sunrise.

Through the treetops, dawn was nearing. Pink fingertips extended from the east, besieging the west, where dark blue skies fought a losing battle, only a few stars remaining to aid it.

Hunter drew a sharp breath as his face twisted, and I knew he wasn't long for the world.

"I'm ready." His brow hardened as he growled.

I nodded, the wolf and I both understood the meaning of his words.

Limping the short distance to where Hunter had shifted, I found the pistol he had carried.

As I returned, I found an entirely new emotion resting over me.

Previously, I would've left, leaving him to slowly die, because me and mine had bled here. Now, it didn't feel right to abandon him to that fate. I felt that his conduct, nearly gentlemanly, had earned him the right to a say in his final moments.

Why did he wait for me to completely change? He could've ended the fight before it started, shredded me before I was able to defend myself.

There was no time for me to ask though. He had allowed me the chance to fight fairly, facing an uncertain outcome. It seemed right, just even, to allow him an escape from slow death.

Gently, I put the barrel to his head.

He shocked me as a gentle curl lifted a single corner of his mouth. "Thank you, Council."

I froze, the gun in place against his head, as his words rattled inside of me.

He was thanking me? Perhaps it was blood loss, clouding his mind and tongue. Why would he thank me for this?

His smile remained, and had he possessed the capability, he looked as if he would've laughed.

Why?

"You would've done well in The Resistance." He whispered.

I recoiled at the words.

"Resistance?"

"Do it." He drew a deep breath, knowing it was to be his last.

Wasn't this… weren't these simply rogue wolves? To call yourself The Resistance would imply something more, more than a simple congregation of rogue wolves.

My eyes fell for a moment, drawn by a bit of color that didn't belong there.

On his right arm, exactly where I wore my own, was a light blue Council shield, overlaid by a black paw print, two black swords crossed behind.

"He was Council."

A thousand questions flooded my mind, but at the forefront, one truth blazed.

"Let him rest."

I squeezed the trigger, interrupting the morning's peace with a single gunshot. Nearby birds sprang from their roosts, taking wing into the bright morning sky.

As I pulled on my reserve clothing, I heard Hunter's words.

"Resistance?"

This was supposed to be a group of rogue wolves, no one said anything about Ex-Council wolves.

Who, or what, was The Resistance?

I reached a damaged hand into a pocket of the trench coat and felt the set of keys…

Time to finish it.

"Let's get this done, wolf." I turned towards the cells. *"Let's go home."*

With these words, I felt the wolf begin to shrink away, having done his part, aiding me when I had called him.

"Thank you, wolf."

I felt his warmth fade away, drawing back into the abyss, and as he left me completely, guilt found me.

A sudden knot of disgust formed within me as I looked to my hands, covered with the blood of five lives.

I had watched, felt, each act my hands had committed, two men freed of blood at the edge of a knife. I hadn't felt guilty. I had pulled the laces from Jordan's boots, used them to rig the grenade to the tripwire that killed two others, again devoid of all emotion. My teeth had torn Hunter's throat away, and still I felt nothing.

Now, the armor of the wolf falling away, I felt everything.

The only act that granted the faintest respite, was easing Hunter's passing, but that did little to cast off Jordan's eyes.

They were young, full of life, but in their final moments, they had been full of only fear, and as the light faded from them, they asked a single question.

Why?

In horror I recalled licking Jordan's blood from my hand, suddenly falling to my knees and doubling over as the memory purged my stomach.

I spat, trying to clear the expulsion from my nose and throat.

"Why didn't I feel like this before? I'm not new to killing anymore, I've taken life. Why is this happening now?"

I tried to steady myself, staring into a puddle of my own vomit.

"Can I do this?"

A murky answer ventured from the rift inside of me, my mind forming the words of the wolf.

"You already have. You learned how to do this in training, tonight was merely an exercise in application. Stay the path, and the day will come that you find your prowess has matched that of my own. On that day, you will become—"

A sudden metallic rattle in the grass beneath me drew my eyes, and I found the cell keys laying amongst the green blades, fallen from my pocket.

I silenced the wolf as I scooped the keys from the ground, knowing that I was facing a reckoning of my own creation, but more so, that three people waited for me.

"Maybe this is what they meant, whoever said that the end justifies the means?"

I felt like whoever said that was probably talking about things on a much larger scale, but this felt pretty large to me.

As quickly as my mending body would allow, I moved towards the last remaining building in the settlement.

28

To Save A Life

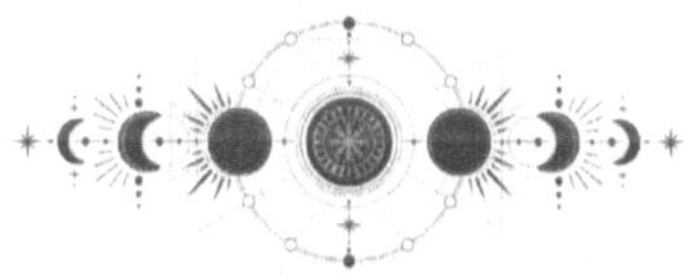

In the early morning light, I rounded the concrete corner, finding a wall of metal bars serving as the face of the structure. A cement wall divided the building, forming two separate cells.

In the nearest were the forms of three people, all staring at the concrete floor they sat on.

Only one pair of eyes moved to look at me.

"So, are you our executioner? Or our Savior?" A man built like a pro football player stood, shielding the others, a red headed young man, and a frail blond woman.

I quietly answered as I shook my head. "I'm afraid I'm truthfully neither. I'm Fenrir, Alpha's new support gunner."

I guessed at which key would fit, and slid it into the lock. To my relief, it turned.

Most of the pain having departed, I opened the door. "Come on, let's get you out of there."

No one moved within the cell, and the big fellow addressed me again.

"How do we know we can trust you? You could be with them, just walking us out of our cell to be hit by a firing squad."

I looked at him through the bars, my eyes wide in awe. "Have you heard what's been going on out here?! There was an explosion if I recall correctly, not to mention one hell of a fight that I'm certain was fairly loud."

"Yeah?" He answered me with his own irritation. "Well over the past few days, it seems like shit blew up just for the hell of it, gunfire in the dead of night; screams and battle cries to keep us up and disoriented. We've all been half starved, Red's nearly died from dehydration, and we haven't seen Ghost in over twenty-four hours. So, forgive me for being skeptical of the man who wears the enemy's uniform."

"Last I knew of Ghost, he was recovering in The Citadel's infirmary, and I can only assume the commotion you heard was Alpha squad trying to break you out. That's when we got him."

He was quiet for a moment, the mention of Alpha squad seeming to sway him. "What's your plan for getting out of here?"

"The pickup seems functional, you can take it back." I looked at my watch, it was 0645. "I found papers about a shipment coming in at 0800, I don't know if it's this morning or not. If it is, I'm taking it back to The Citadel."

"And if it doesn't?" The woman asked as she and the other young man stood, both quite a bit shorter than the man between us.

"Then I'll be along later, I heard chatter about reinforcements showing up here inside of forty-eight hours. If the shipment doesn't show up today, I can't chance waiting for it."

None spoke for a moment. It seemed they still didn't fully believe me, like it was too good to be true, or too easy. I couldn't blame them.

The man in front, whom I took to be Slade as he matched Marcus' 'linebacker' description, pointed to my arm. "Let's see your mark."

I slid my arm out of the trench coat and raised my sleeve to reveal my tattoo.

They seemed to accept the mark despite its color. Perhaps they already knew what it meant.

With a nod the big guy spoke once more. "Behind me here are Red, and Edge." He gestured to them as he named them. "I'm Slade."

I smiled. "I assumed as much from what I've heard out of Knight and Marcus."

In speaking of his sister, I saw trust fall onto Slade. If he'd had any remaining doubts, they were laid to rest.

I looked to the others as they stepped from behind Slade.

I gauged Red to be about twenty years old. A snowy complexion drastically transitioned to flat red hair, no doubt how he chose his call sign.

Turning to Edge I found she wore slim framed glasses over steely gray eyes, nearly silver. Her face was well-defined, a little sharp, though quite pretty, beneath dishwater blond hair pulled back into a ponytail, though a few bangs fell free.

Slade himself was capped with dark brown hair. His build certainly fit Marcus' words, massive and powerful, standing a good three inches taller than myself.

As they ventured from the cage, Slade took Edge's hand, gently pulling her close as he looked to her affectionately, seeming to say that he couldn't believe they were being rescued.

"Hard to believe we're all that's left." Red said quietly.

"Were you all in one squad?" I asked.

"These two are what's left here of Delta." Slade shook his head. "Red was their marksman, and Edge is about the best tech specialist you'll find in The Council… I was Bravo's combat engineer."

His gaze fell to the ground.

Edge tenderly took his arm, wordlessly offering comfort, though the action alone spoke volumes.

As I shifted my pack, I remembered the contents. "Edge, you're a tech specialist?"

She nodded as Red stepped towards the far side of the cell house. "That's right."

"If you're up for it, there's a laptop in here," I removed the pack, "think you could dig up when that shipment's coming in? Provided it's in here?"

"I'll see what I can do." She nodded. "If the battery holds out."

She took the offered pack, quickly reaching inside.

"Hey, hey!" Red stammered excitedly. "There's someone in here!"

Rushing past the dividing wall to Red's side I turned, my eyes falling to the floor, to the unmoving form of a woman.

Her face was largely hidden beneath bloodied blond hair. A single short braid hung from the temple of her hairline.

Her chest rose with a sudden quake as a groan escaped her pale lips, fainter even than her alabaster skin.

Had it not been for these faintest signs of life, I would have thought her dead.

Quickly I unlocked the door, drawing close to the battered young woman.

I knelt down, carefully inching my hands under the bruised girl's back and knees, gently lifting her from the concrete floor. Her eyes barely opened, though it was far from a conscious act.

As I stood, her hair fell from face, and I found myself stricken.

An elegant jaw, though by no means frail, paved the smoothest trail to a slender chin, a stand for curved lips.

At an earlier time, there would've been no doubt of her beauty.

No longer.

Ugly bruises covered what was visible of her body, and her right jaw bore an ugly purple blemish, roughly the size of a clenched fist.

I stepped from the cell, moving to lay her in the light and assess her wounds. Easily as I could, I laid her down on the grass... she wore only a pair of jeans and a tattered shirt.

I shook my head. *"Doc, I wish you were here."*

Her entire body was covered in bruises. Some were old, a sickly shade of green, while others seemed new, an intense shade of blue.

"Who would do something like this?" Slade looked over her.

Red popped his knuckles. "Someone I'd like to get my hands on."

"But why would they?" Slade shook his head. "She's human. A wolf would've healed, and the sunlight proves she isn't a vampire."

I looked to Edge, pushing keys on the laptop. "Anything on her in there?"

She shook her head. "I can't just look at it and break in, Fenrir."

She pulled at her boot for a moment, coming away with a small USB drive. "Give me a few minutes okay?"

I nodded as I looked to her boots, surprised that the USB had been overlooked when they were captured.

"Why would they beat her like this?" I looked back to the girl.

"Fenrir," Red pressed his fingers to her neck, "her pulse is weak. We've gotta get her help right now. She may not even survive the trip, but it's the best shot she has."

"She wouldn't make it, she's too broken." Slade's tone softened. "She's not gonna' make it... Unless..."

"What?" I looked to Slade's narrowed eyes.

"Forget it." He shook his head. "It's against directives, and you probably wouldn't care for the idea."

"Say it, please." I implored.

"We could change her." He quietly spoke.

"What?" I couldn't believe the words. Knowing his story and my own, it was highly unlikely that this would have a sunny outcome.

"That's the best shot she'll have at living, Fenrir."

"That's not... she'd survive but... she'd be like us."

"I never said it was the best thing, or even the right thing," Slade stared at her, "but it's the only way that she doesn't die, and given her state, she still may."

As I looked down on the girl, the fact that it was against protocols was the last thing on my mind. I could keep her alive, but would it really be living? Her normal life would end, stolen. She would be a wolf, never able to return to her family, her friends. Would death be better if you can't live freely? I knew what the Council life brought with it, how could I force her hand in that? But she had so much life left to live, she didn't look twenty years old yet, and she wouldn't be alone, she would have us, The Red Moons. Or maybe one the towns?

What was right? To save her life, and destine her to The Council? To let her die, and that be the end of her story all together?

The wolf didn't stir at the thought of one or the other, leaving me to make the choice on my own.

How many lives had been lost here? Ten? Twenty? Would one more matter? Would the earth recognize the blood of one more? Would it see that human blood lay among that of wolves? Would it care?

I knew the answer. The world, the earth, wouldn't care if another body laid dead here. And none could say how many lives had been claimed here. She would just be another.

But her one life was one more than I could stand to let go.

By my will, five had died here.

By my jaws, one would be saved.

"I'll change her." I said. "I can't let her die like this."

Slade nodded, kneeling next to her. "To do this, you must truly want her to become a wolf, otherwise the toxin won't drop. You won't feel any different, but it'll get sour at the tip of your tongue, that's the toxin."

"Okay." I nodded. "Hold her arm."

I looked down to the woman. "I hope I'm doing right by you. I hope that you would've chosen life over death. And if not, I hope you can forgive me."

I moved out of sight of the others, and slid off my clothes. I closed my eyes, feeling the warmth of the wolf and the transformation moving my muscles, expanding my bones.

Returning to the others, I saw before me not a woman whose life I'd be ruining, but one I'd be preserving.

Looking down at her beaten form, my massive paws near her chest and legs, I felt only right in this.

Slowly, I bent down, bringing her arm into my jaws.

Slade looked me in the eye, still holding her. "Easy now, or you'll take her arm off."

I tightened my hold only marginally before tasting blood. It wasn't sweet like I had tasted before, it was simply blood. The blood of a woman that only had a few moments of humanity left.

A gentle tingling hit the tip of my tongue. It lasted only a second, and as the sensation retreated, I took my jaws from her arm.

I pulled away from the group momentarily, returning once I was dressed.

A set of nickel sized puncture wounds lay on her black and blue arm.

"How long do we have to wait?" I stared down at her. "Until we know?"

"We'll know pretty soon." Slade crossed his arms. "The bruises should–"

Her breath suddenly caught, a light tremor taking her shoulders before a heavy exhale escaped her, and her chest failed to rise again.

Slade pressed two fingers to her neck and shook his head.

I turned away.

"If I hadn't waited, if I had just done it to begin with. Dammit!"

"There's nothing obvious on here about the girl, Fenrir." Edge softly frowned. "Maybe with a little more digging I could turn something up?"

"It's alright, Edge, wouldn't have made a difference anyway." Slade stood, softly speaking. "She was... She was just too weak."

"The shipment?" Red asked as I squatted, bringing my hands to my forehead.

Tapping keys accompanied Edge's reply. "Due today, 0800."

"What exactly is this shipment?" Slade moved behind Edge, peeking at the screen.

"Silver bullets and Anver." I slowly stood as I tried to push the young woman's face from my mind.

The seriousness of the matter surged across their faces, yet behind that lay unmistakable injury.

Slade's following words explained the reasoning. "So... We weren't the reason this operation was authorized. We were just a bonus, weren't we?"

I nearly smiled, almost laughed as my head and heart raced over who would break first.

"This operation was never authorized... I chose to come back. I wasn't going to leave you. Even though I didn't know any of you, I knew what you mean to my friends. Last night I learned about a shipment coming in, then I found the papers detailing the cargo. If it wasn't for the fact that The Red Moons could use it, I'd leave with you, but I can't, not when I know that we're all but out of Anver."

Red looked to the others, then back to me. "Looks like Phoenix made a good pick. Didn't even know us and still risked your neck. To just say thanks doesn't really seem to cover it, but... thanks."

I lightly nodded to the group. "Take the pickup and get home. I won't be far behind."

Slade looked around the group, and it seemed they were all wordlessly in agreement.

"Believe we'll stay, Fenrir."

I smiled. Not because I'd have help, but because I knew that they didn't want to leave me alone.

I looked over them. "Alright."

* * *

Standing beneath the pine tree, I glanced at my watch. The shipment was due any minute.

Red and Edge were both leaning against the burnt hut, having hidden the bodies, trying to look as if they belonged and that nothing was amiss.

As we waited I found myself wondering what the young woman was like in life, and still trying to figure out how she ended up in that cell.

"Think I hear it." Edge nodded to the hilltop.

I did what I could to appear natural as a red and white ambulance crested the ridge, continuing down the dirt road.

One man, heavy set with aviator glasses and a bushy mustache was the only visible person. On the arm of his jacket, just above a medical cross, was the same shield I now wore on my trench coat.

There was no doubt he was part of the same group.

The Resistance.

The window rolled down as Red and Edge walked around the vehicle, greeting the driver who spoke quickly and rather angrily.

"Where do you want it?" His voice betrayed a macho attitude as he fidgeted with his phone.

Red replied. "Right there is fine."

The driver stepped out of the ambulance and began walking towards the rear of the vehicle, ahead of the others.

Edge surprised me as she suddenly sprang forward, taking hold of the driver's head and wrenching it around with a series of unsettling crunches.

There was no fight, not the briefest of contest. In less than a second, she had snapped his neck.

He fell to the ground and it became clear that Edge was no stranger to combat as she turned around.

"Let's get the hell out of here." She showed not the slightest hint of hesitation, nor the faintest glimmer of remorse.

"Is this what awaits me?" I asked. *"To become so cold that I can just claim life?*

Slade nodded, waving the others in as I looked around the compound.

This place was, technically, my greatest achievement, but it felt like my greatest failure.

"I'm sorry miss... Whoever you were."

I took the driver's seat, and as Slade joined me in the cab, I fired the engine and spun the ambulance round, finally leaving the outpost that had served as my baptismal.

It felt like more of a crucible, a furnace that broke me down, leaving me yet to be molded. I had taken life, and now I had to deal with that, sort it out with myself. This was the path I had chosen for myself, but faced with the realities of it, I had begun to falter. The wolf had pulled me through, the wolf had saved the operatives, not me. I was there, but he was at the helm.

I recollected his words.

"Stay the path."

It was too late to change course. I was part of The Red Moons, and more than that, I had found Frost. If I left, I would always wonder what became of her, if she was okay. If I stayed, I knew that my wolf would keep her safe. I couldn't turn away now. I would stay the path, I would learn from the wolf, I would become strong enough to fight on my own, but before I could do that, I had to learn to deal with taking life.

The wolf had no qualms in the matter, though I doubted that he could teach that particular skill. I'd have to sort that one out on my own.

"I'm with you wolf." I spoke inwardly. *"Teach me, but be patient. I don't have to tell you that I'm new to this."*

A dark growl formed words in my soul. *"The mightiest mountain appeared as a pebble when it first broke the crust of the world."*

I nodded with understanding as I looked into the mirror, looking upon the operators in the back of the ambulance.

We had *actually* pulled it off. The operators that had been my sole reason for returning were safe. Three lives had been saved.

Hunter's words suddenly echoed in my ear.

"Little more than students."

The word "students" still chewed at the back of my mind.

I hoped he had lied, that I hadn't just claimed innocent lives.

"You good?" Slade's question echoed in the cab.

I quickly nodded as I answered. "Yeah."

"You sure?" He continued. "Most operators wouldn't look sad about doing what you just did."

I shook my head as I frowned, knowing that my thoughts had rested on my face. "The man in charge there, he told me that the men I killed were little more than students. I guess it's gnawing at me a bit."

"Cadets," Slade roughly equated the term, "don't wipe out two squads and nearly a third. He was toying with you, Fenrir, trying to get into your head. Let it go."

A faint droning suddenly caught my ears, deep, full of base. I looked around the cab for the source of the sound, finding nothing.

"I hear it too, Fenrir." Slade looked out of his window.

I pulled over as Slade opened his door and stepped out.

I too left the vehicle, instantly finding the source of the humming. A large aircraft was flying above us, a military plane.

Its flight path took it straight over the settlement and as the rear doors of the ambulance opened, the others taking an interest, the cargo ramp at the back of the plane opened.

We quietly watched as a massive silver cylinder ejected from the now rapidly climbing craft.

The canister dove slowly as a parachute deployed from its tail, and almost gracefully it descended towards the compound.It disappeared behind the trees, and seconds later it seemed the sun had hit the earth.

A massive fireball erupted from the bowl, no doubt incinerating the remaining buildings and every tree nearby. The blast following was deafening and even though we were nearly two miles away, the ground shook viciously.

The fireball quickly choked itself out, leaving a giant plume of smoke.

"That was low yield?!" I thought as I remembered Phoenix's request.

"What the hell was that?!" Edge asked as she turned to us.

"A Daisy Cutter." Slade answered.

"Was that ours or theirs?" Red asked.

"Surely it was theirs." Edge shook her head.

"Right." Red nodded. "Couldn't have been ours. How would they have known we were out of there?"

I shook my head. *"They didn't."*

Hostile Homecoming

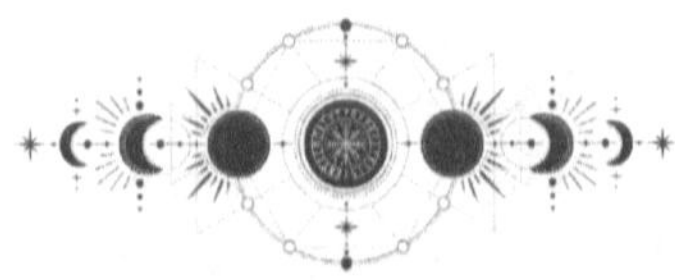

10/17

0950 Hrs.

As I came to a stop before The Citadel, my stomach set to churning. I had done what I set out to do, but now, now I had to answer to The Red Moons.

To Phoenix.

"I'll get the door." Slade slid from the cab, quickly stepping inside, reappearing moments later as the bay door lifted.

As I inched the ambulance forward, I couldn't deny I was nervous.

I had broken orders, and I knew that wouldn't go without consequence.

Maybe, just maybe, saving the operators and bringing in this shipment would buffer the inevitable disciplining.

The ambulance squeaked to a stop as the door lowered, caging me in with my apprehension.

As I stepped from the cab, the rescued operators drew near. Smiles finally started to appear on their faces, making it back to The Citadel seeming to be their final hurdle.

It seemed that only now did they truly believe that they had survived the ordeal.

"What now?" Red looked to me.

"You're on your own now, but," I looked up the stairs to the infirmary, "that'd be my first stop."

The stairs clanged as we ascended, forewarning the nurses that they had business.

As our mob filed through the door, the two nurses looked up from their desks, a look of shock taking them as they rushed to us.

"When did– How?" The blond managed.

Red smiled as he nodded towards me. "Fenrir."

The other nurse, Rachel, quickly pointed to now unoccupied beds. "Everyone have a seat, we'll tend you as fast as we can."

"Look to the others first." I had every intention of slipping away to find Frost. "I–"

"Fenrir!" A man's voice suddenly called.

I turned as the door flew open, finding Marcus, brown eyes burning with anger as he slowly advanced.

He limped a bit, everything not yet mended in his leg.

For a moment I was sure he would plow straight into me, and when he abruptly stopped before me, I found hardly a breathes space between us.

"Do you know how it looks on a Lieutenant when one of his squad goes rogue?" He fumed. "It makes me look like shit, Fenrir."

Slade seemed to take personal offense with the words as he stepped forward, pulling Marcus' eyes.

"Are you serious?! Don't worry about the operators you left it that compound, they'll just rot! Who cares so long as your porcelain ego doesn't get chipped, right?!"

"You don't know what's on the line here, Slade. Watch your tone." Marcus' face twisted as his anger grew, stoked by Slade's assault.

"Or what? You're not my Lieutenant, so don't assume you've got any hold on me or–"

"I am the *only* Lieutenant!" Marcus roared, the situation rapidly deteriorating, only a matter of time before they came to blows.

"What the hell does that mean?" Slade shook his head. "You're the only one left so we all have to do as you say?!"

"That's enough." A stern voice echoed from the doorway.

All heads turned, finding the frays newest contender.

Doc.

His judgment fell upon the crowd as his eyes traveled over us.

"This is a place of healing, not stupidity." His voice was little more than a growl. "If you cannot contain or conduct yourselves with the decency of adults, leave."

There was no counter to this, even from Marcus, much to my surprise.

Marcus would tolerate these words from Doc, one of his underlings, but not from an operator that belonged to a different team?

I wondered if there was bad blood between Slade and Marcus, though being unable to recall any mention of it quickly led me to question what power Doc possessed over them.

His blue eyes darted to me. "Phoenix wants you and Marcus downstairs, now. I would advise you not to keep him waiting."

* * *

Marcus had remained quiet after Doc's scolding, and I could still hardly believe that Doc's words went with consequence.

Marcus pushed through the door ahead of me, and as he straightened to attention, Phoenix stood behind his desk.

"Welcome back, Fenrir." Phoenix's hard eyes said everything but that he was happy to see me.

"Would thanking him be polite? Or would I sound like a smartass?"

Phoenix looked to Marcus, his scowl remaining. "Would you care to tell Fenrir what the charges are against a Lieutenant that can't hold his squad in check?"

Marcus grimaced before clearing his throat. "Lieutenants that perform inadequately, conduct themselves poorly, or prove to be insufficient squad leads will be demoted, pending transfer to another unit so that there will be no conflict upon the promotion of a previous subordinate."

"That's right." Phoenix looked to me. "You've cost Marcus his rank, well done, Fenrir."

I shook my head, narrowing my eyes as I wrapped my head around this notion. "You're punishing him for something he had no control over?"

"More *someone* he had no control over." Phoenix growled.

"You're demoting him and kicking him out?"

Phoenix turned away from us, looking at papers atop a filing cabinet behind his desk. "Now, Marcus, tell Fenrir the charges leveled against a rogue wolf."

I was fairly certain I knew that answer.

Again Marcus supplied the handbook given specifics. "A Council soldier breaking orders and moving freely among the populace unchecked shall be labeled a traitor and has achieved the status of Rogue, as they are defined likely, and so carries the same charge. Death."

Phoenix still didn't turn to us, though if he had, he would've found my eyes burning just as vividly as his.

"To be a traitor would have been to leave our people to die." I minced no words. "I did what needed to be done."

"No!" Phoenix spun to me, leveling a finger to my eyes. "You did as you pleased! Against the orders of your Captain!"

I nearly smiled as I looked to the ceiling, knowing that I was likely only a few short words from an ass kicking at best.

"I completed the orders you gave Alpha. I realize that I disobeyed you, but I couldn't let them die, not when I was still sound enough to try to get them."

"Mmm." Phoenix grumbled as he snatched a pen from his desk, quickly returning to his papers.

"You are a rare caliber of wolf, Fenrir," Phoenix scratched at the parchment, "but your actions cannot be ignored. I need someone who is capable of following orders, not a freelancer. That alone is what separates us from the rogues."

This was growing into an unusual ass chewing, and I began to consider that, since I still drew breath, the death penalty may have passed me by.

"Marcus," Phoenix continued writing, "previous to Fenrir's infractions, how would you appraise his conduct?"

Marcus let out a heavy exhale as he raised his eyes in aggravation. "Prior to recent insubordinate acts, Fenrir possessed both stellar conduct and an aptitude desirable for continued service."

"Marcus," I quickly whispered as I leaned towards him, "what in blue blazes is going on?"

"Shh." He side-eyed me.

"Fenrir," Phoenix pulled a new sheet to the top of his stack, "how would you appraise the ability and aptitude of Marcus as your Lieutenant?"

"Uh… Marcus is a—"

Marcus gently kicked me. "*Lieutenant* Marcus." He raised his brows.

"I mean, Lieutenant Marcus, is a good squad leader." I stepped away from my strangely behaving Lieutenant.

"Do you trust and respect his judgment, as well as mine?" Phoenix asked.

"Yes." I nodded as I attempted to look over Phoenix's shoulder. "Is this a report?"

"Two in fact." Phoenix set down the pen momentarily. "Marcus' and yours, to be submitted to Council records."

"Is that to say that *they,* The Council, will decide our sentences?" I asked.

"Not hardly. Your charge is left to the Captain of the unit, and the respective Lieutenant, as they have the most knowledgeable grasp of your character. I alone will decide Marcus' punishment."

"Marcus is a good Lieutenant, Phoenix." I shook my head. "You'll only hurt the unit if you send him away. He had no hand in what I did, in fact he was bedridden when I left."

"I am well aware of that, Fenrir." Phoenix nodded.

"As far as myself, I don't feel as if I went rogue—"

"And that is also accurate, Fenrir, a rogue wouldn't have gone after captured comrades, nor would they have returned. You did not go rogue.

AWOL, but not rogue." He paused.

"It was the right thing to do." I frowned. "Same as taking the shipment."

"Shipment?" Phoenix repeated.

"The ambulance." I thumbed over my shoulder. "It's full of Anver and silver bullets."

For once, Phoenix's tongue was still, and his expression changed from belittling to intrigue. "You brought it here?"

I nodded, feeling as if the bizarre exchange was drawing to a close. "Still in the ambulance."

"For the love of all that is good and holy... What do I do with you?" Phoenix quickly said before looking up to Marcus. "Tell Frost that the two of you will no longer be making the supply run. We'll speak later."

As Marcus left us, I couldn't help but feel the need to speak further on his behalf.

"Phoenix, he didn't–"

He silenced me with a raised hand before quietly replying. "I know he did nothing wrong, Fenrir, but he is destined to be a Captain one day, perhaps even surpassing Captain. He may be a commander, or God willing, a Councilman. He was never in any danger, Fenrir. This was just a way to expose him to the realities in store. Once he becomes a Captain and leaves us, as he one day will, he will still have superiors to answer to, and they will question him on the conduct of his officers and their men."

This drove home a new concept I hadn't even thought of. I had likely gotten Phoenix in hot water as well.

"Are you also in trouble now?" I sheepishly asked.

"No." He smiled as he shook his head. "This incident was small and is easily contained."

"What about my punishment?" I asked. "You never really got around to telling me that. I'm not so dense as to believe that I'm off the hook. There has to be something."

"And what am I to do with you, hmm? Lock you in the taming unit for a week. No food or water? Dish duty with Cookie?"

I knew he was asking rhetorical questions, and as I looked to the floor I wasn't sure I wanted the answer to the question I was preparing to ask.

"What is the punishment for breaking orders, to a lesser degree than becoming a traitor? Citadel whipping boy for a while? Old fashioned ass kicking?"

"Generally yes, to all aforementioned, but I can't very well do that to you now can I? You just saved three operatives that an entire squad couldn't secure, and returned with valuable cargo. While the unit wouldn't question me, every operator out there, save perhaps Marcus, would think me both cruel and foolish."

"So?" I tipped my head.

"Get to the infirmary. Make sure our operators are alright, help where you're needed, and make sure you yourself are alright. When everyone is cleared, so are you."

"I–" I stammered.

"Dismissed, Fenrir. You have your orders, see that you uphold them this time," his eyes once more grew hard, "or I *will* put your ass in traction."

30

Stains

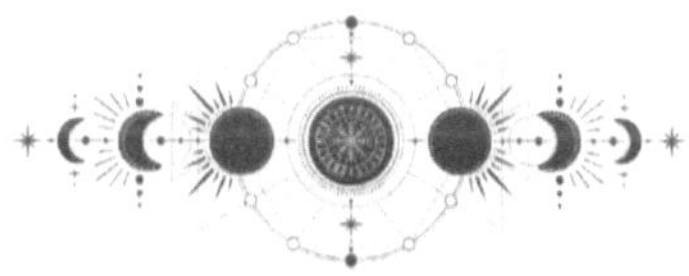

As I stepped into the infirmary, I was relieved to find Red was the only operator remaining. To me it meant that Edge and Slade were well enough that they didn't need any critical attention.

"Ah, Fenrir." Doc looked to me as he hung a clear bag on Red's IV stand. "Happy to see Phoenix didn't maim you."

"Yeah, me too." I chuckled as I advanced on the pair. "You good, Red?"

"Yeah." Red whined as he tilted his head from side to side. "Doc said I was a bit dehydrated, had to put me on a bag."

"It is the fastest way to ensure that you are where you should be, Red." Doc marked on a clipboard.

"Right," Red sarcastically smiled, "more like it'd been a minute since you got to stick someone and you know how much I hate needles."

"You did not have to watch me set the needle." Doc sighed. "That was your own choice."

"I was hoping to puke and catch you in the spew, still might get the chance when you take it outta' my arm." Red retorted.

"I would politely ask you *not* to do that. I just cleaned the floor this morning." Doc smiled.

Red's eyes smiled mischievously. "Don't you have a birthday next month, Doc?"

"Kind of you to remember." Doc nodded as he looked at the IV bag. "Twenty-third of next month."

"Good, good." Red nodded devilishly. "I think the pet store in Davenport sell's *turtles!*"

Doc's face flattened, only briefly before fiendishly smiling. "That reminds me, Red." He quickly stepped to a small medicine cabinet, withdrawing a phial of liquid and another needle. "You need a tetanus booster."

With wide eyes Red began to squirm as Doc approached him.

"Doc, you know that I know that's bull crap, and furthermore," he pointed a finger, "I was kidding about the turtle."

Doc smiled as he returned his tools. "That bag and one more, then you are free to go, Red."

Red settled down as Doc retreated to his desk, the latter bearing a broad smile, knowing that he had Red wound up tight.

"Slade and Marcus scared of needles too?" I asked as I approached Doc's desk.

"Come again?" Doc looked up to me, somewhat confused by the inquiry.

"Well it would explain why they let it go when you came down on them earlier, scared you might stick 'em."

Doc smiled as he shook his head. "No, they simply knew I was right, this is not the place to settle disputes. Especially when we have a perfectly suitable sparring area below."

The door suddenly opened and as I looked up, I found every operator entering the infirmary, most wearing smiles.

Knight was at the head of the pack, also the only one running.

She smashed into me and as her arms wrapped around my chest, I thought my ribs were about to snap. The embrace said it all.

I strained to speak as the air rushed from my lungs. "You don't have to thank me, Knight."

Only when she looked up to me could I see the dried tears on her face. "You dummy."

She let loose of me and I felt the air return to my lungs.

"Please do not add another patient to my infirmary." Doc marked a few boxes off the paper on his desk.

"Well," Slade spoke as he stood between Knight and Edge, holding the latter's hand, "they know the story after we came in, but I couldn't accurately say any more. Then my sister led the charge."

Frost slid along the wall, scraping by the group, and came out front.

"Let's hear it." She smiled as my eyes met hers, locking for a breathless moment.

It felt odd, but it seemed that somehow, her beauty had grown, though she looked just as she had.

"Absence makes the heart grow fonder."

"Well?" Frost raised her brows.

So, I told the story of how I had entered the camp. How I dealt with each enemy. Knight was proud of the knife work, and also the trap I'd left in the security building. The battle with Hunter served as the climax for the tale, leading into the beginning of Slade's retelling.

"I hope you're hungry." Knight grinned as the others began chattering amongst themselves. "Cookie's got the chow line fuller than I've ever seen it."

I chuckled. "I'll call down and have a tray made up."

"Call down?" Confusion furrowed Frost's perfect brow.

"Why wouldn't you come down with the rest of us, we were all kind of looking forward to sharing a meal together." Edge continued.

"I can't leave yet." I answered. "Phoenix's orders. Once Red is cleared, I can leave."

Every eye in the house turned to Doc, who seemed to feel the vast attention on him.

"He needs fluids." Doc said without looking up. "The best way to ensure he is properly hydrated is with the IV."

"Can't he just… drink some water or O-J?" Knight sang as she propped her elbows up on Doc's desk.

"Knight," Doc sighed, "he is a patient in my care, albeit a bit foul tempered, but my patient nonetheless. No."

I smiled as I side-eyed Doc. "Even if it means that you get to pull the needle out of his arm sooner."

Doc looked back to his papers with a slender smile. "Cruel and certainly a malpractice event, though still tempting. Unfortunately, I must stay with my original verdict. No."

"What if someone else took it out?" Slade asked.

Doc sighed once more. "If he agrees to it, you can remove it, and I will clear him. The second bag was more of a precaution anyway and the first is nearly empty, *but,* he has to approve."

"Deal." Slade smiled as he turned towards Red. "Hey Red, wanna' go to mess and get something to eat?"

Red, somehow having missed the unfolding conversation, smiled innocently. "Yes! I am starving!"

"Great!" Slade chuckled as he started walking towards Red. "Let's just get rid of that pesky needle."

* * *

1242 Hrs.

After being cleared, and a rather comical episode that found a light scuffle between Red and Slade, we all made our way to the mess hall.

It was the first time I could recall the whole unit being in one place.

Even Marcus and Phoenix attended, though Phoenix sat at a different table, allowing the operators ample elbow room.

Marcus seemed to have improved a bit, and I hoped that Phoenix had taken the time to explain that he was in no serious trouble, that it was a lesson geared towards Marcus' hopeful future.

Red would still shoot Slade a rather nasty scowl from time to time. In fairness though, I was certain I'd also be a bit sour if someone ripped a needle out of my arm.

Slade was oblivious to the glares however, as his attention was fixated on Edge, sitting across the table from him, to my right.

Knight was right, it was certainly something to be envious of. She sat between Slade and Frost, the latter sitting directly across from me.

Occasionally, between her sips of coffee, I'd catch a small smile brandished in my direction. A part of me hoped that it was just for me, though I knew it wasn't.

She had every reason to be happy, we all did.

The final member of the unit, Ghost, whom I had yet to talk to, came to stand next to Frost and looked to me with a kind smile.

"Don't believe we've met yet." A southern drawl slowed his words as he extended his hand. "I'm Ghost."

"Fenrir." I shook his hand, observing the sprigs of blond hair that protruded from beneath a sandy colored beanie.

Hazel eyes narrowed as he smiled, small creases forming at the corners as he nodded. "I believe I owe you a thank you."

I shook my head. "No more than anyone else. It took all of us to get you out."

"Not just for me." He stared into the coffee mug in his hand. "For getting the rest of us out."

I managed a light smile as I nodded.

"It wasn't me that did that."

Frost seemed to sense that I had struck a wall, graciously coming to my rescue.

"I never did say welcome back." She looked up to me, prompting Ghost to gently raise a hand in parting as he returned to his seat with Marcus and Red.

"Thanks." I whispered gently.

"I'm sorry about what happened, Fenrir." She whispered in return.

My brow furrowed. "What do you mean?"

Slade cleared his throat. "Edge and I told her about… About the woman."

"Oh…" I looked down on the tray, finding my appetite quickly diminishing as the thought of the woman drew back more memories, each of which was soaked in blood.

"Hey." Frost tipped her head, once more capturing me in the depth of her eyes, softly continuing. "I know it may not feel like it right now, but you did good out there, Fenrir, regardless of what Marcus or Phoenix have said. You made a lot of us proud and I'd be lying if I said we weren't a little impressed."

"Well," I smiled, attempting to keep Frost's role secret, "I can't take all the credit."

Even with Frost's assistance however, I knew the real reason I had succeeded.

My wolf, his ferocity and bloodlust.

"Well," Edge looked to Slade as she stood with a partially empty tray, "I think I'm gonna' try to get some rest."

Slade's brows raised as he suddenly joined her. "Y-Yeah. Me too."

As they moved away, a void was created between the rest of the unit and us, leaving Frost and I in semi-privacy.

"Was it something I said?" I chuckled as I looked to my tray.

Frost let out a giggle as she swirled her coffee. "Are you that oblivious?"

"What?" I smiled as I looked up to her.

"What do couples do, Fenrir? *Alone?*" She lifted a single brow.

"Oh." I said as it struck me. "*Oh.*"

A bout of laughter took Frost, and I couldn't help but join in, amused at my own lack of attention.

"Yes," I shook my head, "it seems I am *that* oblivious, but I'm gonna' plead the case as just being a bit tired."

"I guess I'll accept that." Frost teasingly smiled at me.

As I looked down the table, to Red and Ghost, I reheard the words of thanks. I knew I wasn't the only one deserving it, but I was also aware that to make it known would only bring repercussions down on Frost.

"They'll never know that someone helped me along the way. Some of that praise belongs to someone else." I whispered as I looked to Frost.

"Sounds like that someone cared a bit for you, then." Frost bumped the inside of my leg with her own, sending a jolt to my core that I had thought too tired to feel.

"She's just talking, like friends do. Don't make it more than it is."

"Never hurts to have someone like that." I smiled to her, trying to keep my emotions in check.

"And at the end of the day you save the captives and return the conquering hero." She joked in a hushed voice, seeming to try to preserve the semblance of privacy we shared.

"I wasn't trying to be a hero. Just did what was right. They were ours. I did what I'd want to be done if I was in their place." I leaned back.

"You've certainly earned the respect of everyone in the Red Moons, even though you did disobey a direct order. I'd still like to know why Phoenix didn't hang you from the rafters when you got back?" She playfully raised a brow.

"Well, the ambulance full of silver and Anver kinda' buffered a lot of it." I chuckled.

"I think that saving Bravo and Delta are probably what mitigated most of the damage, though I must admit I'm grateful for your surprise shipment. Spared me that pick up you mentioned." She paused, and when she spoke again, she was hushed.

Soft words hung on her breath. "I'm just glad you're back home, Fenrir."

"Didn't leave me much choice after you made me promise I'd come back." I smiled to her, and I felt my grasp on the situation wane as I heard the words of my promise again.

Not that I would simply make it back, but that I would make it back to *her.*

Briefly I glanced to her, to her lips, and an all too familiar hunger took hold of me.

"Did that promise expire when you got back?" She quietly asked, her directness shocking me for a moment.

I could see her eyes softening, and I feared I was letting myself dream as

I thought I saw the faintest hint of desire lying behind the shades of blue.

"Only if you wanted it to." I regained myself as I smiled.

The corners of her mouth tipped up as her eyes searched mine, words teasing at her mouth though none ventured forth.

With a smile she veered away, clearing her throat as color flooded her cheeks. "Ahem. Don't eat too much, okay?"

"No worry of that." I replied as my gaze fell to my hands.

Despite what could only be considered a positive outcome, the weight of the past hours, the lives claimed in that time, the manner in which they were claimed, still lingered in memory.

More than memory. My hands still felt the grip of the knife, the feeling of a wrenched jaw or covered mouth. Heat radiated from my skin, where their hot blood had splashed me.

I still tasted Jordan's blood.

I couldn't hold the wolf totally accountable for those actions either, though I desperately wished I could.

I welcomed him in, and my own sense of vengeance only spurred him on, his anger bleeding into my own, each fueling the other. I wanted them to hurt, I wanted to see the fear in their eyes as I took their life away. Only the presence of the wolf granted them quick death, and had that not been crucial to the success of the rescue, I was inclined to believe that he would've shared my sentiment of painful ends.

"What's wrong?" Frost asked as she dipped her head once more to meet my eyes before looking into my hands.

Her eyes darkened in understanding as her mouth moved with regret.

"What do you see, Fenrir?" She quietly asked.

I shook my head.

"Fenrir," she whispered, "what is it?"

"Blood."

"Fenrir," she spoke quietly, understanding in her voice, "they killed most of two squads. They were far from innocent."

I shook my head. "When I got there, I heard them talking. They were talking about someone not surviving, about having done all they could, but if she wasn't gonna' make it then they couldn't change that. I thought that something happened to Edge, but I think that they were talking about the woman, she was around our age. I think that they were trying to keep her alive, but they didn't want to do what I did, or… what I tried to do."

Again Hunter's voice sank a knife into my gut, Jordan's eyes burning my soul.

"The last man I fought, Hunter. He told me that I had killed four men that were little more than students, and now it's all I can hear. I looked one of them in the eye when I cut his throat, Frost, and every time I close my eyes, I see his. I watched the light inside of him die… How long will it be like this?"

She only frowned as my core tightened, at war with myself, trying not to cry, not to scream in anger at my feeble emotions, at both my weakness and my alarmingly healthy sense of bloodlust, however momentary.

The wolf was my greatest strength, that was certain, but it seemed that when I let him in, merged him with my own will, he only magnified it.

And that terrified me.

"Let's go for a walk, Finn." Frost whispered. "Just you and me."

"A walk?" I asked.

"Mhmm." She nodded. "Some place not here, where we can talk."

"That sounds good." I nodded, standing from the table.

31

Different

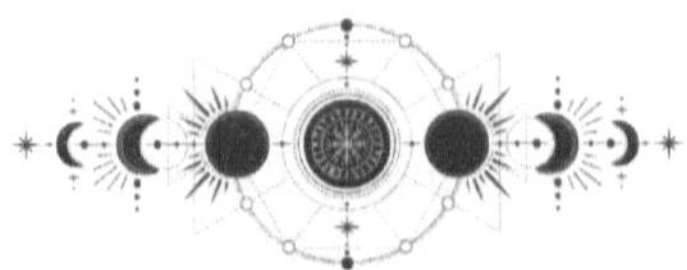

10/17
1330 Hrs.

No one questioned where we were going as we left the chow hall, too caught up in regained freedom and the happiness of not losing any more operators.

I took small comforts in that, knowing that there was a net positive outcome, despite the sins that covered my hands.

As we neared the door of the warehouse, a voice called to us.

"Where are you off to?"

We turned round, facing Phoenix, near the doors of the chow hall.

"Seems the man of the hour ought to stay for his own event." He smiled, though it faded as his eyes met mine. "What's wrong?"

"We're just going for a short walk, Phoenix." Frost nodded. "If that's alright."

His face rose, as if this meant something to him, though he was quiet.

He let out a slow breath, stepping away from the doors and starting towards us.

"Please give us a moment, Frost." Phoenix glanced to her.

She quickly nodded, stepping away without question.

Once Frost had moved an acceptable distance, Phoenix fixed his eyes to mine.

"Are you alright, Fenrir?"

I wanted to nod, to say that I was, but both would've been lies.

"I–" I grimaced before I slowly replied. "I'm not broken, if that's what you're asking, Phoenix."

"It's not." He gently smiled. "I'm asking if you are alright. I know that on the outside you're okay. I'm asking what's inside."

I looked to the ceiling, barely shaking my head. "Inside I'm a mess, Phoenix."

I lowered my eyes to his. "I knew that I would kill them, that I had to. I just wasn't as prepared for it as I thought I was."

"How did you kill them?" Phoenix asked shortly, though without callous.

"What does that matter?" I narrowed my eyes.

"It matters a great deal, Fenrir." Phoenix nodded. "Please answer the question."

"Up close." My eyes fell to his chest as I replayed three deaths, one in particular. "Two with the knife, one as the wolf, two with a trip wire."

"You saw their eyes." He frowned, immediately understanding.

I only nodded.

"It's a hard thing," he said, "watching the life drain away."

Oddly, Knight flashed to mind. This was her forte, close quarters combat. She had to have seen this before, had to have come to grips with this. How was she, the sweetest member of our squad, also among the hardest operatives. What kind of strength did that require? Did I have enough?

"How does Knight do this?" I absently asked.

"For all the love and kindness in her," Phoenix quietly answered, "she holds in a rage that few will ever witness, something you only glimpsed in your training. She is a coin, much like your weapons expert."

Phoenix smiled as he looked over his shoulder to Frost, reminiscent of a proud father.

"Knight will never be anything but loving to all of you, but when it comes to doing her job, she is the best in The Red Moons. Her steel rivals that of Frost, of Edge."

Suddenly I remembered the driver at the compound, the sheer ease with which Edge snapped his neck.

"Something special about my girls." Phoenix smiled as he looked back to me. "On the battlefield, they aren't the people you know, Fenrir, they are my furies. They fight as if the lives of the people they love depend on it, because they do."

"I care–"

Phoenix raised his hand.

"I know you do, Fenrir." He smiled. "You wouldn't have broken orders, or gotten Bravo and Delta out if you didn't, but there is a difference. You may love the people around you now, but there is a line between loving people when all you've known is peace and when you've bled, killed, and fought to survive alongside a group such as this. You will come to know this, of that I am certain."

"And until then?" I nearly scoffed.

"Go on your walk with Frost." He nodded with a kind smile. "And above all else, be honest."

"I– Yes sir." I nodded.

He gave my arm a light pat. "You'll be alright, Fenrir, just look to your team. They won't let you down."

He turned away, moving to Frost, where they too shared a few short words.

At first it seemed business-like, a quick exchange of words.

"Probably telling her I'm a basket case. As if she doesn't already know..."

Her eyes suddenly fell, a small smile taking her lips.

She gave another quick nod before patting her pocket.

With that, the conversation concluded, each going their separate ways.

"Well," she asked as she drew near, "did he give you a 'dad' talk?"

"Kinda." I managed a small smile. "I think that's what it was. In a nutshell, and in his own way, I think he tried to tell me that it'll get easier with time."

"Still want to go for that walk?"

I looked to the door, only a few steps away.

"Phoenix seemed to recommend it, and I'm still far from being okay."

"I wouldn't turn down the chance to get out for a while." I answered.

"Okay." She smiled, a little more than I had expected. "Let's get going then."

I followed her out into the light of day, and as I pushed the door shut behind me, I took in a lung full of autumn air.

It was a little thing, and though I couldn't say if it was the sunlight or the atmosphere, I felt a bit cleaner.

I chalked it up to both. The warmth of the rays and being out of the still air of The Citadel.

"Is that all the further you're gonna' make it, Finn?" She called.

I opened my eyes, unaware that I'd even shut them.

"Sorry." I stepped to, following her into the trees.

"Not packing any butter knives are you?" I asked.

She let out a soft giggle. "Not today. No need to add injury to injury."

"Hmpf." I nodded. "Just making a–"

"I know." She slowed, matching my pace as we traversed a stand of small trees. "What did Phoenix say if you don't mind me asking?"

"He asked how I was. Then how I killed them." I answered.

She nodded. "To which you said?"

"Close quarters for the most part." I replied.

"Explains why it's just hitting you now, I guess." She continued on. "To be honest, I expected this to come up during your training, especially after what happened at your farm. Killing takes a toll, Fenrir, and you took your first life some time ago. I was a bit surprised when you didn't go to pieces on the ride back that night. I mean, you did, in a way, understandably so, but it never came up again. Not once did you seem to take stock of the fact that you had killed those vampires.

"Then we made our move on the compound and you still didn't blink. You gunned down a wolf at point blank range. There was no doubt that *you* killed him, yet you came out of it unscathed."

I nodded, unable to say anything.

She wasn't wrong, and I didn't simply overlook their deaths, it just didn't seem to hang on me.

I lost Vivian that night, and the guilt I felt for her death blotted out any weight from killing those vampires. Not that there really was any. I acknowledged that I took life, and I knew that I'd never be the same, but my brain was too fixated on Vivian. I was too wrapped up in what she'd become, and what it meant for me if I ever found her, to feel bad for killing those vampires.

As for the compound, the wolf implicitly, that was pretty cut and dry as far as my brain registered. The preservation of Marcus' life, and my own, hinged on that wolf dying. It had to happen.

"I guess," I finally answered, "in those times, I was too busy being occupied with the people around me, trying to keep them safe, and coming to terms with what it meant to fail."

The contradiction of my words struck me just as quickly as Frost picked up on it.

"So what was the difference about this?" She calmly asked.

"I–" I shook my head.

I knew what the difference was. I just didn't want to say it, hear it out loud.

I wanted to hurt them, it wasn't enough to kill them. They had hurt my team, my friends, my family. I intended to make it a point to ruthlessly extract my pound of flesh. For a brief time, when I called upon the wolf, and in the moments leading up to, I wasn't Rainer anymore.

I was a monster.

"I don't know." I answered.

"Be honest." Phoenix's words blazed in my mind.

Frost made no response as we walked, save a nod, taking a different approach than she had with my knife training at the farm. She didn't pry, nor did she make suggestion. She simply let it be.

The trees opened up a bit, giving way to a small meadow. On the far side a small stream gurgled, feeding the dark green clover that the cooling year had yet to claim. A short oak log lay a few yards from the creek, and as I noted the worn trail through the greenery, I gathered that this was a place often visited.

"Sit?" She asked, gesturing to the trunk.

"Sure." I nodded, stepping over the log to sit on the ground, resting my back against the ridged bark. Surprisingly, it wasn't totally uncomfortable.

The log gently shook as she sat down, her legs next to me.

"I come here when I need to think, or just want some space." She said, never looking down to me, fixing her eyes on the moving water. "You don't have to say anything, Finn. We all deal in our own way. I'm just here if you need me."

"*If?*" I smiled at the clover just before closing my eyes, moving to lay my head back. *"No question about that, Frost."*

My head had just reached the log when a particularly sharp ridge forced me to turn, not much, but enough that the denim of Frost's jeans came to kiss my cheek.

My breath caught with the unintentional touch as I waited for her to awkwardly pull away.

She didn't though, she remained still. There was no jerk of surprise, no push of air to convey shock or otherwise. For the moment, she seemed at ease with me resting against her.

My chest hummed as her warmth transferred through to me, and I couldn't begin to measure how thankful I was for her.

She was becoming something of a fixer for me, keeping me together when I threatened to go to pieces, an anchor keeping me steady when I was fighting not to be swept away.

A happy exhale escaped me, a cleansing breath that carried out a bit more darkness, brushed away as my fingertips played at the clover leaves.

"Is Hunter haunting me?" My brain still rattled. *"Was he really just trying to get in my head? Guess if he was, it worked."*

I still heard his words from time to time, but I couldn't shake the sense of knowing that what he'd said was only part of it.

I was scared of what I felt, what I did. I couldn't fathom where that line lay, the border between being what I was and being a werewolf from legend. The only difference between what I did and the legendaries was that the human part of them wasn't supposed to know what they were doing.

That only made it worse.

I knew exactly what I was doing and still felt that it wasn't bloody enough.

I couldn't help but feel that I was worse than the legendaries. They couldn't control what they did, the wolf was at the helm.

A word screamed in my mind, and it threatened to break me.

"Evil."

It wasn't the only word that fit, followed rapidly by "Devil, Hellish, Demon", and every word shook me to the core.

"This can't be what I am." My breath grew quick, shallow. *"I won't allow this. If this is what the wolf does to me then I don't want him. I was going to shoot Hunter and Irving in the back. I was going to **murder** them!"*

In recent hours, I was grateful that I hadn't. Despite being throttled in the fight, it was at least an honest fight, equal chances at life.

"Is there really such a thing as a clean kill? Can a person be clean, redeemable when this is what we do? Or are we just forsaken outliers."

In the span of a few short seconds my morality, my wolf, and my Christianity all crashed together, each competing for focus in my mind's eye, none being the clear victor.

Frost's hand gently fell to touch my face as I clenched my eyes, holding the tears that scorched my eyes.

Bittersweet was the moment, the cool touch of her fingertips holding back the fire that raged in my soul.

"What did I turn into in that compound?!" I screamed. *"What did you do to me?!"*

"I wasn't like this before you!" I cursed the wolf. *"I never wanted to hurt anyone, anything!"*

If a part of me was lost the night I killed those vampires, then the entirety of my being had been destroyed in the confines of that compound.

"I–" My voice shook as I finally spoke. "I wanted to hurt them, Frost, to make them pay for what they did."

"That's a pretty human response, Finn." She softly spoke. "Anger is a very real thing."

"It wasn't anger." I shook my head. "It was revenge."

The old proverb about he that seeks revenge digging two graves came to mind, though it suddenly had a different ring to it.

"Because of what they did to you." Frost stated. "That's underst–"

"Not me." I cut her off, past the point of carefully choosing my words. "Because of what they did to you."

"To me?" She whispered.

"All of you." I opened my eyes, the tears having melted away, leaving a dull ache in my eyes. "Phoenix said that in time it'll get easier because I'll love you more, but I love you now. It's not the killing that bothered me."

I looked to the sky. "It's what I felt. I wanted them to suffer before they died. I was a monster, Frost."

She didn't say anything, her fingertips gently playing at my neck, offering any comfort she could.

"What do you feel," I asked, "when you use the wolf, Frost? When you call it out of whatever hole it lives in?"

"I–" She hesitated. "I don't understand, Fenrir? What do you mean 'when I call it out'? It's always there for us to use when we need it."

I lifted my face, my eyes slowly moving to hers as I realized that something was very wrong.

"You don't feel it? When it moves, guides your hands? When it–" My words faltered as it registered that I was alone in this.

I turned to look at the clovers as a question I had asked before returned to me.

"What are you wolf?"

"Fenrir," Frost knelt next to me, "what you're saying sounds a lot like someone who is struggling to control their wolf, but I watched you tame it that night."

"I didn't *tame* him, Frost." I tried to find words that made it clear. "He didn't bow to me, I didn't leash him, or any other means of control. I talked to him and he understood. We are one unit, there is no him and me where he is just on a tool belt waiting for me to draw him. He's alive, I can feel it when he moves, when I'm angry or upset, or even if someone says something that upsets him."

"The things I've been able to do that I shouldn't have." My mind cleared.

"He helped that night on my farm." I nodded as my eyes settled on the churning stream. "And in my fight with Knight. Again when I went back to the compound. I call on him when I need him, and even though that sounds like what you just said, it's obviously not the same. Your wolves are kept handy, and give you size and strength. Mine's…"

I fell silent as I looked to my arm, the sleeve of my shirt, to the mark concealed beneath.

"Do you think it might have something to do with the mark?"

"I don't know." Frost shook her head. "I haven't heard anything like this before, Finn. Do you know what your mark–"

"It means I'm a pureblood." I said, unable to keep from sounding disappointed. "That's why Marcus was in a foul mood on the mission. Phoenix told him, and I think Marcus, whether he meant to or not, put me in the same scope as his brothers and sisters."

Frost frowned. "Honestly, Fenrir, I don't know why your wolf is the way he is. It could be a result of being a pureblood, but I can't say with any degree of certainty."

I pushed breath from my nose as I scoffed. "Great. Whole 'nother level of jacked up then. Whole different kind of beast."

"Does he try to get out?" She asked. "I mean, do you still fight to keep him in?"

"No." I whispered as I shook my head. "I just ask him for help when I need it, and he always answers. He was the reason I beat Knight. It was almost like he knew his way with blades, like he had used them before, but that couldn't be, right? Not if he's only as old as I am. You're the last person I have to tell about my lack of being a knife fighter. With him though, I was. With Knight, and in that compound. I felt him, his energy, all of his rage, seep into me."

I looked at my hands as I flexed my fingers. "Mostly here."

Frost's eyes fell to my hands, just before she reached down, taking my right.

"And now?" She asked.

"No." I managed a small smile as her fingertips played at my palm, dropping lightning everywhere they touched. "It's just me now. He's gone back to wherever he comes from."

"That's so…" Her voice trailed off as she looked across my palm.

"Weird?" I grimaced. "Yeah, I'm just now learning that too."

"Mm-mmm." She hummed as she smiled at me. "I think I'd call that special, Finn. *Especially* if he's anything like you make him out to be."

"Special? More like FUBAR. A hazard. A liability."

"No." I frowned as I shook my head. "He's dangerous, Frost, and I don't know what side of good or bad he belongs to."

"And that's something you're alone in?" She asked sarcastically.

"What separates us from *bad*, Finn," she smiled, "is what we do with our wolves, and I'm not worried about you going to the dark side anytime soon. You've got a good heart, Fenrir. You wouldn't be tearing yourself apart otherwise."

A new pang of guilt hit me, her kind and supporting words bringing up an accidental glance I'd stolen only hours before.

"Why'd she have to go and say that?"

I hadn't meant to look.

"About that." I pursed my lips. "There's something I feel like I need to tell you."

"Oh?" Her grip on my hand remained as her eyes locked with mine, and I noticed a hint of excitement hidden in the blue.

"Yeah." I smiled, just barely, as I brought my free hand to the back of my neck. "I uh, may have seen a little bit, when you were getting dressed last night."

Her grasp on my hand tightened as her kind eyes turned icy. "Pardon?"

"I didn't mean to." I glanced to my hand, well aware that carefully chosen words were the only thing preventing it from becoming a sieve. "I thought I heard someone coming up the stairs, and I looked at the door. From the corner of my eye I–"

"And you didn't say anything?" She asked, surprisingly rather calmly.

"She doesn't seem mad." I thought curiously. *"Not happy by any means, but–"*

"When could I have brought that up?" My smile inched back across my face, finding humor in her question. "Just now? In front of everyone?"

"There was a whole car ride back to that compound, Finn!" Her pretty eyes widened as she observed the obvious opportunity.

"Still using my nickname." My chest hummed.

"And what might've been the result of that, Frost?" I gently closed my hand, wrapping her fingertips. "It could've been the last time I saw you. I didn't want to spend it with you upset, or with us fighting. And I'm glad we didn't, because I may not have had the opportunity to make our promise."

With the mention of that promise, her eyes, her hands, everything about her, softened.

A light smile lifted a corner of her mouth, and I couldn't help but match it.

"That promise is what got me home, Frost." I quietly spoke as she looked down to our hands, content to leave them entwined. "Are you angry with me?"

"I should be, shouldn't I?" Her cheeks began to turn rosy as her smile grew. "I'm not though."

"I'm–"

"It didn't expire, Finn." She blurted, keeping her gaze on our hands for a moment, before her eyes moved to meet mine. "The promise. You said it only ends if I want it to. I don't want it to."

My tongue fell slack as my heart stalled, feeling her hand leave mine and take my side as she leaned in towards me.

"Is– " Every wire in my brain shorted. *"Are we–"*

My heart kicked into overdrive as her other hand took my neck, gently pulling me towards her.

Our eyes locked, hers calm, confident, certain that this is what she wanted while mine surely screamed a concoction of excitement and borderline terror.

Once more the shards of blue ice radiated in her eyes, setting my chest alight, pushing the air from my lungs as I rose to close the distance.

"Is this really happening?!" My heart hammered in my ears as her eyes fell to my lips, the space between us all but gone.

I drew in her breath with my own, a cool air of mint.

I swallowed nervously as I brought my hand to the side of her face.

A harsh buzzing filled the air, stopping Frost in her tracks as she looked down to her pocket.

There was no denying the disappointment in her sigh as she pushed a phone from her pocket, answering with a swipe of her thumb.

"This is Frost." She pushed the phone to her face.

I could make out a woman's voice on the other end of the line.

"I'm with Fenrir." Frost replied before her eyes fell to the earth, turning serious. "We'll be right there."

She sighed as she hung up the phone.

"Edge needs us to come back."

"What?" I fought to keep my voice from breaking.

"Sadly." She half smiled, offering me her hand.

As she pulled me to my feet, I looked down on her.

"Just kiss her!" My heart screamed. *"It only takes a moment!"*

As much as it pained me though, I knew something was amiss. It had to be, otherwise it could've waited.

"Alright." I sighed, miserably failing to conceal my disappointment. "Let's go."

Her hands left mine as we started back towards the Citadel, and I found my heart still pounding its message in my ear.

"It's important." My feet crunched fallen leaves, I retold myself. *"Edge wouldn't have called otherwise."*

"Maybe later tonight we could take another walk?" Frost softly asked.

"Oh yeah?" I hoarsely chuckled, her words pushing everything else from mind.

"Mhm. I want to hear more about this wolf of yours."

"What?" My feet fell still as my ego took a blow, having hoped that this proposed walk would find us continuing our latest topic.

"Keep walking, Finn." She giggled as she shot me a teasing glance.

"She knows exactly what she's doing." I chuckled to myself. "What do you want to know?"

"It's just…" She smiled as she shook her head. "I never knew this was a thing, and the fact that no one else is like that…"

She turned to face me, and for the first time in knowing her, she looked her age. A girlish cuteness took her face as her eyes sparkled. She was fascinated, daresay infatuated, with the wolf, with me.

"I don't think I'm all that special, Frost." I couldn't help but still feel that she mistook the nature of my wolf. "I'll give you different, but not special."

"I beg to differ." She said matter of factly as she offered up a stunning smile. "You *are* different, that's a fact, but special is a matter of opinion. And to me, you're both."

Once more slack jawed, I scrambled for a coherent response. "Just because of the wolf right?"

"Amongst other things." She smiled. "That good heart helps."

"How can you believe you know me well enough to make that judgment?"

While I was flattered that she held me in such high regards, it didn't seem possible that she could know me that well so soon.

"You trained me, we fought together once, and then you sent me off on my own. It's only been a few months."

The wolf suddenly stirred, catching me off guard as he sent a shudder through my core. I recoiled as he moved, his feelings twisting into things I understood, raising a valid question.

"Finn?" Frost's tone bordered alarm. "Are you okay?"

"It's nothing." I shook my head. "He… moved around, that's all."

"Just like that?!" Her brows raised. "Does this happen often?!"

"Kinda." I chuckled. "When it's something important."

"What's important right now?" She stifled a laugh, though I noted the wonder in her voice.

"Did she really just ask that?" I laughed inwardly.

"Nothing worth bringing up at present." I smiled, unsure how to explain what the wolf had pushed to me.

That didn't I feel the same about her? That I was certain she also had a heart of gold, layered beneath. And hadn't I only known her a few months?

I sure couldn't argue with him.

32

The Truth

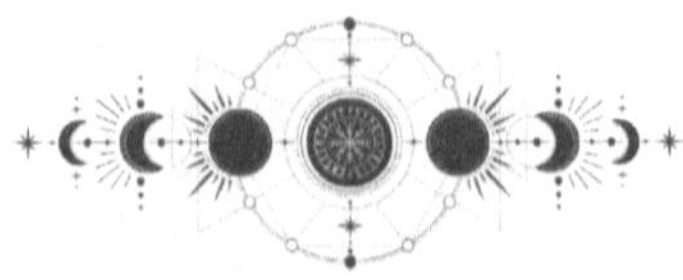

10/17
1500 Hrs.

"I'll be right back, Fenrir." Frost nodded back to me as she opened the door to the crew quarters.

As she stepped in, I spotted Slade and Edge, both at the table in the corner of the room.

"Close it please." Slade's eyes met mine, just before Frost pushed the door to.

"They knew I was coming didn't they?" I slumped down on the stairs, suddenly not so at peace with the interruption of Frost and I's moment.

My body still hummed with the charge she had put into me, I could still feel her breath on my skin.

"It was so close." My heart ached.

I could hardly believe it. It seemed so sudden. One minute we had just been talking, the next...

"What happened?" I smiled to myself, trying to wrap my head around it.

"When did she start to feel like this?"

Voices rumbled through the door, too muffled to pick up anything legible, but they all had a part to speak, and all of it was in a hurry.

"What's going on in there?" I wondered as I looked to the door, the seconds growing to minutes.

The voices grew only slightly louder, alluding to flaring emotions.

I was contemplating reaching for the door myself when quick steps silenced the thought, someone rapidly moving on the door.

"Fenrir," Frost cracked the door, pausing to check the rest of the warehouse, finding only me, "get in here."

There was no mistaking the concern in her eyes, having replaced the joy that had lingered in them only minutes before, and with no lack of apprehension, I feared my recently acquired happiness wasn't long for the world.

"What's wrong, Frost?" I quickly stood, wondering what could've marred what should have been, by all rights, a day that found everyone in high spirits.

"I–" She frowned as sadness took her eyes. "Just get in here."

As I followed Frost into the living quarters, I found Slade still sitting at the table, his head rocked forward in his hands.

"Are we *sure* we want to do this now?" Slade asked without looking up, seemingly oblivious to my presence.

"Might be the only chance for a while." Edge replied. "Everyone is still out and about, so if we're gonna' do it, best be quick about it."

"Okay." Slade's eyes met mine, and I found the same gloom in them that I had witnessed in Frost's.

"Something is very wrong here." I put my hands to the back of a chair as Slade quickly moved to a footlocker, digging to the bottom of it.

"Might as well sit." Edge said as she took a seat herself.

"What's going on?" I pulled myself up to the table.

"Just hang tight," Slade replied as he wrestled with the locker, "and you'll see for yourself."

He lifted a laptop from the box, and I recognized it. It was from the compound. I assumed it had been turned over to Phoenix, and I was shocked that it hadn't been. Several concerns rose to mind, and I wasted no time in asking.

"Phoenix know you have that?"

"No." Edge took the laptop as Slade sat next to her, flipping it open.

"Shouldn't he?" I asked.

"Just… Hang on, Fenrir." Edge said somewhat impatiently. "There are some things that we've decided you should see."

"Can't those be tracked?" I asked.

"Don't worry about–" Edge radiated frustration as she tapped at the keys. "That's taken care of."

"And why the secrecy?" I asked as I looked to Frost, assuming that she learned something about this during their conversation.

"Fenrir, stop." Frost whispered to me as Edge spun the laptop around.

Before me was what appeared to be a daily operations log, sent forward to some commander. Edge had scrolled through text, to the point where she wanted me to begin.

"Oct. 9th

Council assault commenced at 0300 hours. Camera's picked them up before they were within striking range. Neutralized majority, captured four, placed in holding cells to await prisoner transport. Insignia is consistent with The Red Moons. Resistance casualties are manageable but damaging enough that a significant portion of the outpost has started back to Headquarters due to major injury. Until we receive reinforcements we will be running on essential personnel. Priority- Anver, ammunition.

Oct. 13th

Intercepted unarmed Order transport at 0115, few troops, two human females. One DOA. The second was placed in the remaining holding cell, pending medical care. Priority- Medical personnel, prisoner transport, Anver, ammunition.

Oct. 16th

Second Council assault 0130. Cameras again detected the attack. Re-pelled with heavy small arms fire. One captured Council soldier was taken while out of cell receiving medical care. We have sustained heavy casualties. We're down to the wire, Whitedeer. If they coordinate another assault, we <u>WILL NOT</u> be able to hold the outpost. We need reinforcements asap. The girl has gone untended and is largely unresponsive, she will perish without due attention. We need help, Whitedeer."

"If this is Hunter, then he's desperate, he's speaking plainly."

"I've got a handful of research recruits here, and all I know is basic trauma care, which is useless to her. We've managed to get some water in her but that's it, she's too damaged to eat solid foods. She needs exfil'd now, and we desperately need support. Recon op's have been completely halted, and research has all but stopped as well. I know I've had reservations about working with some of our vampires in the past, but I will take anyone you can send, Whitedeer. Our lack of manpower is made even worse with the fact that we've got three trained Council wolves locked in holding cells meant for nothing more than holding newly turned wolves and vampires for a few days. We're not equipped to be a Res-Rec installation and a long term stockade."

"He wasn't lying." My heart dropped, leaving me knowing why Frost and Slade had looked at me the way they did.

"I killed researchers." I slammed my eyes shut, balling my fists on the keyboard. *"Recruits."*

"Students." I heard Hunter's voice.

I had killed young men who had likely never taken a life, who probably had no intention of doing so. They were what was left after their fighters had either left or been killed.

They never stood a chance.

"Fenrir." Frost gently laid her hand on my arm, leading me to open my eyes.

Her eyes held my sorrow, but they couldn't fathom my guilt.

"There's more." She whispered.

"More?" I looked back to the screen, bringing a hand to my forehead. *"What more could there be?"*

"What else is there?" I quietly asked.

"Aside from vampires working with wolves?" Slade asked.

Whether I was too tired, or had been rendered too numb, I wasn't sure, but I couldn't muster a response to Slade's valid question as I stared at the screen.

No reports followed the last I'd read, obviously I knew why.

"Seems we weren't simply dealing with Rogue wolves." Frost said as I leaned back in my chair. "So, who is The Resistance?"

"We're not entirely sure." Edge shook her head. "Evidently a group of wolves and vampires, though I don't really understand why Hunter would say he had issues working with vamps if he belonged to the organization."

I nodded as I realized the answer, shedding light on the issue for the others.

"Hunter was Ex-Council." I crossed my arms. "He had the mark on his arm."

Slade grimly looked to me. "Must've had some bad dealings with vampires beforehand."

I nodded, a question remaining.

"Why did help never come for the woman?"

The impending reinforcements and shipment would've taken care of most of their needs, but it didn't do much for the woman.

"Unless..." My mind reeled. *"The shipment. It was an ambulance... They were going to get her out of there. What if the driver was actually the requested medical personnel? Drop the shipment and pick her up?"*

Not only did I kill researchers, I had killed the man possibly dispatched to get the woman to help.

"I never would have had to bite her... She may have survived with medical attention."

"Damn." I breathed as I shook my head.

Again I saw Jordan, his brown eyes, again they stared at me, asking me why...

The band of freckles across his cheeks and nose... Why didn't I see them then, why didn't I take time to notice the short sprigs of facial hair on his top lip? How soft his face was... Why didn't I *see* him?

"You were not meant to." A dark growl rumbled from my core, the unknown snarl jolting me with its sudden invasion. I didn't know this voice, it was not that of my own, nor was it what I felt when the notions or thoughts of the wolf took shape as words in my mind.

It was a real voice.

"Here, Fenrir." Edge said as she briefly took the laptop from me, pulling me free of the invaders words.

When the laptop returned, I found what appeared to be more status reports, though lacking dates.

"Just read it, Fenrir." Edge said quietly.

It was all I could do to hold myself upright in the chair. I didn't want to read another word, each letter threatening to reduce me to rubble. If it was ever anything but, it was now clear to all that my heart was firmly entrenched upon my sleeve.

"As instructed, we've been monitoring and investigating disappearances around our area of operations. In the past six months the total number of disappearances numbers at forty-two."

I stopped reading for a moment, taking issue with the presented figure.

"Forty-two disappearances?" I shook my head. "Someone would have looked into this with that kind of number. Right?"

Slade killed my prayers as he shrugged. "It depends on the size of their A.O. If it was composed of several states, or pieces of, it could go unnoticed. Where we're positioned here, you could be in one of four states inside of two hours."

I frowned as I forced myself onward.

"Of the forty-two, approximately ten were located alive and well inside of a week. From the remaining thirty-two, six were found deceased in or around our A.O. Two of the said six were found to have an unknown cause of death. Both victims sustained multiple puncture wounds to the neck, bottom of upper arm, and on the thigh above the femoral artery. Cannot confirm if this is Order activity or the work of rogue vampires. The Remaining twenty-six missing persons we have been unable to locate. Tracking operations are on the precipice of futile. Our teams report that sixteen of the trails end with the smell of wolf, our only conclusion is Council. The other ten missing individuals we have been unable to trace entirely. End of report."

Beneath the official report was what seemed to be a more relaxed communication to Whitedeer, though I assumed it was from a time prior to the previous messages. Hunter wasn't yet asking for help.

"Whitedeer, there are no confirmed Order units in the A.O. Excluding what we know to be vampire related, and the genuine handful of missing persons cases, the rest are indicative of the Council. We know that they're fond of roadside smash and grabs, and that's only speaking of the trails that we can't follow. We're looking at twenty-six possible Council abductions, sixteen at a minimum, that's exponentially larger than the team we relieved reported. This isn't just picking up a few homeless folks here and there to replace troops, this is significantly bolstering ranks. If history, wolf, vampire, or human, is a sign of any kind, this sort of action often precedes a very aggressive offensive. The facts are here Whitedeer, The Council is stealing people, and if they are conducting this practice elsewhere, well you see where this is going."

Beneath this piece was the first bit of text I'd seen from Whitedeer.

"Hunter, I share your concerns. I'm aware of The Council's methods of recruitment, and much as I know you would gladly head the counter operation, I must remind you that your outpost is strictly forbidden to engage in combat operations. Your utmost priority is to monitor your A.O. and continue your recon operations. Latest intelligence suggests Trick Jaw is operating inside your A.O. I cannot stress the importance of verifying his location. Neutralized, his absence would deal The Order a critical blow, though that says nothing of the pending results of your research staff. Your outpost is to continue research into the cures. A cure to vampirism or lycanthropy, one or both, is paramount. If an antidote is produced, the actions of The Council and The Order can be undone. Your compound is shouldering a great deal of burden right now, Hunter, and as soon as possible, I'll have additional assets in place. Until that time, however, you must keep your course."

As I pulled away from the screen, my mind melted, a mess of names, of goals, all cut down at the points of my knife and teeth.

"They weren't even looking for a fight. Res-Rec." Hunter had called it.

"Research-Recon. Res-Rec." My brain translated.

"The only things they looked for were a cure, missing people that The Council had taken, and one Order operator."

I looked back to the screen.

"Trick Jaw."

The Council, the organization I believed to be acting on humanities behalf, seemed to be doing anything but.

Any research was likely destroyed in our attacks, and I'd never heard mention of this Trick Jaw, nor had I seen any notes on him in the security room.

"The Council though..."

"Is this true?" I slowly looked to Frost, praying that she didn't confirm it. "Is this what we do?"

Frost shook her head. *"We* never have. We're a combat group, not recruiters. We don't deal with humans, hardly ever. We were all taken in by Phoenix."

I nodded. "I wonder if Phoenix is aware of this?"

Edge shook her head. "Phoenix wouldn't serve in an organization that he knew did this stuff. All he preaches is 'Good of humanity'. He's probably got no idea about this, he's only a Captain."

"Slade?" I asked his opinion.

"We've been thinkin' on this since Edge began digging into this damned thing. Best we can figure is to talk to Phoenix. See what he has to say. Maybe when he hears this, he can make sense of it. He's too low a rank to change anything, he can't change how the Council runs, but he could probably rally other units to stand with us against this."

Alarms went off in my head. "What if he does know about it?"

"He can't." Frost said. "There's no way."

I sighed. This had trouble written all over it, capital T and all.

"I shouldn't have to say that this is a bad idea." I brought my hands to my face.

"We know it is." Edge said. "That's why, whatever we do, us four, we're doing it together."

I sat quietly for a moment, wishing I had never touched the laptop.

Now I, *we*, knew the truth.

"This is what they were talking about." I shook my head. *"When Frost came in here. They were questioning whether or not I could be trusted with this. Why did she say yes?"*

"Because she trusts me." I let my hands down.

"The more of us approach him about it, the better." Frost looked to Slade. "Knight?"

Slade shook his head as his brows hardened. "I won't drag her into this."

"Doc?" I asked.

"Ghost is due for a check up." Edge said. "Doc may very well side with us, in fact I know he would, but you'll never pry him away from a patient."

"Red?" I tried.

Slade shook his head. "You'll never get him to go before Phoenix on something like this."

I sighed. There was one name left.

"Marcus?"

Frost scoffed. "A legacy child with dreams of grandeur? Whose sole purpose in life is to climb The Council ranks to the point of *actual* Council member?"

I almost chuckled. "So, us four."

Frost nodded. "Us four."

"Together." Edge replied.

"That'd look great on a poster." Slade sighed with sarcasm as he frowned at me. "Don't suppose you also scraped up some cures? Or found out anything about this 'Trick Jaw' character?"

I shook my head.

"Yeah, I didn't figure." Slade looked down as he rubbed his face. "Just might've been handy for when Phoenix flips his lid over this."

33

Before the Captain

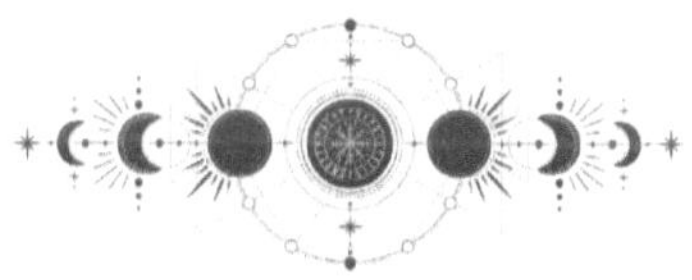

10/17

1600 Hrs.

The four of us stood in front of Phoenix's desk, his eyes suspiciously traveling over us in a moment of near clairvoyance.

"What's the issue here wolves?" He asked, his voice revealing that he was certainly on guard.

"Captain," I spoke slowly, unsure how to proceed, "while I was in the outpost, I secured a laptop, a laptop that contained logs from the outpost captain to a Commander Whitedeer, as well as several observation logs. We didn't know any of that until we were able to look deeper into the laptop here–"

"Here!" Phoenix shouted as he stood. "You brought a captured piece of tech *here*?! Where it could be tracked?!"

"I took care of that, Phoenix." Edge spoke up. "Please, hear us out."

Phoenix turned his raging eyes back to me.

"Go on." He growled.

"Documents in the logs seem to show that The Council is abducting people, humans." I continued. "Wolves don't feed on people, so the only reasonable explanation is that The Council is taking people to make them wolves, soldiers for The Council."

Phoenix's demeanor instantly changed. He became quiet, reserved.

It was news to him.

He took in a breath before speaking, much more calmly than he had prior, almost whispering. "The laptop should've been brought straight to me. Whose idea was it for Edge to look into it?"

I began to speak, and he raised a finger to me. "Fenrir, don't. From the moment you returned until just earlier you were busy, so don't lie to me."

"I asked her to, Phoenix." Frost said. "I thought we might be able to find something to help us. I never thought we'd uncover this."

Phoenix only nodded. "Who else knows?"

"Just us four." Frost again took the lead. "Fenrir and I found out while we were– after we left the mess hall. We knew we had to come to you with the information."

Again, Phoenix nodded. "And what would you have me do? I'm only a Captain."

"We know, sir," Edge said, "we assumed you didn't know, seems we were right. Our only remaining option, what we four believe to be the *best* option, to actually uphold what you teach, protecting humanity, is to find other units that will help us change this. This… This isn't what we fight for, Phoenix."

Phoenix looked to his desk and blew air from his nose in a quick puff. "Words so easily spoken."

The room was quiet for a time, until Slade spoke.

"So, that's it?" There was no mistaking his aggression. "We're stuck here?"

"No." Phoenix shook his head, never looking away from his desk, countless thoughts no doubt rattling round his head.

"We're not stuck," he said, "but I can't simply call upon other units and ask them to join me in a stand against the *actual* Council. This… This is going to take some planning… and a bit of time."

"So, what do we do?" Edge asked.

Phoenix heavily let himself down into his chair and placed a hand on his temple. "I'm removing our status of combat effective. Right now, I've got two squads at best and both have been through the wringer."

He suddenly stood up. "We're going on R&R."

"R&R?" I asked.

"Rest and relaxation." Slade said.

"A formal way of saying we're hurting and need to recoup." Frost said bluntly.

"Do you disagree, Frost?" Phoenix almost smiled.

She made no reply.

"I thought not." He said. "Get everyone mustered up in front of my office."

34

R&R

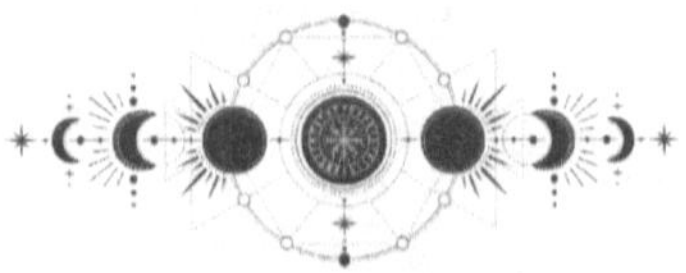

10/17
1617 Hrs.

Everyone had been brought to stand in formation in front of Phoenix's office, and his orders were fairly cut and dry.

"Collect your gear and expect to be gone for a while."

The only exceptions to the orders were Cookie and the nurses, they were to remain at The Citadel, the reasoning withheld from the rest of the unit.

"Think this is going to be a survival exercise?" Knight said as she crammed clothes into a rucksack.

"I hope so. Means we'll have to provide our own food." Red said. "Fine by me, been a while since we've had fresh venison."

My bag packed, I drug myself to the main warehouse.

"Where did everything go to Hell?" I asked as I looked back over recent events.

Training seemed so far passed now, though it had only been a few days.

"I had never expected things to be easy, but this was my first mission. How could I, and only I, have flipped an entire unit on its head within hours of finishing my training?"

"What do you think he's going to do?" Frost stepped up beside me, unknowingly saving me from my thoughts.

"I don't know." I said blandly. "I really don't. I'm glad that he's taking the time to evaluate, but I feel like we're just running from a problem. Whether we're here or there, the issue remains."

"That's pretty much what Edge said too." Frost replied.

"What do you think?" I asked.

"I agree with you." She nodded. "I think Phoenix just needs time to think."

I nodded as I dropped my rucksack into the trunk of the Challenger.

"What we really need to be asking, Fenrir, is what are we going to do if he decides to do nothing?" Frost said.

That outcome hadn't occurred to me, and it was a struggle to imagine it.

How could he do nothing? If he really meant what he said, he couldn't just go along with this.

"I– I don't know, Frost." I finally replied. "I don't think he could just turn a blind eye to this."

"Would anyone happen to know if we are taking our arms?" Doc asked as he gently laid his pack in the back of the van a few yards away.

"Be kind of silly to leave them behind, Doc." Slade coyly smiled as he raised his foot. "You ever seen a two legged wolf?"

With nothing more than a flat face, Doc conveyed just how humorous he found Slade's attempt at a joke.

"I'll ask Phoenix." I nodded as I turned towards his door, giving it a light rap.

"Come in."

Phoenix briefly looked up to me from his desk. "Are things underway?"

"Nearly done sir."

He didn't look at me, just kept rummaging through his desk and various filing cabinets.

"Are we going to be taking our weapons?" I asked.

Phoenix took his time before offering a quick nod. "Best have them in the event we have to respond to something."

"Will we be close enough to respond?"

"We'll only be about an hour and a half away. No reason we couldn't."

"We'll still be pretty close then."

Phoenix nodded again. "We need to stay in the AO, The Council relies on my monthly reports for the news here."

"I see." I nodded, my voice heavy with disappointment.

He immediately caught my tone, failing to let a moment pass before putting it to rest. "I know you want me to make a choice Fenrir, and I suspect that you prefer the option of convincing other Captains to stand with us. That may very well be my verdict, but until I make a decision, I still have to play the part of a faithful Council captain, and all of you still have to conduct yourselves as Council soldiers."

"I understand." I replied, though I didn't like it. Not at all. "I'll be with the others."

"Alright," Phoenix nodded, "and, Fenrir?"

"Yes, sir?"

"Try to get some sleep on the ride." He managed a weak smile. "You do not look well."

I nodded as I turned for the door.

"Well, that perfectly coincides with how I feel."

35

The Safe House

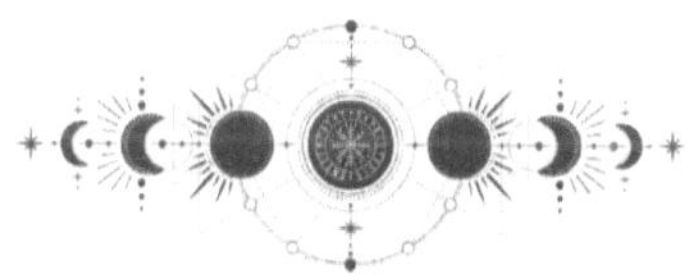

10/17
1810 Hrs.

About an hour and a half and 90 miles later, I woke to Phoenix's voice calling over the radio, though it was largely lost to me.

"What did he say?" I stretched my legs as I blinked sleep from my eyes.

"He said to pull over here." Frost replied.

I looked to the side of the road where a long driveway led to a barn.

"How long was I out?" I asked as we slowed.

"About an hour." Frost smiled. "Not too long. Feel any better?"

"Feel a bit stiff." I yawned. "Aside from that, can't complain. Where exactly are we?"

I looked around, finding one side of the road was flat farmland, dotted with houses and barns. The other, the prettier of the two views, was a mixture of sloping timbered bluffs and sheer rock faces.

"I'm not entirely sure, Fenrir." Frost replied. "I've never been here. An hour and half south of Kirkwood if that helps at all. We haven't come close

409

to any towns, kind of out in the middle of nowhere."

As we came to a stop, I assumed the barn was the safe house. It was certainly inconspicuous enough not to draw attention.

It was a large wooden structure, definitely in need of fresh paint. Large enough to hold three or four tractors. There was no doubt in my mind this place could house both the unit and our vehicles.

As Phoenix stepped forward to open a massive sliding door, I looked to Frost, grateful that despite being in what may have seemed like a tight spot, we could face it together.

Phoenix waved a hand, ushering us in as Frost gently pressed the accelerator, pulling into a sizable bay.

She killed the engine and as we stepped out of the vehicle, I found I was wrong with my guess.

The barn wasn't the safe house, it was just a barn.

An earthen floor that sent dust into the air with every step, and the musty smell of old straw in the loft were the only things that waited in this place.

It was just a barn.

"The van we'll keep with us, your car and the ambulance won't make it." Phoenix looked over at a mounded tarp. "The rest of you can take that."

"To where exactly?" I asked.

"You'll soon see." Phoenix nodded. "And don't worry about the car, it'll be here, under lock and key."

I nodded as I walked to the large tarped form, finding the outline discernible enough to know it was a truck.

I took the tarp in my hands and gave it a hard tug, launching a cloud of dust into the air as a blue pickup came to light.

Phoenix patted my back, suddenly beside me. "Think you can manage?"

"Yeah." I nodded.

Frost and I stepped up into the cab and waited for several operators to take their place in the bed.

We crossed the highway, driving into the bluffs, up an old road that looked like it had been cut into the trees several decades ago. At times the truck pitched and groaned, but it held fast as we climbed ever higher and further away from the highway.

This safe house really was in the middle of nowhere.

* * *

I opened the door of the truck, stepping out before a weathered cabin.

It was rustic to say the least, a fire pit laid before it, an outhouse behind it, and to add a touch of character, a deer skull, having once belonged to an eight-point buck, hung above the door.

Phoenix stepped from the van. "Go on inside and take a look around."

Frost and the others had already congregated near the door and made way as I came close.

The doorknob turned easily, though a bit rusty, and as I stepped inside the cabin I felt as if I were stepping back into the days of settlers and covered wagons.

No one had set foot in the one room cabin for years, dust covering everything in sight. It was a simple, but sufficient shelter. On the right side of the door stood a wood stove, whose duty was no doubt to keep the cabin warm in cooler seasons.

On the left sat a table, large branches serving as legs. Around the table sat benches that had been made of logs, also featuring stout branches to hold them from the floor.

At the rear of the room were two couches and the only window in the place.

The cabin was far from luxurious, but served the purpose that it was built for.

"Home away from home." Phoenix stood in the doorway.

We all nodded as Doc looked around. "Is there enough room for everyone?"

Phoenix shook his head. "Not in this room there isn't."

He walked towards the left couch, turning to a fuse box on the wall above it, something I'd overlooked while initially scanning the room.

Opening it, Phoenix revealed no fuses, but rather a ten-digit keypad. He punched four buttons and we all heard a metallic click. Aside from that, nothing happened.

With a nod Phoenix spun on his heels, stepping to the space of wall between the wood stove and the couches.

He pushed against the cinder blocks and a large section shakily moved back, revealing a set of descending stairs. At the base of the stairs stood a solitary door.

"Everybody down." Phoenix gestured down the stairs.

We all looked at each other, unsure of what awaited us.

Phoenix offered no words, good, bad, or otherwise in the presence of our uncertainty, granting only a curt nod.

I descended the stairs and reached for the bolt that seemed to hold the door shut, and with a small amount of force it pulled free, though the same couldn't be said for the door.

I tried to gently push it at first, earning no ground when it didn't budge. Pressing my shoulder against the cool steel, driving with my legs, the door slowly opened. Behind the door was a dark corridor, a blue square shining at the end.

A cool hand touched my shoulder, accompanied by Frost's soft breath. "I'm right behind you."

Her hand fell away as I took my first step into the hall and the wolf illuminated the dark space.

The hallway came to new light, revealing a short chamber that ended in another door, equal in size to that of a bank vault. On the wall beside the door was the blue square, little larger than a hand.

"Stop there, Fenrir, I'm on my way." Phoenix called out.

He made his way past the rest of the unit and myself, approaching the blue panel. Pressing his hand to what I observed to be a biometric touch pad, a heavy thud resonated down the hall.

The door mechanically opened, and light filled the hall, momentarily blinding us. As our eyes adjusted, an immense room came into view.

A gas stove, granite counter, two rows of cots, computer and projector were all the room contained but it was clear that this room was the real safe house.

"Alright," Phoenix pulled attention to himself, "these are the living quarters. Everything else is up top. First priority, I want all arms down here, radios too. You won't need either here, and I need to take stock of our equipment. After that feel free to go outside and move about, but don't stray too far. Until further notice, this is our home. Every night I'll do a headcount. You're free to stretch your legs, but I must stress, do not leave these trees wolves."

We all nodded, making strides to start unloading the vehicles.

"Marcus, Fenrir, a word." Phoenix said.

Marcus and I both stood at semi attention while the rest of the unit filed out.

Only after we three were left in solitude did Phoenix open his pack, extracting what appeared to be a military grade tablet.

"I've got something I'd like you and Marcus to look into."

"I thought this was R&R?" I asked.

"Doesn't mean we can't still be productive." Phoenix replied. "For a while Council intel has believed there is an Order installation east of here, about three miles out. There's a campground in that direction and it's heavily used this time of year. I've checked the local news outlets and there haven't been any reports of missing campers, but since we're right here there's no reason not to check it out. This is recon only, understand?"

"Weapons?" Marcus asked.

"Didn't I just say recon only, Lieutenant?" Phoenix turned a hard eye to Marcus.

"Solid copy." Marcus slowly replied.

"Good." Phoenix said. "The installation is supposed to be in an old ranger station a little northwest of the campground, so if you hit the campground, you've gone too far. First, I want you to confirm whether there even is an installation. If so, I want you to record sentry locations, weaponry, and appraise their numbers. Clear?"

"Clear." Marcus said.

Phoenix nodded. "Well, go on."

***

"What do you mean he's sending you out?!" Frost's eyes blazed.

"He's just sending Marcus and I out on a recon mission, scout out a potential Order post." I held my hands flat at my waist, trying to keep her quiet during our hurried exchange, made private only by the meeting taking place behind the cabin.

"Why not all of us? At least all of Alpha?" She justly asked.

"I don't know, Frost." I shook my head, unable to deny that it felt odd, the notion furthered by the lack of radios and weapons. The situation was made only worse with the knowledge that I would have to leave Frost behind once again.

Frost was largely quiet, her mind moving behind focused eyes.

"I know." I nodded. "Doesn't seem like he's put much thought to it."

With a sigh of aggravation she shook her head. "He hasn't put any thought to it. This is stupid. He's not even *making sense.*"

"What do you mean?" I asked.

"He says he's removed us from active duty, yet he's sending you and Marcus on recon. What do we do if it turns out that there is an Order post? Ignoring the fact that the team is still recovering, you're running on *one* hour of sleep, Fenrir." She shook her hand, a single finger raised. "One. Explain how this makes any sense."

"I'm not arguing with you, Frost." I shook my head. "It doesn't make sense to me either. Maybe he's just trying to keep busy. Maybe it's just taking him time."

Despite her anger, her eyes betrayed her. In their depths, fear, fear of uncertainty, waited.

She didn't feel this alone. Slade, Edge, me. We all felt it. We were all scared of what lay ahead.

"Whatever happens, Frost–"

"Remember your promise, Fenrir." She whispered. "Come back to me."

For a moment, I thought about making a quirky response about us still having to "talk" later. With the worry in her eyes though, I couldn't. She didn't need smooth talking. She needed reassurance.

"No force, on earth or otherwise, could make me break that promise."

36

Unlikely Rebel

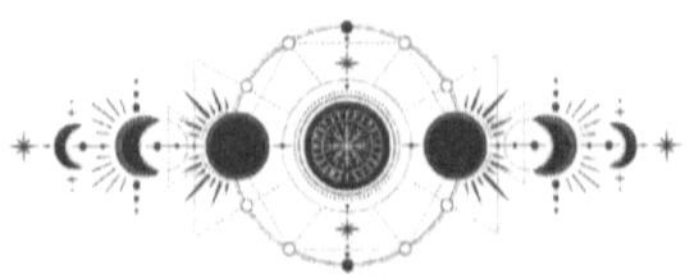

10/17
2105 Hrs.

A short distance into the trees Marcus and I picked up a deer trail leading deeper into the woods.

The trial was soft, commonly used by game of all sorts.

We were making good time east, though it was quiet between us, and I realized that Marcus and I hadn't really spoken since I'd returned from the compound.

No doubt he was furious with me, as he had every right to be. Even if things were okay between him and Phoenix, I had still put him in a bad spot.

Regardless of that, I tested the waters. I needed to know where we stood.

"Awful quiet, Marcus." I said as we walked, just as much to help quiet my mind as to break the silence.

"Not much to say pup. You made me look like shit. I took my ass chewing, and I don't really see much point in passing it on."

"Yeah. Sorry about that."

"Don't be." Marcus briefly glanced back, offering me a smile that threatened to break my heart. "You did good. You did what we couldn't."

As we walked, I briefly considered telling Marcus about what we had uncovered on the captured laptop.

Briefly.

"Gonna' have to pick up the pace." Marcus noted as his strides grew longer, faster. "Your rendezvous with Frost lost us a bit of time."

"At most it was five– Hang on." My interest piqued. "No one saw us, everyone was inside, how–"

"I'm a Lieutenant, Fenrir, part of my job is knowing where my team is, *all* of my team. Still like to know how you weaseled your way past her icy exterior."

"That's a little harsh isn't it?" I ducked under a low branch.

"Is it?" Marcus nearly chuckled. "You seem to have forgotten some of your time with her at the farm."

"I just took it as something to help me. I took it for what it was, training. She wasn't actively attacking me."

Marcus seemed to process the words before replying.

"No," he agreed, "quite the opposite in fact, she nearly praised you when I asked her how you handled the wolf."

"What?"

"Mhmm. First time I recall anything like that actually, of course you have been near the epicenter of many firsts for our unit." His tone bore a striking resemblance to humor.

Marcus suddenly stopped and turned on his heels, looking to my hip.

"Good. You've still got your holster." He reached into his jacket, extracting a large frame revolver and holding it out to me. "Cylinders full."

"Thought we were going unarmed?" I said as I took the revolver, minding the hammer as I strapped it into the holster.

Marcus shook his head as he drew another pistol, what looked to be a Beretta, from a cargo pocket and dropped it into his own holster. "Not a chance. Not when there's the possibility of running into trouble. Phoenix isn't thinking straight, something's got him off tilt. First Phoenix wants all the weapons, then radios. After that he decides to send us out on a recon mission. With no weapons or a radio. That doesn't add up. We never go on any kind of assignment without both. Something's not right, this whole R&R thing's not right. You know anything about it?"

"No." I lied.

I really wanted to tell him *now*. His notion hit the nail square on the head, but Frost and the others had all elected not to say anything to the others, *especially* him.

Still, it felt wrong to lie to him, to make him question his own instincts.

"Time will tell I suppose." He pulled a radio from his pocket and switched it on, then hit a small button on the side, producing a quick quiet beep.

"Never figured you to break orders Marcus, let alone two."

"Like I said. Something's not right, and I believe, whether or not you know, or if you're simply refusing to say, you are, yet again, at the center of it. The Red Moons have been turned upside down since your arrival. Phoenix would have beat the hell out of others for pulling what you have. Yet you get off scot-free. And then we go on R&R? Something's wrong."

His instincts were definitely on point, on numerous facts. Set aside the R&R business, and still Marcus and I found ourselves away from the squad on a recon mission, with one radio and two sidearms, none of which we were supposed to have.

"Won't do much good if they're at any sort of range."

"Got anything a little larger tucked up your sleeve?" I asked.

"If you don't want it, give it back." He growled as he stepped over a fallen pine sapling.

"Take that as a no." I followed.

* * *

The day was beginning to wane by the time we came upon the old ranger station.

Phoenix was right when he said it wasn't far from the campground. It was all of fifty yards to the nearest cabin site.

Marcus dropped his pack as he laid down on a small rise in the woods.

Reaching inside he donned a pair of binoculars, then handed them to me.

"Get eyes on and tell me what you see. Numbers, fortifications, weapons."

"Got it." I raised the binoculars to my eyes, calling it out as I saw it. "Two out walking."

"Weapons?"

"Handguns on their sides."

"No long guns?"

"Not that I can see L.T."

"Insignias?"

"Uh…Brown shirts, badges on their sleeves…Conservation Police. Vehicle is a dark green pickup, same logo, light bar on top. Oh, got a long gun, it looks like a pump gun in the cab."

"Now's not the time to joke, Fenrir."

"Lieutenant," I lowered the binoculars and extended them to Marcus, "I'm not."

Marcus still eyed me suspiciously as he took the binocs and looked for himself.

"Well," He murmured, "crap."

"Uh-huh." I sighed.

"Council intel needs some intel." Marcus said.

Both of us chuckled as he set the binoculars down. "We'll just hang out for a bit, keep an eye on 'em. They'll eventually show."

* * *

2340 Hrs.

"Well?"

"No change L.T."

"What the hell." Marcus shook his head. "We'll stay till daylight. Sun comes up, we'll know for sure what–"

"Red Moon Actual, Black Star Actual, how copy?" The radio crackled.

I spun around and looked at Marcus' pocket, to the radio.

"Red Moon Actual?" I whispered though no one could hear us.

Marcus raised a hand to me as he listened, then whispered. "Phoenix."

"Solid copy Black Star Actual. ETA?"

"Fifteen mikes. Legacy status?"

"Legacy clear and away. Black Star Actual you are green on designated targets. I say again, Black Star Actual, you are green on designated targets."

"Solid copy Red Moon Actual. Green light. Get small."

The radio fell silent.

"What the hell was all that?" I asked.

Marcus looked to me, a ghost of his former self. The color had left his face.

"We gotta' go!" Marcus took to his feet, making rapid tracks towards the safe house.

I gave chase and when I was within a few feet he yelled back to me.

"You hold the Black Stars, Phoenix is mine."

"Phoenix is mine?" My brain struggled to catch up.

"Marcus!" I caught his arm and drug him to a stop. "What the hell is going on?!"

"Phoenix just called in a cleaner squad!"

"What?!" I shook my head. " What does that even mean? You mean to kill everyone?"

"Why would he do that?!"

"We're Legacy! Phoenix sent us away. I'm a legacy, and you…" His eyes briefly fell to my arm, to the mark beneath the fabric. "I don't know, but it's us."

"Are you sure?"

"Get small." Marcus turned back towards the safe house. "It means danger close."

"Damn!" I once again let out after Marcus.

As I ran, I spoke to the wolf, to anything that rattled around inside.

Whatever it was that spoke in me, whatever made it easy to kill, whatever made me *like* killing, whatever liked the taste of blood. Whatever it was, I called out to it, I told it to take hold and no matter what, don't let go.

"Above all else, protect Her."

My mind raced, trying to calculate how long it would take for us to make it back to the safe house.

Three miles.

Less than fifteen minutes until The Black Stars showed up.

Less than five minutes a mile.

Humans in peak shape and tons of training could pull it off.

I didn't fit that bill.

But I wasn't simply human either.

"Marcus!" I snatched the strap of his pack, jerking him to a stop.

"What the hell are you doing?!" His eyes flashed.

"Take this." I handed him my pack. "We're too slow like this. Four legs are faster."

"What?" His eyes widened. "Do you expect me to ride you?!"

I hit my hands and knees.

"I don't give a damn what you do!" I shouted. "Just hold on to me, drop before we get there, so if I take fire they don't hit both of us."

"Are you nuts?!"

"Shut up!" I roared.

For the first time in our relationship, I truly commanded the wolf to venture from the darkness, demanding rather than asking. Heat and confidence seeped into my soul as the wolf accepted my order, taking hold with a vengeance.

"Fenrir," Marcus slowly spoke beside me, clairvoyance once more kicking in, "what do you know about this?"

"Not now." I growled. "I'll tell you, but first, we have to keep them safe."

Fire ripped at my core, the wolf's rage.

The growls of the emerging wolf took shape in my mind, forming no words, though I understood their meaning.

Death.

37

Ambush

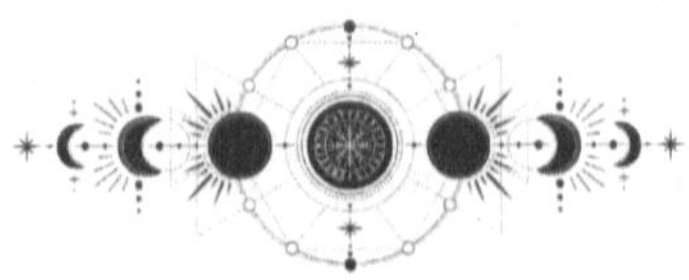

The Red Moons were pinned down inside the cabin, unable to rally any real defense against the sudden onset of raining silver.

The bunker had been tried, the bulk of their weapons contained within, though the scanner would release the door for none but the absent Phoenix.

Countless adversaries laid fire into the building, chiseling away at the front wall of the cabin, The Red Moons doing little to suppress the largely unseen enemy.

The only shred of luck cast their way was in the form of the few rifles they had not yet put in the bunker.

Frost leaned against the wall next to the door as a single target presented himself, quickly cut down as she let out a burst of fire.

"Slade!" Frost jerked her head towards the window at the back of the Cabin. "Get them out of here!"

A few feet from where she stood lay Ghost, a small hole in his forehead, the back of his skull blown away.

The first casualty, throttled as he opened the door to step outside. His body hadn't fallen to the floor before the ridge erupted in a fiery line of muzzle flashes.

Frost was doing well to keep the enemy at bay, hoping to buy enough time for the team to get out of the cabin.

"Gotta' get them out. One rocket or a lucky grenade is all it'd take."

"Frost!" Slade called through the window. "We're clear!"

Her eyes moved over Ghost one last time as she stepped over his body on her way to the window.

With her lack of fire, she was surprised that no rounds tore into the cabin. The cinder block walls were surely shot to hell. It wouldn't take anything special, a standard round would punch right through.

"Why aren't they firing?!" Frost stepped onto the window sill.

On the other side, Knight took her by the arm, helping her down as a solid thud echoed in the cabin.

Frost knew the sound.

"Grenade, get down!" She tackled Knight, pinning her sister beneath her as thunder and lightning spouted from the window.

"That was a flashbang." Frost's mind noted. *"Non-lethal. Why would they–"*

She looked up, frantically searching for wounded, finding none.

"You alright?!" She rolled from Knight, smashing her shoulder to the wall.

Knight nodded, her face covered in dark dust. There was no mistaking the fear in her eyes.

"We need our gear!" Frost's thoughts raged. *"Why would he lock– Doesn't matter."*

"Find Phoenix!" Frost yelled. "He was doing a perimeter check behind the cabin!"

"On it!" Knight nodded, quickly slipping away into the draw behind the cabin.

"Hurry back, Knight."

"Suppress the ridge!" Frost sent out a volley of rounds.

"Thank God I didn't go with him." Frost's mind raced as she replaced an empty magazine.

"Care to go on a quick perimeter check?" Phoenix had asked. "I would not be opposed to having someone along just in case, Knight and Edge could join as well."

"In case of what?" Frost had nearly laughed at the time. "If it's all the same, Phoenix, I'd rather stay with the team. Some of us still aren't quite out of that compound if you get my meaning."

Phoenix frowned, eventually nodding. "I understand. To be honest, it was less about checking the area, and more about having the chance to talk about what we spoke on before. What to do about our current situation."

"Oh." Frost was struck by the ruse. "I– I figured you'd want to talk that over with Marcus. He's your Lieutenant, and he's been here longer than–"

"Even if Marcus wasn't out on assignment," Phoenix smiled, "I still would've asked you, dear. I fear that Marcus will be rather biased on this particular matter. I realize that all of us are going to be conflicted here, but Marcus… Marcus will be more than most."

"Yeah." Frost nearly whispered. "I don't envy you that conversation."

"Mm." Phoenix chuckled. "Sure you won't go with me? It would mean a great deal to me. I value your input, Frost. I don't have to tell you that."

"I know you do." Frost smiled up to the man who stood as her father. "But I don't–"

"Say no more." Phoenix nodded as his hand slid into his pocket. "I won't be long. Just need to clear my hands– Head."

He chuckled with the stammer, an act that Frost had rarely, if ever, witnessed their captain commit.

"If I had–" Frost shook the parting from her head as she released the charging handle of the rifle. *"No time for that now."*

"Pour it on!" She roared.

Red nodded as he leaned around the corner to fire, making a sudden backpedal as a crater formed in his back, spattering Frost's face with hot blood.

By the time he hit the ground the silver had already begun its work. He lay on the ground writhing like a serpent, the blood in his veins boiling silver. He screamed for the first few seconds before running out of air, leaving his locked open jaw producing only coarse grunts and gurgles as he clawed at the ground. As quickly as he'd started shaking, he fell quiet and lay still.

"Shit!" Frost's mind cried.

A round shattered the corner wall near Frost's head, showering her with dust and sharp bits of concrete.

"Dammit!" Frost threw her arm around the building, firing blindly.

"Doc! I need help up here! Slade!" She screamed as she found him lying on the ground. "Are you hit?!"

Slade looked up from his prone position as he snatched Red's rifle. "Not yet, but I'd kill for a grenade!"

Slade ripped a magazine from Red's pocket as rounds riddled his friend's body, quickly driving Slade away.

"They're circling!" Frost cried. "Doc, we need to get to the hollow! Can you keep us covered?" Frost called to him.

Doc grimly looked to her over his shoulder, fully aware that he could keep the ridge suppressed, also that it would likely be his final act.

For a moment, he held her gaze.

With a breath of acceptance, Doc nodded. "Go."

"Get ready to move!" Edge prepared to push from the wall next to Doc.

"When I get into cover, I'll lay a base of fire." Frost drove her last magazine into the rifle. "Wait for my word."

Slade shoved his last magazine into Doc's pocket, giving his friend the best chance he could to keep them covered.

"Doc," Slade barely peeked from cover, seeing only brief muzzle flashes dotted along the hilltop, "are you sure about this?"

Doc nodded as his face softened. "My charge is to keep you safe. I can hold them long enough."

Slade's eyes saddened, knowing the words that his friend left unspoken.

Goodbye.

With a final deep breath Frost readied herself to bolt into defilade, picking a sizable oak log a short sprint into the ravine as her destination.

From there she could look back, putting enough rounds down range to keep their attackers at bay, at least until the others could join her.

Her feet started forward, hellbent on the log, though she had only taken a few steps from the cabin before bullets buried themselves in the earth at her feet.

"They're flanking farther back!" She slammed herself back to cover as she yelled. "Nobody move!"

For a moment she was quiet, her mind racing, trying to figure a way to get her and the team out of immediate danger, knowing that every second they remained stationary, the enemy drew closer.

"Keep them from pushing any further! Make your shots count!" She yelled. "When they can't take our flanks, they'll charge. We'll meet them."

Everyone nodded, knowing what this was. A hail Mary, the last ditch effort.

The remnants of The Red Moons moved to fire before the sounds of battle fell silent, cut down by a sudden roar echoing through the trees.

For a minuscule moment, all was quiet.

Her breath still ragged, Frost chanced a glimpse around the chiseled cabin wall.

"Frost," Slade whispered, the sudden silence putting an eerie hue to the lingering gun smoke, "what is it? Are they shifting?"

"No." Frost simultaneously answered Slade, and her own fears.

No weapons fired, but Frost was sure that every soul on the battlefield had eyes locked onto the wolf at the edge of the clearing.

Through the smoky haze, only its head and front quarters were visible, like it was part of the sulfuric cloud itself.

Crimson droplets fell from its dark coat, bleeding from cuts and gouges scored over its body, numerous incisions from the undergrowth it had cut through.

Frost's breath caught. She recognized the wolf, yet as she looked into its eyes, she found no trace of the man within this creature. They were not the eye's of its host, once familiar and bright, now dark, full of fury.

It snarled, gleaming fangs clacking together, harshly meeting and relaxing, eager for the blood that this fresh battlefield promised.

It turned, examining the battleground, and under its gaze, fear settled over the field, none safe from its clutch.

Frost's heart raced as she felt a primal terror grip her core.

She had seen this before, against rogues, afflicted that had lost control of the animal within. When it took them, they were powerless to resist, unable to regain themselves until the wolf had done its bloody will.

"He's hunting." Frost's mind hummed as a chill rolled down her spine, sending prickles to her skin.

She knew she needed to raise the rifle, in case the wolf came at them, but her hands refused to move, unwilling to devote this beast to destruction, unwilling to devote him.

"Be still." Doc calmly spoke as he rested his rifle barrel against the wall of the cabin, training the sights on the wolf.

"Doc–" Frost started.

"Only if he charges, Frost." Doc's trigger finger rested along the frame of the rifle.

"Do not make me do this, Fenrir." Doc silently willed his thoughts to his friend.

Fenrir had taken control of his wolf, and never had Doc heard of a wolf overpowering its host after dominance had been established.

"But this," Doc thought, *"this looks different. Like m–"*

The wolf's eyes held on The Red Moons an unsettling moment too long, driving a spike of fear into each of them before it looked away.

Its gaze rose to the high ground, where the enemy remained motionless, equally stricken.

Frost sickened as she stared at the wolf, noticing the faintest lift at the corners of its mouth.

It was smiling.

"What is this?!" Frost's mind screamed as the wolf drew back into the

smoky wisps.

As its face vanished, Frost caught two twins of moonlight peering from the haze.

"On guard." Frost's voice shook.

"Who's at the helm?" Slade asked as he spun to the fog that had moved behind the cabin.

"I–" Frost's voice nearly failed as she fixed her rifle on the ridge. "I don't know."

"I can't see the–"

A shrill roar stung the air, putting ice to vein as a woman's scream rang from the ridge.

Frost looked up in time to see a surge of bright blood take to the air, the vivid red cutting through the murky atmosphere.

A sudden wind coursed over the battlefield, clearing away the veil, revealing a dozen soldiers at the top, their barrels quickly traveling towards Fenrir.

"Light 'em up!" Frost's rifle screamed slag and white light.

"I've got you, Finn."

The reports spurred the wolf into action. In a few quick leaps it came down on the nearest soldier, tearing her apart in a bloody mess as rounds began to fly anew, restored by The Red Moons, capitalizing on now exposed enemies.

The remaining soldiers seemed oblivious to the riddled bodies that fell around them, left to face down the charging wolf alone.

As the last soldier in sight fell to the jaws of the wolf, it seemed that others, out of sight, had drawn the wolf's attention.

The wolf pursued its quarry over the ridge and a new roar reached the cabin survivors.

Over the rise, out of sight, wolves were at battle.

The Red Moons stared at the ridge, where they had last seen the wolf, breathlessly waiting for it to reappear.

Edge looked to Frost, breaking the eerie silence with a shaky voice. "Was that Fenrir?"

"No," Frost replied in an equal voice as she shook away trembles, "it wasn't."

"Ammo check." Doc said as he dropped his spent magazine, his last magazine. "I'm out."

Frost cleared her throat as she looked to the open bolt of her rifle, seeing the plastic lift of the empty mag. "Me too."

"Same here." Slade frowned. "We should get to the–"

"Hey!"

They all turned to see Marcus round the corner of the cabin.

"Thank God you're all okay." He breathed.

Frost grimaced. "We're not. Ghost, and Red..."

Marcus shook his head. "Damn..."

"I found him!"

All spun to find Knight coming up the hollow behind the cabin, Phoenix trailing close behind.

Seeing Marcus, Knight let out a heavy sigh of relief before noticing the absentee. "Fenrir?"

Time froze as the team watched Phoenix raise his pistol. The barrel let out a single bark, shock rippling through Knight's face as her chest opened.

"Hannah!" Slade screamed as he broke from the group, rushing to Knight's side as she fell to the ground.

Knight's face twisted in pain as Slade rolled her to her back, quickly trying to assess the wound.

Slade had barely exposed the injury before the surrounding veins began to turn a heavy blue.

"It's too close to her heart!" Slade panicked as Frost took a step towards Phoenix, the pistol jerking to her in response.

"Hannah, hold on." Slade begged as he turned to Doc, opening his mouth to cry for Anver as the realization struck him.

Everything was locked away.

In a long breath, Knight fell motionless in the leaves of the forest floor, her brief suffering reaching its merciful end.

Helplessly, Slade watched as the light faded from his sister's eyes.

Slade sobbed as he cradled his sister's body, stricken of the ability to do anything but bury his face into her still form, unaware that the handgun had shifted to him.

"No!" Frost screamed through tears as she rushed forward, placing herself between Slade and Phoenix.

Phoenix quickly backtracked a few steps, maintaining the gap between them.

"Why couldn't you have just gone with–" There was no mistaking the anger in Phoenix's eyes. "You weren't meant to be here. You should've been spared all this."

"Why?!" Frost's voice broke in her scream.

"A clean slate." Phoenix's eyes clung to Frost, ignoring all else, like she was the only one that existed. "What you found, has always been an occasional happening. You can't fight a war without soldiers."

"You–" Frost shook. "You knew?"

With no more than words, Phoenix reduced what little fortitude Frost retained to rubble, wrecking her, threatening to send her to her knees.

"It's not too late." Phoenix ignored her question as he held out his free hand, his eyes darting from her to Marcus. "Marcus, you, Fenrir. You three are the chosen survivors. The others–"

"What are you talking about?!" Marcus roared. "This is your family, Phoenix! We would've followed you into Hell if you had asked it."

Phoenix nodded. "I know. Now, the two of you, come to me."

"No." Marcus' voice cut the air as he stepped before Phoenix's barrel, shielding the others as best he could.

"Marcus." Phoenix growled. "Make no mistake, my orders are only to *try*."

"I won't leave them," Marcus' eyes burned of defiance, "and I will kill you for what you've done."

Phoenix's mouth turned up as he grinned, sudden bloodlust glistening in his dark eyes. "And so I tried."

The frame of the pistol twitched as Phoenix pulled at the trigger.

With wide eyes Phoenix briefly looked to the fouled pistol, quickly casting it away as Marcus began to shift.

In seconds both had turned to wolves, Phoenix obviously at the advantage. He towered two feet above the sandy colored Marcus.

Outgunned, Marcus was forced to the defensive, using his smaller stature and agility to dodge and evade the massive jaws of Phoenix as he nipped and bit at the great gray wolf, occasionally scoring a hit.

Phoenix knew he had size and strength on his side but as large as he was, he didn't have a chance at outmaneuvering the nimble Marcus. He was a seasoned fighter though, aware that patience was key.

Marcus dodged behind him, just in time to catch a hard hit from Phoenix's rear legs. The hit came square into Marcus' ribs, bones audibly breaking as he was launched against the unforgiving wall of the cabin.

Marcus crumpled into a heap, unmoving except for the rising and falling of his shattered ribs as he drew breath.

Phoenix slowly approached the downed wolf, observing its chest rise and fall, waiting for it to stop, slowly moving in when it didn't.

Marcus' eyes shot open to the massive wolf standing over him. In an effort to back Phoenix away, Marcus brought his jaws down onto the leg of the wolf.

Phoenix jumped back as he felt teeth sink into him, tearing at the flesh, gnawing at the bone. Try as he did to retreat, Marcus refused to let go.

In a flash of fur Phoenix brought his free paw down onto Marcus' head, raking the flesh from his leg, but breaking the grip Marcus had on him.

Marcus' vision flashed, the tremendous force coming down on him, leaving him stunned, paralyzed.

Phoenix took the opportunity for what it was, the end of the fight. He bent down, jaws wide, and took hold of Marcus' back just behind his shoulder blades.

Marcus felt the air drive from his lungs as he was lifted whole bodily into the air.

Phoenix pulled him from the earth, holding Marcus just high enough that his front paws couldn't touch the ground. In a quick, fluid motion

Phoenix swung his head, choosing with deadly precision the exact second he let Marcus go.

Marcus flew only a few feet before wrapping around a nearby oak, the cracking of his spine echoing through the trees.

That moment, the wolf departed Marcus, a man before he hit the ground.

Phoenix resumed his human body as he looked down on Marcus, shaking his head. "It didn't have to be this way."

Phoenix turned to face the rest of his former unit, lacking any weapon, but confident in the fact that he was still very much armed.

Frost stood, the suggestion of tears purged from her eyes by anger as she spoke before the rest of the unit. "I'll kill you!"

Phoenix smiled as he clenched his hands, making hard fists. "Let's see how good you really are."

Phoenix cocked his legs, preparing to make a shift mid charge, relishing the thought of facing off against Frost when her eyes suddenly left his, fixated behind him.

Phoenix turned, looking to a nearby rise, where stood a black wolf, rays of light from a yellow moon draped over it.

Blood dripped from its jaws, remnants of the enemies it had routed, and Phoenix had the inkling that it hungered for more.

"Fenrir." Phoenix attempted to reach his pupil, buried somewhere deep inside the hound before him.

He took a cautionary step back as the wolf slowly advanced. "Fenrir, I know you can hear me. You can still get out of this alive."

Phoenix sensed he would have to work hard to get to Fenrir, and he had just the ticket.

* * *

Heat rushed through my body, absolute hatred flooding my being. Every question I'd asked Phoenix… Every answer he'd ever given… Lies.

The wolf told me the truth, the truth he had always known.

It all fit together, save one piece of the map.

The group of robbers had a run in with a wolf, a robber was infected. Phoenix neutralized the entire gang to prevent knowledge of wolves getting out, and also to keep a bank robber from becoming a wolf.

I picked up a scent that led me to 411 Pine, where I found the damage. That very scent led me to the next scene, where I found the car and unknown gunman.

But he wasn't unknown, the wolf knew when first we met, when I came to call the man "Not Francis." The wolf knew it was Phoenix, fresh from killing the infected.

That night, Phoenix could sense the presence of another wolf, of me, but could find no scent of Red Moons, and I certainly wasn't a bank robber.

Only Phoenix's love of the Council had saved me then. He had no way of knowing anything about me, if I had claimed human life or not, and if I hadn't, I could be a possible recruit.

I, nor the wolf, could say why he hadn't taken me at that exact moment. I suspected he didn't want to take any actions that might spark the wolf's anger, choosing instead to bide his time.

The police found out I was at 411 Pine, and brought me in.

Phoenix wanted to find out what was going on, he learned I knew absolutely nothing, only that I was a wolf, but hadn't killed anyone.

Then, the perfect opportunity provided, he used fear to convince me that I'd be safer going with him, earning himself a new recruit. It was only a bonus when he learned I was a pure blood wolf. Then we hit the settlement.

The remaining piece of the puzzle was the very first.

"Who, and where, is she?"

* * *

The rest of the pack stood frozen, holding a tight breath, waiting to see who was in control. Fenrir, or something else.

"Fenrir, don't you forget all I've done for you. Where would you be if not for me? You'd be dead, another rogue wolf! But look at you now,

433

you're so much more now." Despite knowing he dwarfed Fenrir in wolf form, Phoenix wasn't certain that the human side of Fenrir was the one in control anymore. He could no longer speak with any certainty as to Fenrir's capabilities, unable to calculate the outcome of a fight where he no longer knew his foe.

"Listen to me, Fenrir," Phoenix began to stall as he continued a calm retreat, "we were friends, you and I."

The wolf momentarily took its eyes from Phoenix, looking to the survivors. Its gaze fell upon the face of each operator, before finally resting upon Frost.

It stared at her for a time, simply observing her.

The wolf let out a heavy exhale, as if in relief.

Its gaze shifted to find Red, then Marcus, and finally Knight, still wrapped in Slade's arms.

A low growl ventured from the wolf's jaws as it turned back to Phoenix.

The wolf slowly advanced, and Phoenix knew that now was the time to play his trump card.

"Your father lives, Fenrir! He's a Councilman. You are a legacy child! You don't have to die with–"

The words didn't have the desired effect, in fact they had none at all.

One slow, deliberate step after another, the wolf's jaws inched closer.

His saving throw spent, Phoenix scrambled for something, anything, to stop the black wolf.

He looked to Frost, aware of their strengthening bond. "Frost–"

The wolf jumped as the words broke Phoenix's lips, bloodied teeth ready to devour Phoenix and all his betrayal.

Its jaws came to rest on the fur of Phoenix's left flank, having turned to flee as a wolf, seeing that his efforts had been in vain.

Phoenix, in a reflex he'd developed many battles ago, turned and sank his teeth in the black wolf's shoulder, hoping to slow down his adversary.

In an instant the black wolf turned loose of Phoenix's flank and brought its jaws to Phoenix's throat, fighting for the jugular against his suddenly terror stricken opponent.

Phoenix wrenched himself free from Fenrir, losing a large bit of fur and a chunk of flesh though escaping major damage.

Phoenix bolted down the hollow, Fenrir quickly following and closing the gap.

As Phoenix ran his body began to ache, the initial adrenaline surge from his fight with Marcus wearing off, though as he turned back, he was fueled onward, bearing witness to what truly pursued him: an unwavering Hell hound, rapidly closing the distance.

Phoenix pushed his torn body to it's break point, his lungs burning for breath, his tattered leg screaming with every step. Time was running out, and he felt himself begin to waiver, as the churning of water reached his ears.

His saving grace.

If he could break Fenrir's sight line and get across the water, he'd have a chance. Fenrir would have to go on scent, which he would lose at the water.

Energy renewed, Phoenix darted between the trees, crossing draw and ridge, doing everything in his power to evade his pursuer.

Fenrir's chasing steps had gradually fallen away, leaving Phoenix with a glimmer of hope as he crested yet another rise, looking down on a sizable stream more turbulent and akin to a small river.

"This is it!" Phoenix urged his legs onward, splashing into the rushing water. *"He's lost line of sight, now–"*

With the force of a freight train Phoenix was sent into the churning water, as Fenrir throttled him from his feet.

Pulling himself above the rapids, Phoenix stood to face an unmoving Fenrir.

"Was he waiting for me to get up?" Phoenix bared his teeth. *"Why would he do that? The fool."*

Knee deep in coursing water, Phoenix decided there was but one way to get out of this alive.

With a thundering roar Phoenix lunged, banking on his size to over-whelm the smaller Fenrir, to hold him beneath the waves until there was no fight left in the black wolf.

"I would have saved you, Fenrir, but you wouldn't allow it. You, Marcus, Frost. They wanted you three alive, wanted to salvage what they could from this broken unit. Now Frost is lost to the wind, Marcus is dead, and you, are soon to join him."

It was with nothing but surprise that Phoenix's jaws slammed together, full of nothingness.

In a blur of black, Fenrir was on him, jaws locking on his neck.

Phoenix felt the teeth digging in, ripping and tearing as Fenrir viciously shook him, dragging him to the water.

Going under, Phoenix's mouth and nostrils filled with water as he kicked for purchase. Panic ran through him as his lungs begin to fill, driving his thrashing legs all the harder, finding neither Fenrir nor the rocky bottom of the river.

Fenrir's jaws didn't loosen, didn't shoulder for a better grip, there was no need. If Fenrir's teeth didn't clip the jugular, Phoenix would drown.

Fire took Phoenix's throat as he felt his windpipe collapse, suddenly struggling with everything he had left.

Claws swung wildly, trying to catch something, anything.

"Where is he?!" Phoenix's mind screamed as he began to fade.

Phoenix felt his face rise from the water, only briefly, as with a final rip the fight left him. His head fell to the bank, and he watched as blood drained from him, trickling to the river, watching as the waters ran red.

* * *

I could still control myself, my guest only helping me through the battle. The soldiers had all fallen easily enough; several had turned and ran for me to simply run down. Only two sought to face me as wolves, and they fell just as easily as the others.

All the while I fought, one thought drove me on.

Frost.

Despite the fray, every round fired, I found her.

I kept my promise.

But that wasn't enough to save them all.

I learned what betrayal cost.

All the rage, every drop of molten hatred, flooded my veins, marking a single target.

Phoenix.

He had been a surprise, of all the things I had anticipated, I hadn't expected him to run.

It made no difference though, fight or flee, him getting out alive was never an option.

As I chased, his scent filled my nose. It was different.

"Is this what terror smells like?" I asked the wolf.

He made no effort to answer as he told me to turn from his tail, try and overtake him from the side.

The wolf told me to end it right there, rather than rolling him from his feet, but he was still much larger than I, and I wanted every advantage.

Yet as he fell beneath the water, my feet became rooted. Something inside me, not entirely unlike the wolf, told me to wait, to let him stand. To face him proper.

"He doesn't deserve the courtesy Hunter afforded me." I thought. *"This doesn't need to be a fair fight. He just needs to die."*

I wanted him to feel fear before I ripped him apart. It didn't matter how he met his end, so long as he did in very short order.

Wishing for nothing more than to tear into him as he floundered, I found it curious that still, I waited.

In regaining his feet, I found his demeanor had changed, and I sensed that the end was drawing near.

Once more he surprised me. He charged, headlong, a final charge to end it.

It was almost too easy, predictable. An imbecilic, daresay rookie, maneuver.

Marcus' drill carried my feet to the side, Phoenix replacing Scarecrow.

I brought my jaws to his throat and clamped down as hard as I could, then threw every ounce of my being into ripping out his throat.

The savage wrenching brought him down, splashing my face with water, and I knew I had him.

"Just take in a breath, Phoenix. It'll be the kinder of the passing."

Still he struggled, and I knew eventually, one of his paws would find an anchor.

The time for drowning him had passed, and as I lifted him, I used his own body weight to ensure a killing tear, the force of which dragged his head to shore.

As the life drained from him, hatred faded from me. Pain, it seemed, was all that remained.

"Why did he do it, wolf?" I stepped to the bank, seeing the faces of Red, of Marcus, of Knight. *"How could he?"*

No dark rumble formed words in my mind, the enveloping silence held at bay only by a babbling creek nearby.

As Phoenix's body returned to that of a man, I thought about the speed at which he had shifted. It was fast, the fastest I had yet seen, faster than any of us in the unit, faster than Hunter even.

How could he change that quickly?

I inhaled petrichor as a hand touched my side and I looked down to Frost.

She was scared, unsure whom she spoke to.

"Fenrir?" She looked into my eyes as I let the wolf go, shrinking before her.

"It's me, Frost." I met her eyes, immeasurably grateful to the wolf that she was okay.

"Is it you?" She searched my face for an explanation.

"Yes." I softly said. "The wolf's let go."

"That doesn't–" Frost shook her head as she lowered a pack to the ground.

It was my pack. I had given it to Marcus.

I shook my head as I pulled on my jeans. "Frost, I'm–"

"The world will seek to kill you now." A hoarse whisper sent a gasp from

Frost's lips and a shiver down my spine as I turned, finding Phoenix just like Hunter, still clinging to life.

"You're already dead." Phoenix snarled.

As I looked down on him, I shook my head. He wasn't the first wolf I had torn to shreds, though despite his great size, he was certainly the lesser of them all.

"Funny words coming from you." The wolf clawed its way back to the surface, seizing my throat.

"You have nowhere to go." Phoenix gargled, nearly smiling as he rolled to stare into the tree tops. "Not even your father can save you now."

"We don't need saving." I glanced to Frost's side, Phoenix's handgun resting in her holster.

"And," the wolf continued, our voice full of calm malice as I gently lifted the pistol from Frost's leg, "you still drawing breath is an insult this world will no longer suffer."

A final shot rang, silencing the mouthpiece of deceit, ignoring the dull pain in my left forearm.

Lowering the gun, I stared down at the lifeless corpse that I once would've called a friend, now revealed to be nothing more than a murderer.

"How did you know?" Frost quietly asked as I pulled on the remainder of my clothes.

"If it hadn't been for Marcus' suspicions, we never would have." I sat in the leaf litter as I pulled on my boots. "He brought a radio out with us, and we caught Phoenix's orders."

"This was all a set up." Frost shook her head as her eyes creased in agony, disbelief and denial swirling around her. "How could he–"

"Frost! Fenrir!" A shout echoed down the hollow.

It was Edge.

"Marcus is alive!"

* * *

Frost and I fell to our knees beside Marcus, finding it difficult to believe he was still holding on. Blood trickled from his nose and left ear, and that said nothing of what was undoubtedly broken inside.

His chest rose and fell, but that was the most motion he produced.

He was shattered, covered in blood from numerous wounds, and one of his eyes was sealed shut under an ugly red swell.

"I do not know how much longer he will be with us." Doc knelt across from us as he looked over Marcus. "There is little I can do for him."

"What hap–"

"He fought." Doc cut me off as he looked up to me with hard eyes. "His spine is broken, but that is all I am certain of."

"No way of telling if it's the cord or the vertebrae." I thought as I looked to the dead leaves under foot, looking over the bodies.

Nearby, Slade still clutched Knight's body and I felt a pang in my gut as I knew never again would I see her frequent smiles; never again would I hear her laugh.

I shut my eyes, knowing I'd never truly know those counted among the dead.

"Keep him alive." I looked up to Doc.

"I can try Fenrir, but without my bag–"

"Where is it?" I asked.

"Locked in the bunker with the rest of our gear." Edge answered from Slade's side.

"It will open only for Phoenix's hand." Doc frowned, noting the hand scanner at the bunker door.

I nodded as I looked down on Marcus, sadness and smoldering anger shouldering for rank in my chest. "Hold on Lieutenant. Don't you quit on us."

I stood, making my way to the remnants of Phoenix's clothes, quickly spotting what I sought.

"Where are you going?" Doc asked as I turned back to the hollow.

"Phoenix is gonna' open the door for us." My fingers tensed around the handle of his knife.

* * *

For the first time in recent memory, I welcomed solitude as I moved among the trees. In previous days and weeks, I found comfort in knowing I was surrounded by friends, by family. Now, that family was shattered, torn asunder by the man that most of us considered the one that saved us.

I hadn't always agreed with Phoenix's decisions, obviously electing to blatantly ignore certain orders, but I understood his words, the concept at their root.

But not this.

My head pounded as I approached the still body of our former captain. *"Was I the cause of this?"*

Of course I was.

Had I never gone back to the compound, the events of this forsaken place would never have come to pass.

But I did, and so did they. Now I had to deal with the consequences of my actions.

The heat of the wolf shadowed over me, though differently than I had ever experienced.

This wasn't the furnace of a raging creature, but the warmth of comforting, a reminder that I wasn't alone, that my suffering was shared, and it revealed to me a simple truth.

Looking down on Phoenix's corpse, I shook my head. "I didn't cause this. You… You did this."

I knelt down, knife in hand, and set to work.

"You did this, Phoenix. You, who let us see you as some sort of savior, were nothing more than a pawn, a piece on The Council's board. At the end of it all, you were only ever one thing. You were a liar. Everything since I arrived, lies, words transmuted into weapons of manipulation, aimed solely at generating compliance. And when your words began to fail you, you aimed to shatter my core, claiming my father was alive. I know better. I threw the first handful of earth when those two coffins were laid side by side, before a solitary head stone."

Bloody trophy in hand, I stood over the departed Phoenix.

Setting back towards the cabin, I shook my head. *"There was a time when cutting off a man's hand would've made me sick... What've you done to me, wolf?"*

* * *

Reaching the top, Doc and I rushed into the cabin, towards the supplies that Marcus desperately needed.

"Just get your pack." I spoke as we raced towards the hand panel. "I'll get our gear."

"Right." Doc barked.

"Alright, here we go." I breathed as I pressed Phoenix's hand to the panel.

There was no mechanical release, the door didn't hinge, there was nothing.

"Oh, come on!" I adjusted the fingers, making sure each of the pads were on the screen.

Still nothing.

"Get Edge." My heart began to race. "Now!"

Doc didn't answer as he spun on his heels, returning to the others as I stared at the panel, too scared to try again in the event the door had a lock-out feature.

In short order, Edge reached my side in the hall.

"What's it doing?" She asked.

"Nothing." I shook my head, trying to keep calm as I felt the seconds ticking by.

"Let me see." Her eyes locked onto the screen as she nodded, taking Phoenix's paw from my grasp.

Stepping aside, I watched as she meticulously laid every finger to the panel, achieving the same result as I had.

Her eyes darted around the panel as she pushed out a breath, dissipating tangible frustration.

"Can you pull the panel and make it work from the inside?" Doc calmly asked.

"No." She shook her head. "Panel must've been installed from the other side. All the hardware's contained in the wall."

"No other way of removing the panel?" I fought to keep my voice at tolerable levels.

She shook her head. "Nothing short of ripping it out in pieces, and if I do that it may deadlock the whole damned thing."

I nodded, the drumming seconds growing to minutes.

Edge's eyes fell quickly, looking down to the severed hand.

Without a word, she knelt down, clamping the hand between her own.

"What are you doing, Edge?" Doc asked.

"May have a temperature reader in it. Some of them do, as a safeguard for, well, this. If I can get the hand warm enough…"

She pressed it back to the screen.

My breath caught as the screen pulsed blue.

"Please God, don't–"

The pin released, the door slightly coming ajar.

"Go!" I planted a hand on Doc's back.

In a matter of seconds he was in and out, blazing past Edge and I.

"Thank God." I managed a small smile in Edge's direction.

"We better." Edge nodded as she stepped into the vault.

By the time Edge and I made it back top side, Doc had already feverishly set to work, wasting no time in getting the as of yet unconscious Marcus on a backboard and fitted with a neck brace.

"Did he wake while I was gone?" I asked Frost, my eyes never leaving our barely breathing Lieutenant.

"No." She quietly replied as Doc pushed a syringe of fluid into Marcus's arm.

"He is fighting for his life." Doc cast aside the spent instrument. "Rather the wolf is. The best thing we can do is give him time, and move him as little as possible."

"Doc, we can't stay here." Edge whispered. "When neither Phoenix nor the Black Stars make a report, more will come."

"And we can't go back to The Citadel." Frost whispered. "They're likely already there."

"That is highly probable." Doc's sad eyes held fast to Marcus.

"Where can we go?" Slade barely shook his head, gazing through shell shocked eyes that seemed to penetrate the earth itself.

"The Farm?" I recalled that it was said to be Red Moon knowledge only.

Frost nodded. "We could. Council doesn't know about the place. We could rest, decide what to do next."

I looked back to Doc. "Will he survive the trip?"

Doc painfully shrugged. "I cannot say with any degree of certainty. If we move him, even with the braces in place, he still may not even make it to the highway. That said, if we remain here, none of us will survive."

"Then it's settled." Frost slung her rifle over her shoulder. "The Farm."

38

Final Resting Place

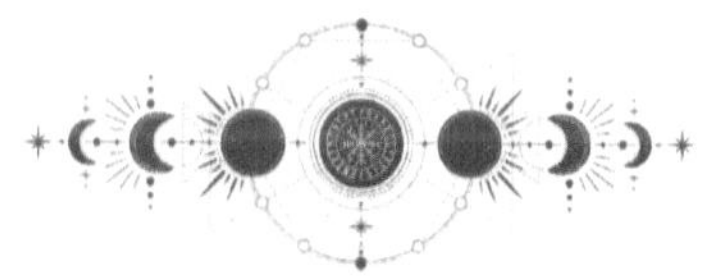

10/18
0500 Hrs.

The Farm once more welcomed us, though it was a much gloomier reception than when I had first visited the place.

As I stepped from the car, the farm didn't feel the same. No longer did I recognize it as where I had earned the right to call myself an Alpha operator.

Now Alpha's Lieutenant barely clung to life, holding on only by the grace of God and the constant attention Doc administered.

The kitchen table became Doc's infirmary, Marcus placed atop it. Doc posted up nearby, ripping through medical books and journals, endlessly searching for some way to help Marcus.

He knew the truth though, so did the rest of us.

There was nothing we could do to help Marcus, his life hung on the shoulders of his wolf, and I prayed that his wolf possessed the same ferocity as mine. That was the only way he would survive.

The farm that forged us, the operators, would hopefully do so again, repairing those of us that remained, and permitting rest to those that had fallen.

Three holes we dug on the banks of the lake, three graves that we laid them in.

They were arranged east to west at Slade's request, Knight's favorite time of day was the dawn, when the stars shone alongside the sun.

We laid her in the most eastern grave, next to Red, followed by Ghost.

As we laid Ghost to rest, I realized I had only spoken to the man once, and my dealings with Red were scarcely more than business. I had never seen the two of them in a sincerely informal setting, like I had Knight.

What had they been like?

Slade left us for a time, as we began pushing earth over our friends. Shortly after, he returned with three wooden crosses and a sledge hammer.

He drove each of the crosses into the untouched earth, at the head of each operator, then produced their bracelets from his pocket.

One by one, he hung their armbands on the crosses, starting with Ghost.

No words came from him as he walked down the line, depositing Red's bracelet.

He came to stop at the final monument, that of his sister.

He drew in a deep breath as he tenderly positioned her tag, and with it, the chain necklace she had worn, now bearing a brown cross.

No tears sprang forth, no tender farewell, his voice stolen by sadness, by guilt. The guilt of surviving his younger sister, whom he had led into this war.

He joined us at the feet of our departed and folded his hands before him.

No one spoke, no one muttered final rights.

None knew what to say, burdened with the knowledge that no words would bring them back, and if God was to claim them, he already had.

Slade was the first to leave, turning towards the farm house.

Edge followed closely after him, knowing that now was not the time to leave him alone.

In time Frost too departed, leaving only myself, standing before the graves.

A cool north wind blew at my back, easily penetrating the torn and tattered trench coat I had taken from Nellis.

I grimaced as I looked over the crosses, a lump forming in my throat as I looked to where Knight lay.

"You were the kindest person, Knight. You welcomed me into the team, shared the first meal with me. Cried with me when I was hurting."

I felt hot pools form in my eyes, and I narrowed them angrily, trying to hold myself together.

"When we came here, I cried for someone I'd lost. You dropped everything and hugged me. You were the real support of the squad, holding us all together, always quick to help. You covered us when we were running out of the compound, and helped get all of us to the infirmary."

I slammed my eyes shut for a moment, turning away from Knight, vainly trying to keep in tears.

"I said I went back to the compound to get our people out, but I went back for you, for all of you, Knight. And you're dead because of me."

Through damp eyes I looked over the crosses.

"You all are."

I looked back to Knight's necklace, my anguish renewed as I saw a shimmer of silver beneath the brown. It was covered in her blood.

I gently pulled the necklace from the wooden cross, rubbing away what dried blood I could as I carried it to the lake.

It took only a moment for the water to soften the residue, and as I wiped the blood away, I allowed a few tears to join the calm waters of the lake.

As I stood, I knew that Knight would appreciate the gesture, regardless of how small it was.

I turned back, and as I looked up, I was surprised to find the others had returned.

Slade looked to my hands, managing a light smile and silent nod.

"I'm sorry." I said. "I should've asked."

I held my hand out, returning the necklace.

Slade shook his head, sniffing as he looked at the cross in his hands.

"Fenrir," he swallowed as he looked up to me, "I'd like you to have this, so would Knight."

"Slade–" I shook my head. "Are you sure?"

"I don't know that she ever told you, Fenrir." Edge quietly spoke. "But she was very fond of you."

Slowly, timidly, I stepped forward, accepting the offered gift.

"Thank you, Slade." I whispered as I clutch the small cross.

"Thank you, Fenrir," Slade said, "all of you, for being there for her, for fighting for her, for loving her. You made it easier on her, on both of us."

No one spoke, at a loss for words once more.

"Our Father," Doc broke the silence, having gone unnoticed in joining us and upon looking at him, I found his head bowed, hands clasped low before him, "on this day, we lay three warriors to rest. Warriors who in their hearts fought to protect your children. I cannot believe that we are outside your realm of creation God, you who made everything. Take them home, Lord, let them know no hunger, nor thirst, nor pain. They are your warriors, Father, they fought for no nation, no woman or man, but rather, for every woman, child, and man. You know this Lord, as you know all, and I know in my heart that you have called them, and I thank you for that Lord, but I must ask, if it is in your plan, that you mend what is broken in our Lieutenant, or if that is not to be, please take him swiftly, so that he will suffer no more. Amen."

I nodded. "Amen."

Once more I turned to look over the crosses. "I'm sorry this is where I've led us."

"Don't be." Slade said, much to my surprise.

He was the last I had expected these words from.

"We found the truth." He continued as his eyes held on the crosses. "They know that."

"What truth is that?" Doc gently asked as his eyes looked over us.

Slade nodded before explaining recent events. The laptop, going to

Phoenix, the safe house.

"And we know the rest." Frost quietly concluded.

"Yes we do." Doc took the story in with only a nod before looking to me. "Which begs the question, what now?"

39

Weighing Options

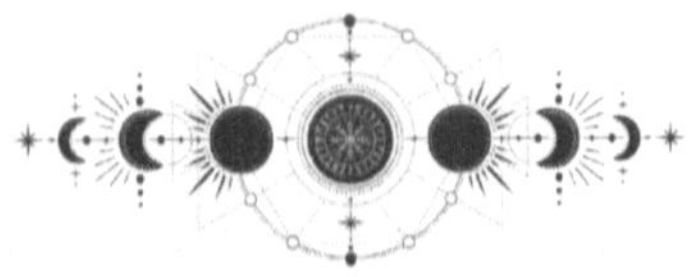

Words were few over the course of the day, everyone grasping at straws in terms of what to do.

That night found us in the farmhouse, Doc settling beside the yet still Marcus while the rest of us dotted the living room.

As I wordlessly stared at Marcus, my mind reeled.

There was nothing any of us, even Doc, could do for him. He needed a Doctor, more-so the equipment at their disposal, but that was never an option to begin with.

We couldn't just take him to an emergency room, it would only be too easy for the wolf to be discovered.

Nor could we return to The Council, not that any of us wanted to.

I knew what *I* was going to do, the idea having gradually taken shape through the day, but I couldn't make that decision for the rest of the team.

I chose Marcus, at giving him the best fighting chance, and that didn't entail remaining at the farm long.

The others, provided they hadn't arrived at the same verdict, had an array of avenues before them by my calculations.

They seemed floored as I opened the evening with a question.

"Who's staying?" I asked.

"What do you mean 'who's staying'?" Frost asked. "Where would we go? *This* was the fall back. We can't go back to The Council, which makes us Rogues, meaning that now, The Council is hunting us."

"I know, but you all know how to blend in. You all have control of your wolves. You could make it out there. You don't have to stay, you could be free. Everyone deserves the right to choose how they live."

With those words, I saw understanding fall over those around me.

"What are *you* going to do, Fenrir?" Frost quietly asked.

"I'll say last." I replied. "Please allow me that."

I didn't want to sway anyone.

Frost slowly nodded and looked over to Edge, only for a moment, and before Frost muttered a syllable, I knew her answer.

"I'm staying." She said.

"Me too." Edge agreed, nodding to Frost.

Slade let out a heavy breath as he took Edge's hand. "You guys are all I have left. I can't leave you."

We hadn't had a chance to look at Doc before receiving his response. "I will be staying as well. I will not leave Marcus."

I nodded, expecting no different.

"That leaves you, Fenrir." Frost once more turned to me, witnessing tangible sadness contained in her eyes. "Do you intend to leave?"

I tilted my head. "Yes and no. Marcus needs help, more than we are equipped to give. I know we can't go back to The Citadel, or The Council, and taking him to a human hospital is out of the question. I'm taking him to The Resistance."

"What?!" Frost's eyes banished sorrow for disbelief. "We just launched multiple attacks on one of their outposts, eventually killing all of their fighters *and* noncombatants. They will kill you if they find out."

"I know the risk, Frost," I frowned, "but Marcus…"

I looked at our Lieutenant.

"The Resistance is his best shot at surviving."

"Fenrir," Slade sat forward in his chair, "I understand you want to help him, but if they find out who he is, they'll just use him as leverage against The Council. They won't help him."

"There is no certainty of that." Doc stared at Marcus, his mind working.

"They're not going to welcome us with open arms, guys." Edge backed Slade. "It'll be an execution, a firing squad."

"Not to be a pessimist," Doc whispered, "but is that so different from what we are facing now? If they could help–"

"We don't know what they'll do." Frost nearly growled.

"But we know that they care about humans." I slowly stood, making my way to Marcus. "If we make our case, explain ourselves, our ideals, our situation, we may find common ground. It could be safe for us, and I don't know any other way to help Marcus."

No one spoke, everyone captive to their own thoughts.

I expected that this was where I would lose most of the team, perhaps even Doc, and my heart wrenched at the thought of losing Frost, but right now, Marcus was foremost in my mind's eye.

"Damn it." Frost suddenly stood, blazing past me before pushing through the door into the night.

My heart wanted me to follow, to tell her that I felt this was the best option we had, but what authority did I have to make this choice for all of us? That wasn't my intention.

I turned back to face the rest of the team, attempting to defuse the situation.

"You don't have to follow me on this," I whispered, "or if you have a better idea for helping Marcus, I'm willing to listen, but I can't just stand here and watch him die."

At the conclusion of my words, Slade shut his eyes, slowly reaching over to take Edge's hand. As he turned to face her, his eyes opened, and a small nod passed between them.

"I'm with you, Fenrir." Slade slowly turned back to me.

"Me too." Edge nodded.

I shook my head, fearful that they supported me out of some feeling of debt.

"Neither of you owe me anything. Please don't follow me because-"

"We don't." Slade cut me off as he gently smiled. "We're saying this because we care for Marcus, and it is evident that you do as well."

"Count me in." Doc spoke behind me, and as I turned to him, I found his hand placed on Marcus' chest, steadily rising and falling with each breath. "I may not be able to fix him, but I will not abandon him."

That left Frost.

I looked to the door, letting out a heavy sigh as I pressed out into the night, hoping that I hadn't lost her.

I doubted I would survive the heartbreak if I did.

* * *

I found Frost kneeling at the edge of the dock, looking out over the lake.

No clouds hung over us that night, and as I approached, distant suns lent themselves to the water.

She knelt amid an ocean of stars.

I stepped lightly, wary of breaking the serenity of the night.

It wasn't until I was only a few steps away that I heard her quiet sniffles.

Witnessing her tears, I could do nothing more than fall to my knees beside her, offering whatever silent comfort I could.

My hands suddenly moved of their own accord, ignoring the danger they invited upon themselves as they took her, pulling her against me.

I braced for a fight, to be pushed into the water, to receive a busted arm at best, a broken jaw at worst.

Yet no strikes came for me as her arms wrapped around my neck, pulling herself into me, and I tried not to acknowledge the energy she pushed into me.

Hot tears fell against my shirt, soaking through to my skin as she sobbed against me.

My heart wept with her as I pulled her closer, every collision of skin sending thunder through my veins.

Every notion of caring was still very much alive in my heart. While I had believed those feelings mute beneath the pain that we both felt, I was sorely mistaken, and I was ashamed that I couldn't ignore it.

Worse still was the knowledge that there were no words that I could say, nothing I could do to quell the storm within her.

She had held herself firm in the immediate aftermath of the ambush, raising her walls in order to stay strong, to keep the others strong as best she could.

She had briefly reverted into the icy soldier that had earned her call sign, but there was too much pent up behind the dam, too much for one person to shoulder.

"You don't have to bear this alone, Frost." I whispered, wishing I could tell her what I really meant. "We're here, all of us are here…"

I felt her head shake against me as she tried to speak. "I couldn't save them."

"They aren't gone because of you, Frost." I lowered my lips to her ear. "Please don't do this to yourself."

"I should've… They…"

"None of us could have known, Frost." I whispered. "Not you, not Marcus, none of us."

"How could he–"

"Don't ask that, Frost. It won't help."

"But I have to!" She cried into my chest. "How could he kill them?!"

I sighed, tracing the line back to where it all began. It had all started with me, but that wasn't the answer she wanted, nor would it help anything to say that my actions had led us here.

I didn't fear her wrath, she possessed none for me. This I knew when she embraced me rather than push me away.

She wanted to know how he could be so calm whilst killing those he had essentially raised.

A father, murdering his children.

The answer tasted too bitter, too cruel to put to words, but I didn't need to.

Frost already knew.

He never cared. Except for her.

I was grateful to him for that, in a twisted sort of way. It made sense when he said to confirm targets. He wanted her alive.

Some part of him cared about her. I nearly voiced that thought, just before realizing that to do so would only add to her pain. To know that he would discard every other life in the outfit, though choose to spare her.

"Frost," I sufficed with a whisper, "I'm so sorry."

"You didn't do this, Fenrir." She shook her head as tears continued from her eyes.

"Shh." I attempted to soothe her.

She softened in my hands, her will failing her, her strength pulled away.

"What are we going to do, Finn?" She breathed.

"The others and I have already agreed on our course." I quietly said.

"That's why you came out here." She turned her head, her gaze falling to the water as if in disappointment. "Where are we going?"

"The Resistance," my chin rested atop her hair as she filled my lungs, "for Marcus' sake."

"How did you convince them to do this?"

"I told them that I knew no other option that gave Marcus a fighting chance, and I did ask them if they had any ideas. When I said I couldn't just let him die, it seemed to strike home."

"Even Edge?" She asked.

I nodded, wondering why she had asked about Edge specifically after I had just said everyone agreed.

"If he makes it, he's gonna' be pissed." She sniffled. "You know that The Resistance is partially made up of vampires."

"But at least he'll make it," I gently replied, "and it seems that they–"

"Hold humanity as the highest priority?" She tilted her head. "I know, you said that already. Have you thought about how you'd even get a hold of them?"

I managed a nod. "A laptop comes to mind, and Edge."

Wordlessly she nodded, fresh tears staining her cheeks.

"Come inside?" I raised a knee. "You're not alone. We're here. I'm here."

"For how long?" She shuddered. "How long until I lose you too?"

"As long as you hold me to my promise, Frost," I whispered, "you never will. Please come inside?"

She shook her head as her eyes shut. "I can hardly stand, Fenrir."

"Hold on to me." I whispered. "I'll stand for both of us."

Collecting her breath, her arms and all of their charge returned to my neck as I took her waist, lifting us from the timbers.

I couldn't bring myself to move further as her face burrowed into my neck, the tears nowhere near finished. She needed this, she needed to let it out.

I swallowed a lump in my throat, helpless to ease her pain. I knew it wouldn't pass this night, nor any in the near future.

"I've got you, Frost." I whispered, welding my feet to the planks, wishing more than anything to tell her that I'd never let her be alone again, I would always be there.

As she rattled against me, my heart broke.

I had to try. "We're going to be ok–"

Her head shook against me, her hands balling into my shirt as it all took its toll. "There's only so much death I can take, Fenrir, only so much fight in me. What happens when I give out?"

"Maybe I can't help your pain, but I won't leave you. I can hold your shields up, keep you standing if you'll let me. You're not alone in this, Frost, take strength in that."

I raised her face to mine, taking her damp eyes with my own. "Then I'll lift you up, brush you off, and we'll face whatever comes our way."

"Together." I gently smiled. "We're going to get through this."

She scraped together the shards of a smile for me as, one slow step before the other, we made our way back to the house.

* * *

"Hopefully they don't drag their feet." Slade looked to Marcus as Edge finished clicking at the laptop. "Not sure how long he can keep this up."

"I'm sure the first thing they'll do is try to back-trace for a point of origin, be that the device or a location. After that turns up nothing, they'll kick it around for a while, and then, hopefully, take it to whoever this 'Whitedeer' is."

"Still not certain that was the best idea, addressing it directly to him." Frost uneasily crossed her arms.

"If Hunter was reporting specifically to him, it stands to reason that he is someone with clout, if only a captain." Doc offered before looking to me. "Though I would advise you not to disclose the exact detail that *you* were the one that killed his friend."

"I think it'd be for the best if I did." I replied. "If we were to join them, and it comes out at a later time that I was the one that ultimately put the installation out of commission, they'd think we intentionally hid it. At that point it's hard to say what would happen."

"You do realize that if we tell them, there is a chance that we'll all be shot right there." Slade rattled.

"No." I shook my head. "Just me."

"How do you figure that?" Frost turned to me with suspicious eyes.

"When you reached out to them, what did you say?" I shifted my gaze to Edge, briefly evading Frost's question.

"I explained that we are an abandoned Council unit that have sustained heavy casualties following an ambush launched by another Council unit and our former captain. I detailed that there are only six of us left, that one of us is critically injured, and that we need help. I didn't mention names, I tried to be as vague as possible while remaining somewhat accurate."

"That's… That's actually really good, Edge." I praised.

"Hard to beat the truth, Fenrir." Her weak smile was tainted by the grim nature of the late evening.

I nodded, returning to Frost's previous question. "If and when they get back to us, we'll arrange a meeting in a public place, plenty of people. I'll be the one to meet Whitedeer, just me. If I haven't made it back to you by a certain time… do what you think is best."

* * *

10/18
1100

For the past few hours, I had sat with Marcus, simply watching his chest rise and fall, giving Doc the chance to catch an hour of sleep.

He had refused to sleep any longer than that, despite my protests.

At the rear of the room, Edge held down the couch, seemingly sharing my inability to rest.

Occasionally I'd hear her fingertips fall to the screen of Phoenix's tablet.

It had been a funny thing. When first I saw her with it, I nearly asked if she had disabled any possible tracking measures on the device. Fortunately I had thought better of it, saving me from opening my mouth.

She knew what she was doing, and maybe something on there would prove useful, if nothing more than a semi-bargaining chip for The Resistance.

Slade, as well as Frost, had both turned in for the night.

I wished with everything that I had that they might actually get some sleep, though I doubted it.

We had all lost friends, but they lost something more in Knight, and that said nothing of how dear they had held Phoenix.

I had heard his praises sung numerous times over the past weeks.

"A good man. Like a father."

I shook my head, still unable to grasp it.

It felt inadequate to say it was cold, and even heartless seemed to fall short of his crime.

With a sigh, I pressed a thumb to my left forearm, once more throbbing in pain. It was like an old injury, something that would go away only to flare up after a bit of stress.

After a moment or two, the throbbing dissipated, only for the rest of my body to remind me of the past day.

I was tired, every fiber begging for rest while my mind fired on cylinders I didn't even know I had.

So much depended on this meeting.

A home for the team, the survivors of The Red Moons.

"Shattered moons." Some tab in my brain rambled.

The sole feasible chance for Marcus' survival, and even that was a bit of a stretch.

A soft thud from the couch led me to turn around, finding a shaken Edge, a pair of headphones draped round her neck.

Next to her, the tablet lay face down.

"Edge?" I softly spoke. "You okay?"

Her steely eyes were focused, staring forward, but I was certain that she was seeing nothing before her.

"What did you find?" I asked.

She shook her head, a tinge of regret taking her hushed voice. "Trick Jaw."

"That operator The Resistance was looking for? Why–" I cleared my throat. "What of him?"

Again she shook her head. "He's not normal."

"What do you mean?" I cast another glance to Marcus as I stood, finding him still doing everything he could.

"You've fought vampires, right?" She brought her hand away from her mouth, though her wide eyes dared not move.

"Yeah." I shrugged. "They're fast, and they're stro–"

"Not like him."

Moving to the couch, I looked to the tablet. "Is it that bad? May I?"

"I won't stop you, Fenrir," Edge's eyes finally moved to mine, "but it isn't–"

She fell silent, seemingly unable to find the words.

I frowned as I reached for the tablet, lifting it as Edge removed her headphones.

"Don't play it out loud." She cautioned.

I nodded as I pulled on the muffs, before dragging the video slider back to the start.

The first few frames were a roughly inserted black screen, giving a brief rundown of the following video.

Date: _06/06/21_

Hours: _0342_

Unit: _Red Moons_Charlie Team_

Target: _HVT 762307_

Alias(s): _Trick Jaw_

Helmet Cam Op:_Lt. Absinthe_

"Charlie team? The Red Moons were hunting him too?"

The screen flickered, resuming in a green hued infrared recording from a helmet mounted camera.

Four more operators moved in front of Lt. Absinthe, advancing towards what looked to be a brick structure of some sort.

"Watch your spacing." A woman's quiet voice crackled beneath the camera.

As they moved, slightly fanned out, I noted the differences between Charlie squad and what we had been.

They *looked* like soldiers.

Ballistic helmets, digital camouflage, kitted firearms complete with suppressors, optics and, judging by the beams that darted along with their muzzles, lasers.

"This isn't at all what we looked like." I watched as they approached the door.

Reaching the door, three of the operators posted up against the wall on the hinge side, while one pressed on the other.

Absinthe knelt down off kilter to the door, training her rifle on the frame.

"Get it, Zeus." Absinthe spoke.

The odd man out, Zeus, quietly let his submachine gun down onto its sling before digging into a pouch strapped to his left thigh.

For a moment it was unclear what he'd drawn, but as he put his hands to the door knob, I realized they were lock picks.

In short order Zeus gently turned the knob, barely opening the door for the other three operators to push into the building.

As their boots landed on the floor, I was surprised that I couldn't hear them.

"Maybe the video just didn't pick it up."

Zeus fell in behind the trio, leaving Absinthe bringing up the rear.

Two peeled off into a doorway on the left, while Zeus and the other split into a room on the right.

Alone in the hall, Absinthe once more took a knee, her laser pointing to the end of the hall.

"Keeping the hall clear until the squad regroups." I made a mental note.

Dampened reports and gentle muzzle flashes bounced from the rooms, accompanied by a soft thud, what I could only assume to be a body falling.

No alarm was raised, no cries or screams to alert any remaining vampires.

I was awestruck with Charlie's near muted efficiency while Absinthe and I waited for the team to return.

"How many are there?"

Zeus and his companion returned, remaining within their doorway, one crouched while the other stood as their lasers joined Absinthe's.

A few more hushed rounds were let off, though with the lack of flashes I could only assume that the pair on the left had moved into a different room.

A quiet, nearly inaudible scraping abruptly reached my ears. A short lived chatter, like metal on metal.

"What was that?" I looked around the frame. *"Bug with the audio?"*

I received my answer as Absinthe and the others cast a quick look to one another, though their muzzles stayed on point.

Before my eyes, the video flickered, a quick blink, though my brain told me otherwise.

I bumped the slider back a few seconds, before the blip occurred. When the cut appeared again, I realized that, with a sense of disbelief, that it wasn't the recording.

A shadow blipped at the end of the hall, from right to left, continuing out of sight.

"What was that?" I felt my heart pick up, as I suddenly felt I was watching a horror film. *"No way that was–"*

A subdued hum rang from the left rooms, silenced by a sharp squelch and a heavy thud to the floor as rapid shots let out.

Those too fell silent with a clatter.

Absinthe quietly stood, moving left into what appeared to be a bunk room, past the bodies of two vampires on their cots, one more on the floor.

"Six cots." I noted, assuming that at least two more lay dead across the hall, where Zeus and the other operator had veered off.

A doorway led from the bunk room, running parallel to the main hall, and as Absinthe stepped to the threshold, her breath quivered.

I could nearly feel the adrenaline drop myself as the camera looked down upon two Charlie operators.

Both lay in a pool of blood. The nearest I assumed to have been the second casualty, laying amongst spent cartridge casings.

His throat was gone, torn away in a mess of blood and ribboned meat.

The other, the first to die, lay only a few feet away, and was missing his head altogether.

His wound differed from the first, a perfectly clean removal at the neck.

"Contact!" A yell and gunfire split my strained ears as Absinthe wheeled around, finding Zeus and the third operator putting rounds down the hall.

They're weapons fell silent, muzzles smoking as Absinthe spun into the hall, rifle at the ready.

Nothing waited in the bullet ridden green hall. No standing foe, no crumpled body, no signs of a hit.

"He's the shadow." My mind confirmed as my breath caught.

"Zeus, on point," Absinthe's voice shook, "Blitz, hold the doorway, cover right."

Zeus nodded as he pushed a new magazine into his submachine gun.

A few steps behind Zeus, Absinthe took his flank, ready to cover him if the need arose.

The pair weren't halfway down the hall when Blitz started firing, drawing Absinthe's eyes.

"Conta—" The shadow jettisoned across the hall, taking Blitz with it. A scream rang out, cut short with the sound of rending flesh, just before something flew into the hall.

As it splattered to the floor, I recognized it as a bloodied lower jaw, attached to a large amount of shredded flesh.

"Zeus, on me!" Absinthe barked as she moved to the doorway where Blitz had last been seen.

She jerked into the doorframe, finding Blitz.

Beyond belief, Blitz leaned against the wall, between two bunks, his chest and torso obviously covered in blood, though the camera muted the color.

His gaze was locked onto the floor, and just beneath his head, from the massive opening in his throat, his tongue lay out.

"How—" My mind reeled. *"How is he still standing?"*

Absinthe moved to his side, and only then did I see the long slender blade that held Blitz to the wall.

Completely silver, a small red gem in the pommel and also in the minuscule guard at the hilt.

"It's a sword." My brain rattled. *"A small one, but— He uses swords?"*

A knock echoed in the adjoining room, and Absinthe finally lost her will to continue the mission, back pedaling as she kept her rifle on the connecting corridor.

As she stepped back into the main hall, her voice had lost what little strength it had clung to.

"Zeus, on me."

He cast a glance over his right shoulder as an enormous revolver emerged from the doorway on his left.

In a massive fireball the magnum spoke, taking apart most of Zeus' head and ballistic helmet.

"Zeu—" Absinthe was unable to finish his name before a glowing pair of eyes flickered in the darkness of the bunk room, only a fraction of a second before he tore into the hall.

A scream broke her lips as the short sword drove into her shoulder and she was slammed to the floor.

"She never got a shot off." I breathlessly watched as Absinthe squirmed and tried to fight back before she recognized her fate.

We both waited for the final Charlie operator to meet her end.

Suddenly he came into focus, his face.

Having pinned Absinthe to the floor, kneeling on her good arm and having disabled the other, he seemed to take the opportunity to relish in his victory.

He knelt closer, a face forming from the grains of the infrared light.

Save two dark eyebrows, he was completely clean shaven, a set of three scars running from his left temple to the bridge of his sharp nose.

His dark eyes shifted from Absinthe's face to the camera, knowing someone was watching as they burned into the soul of the viewer.

Into my soul.

The green and black feed rendered his eyes as dark orbs, but I couldn't fathom that they were anything other than crimson.

He smiled at the camera, a sickening gesture that revealed his teeth.

"What the hell is that?!" I quickly tapped the screen, pausing the video.

"Is that..." My eyes widened.

On each side of his mouth, the canine and the tooth behind had been replaced by the fangs of the vampire.

"He has two sets of fangs?!"

Slowly, unsure if I even wanted to, knowing what was likely to come next, I tapped play.

His lower jaw hinged open, like that of a snake, as he knelt down towards Absinthe, ducking out of screen.

"Hmm." He hummed, a heavy and slow tone, perfectly calm as he looked back at the camera.

He smiled, fangs gleaming at the camera. "Better luck next time."

His hand wrapped around the camera and with the sound of crushing plastic, the feed died.

That was it, the end of the video.

Letting out a breath, I laid the tablet back down on the couch, next to Edge.

"I warned you." She didn't look up to me.

"What is he, Edge?"

"Nothing we've ever seen, Fenrir." Edge shook her head. "I can promise you that."

My eyes fell to the floor.

"That was 2021. Years ago now. That explains the absence of a charlie squad, but why wouldn't Phoenix make a new one? Some superstition about losing another charlie team, or just that it may be unlucky?"

In my mind, I saw his mouth open, unnaturally wide.

"Guess that explains the name they stuck to him." I pushed the image from my mind, though I heard his name. *"Trick jaw."*

40

The Wolf

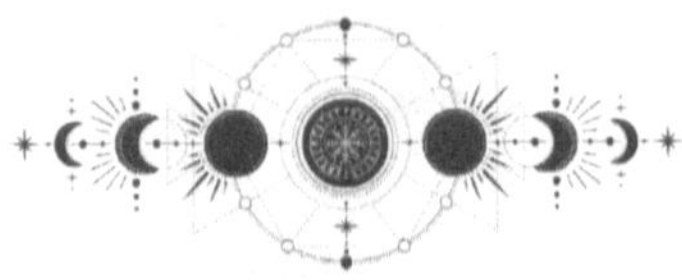

Sleep didn't come easily that night, especially having partaken in Edge's found video.

Eventually though, my eyes grew heavy, no doubt thanks to several days having passed since I got a decent bit of shut eye.

My last lucid thought was that at least I'd finally get a break from the troubles of the waking world.

* * *

"Wake up," a husky voice called from the aether of dreamscape, "open your eyes, Little Lamb."

"Little Lamb?"

My eyes shot open.

I was no longer in my bed, even in the farmhouse for that matter.

I was standing on a transparent pane of nothing, suspended in space, an eternity of stars surrounded me, much like when I met my wolf.

"Yup, this is gonna be a good one." I taunted my dream.

"Do you see me?" A familiar voice called.

"No, but I know your voice." I said.

It was the same heavy, growling voice that I had heard in my head. The voice that replied when I asked myself why I didn't really see the faces of my kills in the compound.

"As you should."

My wolf materialized from the stars. He wore no wounds, no bloody fur, none of the injuries sustained from the ambush remained.

"You…" I couldn't speak, even in a dream I was too awestruck. "You're–"

"You?" His voice rang with humor, though his mouth didn't move. "Precisely why we can speak. We are a single being."

"Glad to see you're healed." I said, having regained my voice as I hoped I'd soon wake from this bizarre place.

"You believe this is a false vision." He stood before me. "This is as true as the lives we've claimed."

"Alright." I scoffed. "You have a name?"

"I am Rainer Hemming."

"Should've seen that comin'." I said, mostly to myself.

"But *we* have another name." The wolf said.

"*We?*" I repeated. "I've only ever had one name, wolf."

"That may be but, with me, you've taken another."

"And that is?"

"An answer you already know, whether or not you recognize it. I come to you now, to tell you that you must align yourselves with The Resistance."

At this point I couldn't help but laugh. "Are you an all knowing wolf now?"

"I, and therefore you, am part of something much larger, something that has yet to reveal itself to you, but will become clear in time."

"What are we part of?" I asked.

"In time." The wolf repeated. "Until then, keep your mind straight, your heart strong. Dark days are ahead Little Lamb, very dark days. And we have only thus served as the catalyst, but there is much more, much greater, coming quickly."

"Cut the shit!" I yelled.

"You've taken a part of me! How dare you think that you have the authority to keep secrets!" My temper failed, stoked only further by his given nickname. *"Little Lamb... He's calling me helpless."*

"If we truly walk together," I growled, "tell me the damned truth!"

The wolf answered, slow and deliberate with every word. "You cannot yet fathom the truth. You are, as of yet, too weak to comprehend or stand against the encroaching storm, and as such explaining further would be a waste. Stay the course, and you will find the part we are to play."

I desperately wanted to wake from this dream, it seemed to be on the verge of madness, teetering on the brink of becoming a nightmare. Try as I did however, I couldn't eject myself from this.

The wolf spoke again. "I have waited months for you to welcome me. When you sought me out in the beginning, when we agreed to walk together, you thought we truly were one. That was not so. Mere hours ago however, we achieved a crucial piece of the bond. You fully trusted me, invited me to take over our body, as you knew you lacked both the experience and the fortitude to do what must be done. As a result, we freed your fellow wolves."

"I vaguely recall licking blood from my hands." I fixed the wolf with burning eyes.

He made not a single move, but I could feel him smile.

"Indeed. The bloody rewards of the battlefield."

I looked down to my hands, finding that they were clean, though I could still feel a thick residue.

"They weren't soldiers, wolf." I clenched my hands.

"That is of no consequence." He replied. "They stood against you, against us. In order for us to succeed, to survive, they could not. In that place you asked me to teach you, and so I did, providing your first lesson that very night. The nature of war is simple, kill the enemy before they kill you. The rest, is simply detail."

"Yeah, but that's where the devil lives." Anger flushed my face as I shook my head. "You don't have to feel what I feel, to see what I see."

"Do I not? You seem to have forgotten others. What of The Black Stars? Were they bloodless? Did they crumble into earthen heaps as we tore them apart? Where is their blood? Where is that of your Phoenix?"

My tongue fell still. I didn't feel their blood. Though I knew I bore it all the same, their blood was weightless, their own actions bringing about their demise

The wolf let out a heavy sigh. "You asked me to teach you, and I obeyed. I carried us through our first battles, through the fields of our home, and the grounds of the compound. You wholly credit me with the preservation of your friends lives, that is not so. *You*, just as much as I, routed The Black Stars, and it was solely you that fell Phoenix, I lent you none of my ability, only direction. Do you wish to know what I see, Rainer Hemming? I see a warrior taking form, molten steel falling from crucible to form, and when our union is cemented, you will feel what I feel."

"Wait." I said. "You said we achieved the–"

"Part of the bond." The wolf's voice growled, irritated that I hadn't heard his words. "You have yet to gain my full strength. Even as a wolf, you do not grasp my power. If I were to grant you control of it now, your body would be torn asunder. What I hold from you is more than many your comrades have experienced, perhaps more than they ever will."

"And how do we get there?" I asked. "How do we reach that point?"

"Stay the course and the day will come that you know every grain of my prowess."

"And until then?"

"We continue on as we do. This is something you cannot force. To do so would be the end of you and therefore, us."

"I see." I nodded as I locked eyes with the wolf. "Other than telling me that there are things that I can't do anything about until the 'due time' arrives, is there anything to be gained from our exchange here?"

"To inform you that we may make such exchanges." The wolf repeated his earlier point.

"Only in sleep?"

"No." The wolf said. "When you think, I will hear, I will answer and offer my counsel."

"You gonna' be pissed if I decide to do otherwise?"

"I have no right. It was your body first. I will never hold your choices against you, I will never fight you, and I will never abandon you. I am your wolf, as you are my human. Where you step, I step, what you touch, I touch, what I devour, so you devour. We are Ulfhednar."

41

Send Off

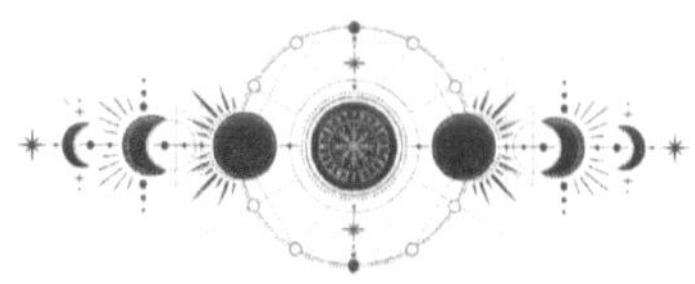

"Fenrir, Fenrir wake up."

My eyes opened, finding Frost at the edge of my bed. Slowly I sat forward, struggling to shift from the dream.

"Sorry." Frost smiled at me. "Didn't mean to startle you."

I shook my head as I rubbed my neck, recalling the wolf's parting words as I noted Frost's tired eyes.

"Have you slept?" I asked.

"No." She shook her head. "I tried but…"

"Yeah." I nodded as I looked to my window, finding it still dark outside. "What time is it?"

"Almost 0500." Frost replied. "The Resistance got back to Edge. The meet's set. 0900 at The Longbranch Diner in Oakstone."

"I know the place," I nodded, "where it is anyway."

"The golden rule with things like this is get there first. I'd like for you to be there around 0700."

I nodded, still not quite awake, still wrestling with the notion of leaving them all here, waiting for word that may or may not come.

"How's Marcus holding?" I chanced.

"Doc's still with him. There hasn't been any change. The wolf still has him unconscious."

"Is that normal?" I asked. "For the wolf to incapacitate its host?"

She frowned as she shook her head. "The greater the injury, the longer the wolf takes to mend, and for the wolf to put him under like this… It means that the wolf would rather go unmoving and try to heal than be able to respond to a threat. It doesn't look good."

"We've gotta' get him to The Resistance." I brought my knees up, hoping that he'd make it long enough to get there. Hoping they'd take us in.

"Rainer." Frost whispered, drawing my eyes at the sound of her voice muttering my name. "Be careful."

I downed a sudden lump of anxiety and nodded, regaining my ability to make coherent words. "I will."

"Little Lamb."

I heard the voice from my dream, and I nearly recoiled in the bed.

"Wolf?" I asked.

"Good." The wolf replied. *"Happy to see you learn faster now than at our first meeting."*

"Oh, no." I thought. *"There are literal voices in my head."*

"You amuse only yourself, Little Lamb." The wolf replied. *"Remember what I told you. You must align yourselves with Whitedeer."*

I made no reply as I hoped that Whitedeer would see reason when I explained why *I* had killed every remaining person in his Res-Rec compound.

I soon learned that it had taken nearly the entirety of the night for The Resistance to reply to Edge. Seemed she was right in predicting they'd take their time deciding what to do with the unusual communication.

Eventually, the meet was set. Oakstone. We were to meet at a diner there, Longbranch. Through a bit of communication, and no lack of scrutiny,

Edge had coerced Whitedeer to meet with me. I was to identify him by a red jacket draped over the back of his chair.

It took no short measure of steadfastness to convince the others that I was going alone, behind the frowns though, and Frost's burning eyes, I saw understanding.

They knew why I wanted to go alone.

The others would stay at the farm, just in case the meeting went south.

I was prepared to leave, taking only the clothes on my back as I stepped from the house, out into the barely existent morning light, most of the stars still present.

Stopping at the corner of the house, I put my shoulder to the wall as I crossed my arms, fighting back the anxiety about the meeting.

"What if they don't accept us? Where do we go then? Even though I'm not in charge, it's me that's gotten us here."

I felt responsible for them.

They had been safe, as safe as soldiers could be anyhow. At least they had a home, an organization backing them, assets at their disposal.

Now we were all we had.

"And I may not make it back."

I took in a deep breath of pine as I looked around the place for what I knew could very well be the last time. Out in the darkness, the distinct croaking caw of a raven let out.

"Fenrir." Frost softly called to me, following me out into the dimly lit morning.

"Hey." I smiled as I shouldered off the wall, turning to face her. "Everything okay?"

"Mhm." She nodded as she came to stand next to me. "You?"

"Enjoying what some would consider a luxury." I smiled, though the good nature of the repetition went unnoticed.

"I just didn't want you to leave without getting the chance to say thank you."

"Thanks for what?" I tilted my face.

"Last night, on the dock." She said quietly, and I could sense the shame in her voice. "You could've turned around, you didn't have to be there."

"Couldn't really just walk away, Frost." I tried to smile for her. "You should know that by now."

Her eyes gently brightened as they smiled. "So, you would've done that for any of us?"

"I'd like to think so," I smiled as I met her eyes, "but I know I would for you."

She shook her head as she scoffed. "Why, Rainer? Why does it have to be you?"

"Frost, we've been through this." I felt terrible as I leveraged the team against her. "Doc has to stay with Marcus, and I won't ask this of Edge or Slade, I won't separate them. They just got their freedom back, together. I won't potentially send one of them out to never come back. And you have to stay. The team needs a strong leader."

She didn't reply as she looked away, but she didn't have to. Her softening eyes betrayed her, made it known that she didn't care for this plan.

Much as it pained me to use the team like this, it granted me the small bit of certainty I needed.

It kept them safe.

It kept *her* safe.

"A strong leader would go to this meeting instead of sending someone else." Frost frowned through a wavering voice, near tears once more.

"Frost," I continued, this time softly uttering truth, "I need to do this for the team. I got us into this mess. If there's a chance we can get out of it, I need to try."

"And what if you don't come back?!" She turned to me with tear filled eyes just before looking to the earth, a bit of hair falling over her face.

"What if *I* need you to come back?" She whispered. "What if–"

"Still holding me to my promise?" I gently smiled, brushing her hair aside before lifting her face, fighting to ignore the lightning that flowed through my fingertips.

I looked to her lips, hunger once more filling me.

"No." My mind quietly hummed. *"She's still hurting."*

Still I found myself tense, though the impending meeting had largely fallen from my mind.

Her breath brushed my face, setting my heart to a rapid beat, as crystalline shards sparkled in her eyes.

"But I may not see her again..."

"Frost," a fit of nerves raged in my stomach as I grasped for courage, "I want you to know–"

Her hands suddenly flew to my neck as she stood on her toes, pressing her lips to mine.

Velvet twins sent a current through me, forcing my eyes shut as my hands took her waist, pulling her to me. I turned, pinning her to the wall as my mouth popped with the mint of hers.

She held me close, refusing to let go as she pushed against me, my nose gently brushing her cheek.

It was no subtle thing, no tender touch.

It was splitting the atom.

My heart thundered as her hand moved to my face, her warm thumb teasing my cheek as she pulled away.

Her eyes slowly opened, finding both of us speechless, breathless, and certainly wanting.

Her thumb, never having left my cheek, gently ran over my lips, slightly parting them as I struggled for air.

"What do I do now?!" My brain fractured, forgetting everything in the world around us. Vampires, werewolves, The Resistance, it all fell away.

I wanted nothing more than to lose myself in the taste of mint and her soft lips.

"I–" I found my voice, only for her to place her thumb on my lips, silencing me once more before she wrapped her arms around me.

Her chin rested on my shoulder, as the lips I so desperately wished to taste caressed my ear. "Make sure he gets back to me wolf, just like before."

He stirred for a moment, lacking every hint of anger, of bloodlust.

My core warmed as the wolf felt something I wasn't certain he had ever felt in his existence.

He felt Joy.

42

The Resistance

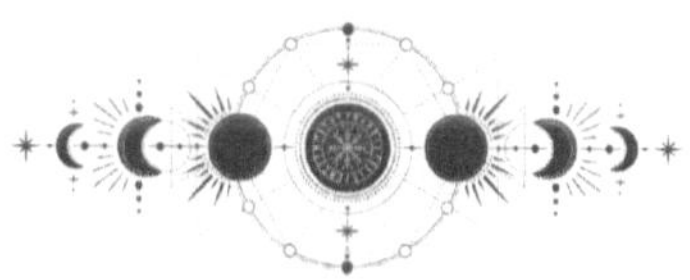

10/19

0715 Hrs.

I found that the Longbranch diner was like every other small town cafe, and given the hour, I was surprised to find so few patrons had gathered.

That said, I was further surprised to find a man facing away from the door, a red jacket draped over the back of his chair, a black cowboy hat atop his head.

Frost had insisted on me taking an earpiece, so they could listen in on the conversation.

"He's already here." I said with the release of a breath. "Here we go."

Slowly I moved around to face him and found a young man of onyx skin, who appeared to be not much further in years than myself.

Neatly kept black hair vanished beneath the cowboy hat, the shadow of which made his coffee eyes all the darker.

"This seat taken?" I asked.

"I'm waitin' for someone." His friendly reply was laden with a southern drawl, and as he spoke I noticed his long canines. "Though he isn't due to arrive for another two hours."

"That would make you pretty early." I said.

"What brought you to my table, stranger?" He politely asked.

"Your jacket caught my eye." I replied.

"And that," his demeanor began to shift, "would make *you* pretty early yourself."

"Golden rule is to be the first there." I shrugged.

"That it is." He offered a hint of a smile.

"Guess I should've been here an hour ago."

He shook his head with a chuckle. "That's a lost cause, stranger, I've been here since 0430."

"Ah." I said before gesturing to the chair. "May I?"

"Please." He said.

He waited until I had taken my seat to look to a pretty redhead behind the dining bar. "Two coffees please, Tammy."

The redhead nodded with a smile. "Coming right up."

"I was under the impression that there would be more o' you, and one in dire straits." He looked back to me.

I nodded. "There are, and there is. They're in another location. We agreed to a one on one, Whitedeer. I had no intentions of doing otherwise."

He nodded as he tipped his head forward. "That rules out a hit, and I appreciate your integrity. But I must ask, what if this was a hit on all of you?"

"All the more reason for me to come alone." I answered.

Whitedeer's eyes smiled a bit.

"How long you been with the Council?" He asked.

"A few months." I answered. "Feels a lot longer though."

"I'm interested in hearin' your story." Whitedeer said as our coffees arrived "But before, are you on a time constraint here?"

"We have time to talk." I nodded before sipping at my coffee.

"Very well." Whitedeer said. "What's your call sign?"

"Fenrir." I answered.

"Fenrir." He nodded. "Well, let's hear it, what brought you to my doorstep? I understand there was something of an ambush on your unit. What led up to that?"

"We…" I hesitated, trying to pick my words carefully, "began to question things about The Council. Our captain organized some time off for us, also set up another team to hit us off guard."

"Why did you start to question The Council? Most of the time Council operators are rather die hard, borderline fanatics."

I let out a heavy exhale. I was hoping to have a bit more time with Whitedeer before coming out with the make or break details.

"We secured a laptop from a Compound, one of yours. In it–"

"Say that again?"

In that moment, I was certain that I would never see Frost again.

I began slowly. "My unit launched several attacks against a compound that we believed to be a collection of rogue wolves, only later did we learn it was a Resistance installation. Once we had the laptop."

"Where was this compound?" Whitedeer asked, his tone growing firmer.

"Nearest town was Kirkwood."

His dark eyes hardened, and I knew.

"The Red Moons?" He asked.

I let out a heavy sigh. "That was us, up until the ambush."

"You are either very brave," he pointed a finger at me, "or you are an idiot."

"I'm not so brazen or dense to claim to be either. The fact is, we're on our own, and we need help."

"Alright," he raised a suspicious brow as he pushed away his mug, suddenly losing interest in it, "let's hear the rest o' your story."

"To fully explain this will take a bit of time."

"Something you claimed we had." His brown eyes simmered.

"When I went into your installation the second time around, against orders to free our operators, I was still under the impression that it was a concentration of rogue wolves. Fast forward to where we get out of the installation–"

"You mean skip past the part where you killed some of our most promising researchers and one of our most senior operators who was on the brink of leaving the field?"

"Yeah." I gulped. "Past that. One of ours dug into the laptop we took from the camp and found an operations log from Hunter to you. You know all of that, then she–"

"Refresh me on the operation log, prove to me you read it."

"I can't give you a word for word, but where I started reading was after the first assault, where some of ours were captured. Then it said that they had intercepted an Order transport with two women, one was already gone, the other was secured. Somewhere in there Hunter stressed that they were vulnerable to another attack and requested medical attention for the human girl. Is that good enough?"

"It will suffice." Whitedeer said. "Out of curiosity, what became of the surviving woman?"

I frowned, her death still weighing on me, and I doubted there would be a time that it didn't. "She was very weak. She didn't survive."

"That is… unfortunate." He frowned as he nodded. "So, how did you learn the truth?"

"After reading the logs, my teammates found a document detailing the secondary function of your installation, recon, to monitor disappearances in the area. I don't recall the exact figure, but a large number were believed to be Council. There was a description on how The Council sometimes obtained troops, kidnapping and turning individuals. A group of us decided to speak to our captain, Phoenix."

Whitedeer hesitated for a moment, as if trying to put a face to the name. "This… Phoenix. Still alive?"

"No." I said.

"How did that come about?"

"I killed him."

"Oh?" He asked.

"We'll get there." I said. "After we spoke to Phoenix about The Red Moons doing something about the kidnappings, he suggested we all go on R&R, so he could think it over. When we got to the safe house, he requested all radios and arms be turned in to him, for inventory purposes. Then he sent Marcus, our Lieutenant and legacy child, and I out on a bogus assignment to get us away from the safe house. Then he called in another unit, The Black Stars, to kill The Red Moon operators still at the safe house."

Whitedeer raised a hand for me to stop. "A question there. Why would he want *you* away from the safe house with a legacy child, especially when you were among those who asked him to petition The Council."

"Before I killed him, Phoenix claimed I too was a legacy child, that my father was a Councilman, though I know both of my parents to have been killed in a car accident when I was younger."

Whitedeer nodded. "So, Phoenix ordered both of you away."

I nodded. "Marcus, our critically wounded man, knew something was wrong. He took a radio and two sidearms. The radio was the only reason we managed to make it back in time to save what was left of The Red Moons. Marcus told me to deal with The Black Stars–"

"An Omega unit." Whitedeer said as if I should know what it meant.

"A what?" I asked.

"An Omega unit." He repeated. "Red Moons, Black Stars, both are Omega units."

"I don't follow."

"That is… odd. No matter though, carry on." He nodded.

"I did as I was instructed and dealt with The Black Stars. Meanwhile Marcus went after Phoenix and…"

"Failed." Whitedeer said, devoid of emotion.

I nodded. "Then I made it back, where Phoenix and I… Afterwards the remainders of The Red Moons took stock of our options. We decided The Resistance was our best option. And here we are."

"How many are you?" Whitedeer asked.

"Six, counting me. Is that a sufficient recount?"

Whitedeer nodded before tapping his ear, activating an earpiece I hadn't noticed before. "What do you think, Whitedeer?"

I was dumbstruck as I realized the individual sitting before me wasn't the man I had believed.

The man sat and listened for a moment before standing and looking around. "We're good ladies and gentlemen, he's coming with us."

Every person in the room stood and turned to face us.

He looked down to me. "Call your squad in Fenrir, Whitedeer has guaranteed your safety, and from what we've all just heard, you'll fit in fine. I'm Cowboy by the way."

A question formed through the flurry of nonsense rattling round my skull. "That's it? I just told you that we are responsible for your compound and–"

Cowboy nodded through a frown. "It's not very often Fenrir, rather rare in all honesty, but you aren't the first to come to us after claiming Resistance lives. As a soldier, you followed orders, and in finding the truth, you also found doubt. That's normally how it goes. Most of the time when this happens, we get one or two at most, I've never seen six people make it out of a Council ambush. You're all very lucky, whether you realize it or not. And, you were forthcoming in what took place. Whitedeer looks well on that. Not much on tardiness though, so let's not keep him waiting."

Acknowledgments

I have to start by thanking God. Since a young man, I've always found myself back at a keyboard. The Lord gave me this drive, this passion, a love of stories and of storytelling. Now, one book finished, I can confidently say I have no intention of turning away from it. If there is to be any honor or glory or praise in this work, in this art of storytelling I am so committed to, let it be reflected to you, Lord.

It's only fitting that next I thank my amazing wife, Felicity (I went through great efforts to find a place where your name fit in this work). Without your help, this book, and those destined to come after it, never would've seen the light of day. From innumerable pieces of advice and being the sole designer of the cover art, to keeping the kiddos occupied while I was working, you are just as responsible for this work as I am. If anyone should ever ask, this book, this series, and every other piece of literature I publish, is not written solely by me. These are *our* books. I thank the Lord for every moment that we spend together. I love you, Felicity, and I can never say thank you enough for all you have done.

To my beta readers, Liberty, Ethan, Ben, Destiny. You've all been instrumental in this book becoming what it is, be that in suggestions given or even being models for certain characters. (Ben, I am sorry that your inspired character doesn't make an appearance in this entry.) I hope that as you turn these pages, you can find bits and pieces of yourselves, both in the text and in it's characters that I have striven to breathe life into. Your fingerprints undoubtedly dot these pages, nearly as much as my own. Thank you all, so much.

To a few friends that I haven't seen in quite some time. John, Benji, Daniel, Elizabeth. The four of you listened to my ideas when this book was still conceived as a standalone piece, rather the first of a series. For those of you that don't know, that's been a while. When I first started rambling about this or that, you listened, and you all asked some great questions, though at the time I wasn't always happy when you stumped me for an explanation on a certain part of my created world. In doing this though, the four of you very nearly laid the foundation of this series yourselves. The rules of the world fell into place, the whys and the hows. For this, I can't thank you enough.

A special thanks here, to Mom. For helping make me the hard-headed cuss I am today, just know I got it all from you. You instilled a sense of "no surrender" in me with that mettle of yours, greater than that of most men I know. If it wasn't for you, this book, and a lot of other endeavors in my life, may have been cast aside at the first inconvenience. Fortunately, I've got you as a Mom. Love you.

To all those who ever believed in me, I am grateful. I know that this vague thanks may seem well… vague, but the fact of the matter is that there are so many of you to thank that this would quickly become nothing more than a list of names. While your name would certainly be on the page, it feels rather empty. So in efforts of avoiding that, I say this. To those that believed in me (You know who you are), thank you for your constant encouragement and support.

Last, though certainly not least, to you, the reader. I thank you for taking the time to peruse these pages, and if you have found some deep meaning in these words, I am happy to have had the opportunity to gift you that. If you haven't however, I hope that you have found at least some bit of entertainment as, in the end, that is what I mean to do. If there is one thing I can give you in thanks, let it be this, believe in yourself. Chase those dreams, God gave them to you for a reason.

About the Author

T.C. Weaver is a small town man, a full time Christian, Dad, and Husband. When not working or writing, Weaver enjoys getting away from the bustle of the world, making time for his family and him to spend in the great outdoors. A devoted nature and history lover, he takes inspiration from the world around him and events in the past, finding ways to twine both of them into the stories he creates.

You can connect with me on:

https://www.facebook.com/profile.php?id=61565223209526

https://www.instagram.com/t.c.weaver/?hl=en

www.ingramcontent.com/pod-product-compliance
Lightning Source LLC
Chambersburg PA
CBHW022014300726
48970CB00003B/889